The Christie Caper

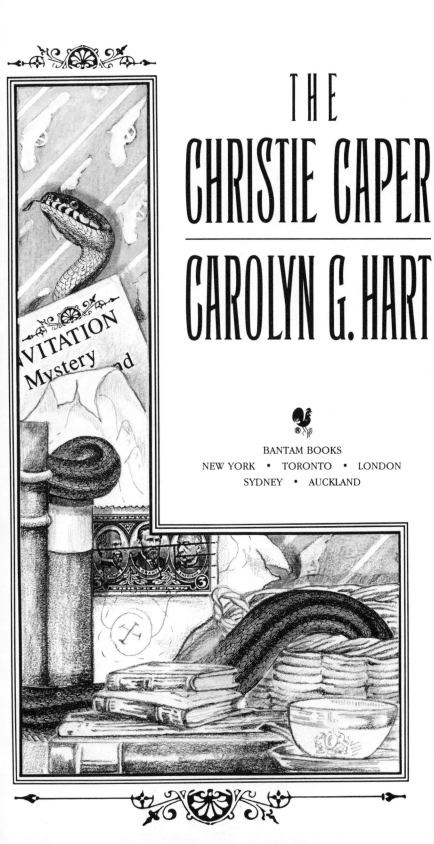

THE
CHRISTIE CAPER
CAROLYN G. HART

BANTAM BOOKS
NEW YORK • TORONTO • LONDON
SYDNEY • AUCKLAND

THE CHRISTIE CAPER

A Bantam Book / August 1991

BOOK DESIGN BY MARIA CARELLA.
CHAPTER-OPENING ILLUSTRATIONS BY VIQUI MAGGIO.

Library of Congress Cataloging-in-Publication Data
Hart, Carolyn G.
The Christie caper / by Carolyn G. Hart.
p.   cm.
ISBN 0-553-07404-0
I. Title.
PS3558.A676C49   1991
813'.54—dc20   90-26021
CIP

Published simultaneously in the United States and Canada

Bantam Books are published by Bantam Books, a division of Bantam Doubleday Dell Publishing Group, Inc. Its trademark, consisting of the words "Bantam Books" and the portrayal of a rooster, is Registered in U.S. Patent and Trademark Office and in other countries. Marca Registrada. Bantam Books, 666 Fifth Avenue, New York, New York 10103.

PRINTED IN THE UNITED STATES OF AMERICA

RRH   0 9 8 7 6 5 4 3 2 1

In honor of Agatha Christie,
the world's greatest mystery writer.

My thanks to Barbara D'Amato and the Malice Domestic Mystery Convention for permission to use portions of the "Agatha Christie Treasure Hunt," which Barb and I co-authored for Malice Domestic I, April 1989.

And my thanks to Dorothy Cannell for sharing memories of Garden Fêtes from the coconut shy to the lucky dip.

CAST OF CHARACTERS

NEIL C. BLEDSOE
Sarcastic, brilliant, unpleasant, the rugged critic is definitely looking for trouble.

VICTORIA SHAW
A soft-spoken, kindly woman, but she has not forgotten and she will never forgive.

HENNY BRAWLEY
Mystery reader extraordinaire, she looks forward to the conference and showing off how much she knows about Christie.

KATHRYN HONEYCUTT
She hated to think ill of anyone, even her nephew, Neil Bledsoe.

JOHN BORDER STONE
He couldn't wait to arrive at the meeting. His life would never be the same.

ANNIE LAURANCE DARLING
Owner of the best mystery bookstore this side of Atlanta. Lively, intense, determined.

INGRID SMITH
Annie's wonderful assistant at Death on Demand. Always patient, sometimes acerbic.

LAUREL DARLING ROETHKE
Annie's ever cheerful, unpredictable, maddening mother-in-law. In the grip of a new enthusiasm.

EMMA CLYDE
Broward Rock's famous resident mystery author. Suspected of authoring a real-life mystery.

NATALIE MARLOW
Author of *Down These Steps*. Awkward, frumpy, brilliant. How angry is she?

FRANK SAULTER
Chief of police. Thoughtful, honest, worried.

VINCE ELLIS
Young and energetic publisher of the *Island Gazette*.

BARB
Secretary at Confidential Commissions, Max Darling's "counseling" agency.

NATHAN HILLMAN
CEO and Executive Editor of Hillman House, who lost more than a prize author when Pamela Gerrard Davis married Neil Bledsoe.

DEREK DAVIS
He blamed Bledsoe for the death of his mother.

MARGO WRIGHT
Literary agent. She would never forget what Bledsoe did to her.

MAX DARLING
Annie's unflappable, equable husband. "Joe Hardy all grown up and sexy as hell."

FLEUR CALLOWAY
Why did she stop writing? She won't even look at Neil Bledsoe.

JAMES BENTLEY
A conference attendee. He sees the marksman outside Death on Demand, but he can't give a good description.

BILLY CAMERON
Chief Saulter's assistant. The conference gives him a colossal headache.

LADY GWENDOLYN TOMPKINS
Cosponsor of the conference, England's reigning Crime Queen. Sprightly, perspicacious, indomitable.

ED MERRITT
The hotel manager. He wants all this murder nonsense to stop!

BRICE WILLARD POSEY
The pompous circuit solicitor. He and Lady Gwendolyn do not have a meeting of the minds.

JEAN REINHARDT
She remembers Stone's manuscript—"all those missing feet!"

DUANE WEBB
Ingrid's good friend. He tells Bledsoe to bug off.

TERRY ABBOTT
Says Stone had only one problem: no talent.

The Agatha Christie Title Clues at the beginning of each chapter are part of the Agatha Christie Treasure Hunt in Chapter 15, Pages 144 to 153.

AGATHA CHRISTIE
TITLE CLUE

Beware the false face;
Can't trust someone in this place.

———
1
———

reat minds have great ideas. Neil Bledsoe enjoyed a very good opinion of himself, but the inspiration which had struck so abruptly was brilliant, peerless—and the answer to all his problems.

Where the hell was that brochure? Impatiently, he dumped the wastebasket, ignoring the cigar ashes and crumpled balls of printer paper. He found it finally and spread open the wrinkled flyer. Quality printing, quality paper. No expense spared.

The first panel told the story:

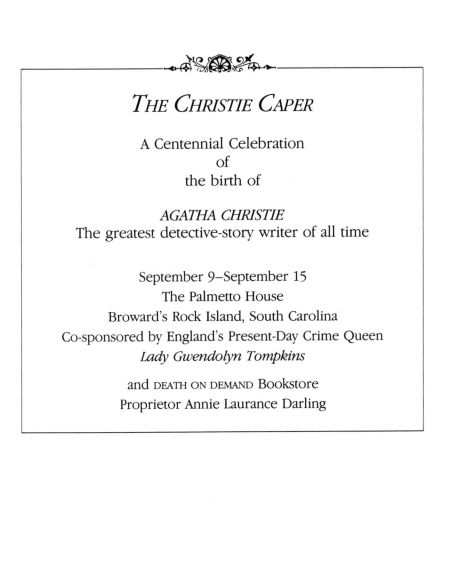

THE CHRISTIE CAPER

A Centennial Celebration
of
the birth of

AGATHA CHRISTIE
The greatest detective-story writer of all time

September 9–September 15
The Palmetto House
Broward's Rock Island, South Carolina
Co-sponsored by England's Present-Day Crime Queen
Lady Gwendolyn Tompkins

and DEATH ON DEMAND Bookstore
Proprietor Annie Laurance Darling

They'd all be there, all those bloody women writers and editors and agents and the damn pansy men who wrote whodunits instead of real blood-and-guts mysteries.

Neil leaned forward, selected a cigar from his humidor. When it was lit, he rolled the oily smoke over his tongue, savoring the pungent, masculine odor that enveloped him. Women hated cigars. So he smoked them everywhere. Especially in elevators. Inevitably, some skinny bitch complained, stabbed a red-nailed finger at the No Smoking sign. Neil took great pleasure in telling her where she could stick it. No-smoking laws were a joke. Was some asshole going to make a citizen's arrest? Of him? He shifted his two-hundred-pound bulk until he could see his dark visage in that prissy damn mirror that Pamela'd put up. All that was left of Pamela.

A face to reckon with. Heavy, black brows drawn in a menacing frown. Florid, acne-scarred skin, tougher than leather. Nobody'd ever mistake him for one of those pansy writers.

And they hated him.

Hated him and feared him.

By God, he'd crash their party. He flipped through the brochure. A garden party, author panels, English dinners, a classic-car display, a Christie Treasure Hunt, a Christie Trivia Quiz, the Agatha Christie Come-as-You-Wish-You-Were Ball. He scanned the list of authors scheduled to attend. Bubbles of laughter stirred in his chest. Holy shit, it couldn't be better. A conference filled wall-to-wall with his enemies. And if they weren't enemies when he got there, he'd make damn sure they were before he left.

The registration form and hotel reservation slip were on the last panel of the brochure. Despite the cigar clamped in his teeth, his mouth split in a ferocious grin as he wrote his name in bold, black strokes.

Oh, Christ, was he going to raise hell.

AGATHA CHRISTIE
TITLE CLUE

Lucky, lovely, rich Linnet.
Luckiest girl in the world—or
is she?

2

Victoria Shaw stood in front of the rural mailbox, the envelope in her hand. Her heart thudded. She'd walked up the lane too fast. Janice kept urging her to have a check-up. But what did it matter, really, how many heartbeats remained? She hadn't cared, not since—

No, no, no. She wouldn't think about it. She would not.

The frail hand holding the envelope trembled. If she mailed this letter, if she attended the conference, wouldn't it reawaken not only the anguish but the poisonous fury that had corroded her spirit when Bryan died?

Not unless she permitted it to do so. She had learned one painful lesson these past lonely years. The mind could be controlled. Not joyfully, perhaps, but effectively. Victoria had been forced to learn that lesson or go mad.

This conference, after all, was at least in part a tribute to Bryan's greatness. Of course, its focus was upon Agatha Christie's legacy to the world of the mystery, but Bryan was one of several authors of classic mysteries who were scheduled to be recognized in a retrospective for their contributions to the traditional mystery.

Bryan would be admired, praised. Once again his books would be talked about, valued.

She could hear the chug of the postman's car, coming up the lane. Quickly, her heart pounding, Victoria yanked open the mailbox, thrust the letter inside.

AGATHA CHRISTIE
TITLE CLUE

Children's laughter, bobbing apples;
Too much talk and murder strikes.

3

enny Brawley paced her study. Where was that damn book? She'd had it in hand just a minute ago! Innumerable sheets from a yellow legal pad, covered with her neat, precise printing, were strewn from one end of the book-lined room to the other. Despite the hour— it was just past midnight—she whistled over and over a rollicking rendition of "Three Blind Mice." She hadn't had this much fun in years! Oh, there it was! Shifting a pile of Christie novels, part of her lovely new bound collection of the Crime Queen's works, Henny flipped open the revised edition of *The Agatha Christie Companion* by Dennis Sanders and Len Lovallo. Yes, yes, yes, here it was, marked by her newest bookmark from Death on Demand, the island's mystery bookstore.

She whistled now in sheer delight. Oh ho, nobody would ever answer some of these questions!

Racing back to the desk and her legal pad, she wrote briskly:

What gave Christie the idea for Thirteen at Dinner*?*

On a separate sheet entitled Answers to the Agatha Christie Trivia Quiz, Henny added:

The monologuist Ruth Draper, 1884–1956, became quite famous in London for stage presentations in which she portrayed a great variety of personalities, ranging from a nagging wife to a peasant girl kneeling in a cathedral. Intrigued by Draper's successful impersonations, Christie's fertile mind came up with yet another devilishly original plot.

Sighing happily, Henny reread her list of questions. Certainly this would be a popular part of the upcoming conference. Be interesting to see how well Emma Clyde would fare. Not that Henny was trying to show that she knew more about Christie than the island's most famous mystery author—although of course she did! As for that British writer—Henny's eyes slitted—Lady Gwendolyn Tompkins, what made her such an authority on Christie? Not that Henny was jealous of Lady Gwendolyn's prominence as a co-sponsor of The Christie Caper. Certainly not. Jealousy was beneath her.

But, dammit, who'd done all the work? Henny Brawley, that's who!

AGATHA CHRISTIE
TITLE CLUE

Where was Agnes Woddell,
Or is this too ob-skewer?

4

Kathryn Honeycutt didn't believe in astrology, of course. But sometimes, you had to admit, it was nothing short of uncanny. She read the horoscope column only occasionally, but this morning's said, plain as day, "An unexpected message will come your way." And here was the letter from Neil, inviting her to come as his guest to a celebration of the one hundredth anniversary of the birth of Agatha Christie. Kathryn would never have expected Neil to be interested in that kind of conference. Why, he'd always sneered at the Christie books, even said they were written with all the pizzazz of a Quaker Oats cereal box. Neil only liked those nasty, gory, brutal novels. Who wanted to read books like that? Kathryn could pick up her morning paper and wallow in rape, incest, and wife abuse, if she wished. She certainly *didn't* wish. But Christie—that was another matter altogether.

Kathryn hurried across the bricked floor of the den to the bookshelves filled with Christies. She reached up and touched the gilt letters on the black spines. Her brand-new set! Neil's Christmas present to her. Sometimes, he could be thoughtful even though she was just a little bit cynical about his motives. Such a beautiful set. Of course, she'd kept her old ones. They were friends from the past. So many favorites. *Remembered Death*—how could anyone ever have thought Rosemary Barton would commit suicide! *N or M?*—look what happened when they tried to put Tuppence out to pasture. Christie loved to make the point that older women saw much and understood much, and the world should take heed of their wisdom.

Kathryn reached up and fluffed her soft white hair. Surprising how many people had commented on her resemblance to Jane Marple. Just because Kathryn, too, was tall and thin with snowy white hair, faded blue eyes, soft pink skin, and enjoyed knitting fleecy baby sweaters. So, of course, she took rather a proprietary interest in all of dear Jane's titles. Especially the first, *The Murder at the Vicarage.*

She opened the brochure Neil had tucked in the envelope and held it close to her eyes. Oh, my goodness, what a wonderful program. And yes, there was a costume party. She would go as Miss Marple, of course. Her white brows crinkled. Too hot yet for tweeds. A summery frock would be perfect. Tea and panels and famous authors—a full week in the company of others who loved Agatha Christie and all her works— oh, it sounded like heaven!

Even if it meant being with Neil.

"Kathryn, I'm ashamed!" She was in the habit of addressing herself aloud. It happened to people who lived alone. "Poor Neil. He really can't help being the way he is." A sweet smile budded on her placid face. "Perhaps," she murmured, "he's changed."

Kathryn did like to look on the bright side.

Though she'd always found that hard to do with Neil. She had always suspected that he'd deliberately left the gate ajar that spring day when Foster ran into the street and was hit by a car. But surely not even Neil was that horrid! It was just that he looked mean, with that scowling, ruddy face. It was certainly unfair of her to judge him by his appearance. Though Jane Marple would surely have done so. Kathryn sighed. Yes, she looked like Jane, but in her heart she knew she was much closer to Dolly Bantry, Jane's closest friend in St. Mary Mead. Jane Marple appraised life in such a Victorian way—rather harsh really. Now, Dolly, she was too immersed in her garden to know as much about the dark side of human nature.

Kathryn's mouth puckered. It had come as such a shock to her last year when that nice young man—really such a charming young man— sold her that counterfeit stamp. Neil had been furious, said she deserved to lose the money. Well, once burned. . . . This last time she'd insisted upon authentication.

She stood on tiptoe to squint at the stamps behind glass that filled the row above her Christie books. The lines and colors, without her magnifying glass, were smudged and indistinct. But there was her latest. She could see the rich violet background. Henry Clay—a premium quality never-hinged stamp. It was another jewel in her nineteenth-century American collection. She'd spent many a tranquil hour these past few weeks studying it through her glass.

Kathryn clapped her hands. How much happiness she enjoyed with her stamps and her books. They both afforded her so much pleasure. Then, her thoughts darting about like goldfish in a summer pond, she peered blearily at the bookcase. Reading wasn't easy now, not even with her trifocals. But she smiled as she reached for *Sleeping Murder*.

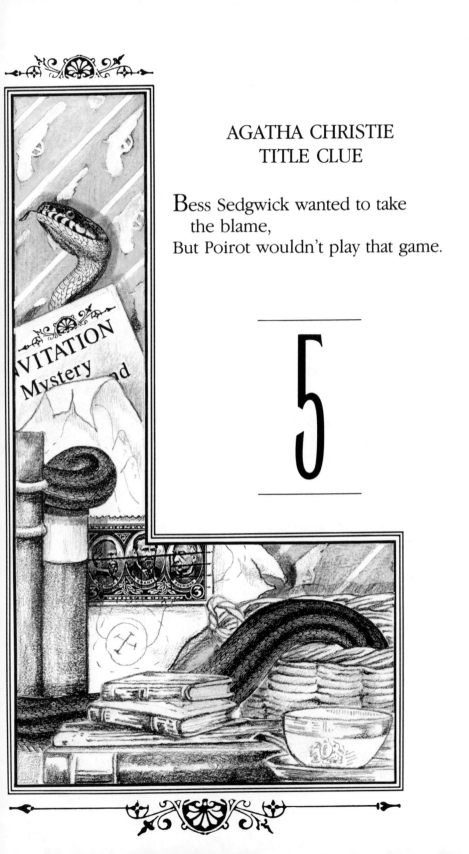

AGATHA CHRISTIE
TITLE CLUE

Bess Sedgwick wanted to take
    the blame,
But Poirot wouldn't play that game.

5

John Border Stone leaned close to the window as the plane circled the field. Palm trees. He'd never actually seen a palm tree before. He couldn't believe his luck. A free trip, entrée to a world he'd only read about. God, it was wonderful. And it was just the beginning. As soon as he did his part—and what a clever piece of promotion—he would be introduced to some top editors, and he would be on his way to success and fortune. Because that was all he needed, a chance for his manuscript to be read.

If he could get his book to the right editor, he had it made. It was ridiculous the way you had to have an agent even to be considered. How did you get an agent if you weren't already published? Oh, he'd heard the same story over and over, "Go to writers' conferences, sign up to talk to agents, tell them about your book." He'd done it and done it. And nobody ever asked to read "The Ashen Prince."

He sat lost in daydreams for a moment, the *New York Times* Best Seller List, higher than Tom Clancy—appearances on the top talk shows, on a first-name basis with Geraldo, Oprah, and Phil—admiring fans following him, timidly seeking *his* autograph.

The jolt as the plane hit the runway brought him back to the present, the wonderfully, incredibly, magically exciting present.

AGATHA CHRISTIE
TITLE CLUE

Be wary of so many accidents;
Fair of face, but a greedy soul.

6

nnie counted the magnums of champagne. Four. Five. Six. Surely that would be enough. She whirled on her heel and dashed out of the storeroom.

"Ingrid!"

"Yo." Her faithful clerk was nimbly transferring plastic wineglasses from a box perched atop the coffee bar to the tablecloth-draped trestle table in the center of the coffee area and trying at the same time to persuade Agatha, the bookstore's resident feline, to leave the centerpiece alone. Despite its expensive price tag ($240), Annie had been totally unable to resist a wax replica of the dining table centerpiece used in the 1945 American film version of *And Then There Were None*, starring Barry Fitzgerald as Judge Quincannon. Agatha swiped one whip-quick black paw at the nearest figurine. Ingrid, careful to avoid the snaking claws, scooped up the cat and placed her atop the coffee bar. "Look at the nice box, Agatha. It's a beautiful box. You love boxes." The elegant black cat made a sharp, chuffing sound, an unmistakable indication of displeasure.

The tables usually in place in the coffee area of the bookstore had been shoved toward the back wall and utilized to display copies of Agatha Christie's books in order of publication (*The Mysterious Affair at Styles,* 1920, the first, and *Sleeping Murder,* 1976, the last) and assorted memorabilia reflecting the exciting course of the Crime Queen's long and productive life. The coffee area chairs were stacked out of the way in the storeroom, behind the ice-filled tubs holding the champagne magnums.

"Do you think we need more champagne?" Annie demanded frantically. "Henny said more than a hundred have already checked in. What if *everybody* comes?" She shoved a hand through her thick, already tangled blond hair. It had seemed like such a good idea when the conference was in its planning stage. What could be nicer than a champagne reception Saturday night at Death on Demand to welcome the early arrivals for Sunday's kickoff of The Christie Caper and at the same time subtly—she had ignored Ingrid's snicker at this statement—introduce all those wonderful mystery readers (the kind who buy *hundreds* of dollars' worth of books at one whack!) to the finest mystery bookstore this side of Atlanta? She had the latest books by Peters, Elkins, Pickard, Barnard, Clark, Matera, and Cannell enticingly displayed right by the front cash register. But last-minute details whirled ominously in her mind. Would it, for God's sake, rain tomorrow afternoon on the Grand Garden Fête on the grounds of the Palmetto House? Had the printer delivered the banquet programs? Were the copies of the Christie Treasure Hunt clues ready? Would Billy Cameron, Police Chief Frank Saulter's assistant, serve as night watchman for the vintage-car exhibit? Had Max checked on the grand prize for the treasure hunt? Max! Oh, dear. She'd promised her unflappable, adorable spouse (Max Darling was definitely Joe Hardy all grown up and sexy as hell) that she would squeeze in a jog before the Saturday evening reception—"So you don't explode before the conference even starts, sweetie." Dear Max, he was so *good* for her, an example of the relaxed life, though she sometimes thought perhaps her husband was just a tad bit *too* relaxed. Did anything ever ruffle him? Max, a jog, the printer. Oh, God, the champagne. Did she have enough? A magnum was 1.5 liters. How many ounces in a liter? Annie didn't even try to figure that one out. But say a hundred people came, and estimate two ounces a glass, that made two hundred ounces. Oh, hell, she hated math. All right, say everybody drank two glasses—

"Agatha, *stop* it!" Annie wailed.

Annie used both hands to remove the sleek black feline from the middle of the centerpiece and to carry her squirming, furry captive to the storeroom and shut the door. Swinging around, she called out, "More champagne! Ingrid, hurry. Go buy at least two more bottles. Magnums."

"Annie, I really think we have enough."

Annie darted to the coffee bar and ripped open the second box of glasses. "I'll do this. Hurry, Ingrid. At least two more. Better make it three."

After Ingrid left, the phone rang.

Of course it waited until Ingrid had left to ring.

Annie stared at the ornate French ormolu instrument. A gift from Max. Honestly, did he think she had rococo taste?

The damn thing rang again.

Annie had for some time now had a love-hate relationship with the telephone. Ever since Laurel Darling Roethke, at that time her mother-in-law-to-be, had enriched MCI with her frequent calls to consult over details for Annie and Max's wedding. Mercifully, that time was behind them. She and Max had now been married for almost a year. There had, of course, been other, later calls from Laurel. Enough calls to instill in Annie a somewhat nervous response to the shrilling of a bell. But, to tell the truth and Annie had never expected it to happen, she positively yearned for this call to be from Laurel.

And not from Lady Gwendolyn Tompkins.

Perhaps Lady Gwendolyn's airplane had been hijacked to Tibet.

Feeling guilty, Annie amended the silent prayer. Perhaps Lady Gwendolyn's airplane could be hijacked for just a few hours, just long enough to diminish the continuing shower of incredibly complicated albeit cheerful suggestions for improving the conference. After all, she'd succumbed to Lady Gwendolyn's siren song about the beauty and majesty of classic cars. But it hadn't been easy to arrange! One of them—the six-seater Nürberg Mercedes-Benz—had come all the way from Pasadena.

Annie yanked up the receiver. She didn't start breathing again until she realized it was a local customer who wanted to know why the latest Eugene Izzi book wasn't in yet and was cheerfully oblivious both to the impending conference and the fact that Death on Demand was closed this Saturday in preparation for the evening's festivities.

She was reaching for the last plastic wineglass when the phone rang again.

There had been three calls from Lady Gwendolyn yesterday. Annie always recognized her caller immediately. The British crime writer's effervescent voice brimmed with eagerness, delight, and good humor—and more good ideas (involving *beaucoup* work on Annie's part) than John Creasey had titles.

With remarkable—considering her feelings—control, Annie scooped up the phone. "Death on Demand." Fortunately, mental images are not, as yet, transferable over telephone lines and no one but Annie could see her personal internal vision of a certain famed English author bound and gagged—eyes still twinkling, no doubt—and securely stowed in the darkest recesses of a French dungeon. Where was it they'd put the man in the iron mask?

The hotel banquet director's voice was a distinct whine. "Mrs. Darling, I understand your concerns for authenticity. But this is *not* England. Lionel—our chef—threw up his hands. Literally, he threw up his hands! Where do you expect him to find kipper stock!"

"Not to worry. The kipper stock arrives tomorrow."

Unless—she refused to relinquish the faint hope—an insanely daring hijacker made off with Lady Gwendolyn's plane. It would, of course, be his last hijacking. Within half a day, Annie was sure, Lady Gwendolyn would have persuaded the miscreant to devote the balance of his life to ecological pursuits.

"Tomorrow." The hotel banquet director sounded glum.

"With Lady Gwendolyn Tompkins. Our co-sponsor. She's bringing the recipes, too. She'll talk to Lionel."

"Lionel is one of the most famous of the Low Country chefs. His okra, crab, and shrimp gumbo is legendary. His she crab soup—he uses pure cream—is beyond belief. He poaches oysters in champagne—"

"I'm sure Lionel and Lady Gwendolyn will work together splendidly. Thank you for calling." Annie hung up, glared at the clock, and pulled out the last glass. She grabbed up the empty boxes, raced to the storeroom, thrust the boxes inside, used one foot to block Agatha, who hissed and bared razor-sharp canines, shut the door, then swung around to vet the party area.

And realized she was panting.

Relax, she ordered herself. It was all going to go smoothly. Of course it would. After all, Lady Gwendolyn wouldn't arrive until tomorrow. That had been the upshot of yesterday's last call. "I do *so* hate to miss your wonderful cocktail gathering—and you know, Annie, you might want to add caviar to your buffet, always such a thrill. I remember my first when I was just a girl—a trip to the Balkans. Perhaps that's why I've always adored *The Secret of Chimneys*. Such fun Agatha has with the Balkans. But I've had a few more thoughts about the fête. Don't you think perhaps a maypole and young girls in soft pastel dresses? They dance in and out.

The girls. Not the dresses. Really, so lovely in the spring. Though, of course, this isn't spring. Or perhaps an animal show—the children, you know, bring their pets. It can be such fun. Sociable dogs and determined cats—don't you think cats are *the* most determined animals? Although, I always feel a pang at calling a cat an animal. And I'm certain my own dear Prince Ladislas would be offended. Of course, he is *easily* offended. A tortoiseshell. Quite majestic. But then, where was I? Oh, yes, an animal show..." Annie had resisted the late addition of an animal show. Undaunted, the author had merrily capitulated. "Of course, of course, I do see the difficulties. Alligators are certainly a complicating factor. Ah well, I know our fête is going to be absolutely glorious. I shall arrive on Sunday at the stroke of three to open the fête, the kind our dear Agatha knew so well. Although at home, fêtes are held on the grounds of the grand houses, not at inns, but one must do with what one has at hand. I'll breathe a tiny prayer that it doesn't rain, but no matter if it should, we will merely pop up our brollies and persevere. Ta ta."

But tomorrow—and the advent of the most energetic author since Isaac Asimov—was tomorrow. Sufficient unto the day.... As for now—Annie smiled. Everything was in place. Death on Demand had never looked lovelier, never held a more heartfelt exhibit. The displays scattered about the coffee area in tribute to the greatest crime writer of all time were superb:

An enchanting reproduction of a photograph of a very young Agatha Mary Clarissa Miller, large-eyed and solemn, with long, softly curling hair.

An artist's sketch of Ashfield, Agatha Christie's childhood home, the rambling villa at Torquay, which she remembered with love her whole life long.

Some of Christie's favorite childhood books, Mrs. Molesworth's *The Adventures of Herr Baby,* Edith Nesbit's *The Railway Children,* and Louisa May Alcott's *Little Women* and *Little Men.*

A recreation of some of the notes Christie made during World War I when studying for the Apothecaries' examination—

GENTIANA: *looks like Russian chocolate*
EXTRACT OF ERGOT LIQUID: *smells of bad meat extract*
COLLODION: *smells of ether—white deposit around cork*

Those days in the dispensary ignited Christie's lifelong interest in poisons . . . and poisoners.

A huge wooden surfing board, circa 1920, recalled Christie's glorious month-long holiday in Hawaii in 1922 with her first husband, war hero Archie Christie. Those were the halcyon days. She and Archie were divorced six years later.

A 1930 calendar with September 11 circled in red, the date of her marriage to Max Mallowan, the young archaeologist she first met in 1929 on her second trip to Sir Leonard Woolley's diggings at Ur.

A poster from *Witness for the Prosecution,* featuring Marlene Dietrich's enigmatic, unforgettable face.

A sack filled to the bursting with bright red apples, the favored fruit of Ariadne Oliver.

A faded photograph of the Nile steamer the *S. S. Karnak.* Christie used the steamer in her thirtieth mystery novel, *Death on the Nile,* her own favorite among her books with foreign backgrounds.

A copy of the Hekanakhthe Papers, found in a tomb near Luxor. These ancient letters by an Egyptian landowner who also looked after a nearby tomb were the springboard for *Death Comes as the End.*

Annie sighed happily and looked beyond the books and displays to the back wall. The September paintings were wonderful indeed. She had no doubt that everyone attending the conference would be duly impressed by the Death on Demand custom of monthly hanging untitled paintings which represented famous mysteries. The first person to correctly identify author and title received a month's free coffee and a free book. (From the current stock, not the collectibles, of course. Annie's generosity didn't extend to, say, a first edition of Robert Hans van Gulik's *Dee Goong An: Three Murder Cases Solved by Judge Dee,* a privately printed edition of twelve hundred numbered copies signed by van Gulik, at nine hundred dollars, or a first edition of Dorothy L. Sayers's *In the Teeth of the Evidence* at eight hundred dollars).

In the first painting, an elderly, black-haired man with an egg-shaped head, catlike green eyes, and a luxuriant mustache stared down at a splotched area on the dark carpet of an English country home bedroom. A soldierly-looking man observed his actions closely. The bedclothes were tumbled and tossed. The fireplace was filled with still-smoldering ashes. Summer roses bloomed outside the windows. A table by the bed had been overturned. Among the debris on the floor were a reading lamp, books, matches, and the finely crushed remnants of a coffee cup. A small purple despatch case with the key in its lock lay on a writing table. The door from the hall was closed as was an interior door. A third door, to a connecting bedroom, hung brokenly on its hinges.

In the second painting, a well-dressed man paused on the threshold of a study, bag in hand, looking back into the room at the dark blue leather chairs, the round table with magazines and journals, the bookshelves, the fireplace. The rest of the study wasn't visible from the hallway. The man's face was furrowed in thought as he gave that last measuring glance and began to shut the door. Approaching him from the hallway was an oily-faced butler.

Annie loved that particular book. Clever, oh, it was clever. But only one of this wonderful author's completely original tales.

The book represented in the third painting was without doubt one of the most unusual crime novels ever written. The hands of the clock in the dining room pointed to twenty-two past nine. The eight guests in evening dress appeared white-faced and fearful, from the elderly, white-mustachioed gentleman standing by the fireplace to the rather handsome young fellow near the French windows that opened onto the terrace to the elderly woman sitting rigidly, hard spots of color in each cheek. Broken cups and spilled coffee marked where the butler had dropped his tray.

The fourth painting told a grim story. An old woman's body lay sprawled on the floor of the modest parlor. The back of her head had suffered a brutal blow. Blood stained her gray hair and the dark carpet. The desk drawers were askew; papers were strewn about. A pale young man—his face reflecting terrible horror and indecision—hesitated in the doorway. A smudge of blood stained one cuff. There was no sign of a weapon.

An elderly woman sat transfixed in the fifth painting, staring through the window of her train compartment at the compartment in a train running parallel to her own and at the tableau of murder: a man stood with his back to his compartment window, his hands fastened about the throat of the woman he was strangling to death.

Perfect, perfect, perfect.

Annie felt a glow of eagerness. Everything was in readiness here at Death on Demand. She glanced at her watch (an el cheapo on a sturdy plastic band; the very word *Rolex* raised her hackles). Almost four. Maybe there would be time for a jog and, if Max were home early, not an unlikely occurrence, other afternoon delights.

She switched off the lights, leaving the bookstore in dimness, and stepped into the storeroom. She paused to pet Agatha, ignoring the low growl, and heard the muffled jangle of the bell at the front door. Annie turned, ready to greet Ingrid.

Light footsteps sounded in the central aisle. A faint scent of lilac eddied in the air.

Annie's eyes narrowed as she peered out of the storeroom. Damn. She should have known.

Enough light speared in from the high windows on the north to illuminate a puzzling pantomime—to anyone other than Annie.

A notably lovely woman, delicately golden hair that glistened like moonlight, blue eyes as dark and vivid as a deep northern sea, patrician features that would be as enchanting at eighty as at eighteen, crouched—dammit, she even crouched gracefully despite her fashionably long skirt—at the center table of the Christie exhibit.

For a long moment, the golden head tilted at a listening angle, then, with a nod of satisfaction, an elegantly beringed hand (sapphires predominating) opened a canvas carryall.

Annie cleared her throat.

The intruder's slim shoulders stiffened.

Annie flicked the switches and light flooded Death on Demand, illuminating every corner, the coffee bar with mugs bearing the names of famous mysteries in bright red script, the cheerful enclave for readers that offered inviting cane chairs, Whitmani ferns sprouting from raffia baskets, and onyx-based brass floor lamps, the softly gleaming gum bookcases lined diagonally to the central corridor.

Without turning, the intruder addressed her in an unforgettable, husky, lilting voice. "Dear Annie, how *like* you to be lurking." Serenely, she bent back to her carryall and busily lifted out an assortment of objects. "I didn't want to be any trouble. Just a *little* thought of mine. A soupçon of *history* adds so much to every aspect of our lives."

Annie stalked across the floor, valiantly repressing a sense of imminent defeat. Laurel was *not* going to prevail. Not this time. She managed to keep her voice pleasant when she stood beside her mother-in-law. "Laurel, I know you mean well. . . ." As she spoke, Annie felt she'd fulfilled her obligation for Christian charity for at least a month. "But this exhibition is in honor of Agatha Christie." She continued forcefully, *"Agatha Christie only."*

Laurel looked up reproachfully. Her primrose-blue eyes brimmed with disbelief, dismay, and acute puzzlement.

Since they'd already fought this battle a dozen different ways on a dozen different days, Annie felt a strong urge to say, "Aw, come off it, Laurel." That she didn't was an indication, she felt, of restraint akin to saintliness.

"After all," Annie continued grimly, ignoring the seductive eyes, "we are celebrating the centennial of the birth of the greatest mystery writer of all time. More than one billion of her books have been published. One *billion,* Laurel."

Laurel smiled benignly. "Of course." An airy wave of her hand dismissed the figure. "But Annie, we cannot," she said gently, "have the chicken without the egg. Now, can we?" She bent back to her carryall and reverently lifted out a facsimile of a 3½-by-6½-inch manuscript page covered with tiny, cramped script. She held it out as a priestess might proffer an icon. "Where would Agatha Christie be without Edgar? Who wrote the very first detective story in the history of the world?"

Annie muttered, "How about Vidocq? For that matter, what about Voltaire's Zadig?"

But Laurel continued to pull items from the carryall, carefully placing them in a semicircle on the center table. In addition to the reproduction of the first manuscript page of "The Murders in the Rue Morgue," the new items included a shiny golden beetle ("The Gold Bug"), a stack of letters ("The Purloined Letter") and (Annie's interest rose. Where on earth had Laurel obtained them?) the November and December 1842 and February 1843 issues of *Snowden's Ladies' Companion,* which had carried "The Mystery of Marie Roget" in three installments.

Finally, with a satisfied murmur, Laurel placed in front of the intrusive objects a sign lovingly executed in calligraphy (Annie didn't even want to know when her mother-in-law had mastered this art):

In the Beginning

"Oh, no," Annie moaned.

Laurel gazed at her daughter-in-law fondly. "My sweet, it is only fitting. As our dear Arthur Conan Doyle said, 'Edgar Allan Poe was the father of the detective tale.' "

"So he did," Annie agreed. "Doyle also went on to say, 'I fail to see how any of his followers can find any fresh ground which they can confidently call their own.' And that's what Christie did. No one has *ever* devised plots as ingenious as hers. Besides, Poe was an absolutely, dreadfully boring writer. As T. S. Eliot observed so aptly, 'That Poe had a powerful intellect is undeniable; but it seems to me the intellect of a highly gifted young person before puberty.' "

Laurel gasped and clasped a hand to her bosom in shock. Her magnolia-soft skin paled.

Annie stepped briskly toward the table.

Dark blue eyes gleaming with unyielding determination, Laurel gracefully interposed herself between Annie and the altered exhibit.

Annie glowered. She couldn't manhandle her mother-in-law. Perhaps she could subtly deflect Laurel.

Annie managed a stiff smile.

"Uh, Laurel, don't you suppose Howard would take great pleasure in adding your Poe materials to his collections?"

Laurel's latest romantic conquest, a multimillionaire shipowner on the island, Howard Cahill, had an enormously varied art gallery in his mansion.

Laurel nodded appreciatively at the change in tactics and shifted her feet so that she was directly in front of the table.

"Annie, how sweet of you to think of Howard. Actually, he and I are working together to build an important collection on Poe. Howard's attending an auction in New York this very week, and Annie," Laurel's husky voice eased into a throaty whisper, "I wouldn't tell a soul other than you, but there's a rumor . . ." She finished her sentence in a whisper, close to Annie's ear.

The scent of lilac swept Annie, and Laurel's breath tickled her ear.

"Oh, Laurel," Annie said gently, "there's always a rumor that someone's found a copy of 'Tamer—' "

"Shhh," Laurel warned, looking about as if competing Poe collectors might be present in the shadows of the silent bookstore.

Annie fought down an urge to bellow, " 'Tamerlane and Other Poems,' " at the top of her lungs. Instead, she took a deep breath, ignored Laurel's encouraging smile, and tried a different tack.

"Don't you think it would be better, Laurel, more fitting, if we planned a symposium on Poe? For *next* year? You can be in charge—"

A thunderous knocking rattled the front door of Death on Demand.

Some summonses unmistakably herald disaster.

Nobody knocks like that merely for admittance.

Annie catapulted toward the door. Oh, God, had the Palmetto House burned down? Was the banquet speaker marooned in Morocco? Were the airlines on strike, stranding travelers across the country?

Annie yanked open the door.

Emma Clyde, the creator of that septuagenarian sleuth Marigold Rembrandt and the nearest equivalent to an American version of Agatha Christie, glared at Annie as if she were a cross between a child abuser and a drug pusher, and growled icily, "What the hell are you up to, Annie Laurance Darling? What kind of little game are you playing?"

The prize author of Broward's Rock Island was imposing even when exuding charm. Emma was emphatically not dealing in charm this afternoon. Her squarish face looked as if it had been hewn out of granite by a broad ax. Bulky and broad-shouldered, she was given to wearing sweeping, bright-colored caftans, summer and winter. Today's orange-and-pink vertical-striped caftan was accented by improbably varicolored hair (pink, green, and orange) bristling in spikes. Anyone else would have looked like a garden party tent topped by peacock feathers, but Annie didn't find Emma the least bit absurd. She found her scary. Annie knew that Emma had been suspected of shoving her nonswimmer, much younger, unfaithful second husband off the stern of *Marigold's Pleasure,* her luxury yacht, several years before. The incident was carried on the police blotter as an accident. Deep in her heart, however, Annie felt certain that the mistress of fictional murder was just as adept at the real thing.

Annie eyed the bigger woman warily. "What's wrong, Emma?"

"As I understand it, as you represented it to me," there was no mistaking the accusation in Emma's raspy voice, "The Christie Caper is intended to be a gathering of traditional authors, an opportunity to honor people who write and enjoy the Classic Mystery."

Annie's shoulders relaxed. "That's what it *is*! For heaven's sake, Emma, what's upset you? You've seen the program. It's going to be wonderful."

"Wrong." The author's lips twisted angrily. Her bright orange lipstick almost matched the vivid spots of anger on her cheeks. "Why didn't you tell me—tell any of us—that Neil Bledsoe was coming? I couldn't believe my eyes when I saw his name on one of the folders at the registration desk."

"Wait a minute. Wait a minute! Emma, I don't know what you're talking about. Who's Neil Bledsoe?"

Emma's pale blue eyes examined Annie like a scalpel searching for nerves. Slowly, the ugly flush began to recede from her square face. "You didn't invite Neil Bledsoe?"

"Emma, it doesn't work like that. You know that. This conference is being run just like all the rest. I snagged a big name to serve as official hostess." Lady Gwendolyn was, for sure, a Big Name. "I sent out flyers to all the writers' groups and mystery clubs and mystery bookstores. The registration fee was fifty dollars, and on the application blank people marked whether they were fans, authors, editors, agents, whatever. Henny took the forms and wrote letters asking writers who had registered if they would like to appear on panels. Oh, and she also asked Bryan Shaw's widow, Victoria, to be on a panel. The only person who received a special invitation is our guest of honor, Fleur Calloway." Annie couldn't keep the reverence from her voice, though she knew it wasn't cool to engage—at her advanced age (twenty-six in June)—in hero worship. But Fleur Calloway—oh, how Annie had loved her books, ever since she'd first discovered them when she was just fifteen. But this wasn't the time to think how thrilled she'd been several weeks ago when Fleur Calloway—*Fleur Calloway*—called Death on Demand to say, in a soft and gentle voice, that she was so delighted to be remembered, even though she hadn't published in some years. Annie had interrupted breathlessly and said, "Oh, Mrs. Calloway, everyone loves your books. They are all in print. You are one of my best sellers."

"Fleur Calloway." Emma's tone was odd. "God, I'd forgotten she was coming. Oh, sweet Jesus."

AGATHA CHRISTIE
TITLE CLUE

Henrietta did her best,
And almost lost her life.

7

mma's stubby, capable-looking hand rested on the steering wheel of her Jaguar, but she made no move to turn the key in the ignition.

Annie wriggled on the hot leather. September on Broward's Rock had its charm, a lessening of summer's hectic pace, but until the winds shifted westward, usually during the third week, the island was as soggy with humidity as Houston or Calcutta. Emma had left her windows rolled down, but it was still muggier than a steam bath in the front seat. Annie could feel trickles of sweat on her face and back.

Emma watched a flight of monarchs. The butterflies drifted lazily over the gleaming emerald-green hood, their black-veined russet wings magnificent in the sunlight. "Beautiful. And so vulnerable. I don't understand people who catch them, pin them to paper." Her voice hardened. "I hated it when they tracked the monarchs to their jungle in Mexico. It's as if our world is intent upon stripping away all refuge, throwing open to destruction every last bit of hidden loveliness." The monarchs fluttered away. "Fleur always made me think of monarchs in flight."

Her hand moved with precision. The motor roared to life, and the Jaguar hummed out of the crushed-shell parking lot behind the harbor-front shops.

"Damn Neil to hell." Emma's voice was as dry and unemotional as always, but still Annie felt chilled. The words were a curse in every sense. Annie had never, in the several years she'd known Emma, seen the author this furious.

"Emma, who is Neil Bledsoe? What did he do?" And what kind of scene was going to occur at her conference, the wonderful conference she'd planned and worked on for almost a year?

The cool blue eyes swung toward Annie questioningly, then back to the road. Emma's voice was neutral when she answered. "It's hard to believe you've never heard of Neil Bledsoe, Annie. But he is a little before your time. The man self-promotes like crazy. He's worn almost every hat in publishing—editor, agent, critic. Everything but write fiction. Oh, he turns out reams of nonfiction, blathering glorification of the iron balls kind of mystery. He worships at the feet of the tough-guy writers." The Jaguar leapt as if stung.

Annie clung to the door handle. "But what has he done that's so awful?"

"What *hasn't* he done?"

As Annie started to speak, Emma held up a hand. Sunlight sparked off the enormous ruby ring she wore. "All right. But I don't know if you'll understand. It all has to do with vulnerability." Another appraising glance from those probing blue eyes. "You don't strike me as being particularly vulnerable. You are—"

Emma paused as she signaled right to turn onto a blacktop road lying in the deep shade of an avenue of live oaks. Ghostly fingers of Spanish moss dangled in silvery-gray splendor. The Jaguar curved smoothly onto the road.

"—a fighter, Annie. Scrappy. You'd tell a bully to stick it." Again, that cool appraisal. "You don't have enough imagination to let anyone play tricks with your mind."

Ordinarily, Annie wouldn't have let that snide comment slide. But she didn't want to distract Emma.

"You see," and the Jaguar zoomed to sixty, "you aren't an author. If somebody told you Death on Demand was stupidly arranged, poorly advertised, and sloppily run, what would you do?"

Thinking of her computerized inventory, her quick turnaround of stock, her thousand-plus mailing list, Annie snapped, "Laugh all the way to the bank."

"Right." Emma's lips almost twitched into a smile. "You'd go on the offensive. If the slam came from a competitor, you'd take out an ad, put in a color graph of your profit margin, list your assets, tout your customer list."

Annie's head bobbed in agreement.

"That's you. But you're a bookseller, not a writer. Just for a moment, pretend you're a writer, a successful one. Very. You write the light, charming kind of mystery that provides a golden circle of peace—just for the duration of the book—to readers who seek respite, readers who are in pain. And there are so many of them, Annie. Pretend you are Fleur Calloway. What would you do if a powerful critic whose column is read by everyone in the mystery world sneered at your books, called them romantic twaddle, dismissed them as silly and juvenile. Described them as arch. That one's a killer. It's better to be boring than arch. Oh, Neil did a superb hatchet job. Used that favorite phrase, 'the author's characters are paper thin.' Said the plots were hackneyed, second-rate Christie, the writing *uneven*. Accused you of making light of murder."

Emma braked briefly as a mother white-tail deer followed by two nearly grown fawns bounded across the road.

Annie pondered.

The sports car picked up speed again. Over the sticky air pumping through the windows and the sun roof, Emma answered for her. "You'd bellow. Tell him to go to hell. But all that would get you is a tag for whining. Americans don't like whiners. If you complained that the critic was a louse and a liar and deliberately trying to hurt you—well, then the cry of sour grapes would go up." Emma's voice was weary.

Annie was puzzled. "Emma, whoever this Neil Bledsoe is, he couldn't really hurt Fleur Calloway. All she had to do was ignore him. Readers adore her books. He *didn't* hurt her! Her books still sell." Annie frowned. "Wait a minute." She knew full well that the Calloway books still sold. Daily. But there were no new Calloway books. There hadn't been a new book in twelve years. "Emma, surely she didn't stop writing just because this guy wrote a snide review?"

"No," Emma said shortly. "It's uglier than that. A lot uglier than that."

Mossy stone pillars marked the entrance to the grounds of the Palmetto House. Not unexpectedly, the small palms, the state tree of South Carolina, lined either side of the road.

Annie loved the Palmetto House, even though she'd endured too many lyrical paeans to its delights from her mother-in-law, who waxed nostalgic about the shutter doors and ceiling fans. But the hotel *was* charming, and Annie was eager for the conference attendees to see and enjoy one of the grand old resorts of the Sea Islands. The three-story cream-colored stucco hotel with its red tile roof and shaded verandas, drenched in late-afternoon sunlight, looked as inviting as a palm-shaded cotton-weave hammock and a banana daiquiri. A turnaround drive swept under the stuccoed portico in front.

Emma didn't slow the sports car as it neared the turnoff for the main entrance. Annie knew she was heading for the parking lot discreetly tucked behind a double row of elegant loblolly pines. The drive through the portico was primarily for arriving guests. There were several cars there now and a bustle of unloading.

"What did Bledsoe do?" Annie asked again, impatiently. She was watching Emma's face, so she saw the transformation, the narrowing of her eyes, the hardening of her jawline.

Emma jerked the wheel hard right. The Jaguar cut swiftly into the drive to the hotel entrance.

Caught unaware, Annie jerked leftward, kept from falling only by the restraining seat belt.

She didn't even have time to scream, it all happened so quickly.

Wind swept through the windows as the sports car snarled forward, faster, faster.

Ahead of them, a man in a tropical white suit bent to open the trunk of a Lincoln Town Car. As the roar of the car rose higher and higher, he whirled around and lifted his arms, as if to stop the metal juggernaut. His mouth opened. The Jaguar and the wind made so much noise Annie never knew if he yelled.

Annie flung out her palms to brace against the dash.

The car slammed to a stop, quivering—inches from the back of the Lincoln. Dust boiled where the tires bit into the drive.

To Annie's right, the man in the no-longer-white suit scrambled to his feet. He'd flung himself sideways into the freshly planted bed of marigolds, flattening a swath of brilliant flowers, and rolled onto a path of crushed oyster shells. One of the jagged shells had punctured his cheek, and a bright spot of blood glistened on his jaw. In the backseat of the Lincoln, an elderly, white-haired woman twisted to stare at the Jaguar, her face slack with shock.

"Sorry, Annie," Emma said calmly. She turned off the motor and sat with her hands loose on the wheel, as self-possessed as Annie had ever seen her.

In the startling quiet after the rush of wind and tires and powerful engine, Annie could hear her own breath. Her hands were trembling so hard she couldn't undo her seat belt. "Emma, my God, what happened? Did the accelerator stick?"

Emma ignored her. She was watching the man she'd almost run down.

His chest heaving, his eyes blazing, he glared at the sports car. He was a big man, barrel-chested and thick-legged, with a massive head that sat almost squarely on huge shoulders. Heavy black brows met above dark angry eyes and a fleshy nose. His reddish acne-scarred skin had a sickly gray undertone from shock. He lowered his head like a bull charging, came around the back of the car, and turned toward Emma's open window, yelling as he came. "Bitch. Fool. What the hell do you think—"

His lips snapped shut. The dot of blood on his cheek trickled toward his chin. His ebony eyes were suddenly opaque.

Both hands—big, brutal hands with spatulate thumbs and hairy knuckles—closed on the window rim by Emma.

Annie was instantly as aware of him as she'd ever been of any man in her life. Not in a nice way. She knew immediately, viscerally, that here was a man who lived his life to suit his own lusts, with no thought or care for those he used. It was apparent in the sensuous droop of his mouth, the jaded disdain of his eyes, the powerful grip of those large hands. She could see it, feel it, and she was horrified to realize he attracted her. A modern Captain Blackbeard, he would attract most women, she knew. He had about him an air of compelling, unbridled, overweening maleness.

Emma tilted her head to look up. "Sorry 'bout that, Neil," she drawled. Her voice held no hint of tension or apology.

His black eyes glittered. "You always live on the edge, don't you, Emma? One of these days you'll go over—and you know what happened to Humpty Dumpty."

"What a tellingly literate allusion, my dear," she replied bitingly. "Just like your reviews."

A muscle flickered once in his jaw. But it was the tightening of his hands on the window rim that revealed just how deep the barb stung.

His lips drew back, exposing blunt tobacco-yellowed teeth, in a savage smile.

"I reviewed a book in the last issue that reminded me of you, Emma.

A serial killer, a killer of shrews and bitches. He liked to cut them into little pieces while they were still alive. He even recorded their screams. But the most fun—"

The car jolted to life.

Neil Bledsoe leapt back just in time as the Jaguar squealed into reverse.

Annie was flung forward then back against the seat, as Emma shifted to low. As the car bolted past the Lincoln, Annie caught a single glimpse of the woman in the backseat. White hair, frightened blue eyes, a wrinkled hand pressed to her lips. The powerful sports car leapt past the parked cars, erupted out of the turnaround, and thundered into the parking lot, white dust boiling in its wake. The Jaguar bucked to a stop behind a loblolly pine.

In the silence after Emma turned off the motor, Annie said grimly, "Next time you plan Death by Car you might inform your passenger." She tried to still her trembling hands.

Emma ignored Annie. With her usual economy of movement, despite her bulk, she unclipped her seat belt, slammed out of the car, and headed briskly for the hotel.

Annie fumbled with her belt, then the latch, flung herself out of the car, and broke into a trot. By the time she caught up with Emma, she felt like a caramel on August asphalt.

"Emma, wait a minute. You can't try to run a man down—oh, all right, you didn't intend to kill him—but you can't race a Jaguar at someone in an obvious attempt to scare the pants off him and not even give any explanation. What are you doing? What are you going to do? Emma, what the hell are you up to?"

"Don't be tiresome, Annie." Emma yanked open one of the side doors of the hotel, and they plunged into the dim hall. "I got Neil's attention—and I enjoyed it. God, I didn't want to brake. I didn't *want* to."

It was cool in the shadowy hall, but not cool enough for the chill that spread over Annie. Emma almost hadn't braked the Jaguar, Annie felt certain of it.

If she hadn't—Annie fought away a wave of nausea.

She reached out, grabbed the older woman's arm. "Emma, for God's sake, you've got to get control of yourself."

Emma didn't even break stride. She shrugged away Annie's grasp. "It may not be too late to stop Fleur."

"Stop her!" Annie picked up speed, her summer flats slapping against the pink-speckled marble floor.

"If she hasn't arrived," Emma said crisply, "maybe there'll still be time to call and tell her not to come." She sailed ahead of Annie into the wide, palm-potted lobby, heading for the registration desk.

Annie had had enough. She put on a burst of speed and caught the author midway across the marble floor. This time she grabbed and held on to a plump but decidedly muscular arm. "Wait a minute. What are you trying to do, sabotage my conference? She's the American star! She's the main speaker at the closing banquet. People are traveling all the way from the West Coast, just to see her."

"Not if I can help it," Emma said grimly. "Take your hands off me, Annie. I'm sorry about your conference. Fleur is more important than any conference. She mustn't come here. She mustn't see Neil." Emma stalked on toward the desk.

Annie realized, as Emma broke away, that their entrance and sharp exchange had attracted attention.

Despite its age (built nearly a century before as a health spa for winter-jaded northerners), the heavily marbled, ornately decorated hotel had a three-story open lobby at its center. On the west side, the sea side, heavily molded archways opened onto a wide screened veranda that in turn led to an open courtyard. The hotel had removed its huge, dragon-decorated Japanese vases. In their place, in honor of the conference, were Victorian urns with lacy ferns and broad-leafed palms, recalling the innumerable palm courts in the English hotels of the twenties and thirties and the cheerful tea dances.

The main axis of the Palmetto House ran north and south and contained the entrance, the central lobby, the registration desk, the concierge's desk, the restaurants, the bar, and conference and meeting areas. East-west wings stretched from either end of the main hall.

Rattan furniture gleamed brightly white among the potted palms. Much of it was occupied, Annie realized, by conference goers. Her conference goers. They were as easily identified with their brightly be-ribboned identification tags, a red rosette for authors, blue for book-sellers, orange for editors, green for agents, pink for readers, as the island's beautiful laughing gulls, with their distinctive sleek black heads.

And almost every eye in the lobby, some boldly, many surreptitiously, was focused on Annie.

She struggled to look pleasant, amiable, and purposeful, the latter so no one would pounce on her. A woman with a curly mop of bright red hair, an anxious expression, and a blue rosette was struggling to her feet.

Annie plunged toward the desk.

A uniformed bellboy pushed a luggage cart toward the elevator. Behind him, Neil Bledsoe followed. The scratch on his cheek was blood-free now but a noticeably angry red. His glance locked with Annie's. She felt her cheeks flush—and saw the flicker of amusement and satisfaction in his eyes. The bastard. He realized his power to attract women, realized and relished it. She determinedly looked away, toward his companion—and stopped flatfooted and stared. Miss Marple? Oh, no, no, it couldn't be! But damned if the woman wasn't exactly the image Annie had carried in her mind all these years, tall and thin, fluffy white hair, soft shell-pink skin—but the eyes were wrong. Fuzzy, myopic, straining eyes. Miss Marple's blue eyes were sharp and quick, even without her binoculars—for birdwatching, of course. As if mesmerized, Annie turned to watch their progress to the elevator.

Emma walked past the critic and the elderly woman as if they didn't exist.

The woman's eyes blinked nervously. But it was Bledsoe's reaction that unnerved Annie. His ruddy face, the grayness gone, twisted, and his sensuous lips drew back in a smirk.

That triumphant smirk held more menace than open anger.

Then the moment was past. Bledsoe and his timid companion stepped into an elevator; Emma leaned on the desk.

Annie stared at the closing elevator door, then swung to peer toward Emma. Annie felt an enormous foreboding. What was going to happen to her conference into which she'd poured months of effort and moun-tains of devotion? She couldn't let Emma bring it all down, like a willful child striking a carefully balanced pyramid of blocks.

Annie skidded to a stop beside the desk. She was just in time to hear the clerk say, "Mrs. Calloway is not registered yet. May I take a message?"

Emma drummed her blunt fingers on the desk. "Yes. Ask her to call Emma Clyde as soon as she arrives. It is very important," and she gave her home telephone number.

Annie knew it well. She always called Emma when the latest Sarah Caudwell arrived. She exclaimed, "Emma, listen, you can't do this to me."

Emma paid no heed. Thanking the clerk, she turned and headed directly for the bank of telephones.

Annie continued her dogged pursuit. "Emma, wait a minute. This is rash. This is stupid. After all, Fleur Calloway's a grown woman. She's promised to appear."

Emma was rummaging for her telephone calling card through a purse that looked like a portable landfill. "Bug off, Annie."

Annie started to speak, but an icy glare made it clear that nothing would dissuade Emma.

Annie stood uncertainly for a moment, then hurried back to the desk and left an urgent message for Mrs. Calloway to get in touch with the conference registration desk immediately upon arrival.

For the first time, she realized why Victorian heroines often stood in perplexity, wringing their hands. She'd never before in her life felt like wringing her hands and was horrified to find that was exactly what she was doing. Jamming the offending members into the pockets of her cotton skirt, she tried to map out a plan of action.

What in the *hell* was she going to do?

Get to Fleur Calloway first. That was the ticket.

Annie looked back at the bank of phones. Emma was gone. Dashing across the floor, barely avoiding collision with a pair of chattering conference attendees who sported I ♥ AGATHA buttons, she grabbed a phone, scrabbled for a quarter in the bottom of her purse where her change always migrated, and dialed home.

"Hello."

Thank God he was home. Never had she been so glad to hear that relaxed, amiable, unflappable, wonderful masculine voice.

"Max!"

She hadn't intended to wail.

"Hey, Annie, what's wrong!"

"Oh, Max, Emma's going to *ruin* the conference!" She got it all out finally, overrode Max's attempts to soothe, and declared, "Look, here's what we've got to do...."

She hung up feeling better, if not completely confident. Now for the next step.

She hurried toward the south wing, passing occasional clumps of conferees, huddled in tight circles and talking at the tops of their voices:

"... the thrillers aren't her best books, I'll grant you that. But I've *always* adored *The Man in the Brown Suit*." (*Aggressively.*)

"The false face. That's the key to understanding the entire body of Christie's work. Always be on the lookout for the false face." (*Insightfully.*)

"Read Mary Westmacott if you *really* want to know Christie." (*Didactically.*)

"It was cheating. I don't care what anybody says. It was *cheating.*" (*Pettishly.*)

Annie was almost grinning when she reached the south wing. Her eavesdropping reassured her. The conference was going to be a smash. That made her even more determined to deflect the forces so firmly intent upon derailing it.

Although the week-long conference didn't officially begin until Sunday afternoon with the Grand Garden Fête, the registration desk was open for the convenience of the early arrivals. It was situated in the south wing foyer, convenient to both the elevators and stairs. This afternoon the desk was staffed by Henny Brawley, Annie's very best customer and a world-class authority on Christie. She was, Annie thought gratefully, also a world-class authority at this point on the Palmetto House, so great had been her involvement in putting the conference together. Annie didn't know how she could have managed without Henny's assistance, encouragement, and stalwart support. As Annie approached, Henny was energetically stuffing some small object into each of the book bags stacked on a nearby table while talking animatedly to a sandy-haired young man with hazel eyes and a sprinkling of freckles across an attractively snub nose. He wore an orange rosette in the lapel of his blazer. Surely he was too young to be an editor! Not a day older than she, Annie was certain.

The black book bags, provided by Death on Demand, flaunted a silver dagger, the store name, and the motto, also in silver: the *BEST* mystery bookstore.

It wasn't until she was within a foot of the table that Annie identified the objects being added to the book bags: two-inch statuettes patterned after the Edgar Allan Poe awards presented for the best in mystery fiction every spring by the Mystery Writers of America.

Laurel had struck again.

But that would have to wait. She had a crisis at hand.

"Henny!"

Henny's fox-sharp face, flushed with pleasure, turned toward Annie. Her welcoming smile slipped away.

"Annie, what's—"

The scream exploded behind them.

Annie, Henny, and the young man turned startled faces toward the stairs.

Annie recognized the white suit, still smudged with dirt and a few spots of blood, but the sound issuing from that heavy face, the lips stretched back in terror, the eyes sightless from horror, curdled her blood. An elephant's trumpet, the whistle of a steam engine, a peacock's screech, the shrill cry in Christie's "The Mystery of the Blue Jar," Neil Bledsoe's scream incorporated them all.

Startled exclamations broke from the onlookers in the foyer.

It seemed almost to occur in slow motion, Bledsoe's uncontrolled ricochet down the stairs, running, slipping, caroming from wall to railing and back again, that agonized wail rising and falling.

Neil Bledsoe fell the last few feet and landed in the lobby facedown, but with almost inhuman agility he rolled onto his hands and knees, his big head swiveling back and forth. Spittle flecked his lips. He gasped for air, struggled to breathe.

Henny was the first to move. Annie followed close behind.

As she hurried forward, Annie realized, with an instant's sharp disappointment, that the young man had whirled and was running away. He'd had a nice face. She wouldn't have expected him to be that kind of person.

It was Henny who understood what was happening.

"Don't be frightened." Her voice was soothing. She gently touched Bledsoe's shoulder.

"Oh dear, oh dear, oh dear." The tall woman—Miss Marple's sister, for God's sake—darted down the stairs and joined them. "Neil, it isn't real. It isn't *real*."

The dark eyes stared at her without comprehension. Bledsoe's face was ashen with a horror Annie had never glimpsed before.

"The crocodile—"

"Alligator," Henny murmured.

"—it's just a painting, Neil. It just looks real." The woman turned toward Henny and Annie, her shell-pink face puckered with distress. "Poor Neil. He just can't bear snakes and—"

The big man, still on his hands and knees, shuddered. Annie felt a pang of sympathy for him. Surely no one deserved to suffer so. Whatever had terrified Neil Bledsoe must have been dreadful indeed.

"A phobia," Henny said calmly. She straightened, then reached down to tug at his arm. "Come now, we'll see you to a different room. It will be all right." Over her shoulder she directed Annie crisply, "Get a bellboy to pick up the bags from Suite 313—" she nodded at Bledsoe and the tall woman "—and move them next door. I'm in 315. The mural there won't upset him. The surf and dolphins. Very restful."

Annie stared after the trio until the elevator door closed, then hurried to do Henny's bidding.

Darn.

If only there'd been some way to forestall Henny from her thoughtful, saving gesture. The hotel was sold out for the weekend. There were no free rooms. What a wonderful way it would have been to rid her conference of Neil Bledsoe.

But she couldn't be too worried about him after that episode. That attack should be enough to take the starch out of him, no matter how hateful the man was reputed to be. She felt a quiver of shame. Certainly she didn't take comfort in any human creature's bondage to irrational fear, but Bledsoe's phobia surely cut him down to size.

Neil Bledsoe was just a paper tiger, after all. She could relax now and look forward to the wonderful, welcoming champagne party at Death on Demand, the unofficial opening of The Christie Caper, a centennial celebration of the birth of the world's greatest writer of detective fiction, Agatha Christie.

AGATHA CHRISTIE
TITLE CLUE

Jane's ulster droops over a chair;
A rolled-up magazine pokes from
a pocket.

Henny's cheeks were perhaps a bit flushed from the champagne, but as always her superb diction carried clearly despite the hubbub.

"Brava, Annie!" she called. "Brava!" She raised her glass in a toast.

Annie grinned at her best customer. Henny looked marvelous in an off-white georgette blouse with a double accordion-pleated collar and cuffs piped in black and an ankle-length black taffeta skirt. Her softly waved hair sported a new silver tone. On anyone else it would have looked grandmotherly, but on Henny, with her observant brown eyes and fox-sharp nose, the result was an aura of sleek intelligence.

Annie lifted her glass in a return toast and permitted herself a warm glow of pride. The champagne reception at Death on Demand was a rousing success. The bookstore had never looked more wonderful, the heart-pine floors gleaming, the gum bookcases filled to the bursting (she had ordered hundreds of extra books, and Ingrid was ringing up sales faster than Annie could replenish the stock from the storeroom; they'd already sold out of the latest Jonathan Gash), the American cozy area enticing (especially to Agatha, who soon retired to her favorite hiding spot among the ferns), the coffee bar appealing. (Despite the appearance there of a model of a tomb from deep in the bowels of the House of Usher. With a furtive glance about, Annie had grabbed the gritty papier-mâché monstrosity and placed it beneath the sink behind the coffee bar. In the interest of familial harmony, however, she had left untouched the jaunty pink scarf gracing the feathered throat of the stuffed raven on his pedestal just inside the front door.)

The evening's only drawback was Max's absence. Annie kept a sharp eye on the opening door, but her tanned and handsome husband didn't appear. (Lightly tanned, of course. Max was a firm believer in the evils of too much sunshine, the efficacy of oat bran despite the jibes of disbelievers, the importance of being relaxed, and the dangers of LDL cholesterol. Max espoused moderation in all things. Well, almost all things. Sex, after all, was natural, wholesome, and essential to achieving the most elevated state of relaxation.)

Annie was regretful. Not only because it was always more fun with Max at her side, but also because he had looked forward to the reception with as much enthusiasm as she. But he had been quick to agree that it was essential to reach Fleur Calloway before Emma did. Annie had no idea how far afield that assignment may have taken him, so she continued to glance hopefully every time the front door opened.

She met several first-time authors who approached her shyly, so nervous they were scarcely able to murmur the names of their titles. They didn't realize that most booksellers look forward to meeting new authors. She was especially pleased to meet Natalie Marlow, whose macabre *Down These Steps* had been one of the most exciting debut novels of the year. It didn't especially surprise Annie to find the author of that polished, icy prose to be gawky, almost incoherent with shyness, and tattily dressed. Not even interviews on the *Today* show could lure some authors out of polyester.

The reception lacked the rowdy overtones of others she had hosted (notably one for the cast after the successful opening night of *Arsenic and Old Lace* a couple of years earlier), but Annie could not have been happier: Death on Demand, plenty of books, and wall-to-wall mystery fans.

Lots of islanders were sprinkled among the party-goers: Frank Saulter, the lanky police chief who never missed a Tom Clancy; Vince Ellis, the red-headed publisher of the *Island Gazette*, who had asked for the latest by Linda Grant; and a glum-faced Emma Clyde, who leaned against the horror/science-fiction shelves. Annie tried to ignore the unwavering stare from hostile blue eyes.

They weren't the only blue eyes Annie was busy ignoring. Laurel, lovely in a kelly-green silk with a pink rose print, sent occasional reproachful glances from her station near the Poe collection. When, of course, she wasn't batting those same alpine lake eyes at handsome young men. Howard, Annie thought dryly, better not pursue Poe manuscripts in New York too much longer.

Shortly after eight, Annie took over at the cash register. Ingrid flashed a grateful look and wormed her way toward the back. Annie hoped there were some hors d'oeuvres left. The chiles rellenos and curried shrimp mold had disappeared early, but, when she'd last checked, the oysters wrapped in bacon, spinach balls, and baked clams were in good supply. Max's secretary, Barb, was overseeing the buffet. (Annie had wanted to provide succulent tidbits appropriate to a tea at Claridge's. The resulting bleat of dismay from across the Atlantic had threatened to sever Anglo-American relations permanently. "Neow, neow, neow. Nevah. One does not partake of banana scones in the *evening* in a cocktail atmosphere!" Annie had reluctantly relinquished that dream, but a tea worthy of the Royal Enclosure at Ascot was scheduled for Sunday afternoon's garden fête.)

Occasionally Annie could hear Barb's loud, cheerful voice as she discovered another Georgette Heyer fan. "*Footsteps in the Dark*," Max's secretary confided, "that's my favorite. I *always* wanted to live in a house like that! Oooooh!"

It was that kind of party, a sustained, cheerful roar, with enough distinguishable comments to make clear the nature of the revelers:

"I've never seen a classier deception than in *The ABC Murders*."

"You haven't read 'Mr. Eastwood's Adventure'? Oh, you must. It has the most *delicious* description of writer's block."

"Don't you just love the opening vignettes in *Cat Among the Pigeons?*"

"Her villages were based on Torquay and St. Mary Church in her native Devon. I always tell my students that her domestic realism is right on a par with Dickens's *Bleak House*."

"I've read every one of her plays. Even *Akhnaton*. Her husband thought it was her most beautiful and profound play."

"Don't you admire her use of color in *Appointment with Death*? She captures not only geography through shades of rose but the emotions of the family."

"Poirot may have been a foreigner, but at heart he was the quintessential Edwardian gentleman."

"Poirot *never* had a twin brother. That was an invention from first to last."

"She enjoyed books by Elizabeth Daly, Michael Gilbert, Margaret Millar, Patricia Highsmith, Elizabeth Bowen, Graham Greene, and Muriel Spark."

At twenty to nine, her first moment of quiet at the cash desk, Annie took a deep breath. She resisted the impulse to punch the computer for a total on the evening's sales, then looked up into the unsmiling face of Neil Bledsoe.

It was a moment she would long remember, the smoldering violence in his coal-black eyes, the sullen droop of his mouth, the aura of physical strength barely leashed, the emanation of swaggering maleness. His crisp white linen suit underscored the raven black of his hair and the ruddiness of his face. He was freshly shaven, but already black stubble showed on his cheeks. The scratch from the injury in the Palmetto House drive was barely visible. More than ever, he had the saturnine appeal of a buccaneer. He saw and correctly interpreted the flicker in her eyes. He gave her a long, measuring, bold look, an inviting, knowledgeable, sensual look.

It was as insulting and invasive as a too-intimate touch. And, horrid to realize, as titillating.

Annie felt like a captive paraded for an emperor's pleasure. She met Bledsoe's gaze squarely—and angrily.

The tall elderly woman a step behind him hesitated, a hand lifted in mute appeal.

Bledsoe grunted. "Make up your mind, sister."

"I beg your pardon." Annie's tone was sheathed in ice. She was proud of her self-control.

"That's the trouble with girls like you. You want it, then you don't. Girls who tease can get themselves in a shitload of trouble."

Annie opened her mouth to attack. The general import of his sentence was infuriating enough, but the denigrating use of *girls* in lieu of *women* was the clincher. And there was such a thing as too much self-control. . . .

"Listen, buddy—" she began.

"Neil—" Miss Marple's look-alike spoke sharply but, to Annie's relief, in a distinctly American voice.

Bledsoe ignored her, keeping his blazing eyes on Annie. "You the one running this thing?"

In six short, snarled words, his tone rude, insolent, and patronizing, he propelled Annie from anger to fury.

A suave, Miss Manners rejoinder was not for her. "What's it to you?" she snarled back, forgetting, as Max had pointed out to her many times, the advantages of inhabiting a morally superior plane.

"*You* put me in that goddam room." His obsidian eyes had the shine of vitreous rock and unsatiated anger.

"Now, Neil, it's just one of those things. Not intentional, I'm sure." His companion peered myopically at Annie and once again the resemblance to Miss Marple waned. "I know it's a sensitive matter. So touchy. But, please, don't quarrel." She tugged futilely on his elbow.

Annie stared at Bledsoe blankly.

"The room with that goddam picture," he raged. "You knew what would happen. You did it to me deliberately. And you're going to regret it."

Before Annie could reply, tell him (a) to shove it, (b) that she hadn't known him from a hole in the ground until the harrowing ride that afternoon with Emma Clyde, and (c) that the hotel management had been responsible for room assignments, he'd turned his back on her.

"Wait a minute," she snapped, but Bledsoe was striding away, his companion trailing unhappily behind, her face puckered with distress.

Following Bledsoe's progress down the aisle was like watching blight spread.

Bledsoe did nothing overtly offensive.

If he had, Annie would have been quick to upbraid him, demand that he leave.

In fact, if she'd had to accuse him, she would have been hard put to frame a charge.

He merely walked, arrogantly, down the central aisle, pausing now and then to glance at titles. Or at people. Selected people.

Not a word was exchanged.

Yet blight touched their faces, turned them grim and stony.

Not everyone, of course. Most of the party-goers paid him no heed, continuing their bright, excited chatter.

But Annie easily pinpointed the ones who knew Bledsoe.

There was the chunky mid-thirties man in a tweed jacket, holding an unlit pipe. He had a stiff brush of wiry black hair frosted with gray, horn rim spectacles that had a tendency to slip, and a salt-and-pepper mustache. He wore an orange rosette in the lapel of his light blue seersucker summer suit. Annie was pleased to see an editor who *looked* like an editor. But his mildly studious look, his air of civilized inquiry dissolved, when Bledsoe approached. After an instant of blank surprise, hatred twisted his face. And hatred sat uneasily there. This was a countenance intended for sunrise and summer, an optimistic face creased with laughter lines. The transformation was shocking. The editor put down a just-replenished glass of champagne, untasted, atop the espionage/thriller book section (Annie hoped no one spilled it; the three books on display were pricey indeed: Erskine Childers's *Riddle of the Sands*, John Buchan's *The Thirty-nine Steps,* and Martha Albrand's *Without Orders*), and walked heavily, as if drained of energy and purpose, toward the front door. As he passed, Annie noted his name tag: NATHAN HILLMAN, Hillman House, CEO and Executive Editor. She wanted to reach out, stop him. But what could she say?

The blight next touched the face of the sandy-haired young man who had rushed away from Bledsoe's panic attack that afternoon. She looked at him closely. He, too, still wore the orange rosette in the buttonhole of his blazer, but now, in Bledsoe's presence, he no longer looked eager and attractive. Without a smile, his snub-nosed face appeared heavy, almost belligerent. He jammed his hands into his pants pockets, hunched his shoulders, and headed for the front door. He strode past Annie as if she were invisible. Whatever he saw, it was not here and now, and it was not pleasant. She noted his name tag: DEREK DAVIS, Hillman House, Publicity.

A customer approached her and she lost sight of Bledsoe, but even as she rang up the books (*Someone Is Killing the Great Chefs of Europe* by Nan and Ivan Lyons, *Death of a Fool* by Ngaio Marsh, and *The Gemini Man* by Susan Kelly), she was certain the dark-haired woman hurrying toward the door was another of the critic's ill-wishers. Her stride was too swift for a casual departure. A green rosette this time, an agent. MARGO WRIGHT, Wright Literary Agency, Ltd. Margo Wright was a tall woman with a Junoesque figure. Crow-black hair tumbled to her shoulders in thick curls, emphasizing the dead white of her face. It wasn't a face that would ever be easily read. At this moment, it was glacial and tormented. As she yanked open the door with one blunt-fingered hand, Annie spotted two new books under her arm.

"Miss!" Annie yelped, "Miss—you at the door—can I help you with those books?"

The agent jolted to a stop and looked blankly down at the books, *Full Cleveland* by Les Roberts and *If Ever I Return, Pretty Peggy O* by Sharyn McCrumb. "Sorry." Her New York accent was crisp. "Didn't intend . . ." She shook her head, slapped the books onto the counter top, and hurried out the door.

That was the crowning blow, a lost sale! Annie glared around the room, looking for the cause. Where was the jerk?

It wasn't hard to spot Bledsoe. He was bigger than almost anyone else. He had returned up the central aisle and was only a few feet away, his back to her, studying the contents of the true-crime section. She didn't see his companion.

True crime wasn't Annie's favorite section, although lately it had done a brisk business. Most of her really weird customers gravitated there. The ones who loved real murder cases, wallowed in their graphic evocation of gore and insanity. No crime was too brutal, too vicious, or too degrading for their pleasure.

The jerk had found his niche.

But even as she sneered, she had to admit to herself—deep in the recesses of her mind—that he might be a jerk, he might be a bully, and he might be altogether disgusting, but the damn man radiated sex appeal in the way he stood, the slope of his shoulders. Annie willed her eyes to move past him.

A small woman knelt in the used-book section, gently lifting out one book after another, glancing at the title page, then replacing them. She arranged the books just so, all the spines even. Her fingers lingered on the last volume. There was more than care here. Her touch was almost reverent, as if these books were holy. Annie studied her profile. She was not a young woman. Deep lines etched her gaunt face. The smooth hair drawn back in a plain chignon was so gray it gave no hint of its youthful color.

Bledsoe's deep voice bayed gleefully. "Well, if it isn't Victoria. Long time no see."

A book slipped from suddenly nerveless fingers, tumbled to the floor. The tiny woman gasped and reached for it.

But Bledsoe's huge hand scooped it up, away from her reach. His black eyes flicked over the title, faded black on a brown cover, and he gave a huge whoop of laughter. "*The Clue of the Chattering Parrot*. Oh, sweet Jesus, can you believe they ever sold even one of these! My God, what tripe!"

"Stop it, Neil. Stop it." The woman struggled up from the floor and snatched for the book.

Bledsoe merely held up his arm, and the book was far beyond her reach. "Finders keepers," he crowed. "I think I'll buy this. Be a pleasure to throw it away. Maybe I'll start a new crusade. Buy a lousy book a day and throw it away. That has a nice ring to it, doesn't it. Rid the world of all these simpering, lily-livered cozies."

Annie had had enough. She charged out from behind the cash desk.

"The book," she demanded crisply, her hand outstretched.

Bledsoe shed his joviality faster than Vidocq changing a disguise. His tone changed from jeering to snide. "This *is* a bookstore? You do *sell* these books?"

"Not to you, buddy. Hand it over and get the hell out of here."

It hung in the balance for a long moment. Annie could see in his darkening face the desire to keep after it, to badger and harangue, but Frank Saulter was turning toward Bledsoe. The police chief wasn't nearly the size of the critic, but there was an unmistakable air of authority to Saulter and a grim set to his jaw.

Bledsoe gave an exaggerated shrug. "Sure, boss lady. Stupid to buy this kind of tripe anyway." He tossed the volume toward the cash desk. It struck the rim and tumbled, yellowed pages shaking loose, to the floor.

The older woman, tears sliding silently down her cheeks, scrambled forward. She swiftly gathered the loose pages and the battered book and rose. "Please," she said to Annie timidly, "I'll buy this."

Annie surprised herself. She was never especially demonstrative (except with Max and that was another, private matter entirely). In fact, she had found it hard to master the casual embrace and brush of lips so fashionable among women she knew when greeting friends. But she was touched by the tragedy she saw in that wan face and in the trembling hands that offered the book. Impulsively, she slipped her arm around those too-thin shoulders. "That's Bryan Shaw's last novel, isn't it? I liked it so much. His misdirection is brilliant. Of course, that's no surprise. He was a wonderful writer, and it's going to be such a pleasure to talk about his books at the conference and discuss the contributions he made to the mystery."

It was like seeing the sun burst through clouds and where there had been fog and dreariness there was now a verdant, glowing landscape. Victoria's face glowed. Her eyes glistened; twin spots of pink touched her gaunt cheeks. "Did you read *Chimera*?" she asked eagerly. "That was his favorite of his own books."

"Oh, of course," Annie rejoined eagerly. "Everything hinged on what the dentist *didn't* see. And his characterizations were superb—the banker, the housewife, the sheriff's daughter."

"Ohh." It was a little cry of sheer happiness. "You really did read Bryan. . . . Bryan was my husband."

There was such pride, such devotion in that quiet declaration. Sudden tears stung Annie's eyes. She gave Victoria Shaw a quick hug. "I'm so pleased to meet you, Mrs. Shaw. I want to give you this book"—Annie touched the faded brown cover "—and I hope you'll be willing to speak at the panel Thursday. Your husband's fans will be so excited to learn more about him. He must have been a very fine man."

Over Victoria's shoulder, Annie caught the flash of Bledsoe's sardonic grin. He started to open his mouth. Annie gave a sharp nod at Frank Saulter.

"If you can't stand the heat—" Bledsoe began.

Victoria Shaw's face crumpled.

Saulter jerked his head toward the door. "Time for you to go see a man about a dog, mister. Outside."

The bell above the door jangled. It swung in, and at long last, there was the man in Annie's life, beaming at her and gallantly shepherding the famous Fleur Calloway into Death on Demand.

Despite her sudden sense of dismay, Annie couldn't help being proud of Max. Not even David Niven as Raffles could match Max in a white dinner jacket. He was so damned *nice*-looking, thick, short blond hair, blue eyes as dark as a Norwegian fjord, strong, firm nose and chin.

His companion was laughing up at him.

Oh, God. Earlier, when the party was at its height, before Neil Bledsoe arrived, Annie would have been delighted: Fleur Calloway at Death on Demand!

Now she desperately wondered how to avoid disaster. There was a clot of people near the cash desk: Victoria Shaw, who was edging behind Annie toward the door; Neil Bledsoe and Frank Saulter, Bledsoe glaring at the chief, Frank undeterred; Annie, and now Max and Fleur Calloway.

Annie, her hands outstretched, surged toward the author. "Mrs. Calloway, this is so exciting, so wonderful."

From the back of the bookstore Emma Clyde boomed, "Fleur. Fleur!"

Annie took slender hands, cool and soft to the touch. "You have so many readers here on the island, Mrs. Calloway. I sell some of your books every week. Everyone is delighted that you are our guest of honor."

"Fleur." Louder and closer. Emma was struggling through the crowds toward the front.

And Annie, looking into jade green eyes, had an inkling why Emma, whom Annie had always found so intimidating and, frankly, so self-absorbed, was moved to protect the woman now standing by the front door of Death on Demand. Although Annie had seen pictures of Fleur Calloway, none of them did the writer justice. The photographs recorded the flowing tawny hair, the exquisite bone structure, the deep-set eyes, the slender neck, but they conveyed nothing of her warmth of manner, the intensity of her gaze, the crinkling laughter lines at her eyes and lips, the sense of rapport that was almost physical.

"How could I refuse," the author said in a light, sweet voice, "when you wrote me such glowing letters."

"Sure she wrote glowing letters."

Annie froze at the sound of Bledsoe's voice.

"Your books still sell, Fleur. Though God knows why. The kind of drivel that soothes weak minds, I suppose."

Fleur Calloway's eyes—a clear green as light and delicate as the first spring shoots of cordgrass in the marsh—sought the speaker, sought him just for an instant, then her gaze moved past as if no one stood there, as if the words had never been spoken. She looked again at Annie. The warmth was there, but in it, unspoken, lurked a question.

"He's just leaving," Annie said tightly. "He seems to have come to the wrong place."

"And so have you, Fleur." Emma Clyde pushed roughly past Bledsoe. "Let's give this conference a miss. I've already ordered my crew out to *Marigold's Pleasure*. Made the arrangements this afternoon. We can sail for Tortola tonight."

"Dear Emma," Fleur cried warmly. She embraced the imposing author. "I'm the world's worst sailor, darling. Remember? I never poked a nose out of my stateroom on that mystery cruise to Hawaii. Such an embarrassment. It always made me feel better that Christie had such a time on ships, too. And so, of course, does dear old Hercule." Fleur turned back to Annie and slipped an arm through hers. The delicate yet unmistakable scent of Diva touched Annie. The author looked eagerly down the central aisle. "I've heard so much about your wonderful store. I understand you have coffee mugs with mystery titles painted on them."

She shot a dazzling smile at Emma. "The conference will be fine, love. Don't worry. I'm looking forward to it. And you and I shall stay up and talk until dawn, just as we used to do. But now, I *must* see all of this wonderful haven for mysteries."

Annie found herself drawn down the central aisle toward the coffee bar, her arm lightly grasped by her famous guest. It was like walking unconcernedly up the beach with a tsunami on her heels. Annie glanced over her shoulder.

Emma, her face a sour mixture of disgust, anger, and defeat, glared at Annie, then turned on her heel and yanked open the door.

Bledsoe looked equally furious, but, of course, for an entirely different reason: Fleur Calloway had ignored the critic's very existence. He turned toward his fluttery companion and gestured toward the door, which was closing behind Emma.

Max was frowning, obviously aware that all was not well at Death on Demand.

Annie flashed him a reassuring smile, then gave full attention to her conference's guest of honor.

"...and I'm delighted to see that you have a romantic suspense section. That's marvelous. Romantic suspense is so undervalued today, despite books like *Rebecca* and *Nine Coaches Waiting*. But you know how publishing is, this kind of book now, another kind next year. So difficult for authors. Most of us" —jade green eyes sought Annie's opinion—"are best at a particular kind of book. We just can't change our styles every other year like hem lengths." Her laughter, though, was good humored, untroubled. "Perhaps that might be a good topic for my talk. I'm sure you've noticed the trends. Everything is a series now. Very few thrillers. Oh, the Tom Clancy techno-thrillers, of course, but what we need more of is the kind of novel Mary Higgins Clark is doing—the quiet, domestic suspense, the scraping sound outside the window in the middle of the night."

They had reached the coffee bar. Admiring fans made way for them as they passed. Annie was reaching for the mug with the title of Calloway's most famous book, *I Won't Let You Die,* when the shots rang out.

AGATHA CHRISTIE
TITLE CLUE

Poor Wonky Pooh's mistress
never reached Scotland Yard;
Lavinia was Victim Number 4,
how many more?

9

Not that Annie immediately identified the faint pops as gunfire. The other sounds, which erupted almost simultaneously, seemed far more ominous:

The tinkling of broken glass.

A shrill, choked-off scream.

Deep-throated curses.

Saulter's shouted commands.

But she knew instinctively that trouble—big trouble—had struck Death on Demand, and she was racing down the central aisle toward the front when Max grabbed her and shoved her behind the true-crime section.

Shielding her with his body, he hissed, "Stay down!" then rolled to his feet and moved in a crouch toward the open door.

Annie popped back to her feet, disconnected thoughts tumbling: outside? . . . of course . . . but it sounded like firecrackers . . . firecrackers wouldn't shatter the window . . . oh God, shots!

It was some indication of the terrorist mentality of Americans that no one had questioned Saulter's shouted commands to take cover. In a country where children can be mowed down in a schoolyard with an assault rifle and where American Rifle Association members defend the sanctity of AK 47s from prohibition, an armed attack on a resort island bookstore seemed reasonable enough.

Annie didn't, of course, stay put.

Without even looking, Max waggled a hand peremptorily behind him.

She ignored that. Dammit, it was *her* bookstore.

And it was her south front window the bullets had shattered. Splintered glass glinted on the floor.

Bledsoe, swearing in a harsh monotone, unceremoniously shoved his elderly companion back inside Death on Demand. Once again his white suit was the worse for wear, stained now with sand from the much-scuffed wooden veranda that fronted the harbor shops.

"My goodness," his companion exclaimed in quiet surprise, struggling to sit up, "I'm bleeding." Crimson spurted from her right hand.

Annie darted up to join her, then looked frantically around for something to staunch the flow, but Fleur Calloway brushed past and set to work. "It's all right," the author soothed. "Surface cuts bleed profusely, but it's not deep," and she wrapped the wound in her soft white cashmere shawl.

Swinging around, Bledsoe charged back toward the door. "Fucker shot at me!"

"Stop, you fool!" Saulter ordered.

If Bledsoe heard—and such was his rage, Annie doubted it—he ignored Saulter.

It took the police chief's tackle and Max's block to bring Bledsoe down. It also brought down pink-scarfed Edgar, the stuffed raven, and the hanging beads that separated the children's corner from the bookstore proper.

By the time the three men stopped thumping about in the foyer, Annie had reached the door and was cautiously surveying the veranda, ignoring the stunned comments of those trapped behind her in the bookstore.

No bodies.

From behind posts, rocking chairs, and stubby palmettos, island residents and tourists peered out with equal caution.

"Stay back, Annie," Saulter snapped irritably as he and Max brushed past her and slid through the open door. Max flapped that hand again.

Annie, of course, was right behind them, almost trodding on her husband's heels.

The harbor front looked—except for the cautious heads poking from behind shelter—as it always did. Romantic, charming, inviting—

and dimly lit. The harbor was on the southwest end of the island, a natural curve facing west. The shops followed that curve, overlooking the marina and the boats moored there. Old-fashioned lampposts dotted the sidewalk that rimmed the harbor. They emitted a golden glow with scarcely enough wattage to attract even the most virile moths. As for the varicolored lights adorning the sea wall, they were strictly for show. Down in the marina, sharply bright, businesslike lights threw into stark relief the floating docks and the boats, which ranged from a multimillion-dollar yacht from Monte Carlo to a single-masted sailboat from Charleston. But this illumination only emphasized the calculated duskiness along the boardwalk.

A gaggle of boys wheeled their dirt bikes to a stop beside the steps leading up to the veranda. Youthful voices tumbled over each other as they yelled at Saulter.

"... *saw somebody behind the bushes* ..."

"... *he ran away* ..."

"... *saw him throw the gun. I saw it* ..."

"... *a splash. Wasn't a fish* ..."

Red-faced from exertion, a pudgy young man trotted up to the boardwalk and announced importantly, "The shots came from *there*," and he pointed at the huge mass of shrubbery, sweet-smelling white-flowered pittosporum, that had grown almost twelve feet tall on the bank at the end of the harbor. It marked the site of the island's original playhouse, which had burned several years before. Behind the shrubbery rose tall, dark pines. The newcomer, gesturing in excitement, launched into a labored account of where he'd been when he heard the shots, what he did next, how he'd yelled for help. "Gosh, I never thought when I came to the island for a mystery conference that there'd really be a mystery!"

One of her conference-goers. Annie noted his name tag. JAMES BENTLEY, Brooklyn. She'd noticed him in the bookstore earlier, curly-haired and overweight, absorbed in the hard-boiled section. Annie didn't like his present expression of avid pleasure. After all, someone—and she had a damn good idea who—had shot at her store, and she sure didn't consider it part of the evening's entertainment.

Pounding footsteps down the boardwalk stairs signaled Neil Bledsoe's mad bull rush toward the site. Customers spilled out the front door and gathered around Annie. Harbor visitors who had taken cover now gathered, talking excitedly, pointing toward Death on Demand and the bank of shrubbery.

"Oh, shit!" Saulter exclaimed, sprinting after Bledsoe. He yelled orders as he ran, "Annie, keep everyone inside the store. Get their names. Call Billy. Max, round up everyone who was in the harbor area!"

It took most of an hour to sort it all out. Billy Cameron, Saulter's assistant, roared up to the harbor area on his motorcycle and took over from Max the task of collecting the names of those who had been walking leisurely on the boardwalk when the gunfire erupted. Annie dutifully herded her reception attendees back inside Death on Demand and as tactfully as possible obtained names, addresses, and phone numbers. Aside from a few island residents, most were registered at the Palmetto House for The Christie Caper. Laurel offered to help, but Annie felt that Laurel's death's-head fountain pen (ivory?) was perhaps not the most tactful means of transcribing the information. However, she smiled appreciatively at her mother-in-law and suggested that she man the coffee bar. "Free, of course."

"Certainly," Laurel murmured, but before turning away, she shook her head commiseratingly. "Dear Annie, I have this sense" —a dramatic placement of hand over heart—"of gloom. And doom." The husky voice dropped yet another register. " 'While from a proud tower in the town Death looks gigantically down!' " The exclamation point was Laurel's.

"Nobody died," Annie replied crisply. She was proud of her cool, restrained answer because, within, she was seething. Somebody was going to pay for this—and she didn't mean just the broken window. Nobody was going to shoot at her bookstore and get away with it.

Henny looked up from her study of the shattered window. "Somebody sure as hell could have died."

Laurel was on her way to the coffee bar when she saw Edgar beakdown in the glass shards that littered the floor. "Oh, oh, oh." Before Annie could intervene, Laurel darted past her and scooped up the stuffed raven. "Edgar!" she wailed, holding the bird aloft.

Annie blinked. Oh, good grief! One of the bullets had lodged squarely in the center of Edgar's feathered head. Annie was irresistibly reminded of Louisa Revell's *The Men with Three Eyes*. Laughter bubbled up inside her, but the anguish in her mother-in-law's plaintive cry was genuine, so she stifled a giggle and said hurriedly, "Laurel, after all, it's just a namesake. I mean, don't take it to heart. Besides, this will be good for the chief. Now he'll have a bullet to trace," and she briskly retrieved the battered bird and placed it on the counter.

Laurel pressed a graceful hand to her forehead and swept to the back of the bookstore, quoting—and Annie couldn't help noticing how distinct and far-carrying was her diction—" 'What this grim, ungainly, ghastly, gaunt and ominous bird of yore/Meant in croaking "Never-more." ' "

Occasionally, as Annie took names and reassured her guests that murderous volleys were far from routine on Broward's Rock, she heard snatches of "The Raven." While dispensing coffee, Laurel was performing the whole damn poem! Annie refused to look toward the coffee bar. Lord, grant her patience. Grant her endurance. Grant her some means of deflecting Laurel from this latest obsession. Grant her also an end to this stream of anxious registrants whose names she must record. She chafed to be outside, in the thick of the investigation. What had Saulter discovered? Had he got a description of the gunman from the pudgy conference-goer and the excited boys? Had he settled Bledsoe down?

Bledsoe's heroics had surprised her. So often in her experience, bullies turned out to be cowards. Certainly, no one could accuse the critic of cowardice. Not only had he tried his damndest to get to the gunman's vantage point first, he had protected his companion, pushing her to safety, before going fearlessly after his assailant.

And where was she now, the elderly woman who looked so much like Miss Marple but had a distinctly American accent? Annie spotted her deep in conversation with Henny, gesturing with a now neatly bandaged hand. Annie hoped that Fleur's cashmere shawl wasn't ruined.

Max popped back inside twice, once to report no luck in the search for the gunman, a second time to assure Annie that the front window would be boarded over in a jiffy.

Annie whipped through her task as fast as possible without appearing rude. She understood the point, of course. Anyone who had been inside Death on Demand when the shots were fired was automatically *not* a suspect.

The corollary, of course, was equally apparent.

Every person outside was, perforce, a possible marksman.

That would include those who had earlier been at Death on Demand and who had departed before Bledsoe.

Especially those who obviously knew and disliked him.
Like Emma Clyde.

"Scotch and soda?" Max held the syphon in his hand and looked inquiringly at their guests.

Saulter declined. "Coke," he said mournfully. Still on duty, of course.

Seltzer sizzled cheerfully as Max prepared the drinks. Although it was almost midnight, neither Laurel nor Henny showed any signs of flagging, and they'd stuck closer to Annie and Max than Nora to Nick Charles, especially when it became clear that the chief had no intention of waiting until tomorrow before quizzing Annie about that evening's events. For the first time, Annie regretted having rented one of the Carolina suites at the Palmetto House for the duration of the conference. Unfortunately, there was plenty of room for everybody. Annie was in a hurry to get this behind her. Tomorrow was the first day of The Christie Caper. She didn't want an investigation ruining the fun. And she had a million details to check before the fête opened at three.

Laurel slipped off three-inch green heels and tucked her size-five triple-A feet daintily beneath her on one couch. With her head tilted admiringly to one side, she smiled winsomely at the chief, looking like a fifties thriller heroine who had just sighted a ruggedly handsome man.

Rarely, Annie thought sourly, had she met any male who was immune to Laurel's charm. The chief was certainly no exception. There was nothing official about the smile he bestowed on her.

Henny was, for her, unusually unobtrusive. Death on Demand's most passionate customer sat in a far corner of the room. The light shining through the Tiffany shade on a nearby lamp created an interesting multicolored effect on her face and her white blouse. Annie's eyes narrowed. Surely Henny's placement wasn't fortuitous. Nothing was ever likely to be fortuitous with Henny. She was obviously up to her old tricks, assuming the guise of a fictional detective when embroiled in a mystery. Be interesting to see how long Henny could be satisfied with the rather passive role Mr. Harley Quin played in the series of Christie short stories featuring Quin and Mr. Satterthwaite.

Chief Saulter sipped his Coke and surveyed the Palmetto House suite. "Pretty fancy. Haven't been inside since that lady decorator from Atlanta redid everything."

Max smiled happily. "Some wonderful improvements."

White wicker furniture gave the hotel suite an air of casual tropical elegance, which was enhanced by the Gauguin-bright cushions and lush potted ferns. The dramatic focus of the room was, of course, the full wall mural. Each suite boasted an original, one-of-a-kind island scene. In this one, a flat-bottomed wooden oyster boat lay abandoned, its bow jammed into a marsh hammock. Cordgrass rippled around the small tree island like a deck of cards in expert hands. Standing behind the forsaken boat, a black-masked raccoon watched as an elegant white ibis probed the murky water for crayfish. Not a cloud marred the soft blue of the summer sky.

Saulter cleared his throat. "Okay, Annie, I want the lowdown on the stuff at the bookstore tonight. Why was everybody hacked at this Bledsoe guy?"

"I don't know about everybody," Annie replied grimly, "but I know that Emma Clyde has it in for him. Do you know what she did this afternoon?"

Max handed her a drink, and she scooted over to make room for him to sit on the love seat beside her.

The chief put his glass down and flipped open his notebook. "I wanted to ask you about that. Since you were in the car."

Annie was impressed. How had the chief already heard about Emma's car assault?

"Stopped on a dime, I heard," Henny said admiringly.

"Barely," Annie snapped. She'd been irritated with Emma at the time, but now she was furious. Shoot out her bookstore's windows! "Listen, Chief, there's bad blood between Emma and Bledsoe. I don't know any details, but Emma deliberately tried to scare the hell out of him this afternoon, and I think that's what happened again tonight."

"You think Emma shot at Bledsoe?"

"I sure do. This afternoon Emma stormed into Death on Demand, wanting to know why I'd invited him. I hadn't, of course. He registered just like everybody else. According to Emma, he's been vicious to the cozy writers and she couldn't believe he would come to this conference."

"Now, Annie," the chief chided, "there has to be more to it than that. Emma damn near ran over the man."

"But she *didn't* hit him, Chief," she emphasized. "Just like the bullets missed him tonight."

Saulter looked at her sharply, then scrawled rapidly in the notebook. "Yep, I get you. But why the hell?"

"I have no idea." Annie tried to look as limpid as Archie Goodwin defending a pretty girl to his orchid-loving, woman-hating boss. She didn't want to drag Fleur Calloway into it.

The chief looked at her sharply. "Buck Hughes, the doorman, swears it was deliberate. He said Emma drove an ambulance in North Africa and she for sure knew how to handle that Jaguar."

Max spoke indistinctly as he munched a handful of unsalted peanuts. "I'd say Emma's always in control—of cars, herself, her world."

"Dear Emma. Such a *strong* personality," Laurel murmured.

Saulter rubbed his nose thoughtfully. "Spite, huh?" Annie could see the tension easing out of his shoulders. After all, using a gun to scare someone was reprehensible, but it was a lot less worrisome than attempted murder. "It's sure possible. Emma left the store before Bledsoe."

Annie managed not to look as satisfied as she felt. She hoped Saulter went straight to Emma's mansion and rousted her out of bed for a third degree. This appealing vision didn't last long. Saulter wasn't that kind of lawman.

Annie couldn't resist adding, "It almost *has* to be Emma. How could anybody else in the store have known Bledsoe was coming to the reception? And why would anybody come to a conference packing a twenty-two?"

Henny made a judicious *harumph*.

Annie had an instant visual image of Mr. Justice Wargrave, the redoubtable hanging judge in the novel version of *And Then There Were None*.

Henny added a dry little cough. "Necessary to look at all the evidence."

Every eye was on her as Henny delved into her purse and brought out a sheaf of papers. Thumbing briskly, she said, "Aha! Important exhibit here."

Annie snarled, "Barristers offer exhibits. Not judges."

Everybody ignored her. All eyes were on Henny.

Annie immediately recognized the pale apricot sheet Henny thrust at Saulter. It was the third status report Annie'd mailed to all who had pre-registered for the conference. "Back side," Henny instructed briskly. "List of authors expected to attend."

Saulter looked at her inquiringly.

"Bledsoe's listed."

Annie started to protest.

Henny continued decisively, "Nonfiction authors are included. He has a book out on the hero in detective fiction."

Annie subsided. To tell the truth, she hadn't paid any particular attention to names unfamiliar to her when she checked the list that Ingrid had compiled from registrations.

"Point is," Henny concluded in that dry, unemotional tone, "everyone coming to the conference got that sheet and could have known Bledsoe would be here—and brought along a twenty-two pistol. And since Bledsoe's obviously intent on causing trouble, it was a safe bet he'd show up at the reception tonight."

"Oh, dammit," Annie exploded, "you've read too many mysteries!" Everyone looked at her.

Annie bristled. "Well, for Pete's sake, why come *here* to kill him?" A thoughtful silence.

Annie could have reeled off a dozen reasons herself. She ignored her own question, plunged ahead. "A twenty-two," she exclaimed disparagingly. "No serious murderer goes around shooting at people with a twenty-two!"

Her sarcasm didn't impress Saulter. "Dead's dead," he said succinctly, "whether it's a forty-five slug or a twenty-two."

"Reopens question of probability," Henny stated.

Even Max supported the opposition. He patted Annie's arm gently. "Have to face facts, sweetheart." She could have strangled him. After a sizzling look at her well-meaning but infuriating husband, Annie tried another tack. "You're all just being stubborn. Look at what actually happened—*no one* got hurt! Obviously, it wasn't attempted murder at all."

"Because the shots missed?" Saulter asked.

Henny snorted. "Annie, that's dumber than Shaitana inviting all those murderers to play bridge."

So much, Annie thought, for the dry and unemotional approach of Mr. Justice Wargrave. Four sleuths appeared in *Cards on the Table*. As Henny leaned forward, chin in hand, eyes farseeing, Annie nodded. Colonel Race, of course.

Henny's clipped, matter-of-fact commentary confirmed her suspicion.

"One person in front of window. Other already started down steps. Bullets hit six-foot level. Intended victim obvious." Henny glanced at the chief for confirmation.

Max nodded vigorously. "I was facing the front of the shop, and I saw the glass break. Eye-level to me."

The chief riffled back through the notebook. "Bledsoe is six foot two. No one else was on that portion of veranda. His companion—an aunt by marriage, Kathryn Honeycutt—was midway down the steps. The bullets struck Death on Demand south window six feet one inch from floor level."

Annie refused to be quashed. "The bullets didn't hit him!"

"Nope," the chief agreed. "So you could be right. The shots could have been intended merely to frighten him. Thing is, we can't ignore the possibility the shots missed from sheer bad luck. Bledsoe'd stopped to light a cigar. He dropped his lighter and bent to pick it up."

"So that's when Emma decided to shoot," Annie insisted.

Laurel chose this moment to murmur in her unforgettable, husky voice, "There was an iciness, a sinking, a sickening of the heart . . . an unredeemed dreariness of thought which no goading of the imagination could torture into aught of the sublime."

There was, also, understandably, a pause in the conversation.

Henny grinned. "A woman's intuition, that's the ticket."

Max smiled kindly at his mother, an admiring light in his dark blue eyes. Annie pretended she hadn't seen it.

Saulter looked at Laurel politely.

Laurel swirled the ice cubes in her Scotch and soda. "Those heartfelt, wrenching words capture the throbbing essence of my tumultuous, inmost feelings when the moment of crisis occurred tonight at Death on Demand."

"Well, uh, Mrs. Roethke, sure sorry you were upset. Pretty unpleasant, I know."

Laurel sipped at her Scotch. "Dear Edgar captured a like feeling so well in that treasured classic of the ages, 'The Fall of the House of Usher.'"

"Edgar Allan Poe," Annie supplied irritably.

"So you take this shooting seriously?" Saulter asked Laurel.

No voice ever seemed more prophetic of doom than Laurel's husky whisper. Her words fell softly like stones slipping quietly into deep water. "'And, anon, there strikes the ebony clock which stands in the hall of velvet.'"

Annie recognized it, of course. From Poe's "The Masque of the Red Death." But even so, the words sent a chill through her, and the back of her neck prickled with horror. Which perhaps explained her over-reaction.

"Oh, come *on*, Laurel. Somebody potting wildly with a twenty-two isn't quite of the same realm as the bubonic plague. There's such a thing as reading too much Poe, you know." Annie swung toward the chief, managing a tight smile. "Laurel's really *into* Poe, as the saying goes. I think we're all taking this too seriously." She glanced at her watch. "Look, it's almost one o'clock and I've got a big day tomorrow . . ." The big-gest day of her career. Why, oh, why did Laurel have to maunder on about Poe and why did that machismo jerk Bledsoe sign up for *her* con-ference and *how* was Annie going to close this investigation down? ". . . and everything will look better in the morning," she ended hope-fully.

Saulter merely settled deeper in his chair. "Annie, what were you and Bledsoe crossways about at the reception tonight?"

Annie jammed a hand through her sandy hair. "The guy charges in like Rambo and blames me for his room assignment." Crisply, she de-scribed Bledsoe's phobia and the resulting panic attack. "I thought he was having a heart attack, but Henny figured it out. Anyway, he shows up at the reception and starts in on me about the room assignments. As if I knew or cared who he was, or what kind of phobias he might have. Actually, if he doesn't stop acting like such an asshole, I may slip a friendly alligator into his suite. Serve him right."

Saulter tapped his pen on his notebook. "The hotel made the room assignments? Not any of your staff?"

Annie glared at him. "Absolutely. We had nothing to do with it." She flapped her hands indignantly. "Frank, surely you don't think the room assignment was a deliberate attempt by one of us to freak the guy!"

"I have to consider it, Annie." There was no hint of apology in his Low Country drawl. "Because somebody sure as hell shot at him tonight. We found four shells in the pittosporum." (He pronounced it like a true South Carolinian: piss-*poe*-rum.) "No footprints to speak of. Too many leaves and drifted palm fronds. No trace of the gun."

Max leaned forward. "I thought the kids heard a splash."

"And they saw the guy, too, didn't they?" Annie demanded. She still smarted from the slight to the staff of her bookstore. "And we were all inside Death on Demand," she concluded triumphantly.

Saulter cocked his head. Did he think he was Colonel John Primrose? "Was everyone?" he drawled. As Annie spluttered, the chief pointed at her. "Okay, Annie. You're out of it. I saw you. I was watching you because of your set-to with Bledsoe. And you're going to tell me more about that before we finish—and how that woman in the used-book section figures in, too. Anyway, I can account for you. And Max. But it was crowded in there. Somebody could have slipped out the back door, run down the alley, done the shooting, and easily slipped back inside during the panic and confusion right after the shots." He tapped his notebook. "And that includes, among many, Ingrid, Henny, and you, Mrs. Roethke."

Annie's mouth opened in a soundless O. So the names and addresses of those at the reception were taken not to establish alibis, but to add to the number of suspects. Oh, wow.

"Right-o," Henny bayed, still in her Colonel Race persona. "Not accustomed to suspect's role. New experience. Good-oh."

Laurel smoothed back a tendril of blond hair. "One writer even went so far as to suggest," her tone was one of quiet condescension, "that our own dear Edgar was himself the murderer of Mary Rogers!"

Annie muttered wearily, " 'The Mystery of Marie Rogêt.' The first fictional use of a true crime. Young woman clerk in a New York cigar store disappeared, body found in river. Never solved for certain."

Max scowled. "That's absurd."

Laurel beamed at her son. "Dear Max, you agree! Certainly it was absurd to accuse Edgar!"

Saulter's face creased in puzzlement.

Max was more accustomed to Laurel's thought processes. "That's not the matter at issue," he said to his mother. "Look, Frank, it's obvious Mother couldn't have had anything to do with it. She doesn't know a thing about Bledsoe."

"Not true, darling," Laurel trilled.

Now she truly had everyone's attention. Especially the chief's.

Laurel gazed at them all with childlike candor. "So necessary, isn't it, in a criminal investigation to reveal every last tidbit of information, whether or not germane?" Laurel's countenance drooped. "A truly discomfiting experience. Very bad karma. Do you know, I feel confident Edgar would have truly understood the concept of karma!"

Saulter refused to be distracted. "You know Bledsoe?"

"I am acquainted with him. *Not* a memory I cherish." She fingered her gold charm bracelet and a tiny ship clicked against a palm tree.

"That mystery cruise to Rio." She turned wide blue eyes on Annie. "My dear, I was so *glad* you weren't along. Though I *always* treasure your company. Your *serious* approach to life, your no-nonsense attitude, your—"

"Bledsoe was on the ship?" Saulter prompted.

She nodded agreeably. "A speaker. On the mystery. Though, I must certainly say, not the mystery as *I* understand it. All about books with characters named Big Al and Rutabaga Ralph"—a slight frown—"or was it Banana Bob? And the detectives he talked about. *Not* gentlemen. And no first names. Quill or Brill or Spode or Tarker. And drink? My dears," she leaned forward confidingly, "this *enormous* capacity for alcohol, as if that were admirable! And sex at the most unexpected"— her glance paused on her son and she changed course—"a most peculiar, and I might add, unattractive, view of women. No more than chattel. To be used and abused. And the plots seemed—"

"Mrs. Roethke! That's fine. That's enough. You knew Bledsoe from a mystery cruise. Any other contact?"

"No. Not an acquaintanceship to be pursued." A cheerful smile.

Saulter asked abruptly, "What's your opinion of him?"

Laurel placed her fingertips together and looked off, as if into a great distance, her face grave, her demeanor one of unparalleled sobriety. " 'The worst heart of the world is a grosser book than the *Hortulus Animae,* and perhaps it is but one of the great mercies of God that "er lasst sich nicht lessen." ' "

"The closing sentence of 'The Man of the Crowd,' " Annie murmured. "Poe opens the story by saying that it is well said of a certain German book that 'it does not permit itself to be read.' "

"Uh, yeah." Undaunted, the chief scrawled something in his notes. Laurel smiled on them serenely. Max ate the last peanut and stared thoughtfully at the empty bowl.

Annie was still hoping for a quick resolution. "Chief, did the boys get a good look at the gunman?"

Saulter laughed grimly. "Did they? To hear those kids tell it, he was ten feet tall, had a skull instead of a head, was dressed all in black. Unfortunately, they didn't see all that much. They were on their bikes and had just come out of the alley when they heard the shots"—as Saulter related their report, Max idly sketched a map on a cocktail napkin—"which they thought were firecrackers. Then they heard the glass break and saw Bledsoe fall down on top of Honeycutt. The bushes rustled over by the ruin of the old theater, and a minute later they heard a splash. Not much to be seen at night. I'll have Billy go down tomorrow and take a look. Maybe the gunman got rid of his weapon before he ran. Course, there's so much muck in that harbor, it'll be a miracle if we find anything. The harbor hasn't been dredged for almost eight years. Anyways, the boys heard running footsteps. The boys took off for the bushes." Saulter blew out a spurt of air.

Max handed his map to Annie, and she saw at a glance why no one had caught the gunman. A grove of pines stood behind the shrubbery. Easy enough to duck behind a pine and wait until the excitement cooled down.

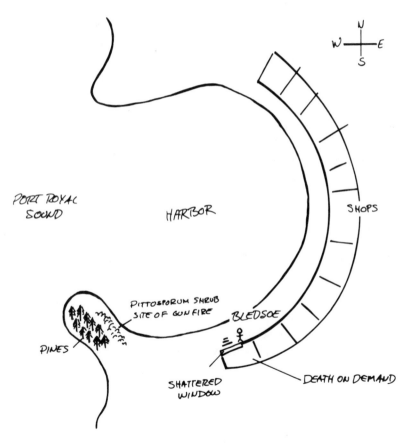

"Damn fool kids. And Scouts, too. Should've known better. I asked Willy Washburn what the hell he thought he was going to do if they'd caught up with a man with a gun."

"But the man didn't have the gun at that point," Laurel interposed.

Saulter glowered at her. "So they heard a splash! Could have been a fish. Anyway, they got to the pine grove and didn't see anybody. That's when they turned around and hightailed it to the shops."

Max popped up to freshen the glasses. Annie glared at him, but he was oblivious. Did he have to be such a good host? They'd never go home.

Henny ate the rest of a fat pretzel and took a sip. "At least we know the gunman was a man."

"Nope." Saulter sounded grim. "The most those boys saw was a figure. They heard a splash; they heard running footsteps. Could be a man. Could be a woman. And the guy from your conference"—he looked toward Annie—"hell, he was worse than useless. Saw *someone*. Could've been tall. Thought maybe short. Yes, it *might* have been a woman. The kind of witness who sees everything but a giraffe in red tights. But, believe me, I'm going to find out. And Annie, you're going to help me. Somebody shot at Neil Bledsoe right after he left your store. You told him to get the hell out. Why?"

"He was rude to another customer," she said briefly.

"The lady who dropped the book?"

"Yes. She's the widow of a mystery writer. The book was one by her husband."

"Is that the book he tossed at the desk?"

"Right."

"What's this widow's name?"

"Victoria Shaw."

Saulter wrote in his notebook, then gave Annie a hard stare. "Was Bledsoe rude to anyone else at the store?"

Annie sighed. "Of course. The man couldn't cross a street without being rude. God, I wouldn't know where to begin."

"Frank?" Curiously, Henny had dropped her role-playing. She was once again herself, bright, sharp, and noticing. "Why on earth are you asking Annie?"

For a moment Annie didn't understand.

It was Laurel who saw it at once. "Surely it is only too simple. Why, who would better know his enemies?"

Max was nodding in agreement.

The chief's corrugated face slowly and painfully turned a dull red.

Annie finally tumbled. "Bledsoe!" she bleated. "Why don't you ask Bledsoe who would be likely to shoot at him?"

A muscle rippled in Saulter's jaw and he spoke through clenched teeth, making him difficult to understand. "...arrogant...pigheaded, obstinate fool...*he'll* take care of it..."

Annie relaxed against the love seat and grinned at Max. If Bledsoe wouldn't tell the chief the likely suspects, certainly it was no duty of hers. Besides, Emma was the ticket....

Annie stretched luxuriously between the silk sheets. She didn't really like silk sheets. But Max did, of course. They *were* comfortable. Silky. And so was her negligee. Max had packed it. Cute of him. He always looked forward to hotel stays and had been especially insistent that they book this suite—actually, the honeymoon suite—for the duration of the conference. They could just as easily have driven over to the hotel from home. Really, extraordinarily thoughtful of Max to be so concerned with the success of her pet project! Insisting it was much better to be on the spot. So much to do tomorrow. Make sure everything was in readiness for the arrival of Lady Gwendolyn.

The bed sagged a little as Max slipped between the sheets. There was a tiny click. Annie opened her eyes, startled. A dim radiance spilled down onto the bed. She looked up. Her eyes widened as she saw her reflection and his in the discreetly illuminated, heart-shaped mirror on the ceiling.

She looked at Max.

He grinned.

And so did she.

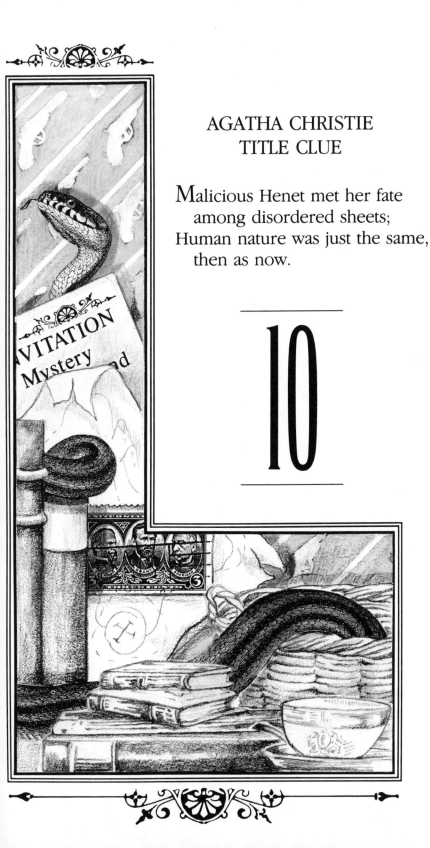

AGATHA CHRISTIE
TITLE CLUE

Malicious Henet met her fate
among disordered sheets;
Human nature was just the same,
then as now.

10

Max Darling stepped back to survey his handiwork. Just a little uneven. He straightened the poster board on the easel next to the registration desk. Good thing he'd planned on being up early. He'd already been accosted by four conference-goers demanding to know when the treasure hunt would begin. Perhaps Annie should have scheduled it for this morning. But she wanted this afternoon's Grand Garden Fête to be the official beginning of the conference. And the emphasis Monday would be on Lady Gwendolyn's presentation about Christie, so Tuesday had seemed best. Certainly, Annie would be thrilled to know how eagerly some of the conference attendees were looking forward to the treasure hunt. Such intense interest was— Max blinked. The portfolio containing the twenty-five treasure hunt posters toppled to the floor and began to inch away from the registration desk.

Assuming it was not being propelled by a poltergeist, the portfolio was exhibiting a mode of independent locomotion foreign to inanimate objects.

Max took three swift steps and grabbed it. Then he saw the almost invisible line and the barbed fish hook.

A tug.

Max tugged, too.

The line was taut and straight for a long moment, then the tension relaxed and the line shimmied to the floor.

Max plunged toward the end of the hall and careened around it.

Halfway down the hall, the door to the ladies' room was slowly closing.

Max grinned, but he also made an instant decision to put the posters in the trunk of his Porsche for safekeeping until Tuesday.

The phone shrilled.

Annie struggled awake. Why in heaven's name was the phone so close, almost exploding in her ear? As she flailed blindly, she realized she wasn't at home, where the phone was a decent twelve feet away from their bed, atop a table next to the chaise longue. Oh, no. She was in a strange hotel room. Although, memory returning, a hotel room with unexpected charms. One eye opened. Where was her playful companion of the night? Probably out for a morning ramble. Lovely, the way the English described a country walk. Not that she was interested in dawn strolls at any time. A successful marriage didn't require Tweedledum-and-Tweedledee coordination of pleasures. Not so long as primary pleasures received due attention. Another piercing ring. She fumbled with the receiver, mercifully cutting off that strident peal.

"Hllmph."

"So sweet of you, Annie, to set the hounds baying at my heels."

Emma Clyde's icy gibe, sans salutation, shocked Annie to full wakefulness. She sat up in bed.

"But I give you a warning, my dear."

Annie's hand clenched on the receiver.

"Although God knows why I'm bothering. I don't feel I owe you anything. But I liked Ambrose. Your uncle was a good man."

Annie tensed. For God's sake, was Emma threatening her? After scaring her to death in that Jaguar and ruining what was left of the reception at the store!

Emma snorted in disgust. *"He* was never a damn fool. Too bad you aren't more like him."

That was too much. "Listen, Emma, Uncle Ambrose would've been ticked off, too, if you shot out his front window."

A weary sigh. "The point, my dear young fool, is that I *didn't* shoot out your front window. I am not the mysterious marksman stalking that odious creature. If you have any sense at all, you'll stop setting the cops after me and start looking for the culprit—or you may truly have a dead body on your hands." A mirthless chuckle. "Not that I wouldn't enjoy seeing that son of a bitch deader than last year's best-seller."

"Oh my God, a 1930 Duesenberg Model J," Max exclaimed in awe. "Just think," he implored Annie, "it has a six-point-nine-liter twin-overhead-camshaft power unit of eight cylinders and a top speed of one hundred sixteen miles per hour!"

Annie had never understood the male passion for automobiles, although a male writer had once explained to her that beautiful cars were like lovely women: fast, laid back, and free as the wind. But this time, she, too, felt the stirrings of enormous excitement and joined heartily in the cheer that rose from the waiting crowd. Nineteen thirty—oh, that was a glorious year for Christie readers, their first book-length view of St. Mary Mead in the incomparable *Murder at the Vicarage*.

As the low-slung, scarlet, open touring car slid to a majestic stop in front of the beribboned poles that marked the entrance to the Grand Garden Fête, Annie blinked back tears of joy.

The Christie Caper had begun.

In glorious fashion.

South of the main entrance to the Palmetto House spread an expanse of lawn. Admittedly it was covered with wiry crabgrass tenaciously triumphing over the island's sandy soil rather than the thickly green, close-cropped grass of an English country house, but it was as close an imitation of the grounds of Nasse House in *Dead Man's Folly* as Annie could manage, and today it looked wonderfully festive with the array of brightly colored tents and assorted games.

The elegant car drawing up to the beribboned poles, often seen on Hollywood Boulevard with Clark Gable at the wheel, was the flagship for a shining line of vintage greats:

An 1897 two-cylinder, four-horse-power Daimler Phaeton. In 1897, Agatha was a well-loved, happy seven-year-old who could entertain herself for hours with imaginary playmates.

A 1902 black Curved-Dash Olds, which looked like a baby carriage on wheels. A wonderful year. Sister Madge married, and Agatha met a friend for life, the bridegroom's younger sister, Nan.

A pale green 1908 Hutton. While recuperating from the flu, a bored Agatha was encouraged by her mother to try her hand at writing. The result: "The House of Beauty," a six-thousand-word short story that contains, as her biographer Janet Morgan points out, a little bit of everything, including death, delirium, the jungle, madness, music, and a black-robed nun.

A gorgeously blue 1910 Alfa with bright red leather upholstery. Agatha's coming-out year. She and her widowed mother traveled to Cairo and spent three months at the Gezirah Palace Hotel, a wonderful season of dances, croquet, and polo matches—and plenty of attentive young men.

A 1924 gray snub-nosed Morris-Cowley (progenitor of the MG), identical to the one Agatha bought with her five hundred pounds in serial rights money for *The Man in the Brown Suit*. In her autobiography, she recalled the purchase of that car as one of the two most exciting events in her life. The second was dining with the queen at Buckingham Palace forty years later.

A jaunty green 1925 Opel Laubfrosch. Agatha patterned the Berkshire estate in *The Secret of Chimneys* after Abney, the ancestral home of her brother-in-law, Jimmy Watts.

A flashy red 1927 Vauxhall. A year of life-altering events, public and personal. The Communist party expelled Trotsky. Lindbergh soloed across the Atlantic. Agatha's marriage to Archie Christie failed.

A luxurious 1928 six-seater Nürberg Mercedes-Benz. Agatha made her first journey aboard the Orient Express that fall.

A classy red 1934 six-cylinder Riley M.P.H. sports two-seater, which could easily be envisaged parked at the Blue Boar. This was a wonderfully productive year, three novels written.

The door to the Duesenberg clicked shut with the precision of a Christie plot. A liveried chauffeur—mauve uniform with gray spats—moved with quiet dignity to open the rear door of the gleaming lead car.

Lady Gwendolyn Tompkins, a petite woman as softly rounded as a rococo cherub, erupted from the car, faster than a jack out of the box. Her pale reddish hair was bound up in a somewhat lopsided coronet braid. Bright blue eyes vivid with good humor and eagerness settled on Annie. "Annie Laurance Darling, at last. What a *pleasure* to be here. Oh, what *glorious* tents. Pink-and-white striped! Just like peppermint. And such a marvelous turn-out. My dear, you've launched us in the most delightful fashion."

Annie was pulled into a soft embrace, overcome with a heady dose of Evening in Paris perfume, and, at the same time, expertly turned to face the waiting crowd.

"Stage front," the author whispered gaily. "Time to shine."

Annie plunged into her speech of welcome. "Lady Gwendolyn, welcome to Broward's Rock. We are honored that you have come so far to serve as the official hostess of our centenary celebration of the birth of Agatha Christie."

A deafening explosion of applause, shouts, huzzahs, and bravas.

Annie began her introductions. The leading lights of Broward's Rock were out in force today, from the mayor to the municipal judge to the entire school board, in addition to the several hundred conference participants. Annie intended to introduce only a few, then get right to the program.

But she knew better than to ignore Laurel.

"Lady Gwendolyn, may I introduce my husband's mother, Laurel Roethke."

"Your Ladyship," Laurel breathed ecstatically.

Annie shot her mother-in-law a look of surprise. It was quite unusual for worldly wise Laurel to evince even a modicum of awe, no matter who the celebrity.

"I've long been an admirer of yours, Lady Gwendolyn," Laurel continued warmly. "Your camel trip into the interior of Arabia. Your expedition to the head waters of the Zambezi. Your war years, parachuting into occupied France—"

Those lively blue eyes sparkled. "My husband always told me I was a world-class fool. Especially as a young woman. I'm afraid I've never been able to resist a challenge—from a mountain to a man. Actually," and she winked at Laurel, "I've never wanted to resist."

"Your modesty does you great credit. But the Legion of Honor—"

Tiny spots of color marked her plump cheeks. "Oh, you are too kind, and you give me far too much credit. My motto is, Do, Don't Think. It's put me in some tight spots a few times. But what's life without challenges? I say," a plump hand, sapphire rings winking from two fingers, gestured toward the crowd, "this *is* a holiday bunch. Shall we start?"

Ingrid, bless her, waited beside the poles with a pair of scissors at the ready. Annie took the scissors and held them out to the official hostess.

"If you will cut the ribbon, Lady Gwendolyn, the fête will open and The Christie Caper will begin."

Lady Gwendolyn waggled the razor-sharp scissors in the air. "I am deeply honored to do so." Her clear, light voice rang out. "Today the peoples of the world are linked from the Himalayas to the Australian Outback. It is quite easy to turn on the telly and see a riot in Rumania, starvation in Zimbabwe, poison gas spewing in Afghanistan. We are bombarded with information and bewildered by choices. Worst of all, so many are adrift from moral bedrock. What then can we deem to be constant?"

The small, blue-eyed woman surveyed her listeners, her plump face puckered with concern.

"There is one constant of which we can be certain and which we can ignore only at the peril of our souls—the nature of the beast. Evil exists. We must combat it . . . always. Here on this island we gather today to recall the life and works of one woman who spoke to every man everywhere. Do we want to understand today's world? Read Agatha Christie. Find bedrock again. In her works, right is right, wrong is wrong. She warns us again and again never to sugarcoat life. And she reminds us that the situations we face, whatever they are, may not be as simple as they seem."

Lady Gwendolyn shaded her eyes against the sun. "Today is a good example, you know. Here we are at a holiday gathering, everyone dressed in their finery. A cheerful scene, much like a winding lazy river on a summer day. But Christie would have us remember that even though water gleams like silver in the bright sun, slime and sewage may undulate beneath the surface. Beware."

Scissors flashed in the sunlight, and the crimson ribbon between the beribboned poles parted.

The happy crowd surged within the cordoned-off area. Lady Gwendolyn trotted up the steps of the gazebo, trailed by admirers. Annie anxiously awaited the verdict as the official hostess eagerly surveyed the area: the bright orange marquee over the tea tables, a hoopla, a skittle alley, a coconut shy, a lucky dip, a fortune teller's tent, and many, many stalls. (Annie had found it impossible to persuade the members of the store's Murder-Most-Read Club to call them stalls. Just a fancy name for booths at a bake sale, one had muttered.) In Annie's own mind, however, stalls they were, and she'd insisted upon proper offerings, including Madeira cakes, bakewell tarts with jam and almond fillings, Eccles cakes (puff pastry with raisins), bottled pickles and onions, rock buns, and fancywork.

Turning to Annie, Lady Gwendolyn beamed. "Smashing, my dear, absolutely smashing." A sigh of pure pleasure. "I've always loved fêtes. I can't wait to try the coconut shy, but I suppose it's time for the performing seal to bark."

"Do you mind?" Annie asked swiftly.

Lady Gwendolyn smoothed back the hair straggling from her braids. "Have you ever met a writer who didn't enjoy meeting her readers?"

The diminutive author settled behind the table that had been placed in the gazebo and began to welcome her fans.

Confident that the official hostess was quite capable of handling her tasks, Annie sped from tent to stall to entertainment, making certain all was well. There were oceans of tea, a choice of elegant and light Earl Grey, delicately scented Jasmine Oolong, or classic Darjeeling. All served from china teapots. There had been a veritable deluge of impassioned suggestions when Annie had proposed silver. "Brackish. *Not* for true tea drinkers. Pottery at the very least, and, of course, preferably china." As for the tea table, ah, what largesse: herbed cheese-custard tartlets, cheese straws, chicken-liver pâté rounds, caviar puffs, harlequin fingers, smoked salmon and cucumber sandwiches, piquant tuna sandwiches, crumpets, Chelsea buns, fruit scones, Shrewsbury biscuits, Cornish fairings, and classic shortbread. At the game booths, Annie made certain there were prizes enough. She had to replenish the Bob-in-Water prizes twice. As for the stalls, Annie was amused to spot Frank Saulter with a Madeira cake in one hand and a clutch of potholders in the other.

That was as close to the tea table as she was to come for quite a while. The last fan greeted, Lady Gwendolyn bounced briskly to her side. "Duty done. Is it cricket for me to play the games?"

It took Annie a moment to understand the request, then she burbled, "By all means, Lady Gwendolyn."

For the next hour, Annie felt like a tail to a spirited kite as she followed Lady Gwendolyn from one entertainment to the next.

Lady Gwendolyn won three Kewpie dolls at hoopla, flinging the plate-size wooden hoops at the stakes with uncanny accuracy. She was unbeatable at skittles, whirling the ball attached by string to a center pole in a wicked circle to knock down the wooden pins. Her finest moment came, however, at the coconut shy. With the precision of Christie skewing social pretensions in *The Secret of Chimneys,* Lady Gwendolyn hurled the soft rubber ball, knocking over a coconut with each toss. By this time, Annie was carrying, in addition to the three Kewpie dolls, a red fire engine, a blue bead necklace, a Victorian dollhouse, a wooden hoop, and a sack full of pear drops.

Lady Gwendolyn adored the Bob-in-Water. She took an especial fancy to the packages wrapped in silver that bobbed in the water of the barrel, hauling out three in a row.

It was with a distinct sensation of relief that Annie held open the flap of the fortune teller's tent for her feisty official hostess.

Carefully stowing her chief guest's booty in Max's care under a live oak, Annie escaped to the tea tent. She rejoined him with a full plate and a happy smile.

Max looked *delicious* in a blue cord suit and a white boater. She resisted the temptation to tell him how handsome he was. She was sure Laurel had already done the honors.

Max didn't quite raise an eyebrow at her generous array of edibles.

"Hungry," she retorted to the unspoken comment, then she concentrated on pure piggish pleasure. When her plate was empty, she looked at her husband.

"More?" he inquired dutifully.

She wouldn't cavil at his tone. It wasn't *quite* accusatory. "Especially the caviar puffs," she called after him.

As she awaited replenishment, she realized that she was surveying the crowd warily. When she spotted Emma Clyde, she remembered why, although Emma appeared quite genial. In honor of the occasion, Emma had abandoned her customary caftan for a truly awesome flowered print (cabbage roses among a plethora of ferns), a pink picture hat, and white gloves. Emma watched with an amused smile as Fleur Calloway, lovely in a pale lilac silk and a matching straw hat, bought a raffle ticket for a set of Lady Gwendolyn's novels.

Emma.

Oh, God, what if Emma was telling the truth? What if she *hadn't* shot at Neil Bledsoe last night?

Of course, she would deny it. Emma's protestations of innocence surely could not be accepted without question.

But if she hadn't—

Anxiously, Annie looked around for the other participants in last night's drama.

Derek Davis's good-humored face was flushed from heat and exertion. The young publicist wasn't having any luck at the coconut shy. He bought three more balls and tried again, finally toppling one coconut at the end, which made his fair face crimson with pleasure. His prize was what looked at a distance like a crocheted doily for an armchair. He offered it laughingly to his companion, Natalie Marlow, the frumpy young author who'd introduced herself to Annie last night at the bookstore. Although Natalie obviously had gone all out for the fête, her choice of attire—a droopy purplish silk with tangerine stripes—made it clear it was a good thing she concentrated on emotions, not fashion, in her fiction.

But, Annie realized with surprise, Derek was oblivious to the author's dowdiness. Annie wondered if the young publicist had any inkling of how revealing his expression was. He was offering not only a silly prize, but much, much more—his eyes looked at Natalie with an emotion akin to adoration.

Natalie didn't see that look because she was overcome with awkwardness. She flushed, twisted her hands, and looked away.

But none of it was lost on Neil Bledsoe.

He sauntered up to the coconut shy, his dark face amused. But not nicely amused.

Annie stiffened.

Kathryn Honeycutt paused beside the fortune-telling tent and looked a fit advertisement, her porcelain-pink face troubled.

Bledsoe ignored Derek. He gave a half bow to Natalie. It was almost a burlesque, but not quite. "Miss Marlow, I've wanted to meet you ever since I read *Down These Steps*. You have a great future ahead of you."

If the crocheted doily had unnerved Natalie, this fulsome praise from an undeniably imposing man undid her. She swallowed jerkily and stared up at him wordlessly.

Bledsoe smiled with the easy, satisfied grace of a panther with its quarry in sight. "I haven't had the pleasure of a lovely woman's company at a country fair in many years. Perhaps you'll allow me the pleasure of competing for your favor, just as a knight of long ago."

Max arrived then and handed Annie a full plate topped by three caviar puffs.

Annie took it and groaned, "Oh, puke."

At Max's startled look, she glanced at the plate. "Oh, no, love, not this. The jerk—at the coconut shy."

Natalie watched wide-eyed as Bledsoe, with the ease and confidence of a superior athlete, unleashed the soft rubber ball and the entire row of coconuts bobbled and wobbled and thudded to the springy ground. He gestured at the attendant. "That bear—the big one with the pink ears—for the lady here."

When Natalie held the huge prize, Bledsoe took her elbow with a proprietary air. "You must come with me and be my luck. Let's try the hoopla."

Natalie did look uncertainly over her shoulder at Derek, but he just stood there, the doily crushed in his hand, his snub-nosed face empty of expression, and then she walked on, with Bledsoe.

"Shit." Annie grabbed a caviar puff and stuffed it in her mouth.

Max squinted in the sunlight. "As you've often told our elegant bookstore feline, don't eat and growl."

"But, Max," the little pastry was so flaky and good it almost melted in her mouth, which should have helped but didn't, "how can she be so dumb?"

"So what kind of guy gives up like that?" Max jerked his head at Derek's receding back. "You go after a girl if she belongs to you."

"Women do not *belong* to men," Annie remonstrated.

"Mmmmh," Max replied noncommittally.

But Annie was looking from face to disconsolate face.

Nathan Hillman, the chunky editor of Hillman House, stood beside the tea tent. He gazed after Derek, shaking his head.

Margo Wright, the statuesque agent, was strikingly attractive in an all-white dress with a layered lace skirt. She broke off an animated conversation in midphrase as Bledsoe swaggered past, one hand firm on Natalie's elbow.

Victoria Shaw, the author's widow, put down her plate with trembling hands, turned, and walked blindly toward the thick and tangled Wildlife Preserve that bounded the lawn on the south.

But it was the transformation of Fleur Calloway that shocked Annie the most. Fleur's face blanched and she looked as though she might faint. Emma reached out to take her arm.

"I say, a problem?" The query sounded at Annie's elbow.

Annie looked down, into alert, discerning blue eyes.

Annie didn't know how to respond. She certainly didn't want to worry her famous co-hostess. Besides, it was too complicated to try and explain: Bledsoe and those who disliked him, the flurry of shots, the uncertainty of what was intended, mischief or murder.

Then, the hair prickled on the back of Annie's neck, and was that from the sudden increase in the onshore breeze and a sharply cool edge to the air or from the brisk summation by the official hostess? "They are so easy to pick out, aren't they?" Lady Gwendolyn's voice was sympathetic and not the least judgmental. "It's as if they were linked by an invisible cord. They are, of course. Quite strong emotion. Hatred, I'd say."

Annie stared at Lady Gwendolyn in astonishment.

The old lady nodded toward the fortune-telling tent. "I heard all about your spot of bother last night. It's always shocking when violence erupts in what *seems* to be a civilized milieu. But as Dame Agatha made so very clear, there is so much evil under the sun." Lady Gwendolyn gripped Annie's arm, her pudgy fingers surprisingly strong. "It's a mistake to think it can't happen here."

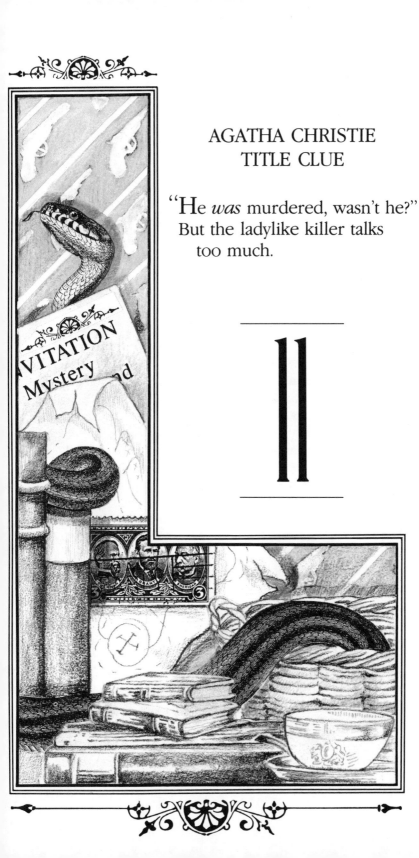

AGATHA CHRISTIE
TITLE CLUE

"He *was* murdered, wasn't he?"
But the ladylike killer talks
too much.

11

The weather had on its most beguiling face Monday morning, which was not always true in September on a barrier island. There was that memorably dreadful Labor Day weekend when it had rained and rained and rained and rained. Eight inches in one day. The golf courses shimmered with lakes, the streets ran ankle-deep, and snakes fled the saturated ground, seeking refuge on porches, in dumpsters, and inside garages. Of course, September always held the possibility of hurricanes. That specter had haunted Annie throughout the months of planning, but Monday dawned with a robin's-egg-blue sky, the silkiest of onshore breezes, and a balmy temperature that only hinted of afternoon heat.

The surroundings sparkled. Their suite was on the third floor in the central block of the hotel. Wings extended from either end of that block. All of the rooms on this, the sea side, had spacious balconies with tile tables and canvas-backed director's chairs. Fiery red geraniums flourished in the twin royal blue vases at the corners of each balcony. The ornately carved columns supporting the balconies added a Moorish flavor. The red-flowered blue vases, positioned at regular intervals along the balconies on every floor and along the roof wall, created vivid pointillist splotches of color against the cream-colored stucco facade.

Their view was magnificent: the red-tiled central courtyard, accented again with royal blue by the fountains on either side, the stuccoed walls that afforded privacy to ground-floor rooms, the crystal clear water of the pool, the creamy gold of the dunes, the age-browned boardwalk, the shiny gray of the strand, and, finally, the glistening green waters of the Atlantic. Seaside flowers and grasses on the protective dunes added delicate nuances of color: the red of winged sumac, the gold of sea oats, the yellow of goldenrod and camphor weed, and the lilac of sea lavender. Overhead a flock of glossy black cormorants, long, stiff tails erect, flapped by, their arrival from the north the only hint of winter to come.

Annie felt a surge of absolute delight. She was blessed not only with a beautiful day and gorgeous surroundings, but with the best of companions. Annie eschewed sentimentalism, of course, just like Tommy and Tuppence in *Partners in Crime,* that delightful collection of short stories in which Christie parodied then-fashionable fictional detectives, including Sherlock Holmes, Father Brown, Reggie Fortune, and even her own Poirot. Annie leaned an elbow on the breakfast table, cupped her chin in hand, and admired her husband, or what she could see of him over the newspaper. Actually, Max and Tommy had a good deal in common, despite their transatlantic differences: good looks but not *too* handsome, good humor but with plenty of steel beneath, good intentions but *never* sappy.

She beamed at the newspaper. A hell of a guy.

Annie almost told him so. But Max was so accustomed to admiration (honestly, Laurel treated him like a crown prince, which got to be a little old) that she broke off in midsentence.

"Max, you're—"

He lowered the newspaper and looked at her inquiringly.

She regrouped and asked briskly, "What are your plans this morning?"

He folded the paper, stretched, and reached for the coffee. "Whatever," he said agreeably. "Do you want me to help Ingrid at the registration table? Or should I make sure our official hostess feels properly pampered? Or shall I mingle and be friendly?"

Annie lifted her cup for a refill, then checked her watch. Just past eight. Although she loved leisurely breakfasts with Max, there was much to do this morning. "Lady Gwendolyn, by all means. I'm sure she's used to lots of attention."

"I like her. Sprightly old gal."

"*You* haven't spent the last ten months on the telephone with her, trying to field a half-dozen brilliant suggestions at once." Honesty forced Annie to continue. "Not that they weren't all wonderful ideas—but I don't have the manpower to produce a Christie play, track down people who knew Christie personally and tape their reminiscences, coordinate a thirties fashion show, and direct the conference all at the same time."

"Full of vim and vigor," Max said admiringly. "She had a hell of a time yesterday. Cleaned the coconut shy out of Kewpie dolls. What will she *do* with the damned things?"

Annie didn't respond to his lighthearted query. Instead, she said soberly, "She looks almost like a Kewpie doll herself, all softness and curves, and she sounds so genial. But, Max, there's an underlying tough-ness—or maybe it's strength of character. I have a feeling that when she looks, she really *sees*. Yet her good humor is real—not because she sees life as sweet and light but *in spite* of the fact that she knows full well how dreadful the world can be."

"Oh, sure," he said quietly. "A gallant old gal, too."

"Oh, God, Max, do you think Lady Gwendolyn's right?"

He had no trouble understanding her thought processes. "That we're sitting on something pretty ugly? She could be. Or she could be overreacting." He poured out the last of the coffee. "All we know is that someone shot out a window at Death on Demand two nights ago. Was it an attempt to kill Bledsoe? Or is your instinct right and was Emma toying with him again? Or was it a random attack?"

A random attack on an island with a year-round population of about twelve hundred? Random attacks in a big city she could understand. She'd read Ed McBain.

On Broward's Rock?

"Not random," she said decisively. "It must have been aimed either at Bledsoe—or at Death on Demand. But," she pointed out emphatically, "nothing happened yesterday. If nothing happens today, I think we'll be okay." But her brows drew down in a tight, worried frown.

"Hey, Annie. Relax. Today's going to be fun."

"I know." She spread her hands helplessly. "It goes around and around in my mind. First, I think it's just a prank—even if a vicious one. Then I get this icy feeling of panic, and I wonder if a killer's just biding his time."

"Cool it, sweetie. You aren't the militia. Frank and Billy will be here every minute today, keeping an eye on Bledsoe. Nobody will try any-thing."

"I hope not."

"Come on, Annie. Smile. This is your great day, the start of the conference sessions. You've worked hard for months, now it's time to have fun."

It certainly was. She felt a spurt of resentment. Why had Neil Bledsoe come to her conference? Just to make some people miserable? It was a heck of an investment of time (a full week) and money (six hundred dollars, which included registration, meal tickets, hotel room, and conference fees) simply to indulge in petty harassment.

"Damn him," she snapped aloud. She didn't have to tell Max who had elicited her wrath. "What if he stalks around the conference like he did at Death on Demand, upsetting people, causing scenes? Or shows off, like he did at the fête?"

"What if he does?" Max speared a chunk of cantaloupe. "I know you want everyone to have a good time, but life is full of unpleasant surprises, and most people handle them just fine." He reached for a second brioche, drew back his hand, murmured, "Actually, this *is* a holiday," and picked up the roll. He didn't, of course, put butter on it, opting instead for fruit spread. He bit into the brioche and mumbled, "Everybody knows he's here now. No more shock value in that. The people who don't like him are prepared. And consider this, only a few people even know or care who he is!"

Annie brightened and began to enjoy her second cup of coffee. Max had a good point. She ticked off one by one the people who obviously didn't like Bledsoe. The editor with the stiff brush of graying black hair, Nathan Hillman. The sandy-haired, snub-nosed young man, Derek Davis. Both from Hillman House Publishers. Was that important, or a coincidence? The imposing, porcelain-pale agent, Margo Wright. The reserved and somehow pathetic author's widow, Victoria Shaw. And, of course, Fleur Calloway. Funny, she looked like she'd seen a ghost at the fête yesterday. But she had known Bledsoe was on the island, even if she hadn't acknowledged his presence at the bookstore. Something awfully grim there, from Emma Clyde's viewpoint. But, Emma wrote mysteries. Perhaps she exaggerated the circumstances in her mind because of her fondness for Fleur.

Sunday afternoon during the fête, each of them had seemed linked to Bledsoe. But the linkage could simply be in Annie's overactive imagination.

"We won't let anything sabotage The Christie Caper," Max insisted stalwartly, once again reading her mind.

·   ·   ·

Annie was all over the hotel in the next couple of hours: the gritty depths of the heating-cooling area of the basement because the air-conditioning was malfunctioning in Meeting Rooms A and B, the controlled hysteria of the catering offices for a last-minute check on that night's dinner à la Lucy Eyelesbarrow, who functioned both as Miss Marple's agent and as first-class cook in *What Mrs. McGillicuddy Saw!*; the mob scene that was the registration table (Ingrid and her good friend and neighbor Duane Webb had the situation under control); the idyllic holiday atmosphere of the Palmetto Court where many conference-goers had elected to enjoy leisurely tea and crumpets while awaiting the opening session, when Lady Gwendolyn would speak on "Christie—Her Life, Her World, Her Work."

Annie trotted happily from task to task. Everything was perfect—and perfectly ordinary. No evil under the sun here. And, glory be, Laurel had apparently switched allegiances. In odd locations, Annie discovered oddments of information about Christie executed in exquisite calligraphy. Taped to the paper towel dispenser in the ladies' room: *Christie began* Death Comes as the End *in response to a challenge from Professor Stephen Glanville, a University of London archaeology professor*. Pinned to a curtain in Meeting Room A: *Miss Marple's most distinguishing characteristic is a profound understanding of human nature*. In the main lobby, a pillar carried this calligraphic information: *The concept of changed or hidden identities is often explored in Christie's fiction*.

Annie was still grinning when she noticed the chunky middle-aged editor and the young publicist from Hillman House deep in conversation with Lady Gwendolyn and Max in an oasis of quiet behind a line of potted palms. Annie raised an inquiring eyebrow as she passed, but her husband didn't even notice her, he was so absorbed in watching the official hostess. Lady Gwendolyn was leaning toward the editor with a most engaging smile. Hillman had the expansive expression of a man busy talking about himself.

Twenty minutes later Annie spotted Max and Lady Gwendolyn making a beeline for Margo Wright. The agent was striding toward the elevators in lavender jogging top and shorts, her face flushed from exercise, a pink headband restraining her tumbling dark curls. (Near the button panel, a card proclaimed: *Christie's favorite home—after Ashfield—was Greenway House, which is located on the river Dart, just south of Torquay*.) Annie eyed the agent and the pursuing duo thoughtfully.

The mob scene at the registration table had transferred to the lobby outside the book room. As Annie tried to calm two collectors who were jockeying viciously for first place in line, she noted Victoria Shaw halfway down the line—smiling eagerly at Lady Gwendolyn. Max, of course, was close at hand.

Behind the closed doors of Meeting Rooms F and G, mystery booksellers from across the country were frantically emptying boxes and filling their tables. Annie didn't even have to peek inside to know that Henny had already finagled her way into the book room and was busy spotting the good buys, ready to grab up the true collector's items at the stroke of ten.

Fleur Calloway, striking in a richly red cotton top and a split red skirt emblazoned with tropical flowers, looked over the heads of eager autograph seekers and waved a cheery good-morning to Annie. The author's light green eyes crinkled in a warm smile. Annie grinned in return. She *liked* this woman.

Lady Gwendolyn, with an ebullient "Good morning, dear Annie," swept past, Max in tow, to join Fleur Calloway.

Lady Gwendolyn obviously didn't believe in letting grass grow under *her* size-four feet. But how could she hope to learn anything important in these brief chats?

If, Annie mentally crossed her fingers, there was anything important to learn. There was, despite Emma's denial, a darn good chance the shooting could be marked down to malicious mischief, not attempted murder.

Annie dashed through the Palmetto Court several times. (Two palmettos bore cards: *Hercule Poirot is buried in Styles St. Mary*; *Of all her books, Christie best liked the beginning of* The Body in the Library.)

It was on Annie's first rush through the Palmetto Court that she'd noticed Bledsoe, lounging at a choice table on the north side. The table was shaded from the sun by the fountain to its left, the wall behind, and the rising tier of balconies above. (The breeze fluttered a card taped to the fountain: *Agatha and Max left Nimrud for the last time in 1960.*) Scattered papers and a dish-laden table testified to an indulgent breakfast. Bledsoe, once again in an all-white suit (Did he think he was Hercule Poirot in Egypt?), leaned back in sleepy contentment, basking under the adoring gaze of Natalie Marlow, whose sensitive face reflected excitement—and more. Annie wondered sardonically how Bledsoe had managed to jettison the Miss Marple look-alike and just how much time he had spent with Natalie since yesterday. His blunt hand occasionally stroked her arm. He looked supremely self-satisfied. His sensual lips parted in a half-smile and his cigar tilted at a jaunty angle. All was right with his world, that was apparent.

All was certainly not right with Chief Saulter's world when Annie almost cannoned into him near the registration table, her vision obscured by an armful of thermoses topped by a stack of island maps with X clearly marking the spot (location, of course, of the one and only Death on Demand, the finest mystery bookstore this side of Atlanta).

"Got a minute, Annie?" the chief asked brusquely. His normally sallow skin was flushed a dark pink.

"Sure, Frank." Plumping down the island maps, she placed a thermos by Ingrid, who smiled her thanks, and shifted the remaining containers. "Taking fresh coffee to the workers. What's up?" She took a quick glance at her watch. A quarter to eleven. Almost time for Lady Gwendolyn's session.

"You got a list of everybody attending the conference?" This query was delivered with all the charm of Inspector Slack. Annie lacked Miss Marple's adroitness at remonstrating without words at rudeness, but her startled look of surprise evidently sufficed. Saulter's flush deepened. "Sorry, Annie. That—" the chief stopped, swallowed, started again with an obvious effort at control—"Bledsoe still won't give us a damn thing. Not a single name. Says he's pretty sure he knows who's behind the shooting, and he'll take care of it. *He'll* take care of it. Who does he think he is? A bloody vigilante?" The chief's face gleamed like copper in the desert sun. "Sorry. Anyway, I need the list. Bledsoe's not going to make a fool out of me. I'll figure out who knows him whether he likes it or not."

As Annie delved into boxes, hunting for the master list of attendees, she wondered at Bledsoe. The man had his psychology all wrong. If he thought obstructionism was the way to choke off the chief's investigation, he was going to have to think again.

The chief stalked off, list in hand.

It was during her final dash through the Palmetto Court that her swift stride checked for an instant in surprise. Bledsoe's table was full now: the critic, the young woman author, Max, and Lady Gwendolyn. Lady Gwendolyn's bright blue eyes studied Bledsoe, who was talking fast and gesturing vigorously as he spoke. Natalie Marlow looked prim and uncomfortable, like a child at the adult table. Max had on his Charlie Chan face.

Annie hurried on to the main conference room. She checked the speaker's table—the mike worked, ice water was available, and clean glasses in place—then tilted the blinds on the east wall to filter the late morning sunlight. The seats were rapidly filling, and there was a genial roar of excited conversations.

"... can't understand the preoccupation of the American media with hard-boiled books! Romantic twaddle, most of them. Reality? Christie was closer to it than ..."

"...Agatha thought Margaret Rutherford looked like a blood-hound ..."

"... she scrapped very hard about the book jackets ..."

"... can't believe it! I found a copy—very fine—of the first American edition of *The Murder of Roger Ackroyd* for less than a thousand!"

"I *love* that movie. I think Margaret Rutherford's marvelous, even if she isn't even a little bit like Jane Marple."

It was a good-humored, holiday crowd, eager for the first session to begin. By golly, everything was going to be all right. So a few people didn't like Bledsoe! So what? The world, as Max pointed out, was full of unlikable people, and you just coped. Annie waved to Laurel and raised an eyebrow at Henny's huge sack overflowing with books. Aglow with excitement, her fox-sharp nose quivering in triumph, Henny raised her closed right fist, indicating some good buys in the book room. It was a bit painful, but Annie knew she couldn't run a conference and scout for titles at the same time, so she grinned, clasped her hands above her head, and mouthed, "Congratulations."

Neil Bledsoe ambled in, Natalie clinging to his arm. Her fashion rating was still abysmal. Today she wore an ill-fitting brown cotton jumper and blue blouse with puffed sleeves. Her lusterless brown hair, which desperately needed to be both styled and cut, hung unevenly, a jagged frame for her thin face. Her eyes were at odds with the rest of the face, almost as if they'd taken up residence there by mistake. They were deep-set, luminous, unforgettable eyes, as richly brown as fresh-turned Texas earth, and they gazed up tremulously at Bledsoe.

The unlikely couple passed within a few feet of Annie. Bledsoe was smiling down at his companion, his knowing eyes focused on her in-tently. His manner exuded sexuality. Natalie was speaking. "You are so different from anyone I've ever known. You make most men seem so—so anemic, so puerile..."

Then they were past. Apparently Bledsoe was going to be safely occupied for the rest of the conference. If Annie could read the signs, and it didn't take the expertise of a sex therapist to figure this one out, Bledsoe had poor Natalie's number. Annie wished he had picked on someone savvier. But it was none of her business.

Augustus Markham, president of Chastain College, greeted her. "Wonderful occasion, my dear. A pleasure to be here." Heads turned to listen. Augustus would be as difficult to ignore as an organ crescendo. "No one will ever equal Christie as a mystery writer. She was a great lady, too, an inspiration to the rest of us. She always did her best. She knew what it was to live."

As his rich voice rolled through the auditorium, conversations fell away.

Annie smiled her thanks and knew it was time. Lady Gwendolyn was already seated on the platform, those inquiring eyes surveying the audience. Annie ran lightly up the steps. At the lectern, she looked out at the sea of smiling faces and couldn't keep from grinning. "You wonderful people, welcome. Welcome to a celebration of a remarkable life. Do you love Agatha Christie?"

"Yes!" the audience thundered, loving it.

"Who wrote the best mysteries ever?"

The shout reverberated like crashing surf, "CHRIS—TIEEEEE."

Annie blinked back a tear. This was no time to get emotional—but what a response! "We are enormously fortunate today to have with us as our principal speaker a woman who is not only an authority on the life and times of Agatha Christie, but a woman who is also one of the premier mystery writers in the world today. It is my pleasure and my honor to present to you—Lady Gwendolyn Tompkins!"

Lady Gwendolyn smiled graciously at the welcoming cheers. She ignored the lectern. Her high, clear voice, without need of a microphone, rolled across the auditorium. "It is indeed a great honor and a great pleasure to speak to you about Agatha Christie. She was a grand woman, and she had a grand life. Christie was brave, gallant, enduring, determined. She knew how to love, how to laugh, in sum, how to live. In admiring her, perhaps we can gain the vision in our own lives to live with the same quiet, unsung courage, no matter what vicissitudes we face.

"...the most British of authors, yet her books are beloved around the world...born September 15, 1890, in the seaside resort of Torquay...fair-haired...the last and late-in-life child of a most genial man and a delightful woman. Her father, an American, enjoyed each and every day on its own terms...a quintessential club man, he loved to offer hospitality, and he loved good food...Agatha's mother was a quicksilver spirit with an unusual and lively mind. Agatha enjoyed the happiest of childhoods at Ashfield in Barton Road. The beloved baby of the family...a big sister, Madge, and big brother, Monty. The early loss of her father...imaginary playmates in the garden...Devonshire cream...dancing school...picnics, rollerskating...a coming-out season in Egypt...

"Archie Christie arrived in her life like a whirlwind, winning her heart...fair and blue-eyed, brave and exciting, Archie was handsome, determined, and impetuous. Agatha once described their mutual attraction, because they were so different, as 'the excitement of the stranger'...the advent of World War I, the end of an era...Archie a flying ace...Agatha a VAD in Torquay...marriage on Christmas Eve 1914...Agatha in the dispensary, learning about poisons...a pharmacist with a fondness for a lump of curare...Agatha starting a detective story in response to a dare from Madge, writing *The Mysterious Affair at Styles*, patterning her detective after the Belgian refugees..."

Oh, it was an old, familiar, endearing story to Annie, but she relished it again.

"The war finally over...some very good years for Agatha and Archie. Rosalind's birth. The wonderful news, in 1920, after she'd almost forgot its existence, that Bodley Head would publish her book. Agatha and Archie's unforgettable tour of the empire. More books: *The Secret Adversary*, 1922; *Murder on the Links*, 1923; *Poirot Investigates* and *The Man in the Brown Suit*, 1924; *The Secret of Chimneys*, 1925.

"Nineteen twenty-six." Lady Gwendolyn tolled the year. "The best of years for Agatha. And the worst.

"A watershed year in the history of the mystery...the publication of *The Murder of Roger Ackroyd*...artful, clever, brilliant...but 1926 brought also the death of Clara, her impulsive, warm, and eager mother. It brought the duty of clearing Ashfield, her childhood home. Grief-stricken, her husband absorbed in golf and business, Agatha worked in a frenzy at clearing the house, sleeping poorly, eating erratically."

Lady Gwendolyn gazed out soberly at her enraptured listeners.

"August 1926: Expecting to go on a holiday to Italy with her husband, Agatha instead is told by Archie that he loves another woman and wants a divorce. Archie had once told Agatha that he hated it when people were ill or unhappy. He was true to his word.

"December 1926: Archie was living at his club, still pressing for a divorce. Agatha, profoundly depressed, lived at Styles and was attempting to write. At eleven o'clock on the night of December third, she drove off into the darkness. The car was found the next day on a grassy slope off the main road. No trace of Agatha. A massive search ensued. Speculation arose that Archie had murdered his wife. The press had a field day, carrying reams of sensational copy. Ten days later, Agatha was discovered at a resort hotel in Harrogate, registered as Theresa Neele. The woman Archie wished to marry was Nancy Neele. Archie came to the hotel, identified Agatha, and whisked her into seclusion, issuing a statement that she was suffering from the most complete amnesia."

The cherubic author posed the familiar questions. "A publicity stunt? An effort to humiliate her unfaithful husband? A mental collapse from stress and heartbreak?"

Lady Gwendolyn was emphatic. "A mind and heart and soul can only bear so much. This was an emotional collapse. Agatha was never able, despite yeoman effort, to recall all that happened during those ten days.

"Put yourself in her place," Lady Gwendolyn suggested quietly to her mesmerized audience. The musical voice fell away, and there was a long moment of silence.

Annie imagined how Christie must have suffered: the loss of a beloved mother, the task of clearing away the mementos of a lifetime, the betrayal by the man she'd loved and trusted, the inability to sleep because of the painful images jostling in her mind, the depression that caused food and laughter and sunlight to lose their savor, the drudgery of work contracted for but now meaningless, the anger and tears and misery.

"Then think," and it was a clarion call, "think how dreadful to collapse in spirit and reawaken to painful reality scarred by a flood of ugly publicity. No wonder that ever afterward Christie shunned publicity, avoided reporters, was cautious in her trust.

"But," and this was a triumphant cry, "she never gave up. Thank God for all of us, she never gave up."

Travel. More books. A ticket to the West Indies, but a chance conversation at a dinner party convinced her to cancel that trip, go instead on the Orient Express to Baghdad. A visit to an archaeological dig. An invitation to return the next year.

"Nineteen thirty, oh, that was a very good year . . ."

Max Mallowan, a young archaeologist at the dig. A trip together. A happy companionship. Marriage that September, beginning a journey that would last forty-six happy years. The first Miss Marple, *The Murder at the Vicarage*.

Lady Gwendolyn moved ebulliently on, totting up the triumphs, the great events, the tragedies of a long life. Happy expeditions to Max's digs. Plays. Rosalind's marriage. The Second World War. The birth of her cherished grandson, Mathew. Sadness at the loss of Rosalind's husband, killed in action. Max stationed so far away in Egypt. So many wonderful books.

Fortune. Honors. Acclaim.

And a peaceful farewell January 12, 1976.

Lady Gwendolyn smiled tremulously, then concluded, her clear voice gentle, "Upon a tall and shining gravestone at the little church in Cholsey, near Winterbrook, are graven these words by Spenser:

> *Sleep after Toyle*
> *Port after Stormie Seas,*
> *Ease after Warre,*
> *Death after Life,*
> *Doth greatly please.*"

The silence held, full of reverence, a moment of shared beauty as delicate as sunlight slanting through stained glass.

Annie, who never carried Kleenex, used the back of her hand to smudge away a tear.

A chair scraped.

The harsh sound was a discordant intrusion.

Neil Bledsoe heaved himself to his feet.

AGATHA CHRISTIE
TITLE CLUE

Suntan in a bottle;
Who took that bath?

12

You know what Henry Ford said." Bledsoe's deep voice was smug. "He said history was bunk. He was right. That's what you've heard today—bunk." His mocking eyes moved from face to face, challenging, daring, taunting.

Lady Gwendolyn's retort was icy and immediate. "Balderdash."

Annie jumped to her feet. But so did almost everyone else in the huge meeting room, all clamoring to be heard.

Annie yelled, "Lady Gwendolyn's every word can be documented. The recollections of family. Friends. Letters. Business correspondence. Every single—" she broke off, belatedly realizing that she couldn't be heard above the outraged shouts and cries of the audience.

Bledsoe strode up the central aisle. He took the platform steps in a single bound. His voice was loud enough, deep enough, to carry to the far reaches of the room. "New sources. Papers hitherto untapped. The *real* truth. What you've heard here"—his voice rose in disdain—"is the *official, approved* biography of one of the world's richest and most secretive women. Find out what's been hidden, swept under the rug."

Annie darted up the steps after him. She skidded to a stop next to Lady Gwendolyn, whose blue eyes observed Bledsoe carefully but without surprise. Annie thought in a flash that nothing had truly surprised the English author in many years.

Henny's voice rang from a near corner. "Nonsense!"

"There is no such source!" Emma Clyde bellowed.

Annie was so angry she trembled. "You aren't going to ruin my conference with this kind of garbage. Get out of here!"

Shouts of accusation, disbelief, query, astonishment.

Bledsoe held up his hand. He was an undeniably commanding figure, his ruddy face flushed and insolent, his sensual lips spread in a taunting smile, his powerful body poised as if for battle. Arrogantly, he surveyed the unruly audience.

Annie's eyes, too, swept the room. Yes, the conference-goers, almost to a person, were angry and vocal about it, except for a few quite still, almost frozen faces with a common expression—the beginnings of relief! The chunky editor, the young publicist, the regal agent, the retiring author's widow, the charming author, each face mirrored a lessening of tension, a relaxation.

Startled, Annie turned toward Bledsoe.

And realized that he was equally well aware of the curious—to her—phenomenon. And it amused him.

Beyond even her fury at his unwarranted attack on Christie, she felt a sudden revulsion. How twisted and dreadful Bledsoe was.

Lady Gwendolyn cut through to the point.

"What," she demanded peremptorily, "do you intend?"

Bledsoe looked down at the august British author, undaunted by her manner.

"I intend that the truth about Christie shall be known." If before he had spoken loudly, now he roared with almost evangelical fervor. "I'm a man who's not afraid to tell the truth. People don't like the truth. They didn't like the truth about James Barrie. Or Mark Twain. Or Georges Simenon. People who like fairy tales are going to fight against the truth about Agatha Christie. But the world deserves to know what kind of woman she *really* was."

Angry shouts sounded against a backdrop of jeering catcalls and whistles.

Bledsoe threw back his head and laughed, his mouth a wide slash against his scarred face. "And by God," his voice rose above the maelstrom, "I'm the man with the guts to dig behind locked doors. You like mysteries? Solve the Mystery of Agatha Christie. I'll tell you how you can do it. Come to the Palmetto Court. Ten o'clock in the morning. Come one, come all. Everybody's welcome."

• • •

Lady Gwendolyn, her face grave, sipped at her tea. As Max finished speaking, she refilled her cup. The tea (Lapsang souchong) was the color of old mud and looked strong enough to fell a horse. Absently, her gaze abstracted, she lifted her cup again.

"So you're telling us," Annie said grimly to her husband, "that we can't do a damn thing!" She flung her napkin down on her barely nibbled lunch and bounced to her feet.

Max spread his hands helplessly. "He's a bona fide registrant of the conference. He's a lawful guest of the hotel. He hasn't *done* anything illegal—"

"Yet!" Annie snarled.

"Annie, you can't libel the dead." Max's voice was gentle, and his eyes filled with pity.

"I've always felt," Laurel murmured, "that the best policy—for those of us among the living—is simply to ignore calumny. So often unkind remarks about one's romantic adventures are simply a reflection of petty jealousy."

"I'm sure," Henny said dryly, "that you have had ample experience in these matters."

Annie furiously paced across the living room of their suite, oblivious to the soft breeze flowing in from the balcony, the caramel-rich splash of sunlight touching the white wicker with gold. She jammed a hand wildly through her thick honey-colored hair. "That's all wrong. Dead wrong," she exploded. "Are you telling us he can say anything he wants to about Christie? Claim she chopped up her dogs for meat pie, fed poison to her cousins, planted plastic explosives in Harrod's, and not a damn thing can be done about it?"

"It's a matter of public policy," Max explained. "You'd never get the truth about people's actions in the past if every statement about a dead person was vulnerable to legal action for libel or slander."

"It's not right!" Annie wailed. "That means the minute you die, *anybody* can say *anything* they want to about you!"

"Truly venomous," Laurel decreed.

"But dead ears can't hear," Henny pointed out.

Lady Gwendolyn slapped a plump hand against the tabletop. "There must be a solution!"

Max tapped the legal pad beside his plate. "The Christie estate might have a basis for an injunction on the grounds of trade injury if Bledsoe tried to publish a book containing unfounded assertions that might damage the commercial value of her books."

Annie stopped pacing and looked hopeful. Laurel clapped her hands excitedly. Lady Gwendolyn leaned forward eagerly, but Henny started shaking her head.

Max shrugged ruefully. "Annie, we are not the Christie estate. Even there, a strong argument could be made that notoriety sells a hell of a lot of books, witness the sales spurt of *The Murder of Roger Ackroyd* after her disappearance in 1926."

"It isn't right," Annie said again, her voice shaking. And she understood so well Mary Drower's angry response to the murder of her aunt in *The ABC Murders*. It wasn't *right*! Neil Bledsoe's attack on Agatha Christie wasn't *right*. It was akin to murder to willfully and viciously try to destroy the image of a gallant and kindly woman whose creative gifts were second to none.

Max absently munched on a carrot curl. "Annie, don't borrow trouble. Bledsoe's probably just raising a little hell. He hasn't actually *done* anything yet."

"What *can* he do?" Henny asked practically. "I think everyone's overreacting. For God's sake, this creep can't hurt Agatha Christie!"

"What about tomorrow? What about his grand announcement session in the Palmetto Court?" Annie paused in front of the island mural.

Lady Gwendolyn's cup rattled sharply against her saucer. "But his threat may be only the tip of the iceberg." She pursed her softly rounded lips.

Everyone looked at her respectfully.

"Think," she commanded her listeners. "Obviously today's performance is just the beginning."

Annie felt as if a curtain had parted. Performance. What an apt description. Hadn't there been, throughout Bledsoe's attack, a sense of unreality, a feeling that his appearance was deliberately calculated to produce a certain effect?

Henny reached for an olive. "Jerk," she said succinctly.

Laurel cleared her throat. "Not attractive. That is, not in his intentions or, certainly, in his manner. But really, not a man to dismiss lightly. Unfortunately, great"—a quick glance at Max—"uh...personal magnetism is not necessarily associated with rectitude. However, if one were to be confined to a desert island and to choose companions solely on the basis—"

Annie broke in. She understood very well indeed where Laurel was heading. But such discussion was not appropriate for everyone present. To be precise, Max would never comprehend the fact that Bledsoe, asshole that he might be, was undeniably a sexual magnet as far as most women were concerned.

"Hunk." Lady Gwendolyn's light voice summed it up.

Annie stared at her in astonishment, Laurel in admiring agreement, and Henny with amusement.

Max looked startled.

"But irrelevant to our present concerns," Lady Gwendolyn continued. "The point is, we must look beyond the moment. We must be aware of the overall picture. Neil Bledsoe's appearance at this conference has been an anomaly from the beginning. Here is a hard-boiled fan at a meeting alien to his beliefs. Why? That's the question to be answered."

"Buttering up his old aunt, in hopes of a legacy," Henny suggested cynically.

A brief headshake, which sent a hairpin flying from the coronet braids, dismissed that suggestion. "Even a cursory acquaintance makes it clear that such an approach wouldn't be in character. No," Lady Gwendolyn mused, "it will be nothing that simple." She tilted her head questioningly, and another hairpin hung perilously from the pale red braids. "Perhaps he plans to mount a vendetta against an enemy from his past?"

"He wants to destroy my conference," Annie moaned.

Max drew a huge question mark on the pad. "Maybe. Maybe not. He's having a hell of a time. That may be all there is to it."

Lady Gwendolyn smiled at Max. "In this instance, I feel confident that the truth, when known, will be quite convoluted. There will be nothing simple here. As we've all observed, there are dark secrets between this man and some of the other conference attendees. There was such patent relief on their part when he attacked Christie. Each apparently feared that Bledsoe's presence here was personally directed at them. But—keep in mind—the Christie attack may merely be a smoke screen."

So Lady Gwendolyn, too, had seen those expressions of relief. But it was possible to be *too* clever. "We have to look at what's right in front of our noses," Annie insisted.

"I'm reminded of an old adage." The author smiled gently at Annie. "A carrot for the donkey. Fools it every time."

Annie had the distinct feeling she'd been called—very gently—a donkey. Her mouth opened, shut. Dammit, how was she supposed to compete with the cleverest living mystery writer?

Annie whirled and stalked to the open doors of the balcony. She stared down at the spouting fountains, then spoke calmly, but there was underlying steel in her voice. "There he is, sitting at his ease in the Palmetto Court with that scruffy writer ogling him like he's a hero."

Bledsoe clearly was in good spirits, talking animatedly, gesturing broadly with his huge hands, then lifting up a tall glass, draining it almost to the bottom, and refilling it from the pitcher. Sangria. Annie thought he looked like a vampire quaffing blood. Probably why he liked the stuff. The young writer, her oddly angled face aglow, hung on his every word. Annie fought away a surge of absolute fury. Anger wasn't the answer. But there had to be an answer.

A waft of Evening in Paris perfume, and Lady Gwendolyn stood beside her. "One has to admit that Bledsoe's an interesting chap. I once knew a Johnny like that. In the war. I always felt he had an ace up his sleeve." Her mouth quirked in a half-smile at once wry and grim that sat oddly on her soft, pink lips. "He turned out to be a double agent." She stared down at the critic. "I shot him." Her tone was matter-of-fact.

Annie drew a breath in sharply and looked down at the small, plump author. The very matter-of-factness of Lady Gwendolyn's statement told volumes about this gentle but indomitable old lady.

She looked up at Annie with troubled but fearless blue eyes. "I have the same sense now as I did then. Danger lies ahead."

Annie had looked forward to slipping into some of the afternoon panels, The Occult in Doyle, Christie, and Rinehart, The Other Wonderful Women—Sayers, Allingham, Tey, and Marsh, Mary Roberts Rinehart—a Quintessential American, and Those Lively Ladies—Taylor, Rice, and Ford. She chalked up missing them as another grievance against Bledsoe—and Lady Gwendolyn. Although, she grudgingly had to admit, the old author's ideas were sound. "Scout the territory," she'd ordered. "We can't operate without intelligence."

Annie's assignment was simple. Find Kathryn Honeycutt. Pump her.

Somehow, it came as no surprise when she spotted Bledsoe's aunt coming out of the session on the occult.

Annie studied the woman who had accompanied Bledsoe to the conference. Kathryn Honeycutt was in her late sixties, probably, and, except for those squinting eyes behind thick-lensed wire frames, almost a ringer for Miss Marple, tall, quite thin, fluffy white hair. Annie suspected that Honeycutt was well aware of the resemblance and cultivated it, wearing a gray cotton dress cut in an old-fashioned way and a fleecy white shawl. Cultivated, too, Annie decided, was an expression of brisk inquiry and lively curiosity which mixed oddly with her obviously poor eyesight. However, she looked pleasant. Though it was hard for Annie to believe anyone with any decency could be a friend of *that* man. But Honeycutt wasn't just a friend. His aunt, someone had said. You don't pick your relatives. Still, why was she with him? Why had she come?

Kathryn Honeycutt stood near the wall and squinted at her program.

The program Annie had worked so hard to create. The program that louse Bledsoe was trying his best to destroy.

"Pardon me. Mrs. Honeycutt?"

A welcoming smile lit the pale thin face. "Oh, Mrs. Darling, this is such a marvelous conference! So fascinating about Mary Roberts Rinehart and the ghost in her house in Washington, D.C. A political boss! Rinehart was quite intrigued by the other side, and made some attempt to contact her husband after his death, but with no success. And I hadn't known about those early stories of Christie's. Even a seance in 'The Red Signal.' And *several* seances in Rinehart's *The Red Lamp.* Odd coincidence on the titles—they sound similar but they had entirely different meanings. And of course, Arthur Conan Doyle devoted much of the end of his life to spiritualism. So sad." A gentle sigh. "Trying so hard to get in touch with his son, Kingsley. Oh, that war destroyed a generation of young Englishmen."

The more Honeycutt talked, the less she looked like Miss Marple. Annie was relieved. She couldn't bear to think of the resident sleuth of St. Mary Mead as a companion to Neil Bledsoe.

"I'm glad you enjoyed the panel." Annie tried to infuse warmth in her voice. After all, she'd once had a lead role here on the island in *Arsenic and Old Lace.* But her acting ability just wasn't up to this role.

Kathryn Honeycutt's face drooped. The happiness seeped away. "I want you to know I *am* terribly sorry that Neil is causing trouble. It makes life so difficult—Neil, you know—always causing trouble. Ignore him, my dear. That's the only thing to do. I, for one, refuse to let my nephew ruin this wonderful week for me. I stopped apologizing for Neil years ago." She looked at Annie earnestly, her eyes hugely blue and fuzzy behind the thick lenses. "You won't hold the way he acts against me, will you?"

"Of course not," Annie said gently.

"Besides, Neil's outburst will be a moment's sensation and then *pouf!*" Honeycutt fluttered her hands. "We all know Agatha Christie was grand. It won't matter what someone like Neil says. No one who's ever read a word of hers will believe anything he says or does."

"I wish that were true, but when people throw mud, some of it always sticks." Annie looked at her soberly. "Will you help me, Mrs. Honeycutt?"

"Call me Kathryn," the older woman responded immediately. "What do you want me to do?"

"Take a walk with me." Annie wanted an uninterrupted session. "Tell me about your nephew."

They followed the boardwalk over the dunes to the beach. Their shoes sank in the soft gray sand until they reached the sleek dampened tideflat. The onshore breeze ruffled their hair, tugged at their clothes.

"Oh, this is just glorious." Kathryn's slender hand, the nails short and unpainted, encompassed the ocean, the beach, the softly blue sky. She twisted her head to look a little defiantly at Annie. "I'm *glad* I came, even though I knew there would be bad moments. There are always some bad moments with Neil." She paused, pointed the toe of her shoe at a tiny sand dome, watched it collapse. "Frederick and I did our best. We tried to treat him like a son. But he was never our son. Frederick's sister, Juliette, was his mother. She—she didn't want him. Neil knew that. You never fool kids. He never forgave her. He wouldn't even go last year, when she was dying." Her voice was almost a whisper. "I'm so glad Frederick didn't know." She shaded her eyes, looked off toward the faraway horizon. "Frederick died five years ago."

"Why did Neil come here? Do you know?" Annie asked.

Kathryn pushed her wire glasses up on her nose. "I'm sure he has a reason." She reached out, grabbed Annie's arm. "Oh, look, look! There's a dolphin. Look at him jump! Oh, another one."

Thirty yards offshore the steel gray mammals arched gracefully in the air, up and over and down, kicking up a spray of foam.

They watched until the dolphins were out of sight.

"Usually it's money with Neil. I thought it probably was again. Sometimes he gets mad at me, thinks I'm extravagant. He says you can't earn interest on money tied up in old stamps." Her lips tightened obstinately for a moment. She stared earnestly at Annie. "The thing about it is, it's my money, and I can spend it any way I want to. And if it's all gone one of these days, that's for me to worry about. But sometimes I'm lucky. Such a surprise. At bingo the other night. The jackpot was carried over from several games . . . I won. I decided I'd surprise Neil since he's paying for our trip. This morning—I asked if he needed money—I felt so sure that was it—you could have knocked me over with a feather, Neil turning down several thousand dollars! Can you believe it?"

They turned and headed back toward the hotel. "So he doesn't need money?"

"Of course he needs money. Just as I thought, he has money problems. But he didn't want a dime from me." The old lady fluttered. "He gave me the funniest look—I guess he never expected me to try and help—he was just flabbergasted! He said he appreciated it, but he had a plan. He said he was going to come up with a lot of money."

As they walked along the boardwalk, their footsteps echoed, just as the words echoed in Annie's mind. *A lot of money . . . a lot of money . . . a lot of money . . .*

Monday afternoons at Confidential Commissions often featured a thoughtful perusal of the balance of the Sunday *New York Times,* a period of contemplation—after all, how could one lead a reasoned life without the judicious, and unhurried, application of reason—and occasionally a relaxed game of darts. It wasn't, certainly, that Max Darling was averse to work. At the urging of his wife, Max agreed that work was real, work was earnest, work could even—he had a little trouble here—be wonderful. As a matter of fact, Max was enormously proud of Confidential Commissions, his quite original business venture. A circumspect ad ran daily in the personals column of both the *Island Gazette* and the *Chastain Courier:* "Troubled, puzzled, curious? Whatever your problem, contact CONFIDENTIAL COMMISSIONS, 555-1321, 11 Seaview, Broward's Rock." Not a private detective agency, since the State of South Carolina had quite particular requirements for the licensing of such offices, requirements Max had no intention of fulfilling. Ergo, his own private counseling agency. No law against counseling. He had been employed to solve several interesting problems. Lady Gwendolyn had been quite impressed with the capabilities of his agency. Of course, he never worked on weekends. Weekends, though tailored around the exigencies of running the greatest mystery bookstore this side of Atlanta, were meant for wind-surfing, love, tennis, love, boating, love, whatever, but, most of all, love. Not that love was limited to weekends, but freedom from work surely meant freedom to play, and if there was a better game in town Max had yet to find it. After a successful weekend, he never felt in any great rush to plunge back into the workday world, so the hum of activity this Monday afternoon at Confidential Commissions seemed odd indeed.

The last of the extra phone lines had just been installed. Normally, of course, it took at least two days for new lines to be activated. Lady Gwendolyn spent ten minutes in private consultation with the telephone company supervisor, who emerged from the session in her thrall, and presto, here came the phones.

The extra tables in his office—workstations for the phones—did crowd the decor. And it was hard to concentrate with Laurel chattering to his right ("so interesting that you've known Mrs. Calloway ever since you both were just girls . . . so exciting to have a window on the life of one of the truly popular authors of our time") and Henny aggressively pressing her questions to his left ("Someone told me Nathan Hillman has quite a temper . . . Not your experience? How well . . . ?"). They'd divided up the list—Bledsoe and all who appeared to be involved with him—among the three of them. He rubbed his ear. It seemed to him as though he'd been on the phone for days, not just hours. And he'd never realized just how uncomfortable office straight chairs were. He glanced longingly at his Italian Renaissance desk, fit for a cardinal. Behind it, Lady Gwendolyn looked just a trifle absurd perched on his red leather desk chair, which she, not surprisingly, had punched into the most upright position.

Of course, it did make it easier for her to let fly with the darts. Her plump arm flashed through the air, the dart sped unerringly for the target, and that aristocratic nose twitched with satisfaction.

Uncanny, how close she came each time to bull's-eye.

Annie's eyes watered. Cigarette smoke always did it to her. She blinked and peered into the dimness of Blackbeard's Retreat. Although it wasn't quite five yet, the hotel bar was full.

And loud.

"So a few of the books aren't wonderful. Three, maybe four. But she wrote more great mysteries than anyone else ever has—or will."

"... be fascinating to know the name of the officer who painted the fresco around the top of the walls of the library at Greenway when the house was occupied by the American Navy during World War Two."

"... wished she hadn't put Poirot in *The Hollow*. She was right, you know. The book didn't need him."

"It gives me the willies—an old lady looking at a fireplace and asking about the child buried behind it!"

"She spent fifteen years writing her autobiography."

Emma Clyde was at the very back of the bar where it was so dark and jammed with bodies Annie felt claustrophobic. She felt a bond with Christie, who disliked crowds, cigarette smoke, loud voices, and cocktail parties. The shy author would have avoided Blackbeard's Retreat like the plague.

Annie felt as welcome as the plague when she met Emma's gaze. Emma's chilly gaze.

No smile. Not a flicker of welcome.

Annie ignored the awestruck fans clustered around Emma. Plunking her palms down on the table, sticky from spilled drinks, Annie snapped, "Dammit, you *did* almost run Bledsoe down. Why shouldn't I think you shot at him, too?"

"I was in absolute control of the car," Emma pointed out impatiently. "I know too much about guns and how bullets can ricochet to fire them in the presence of innocent people."

"You say."

"I do say." So might Mrs. Boynton have spoken to Lennox's wife in *Appointment with Death*. There was the same sense of an overpowering personality that would brook no interference.

Annie met the gaze from those icy blue eyes without flinching. "All right, Emma. I'll accept what you're telling me—that someone else shot at Bledsoe, someone who isn't as punctilious about the safety of others. So you should be willing to help the authorities catch that person."

Emma was the first to look away. She reached down, plunged her hand into a straw purse that looked large enough to harbor a laptop computer, and pulled out a cigarette case.

Annie's eyes widened. She'd never seen Emma smoke.

Emma lifted out a menthol-tipped cigarette. "At conferences," she said brusquely as she lit it.

The minty smoke curled up into Annie's face. Her eyes burned and her nose itched. "Look, Emma, give me a break. I didn't tell Frank there was bad blood between Fleur Calloway and Neil Bledsoe. But now we have to. He has to know what kind of person Bledsoe is, who might have it in for him."

Emma blew two perfect smoke rings. As they dissolved, she smiled grimly. "Annie, dear, I don't have the faintest idea what you're talking about."

Annie tugged her cotton blouse over her head, dropped her skirt to the floor. "Can't stand the smell of cigarette smoke. Feel like I've spent a week with Humphrey Bogart in Casablanca. Look what cigarettes did to him!"

Max, a sheaf of papers in his hand, lounged against the jamb of the open door to the bathroom, an appreciative audience as bra, half-slip, and panties joined the skirt and blouse.

Annie stepped into the enormous peach bathtub and, honestly, honeymoon suite or no, this was beyond expectation. Water plunged with the explosiveness of the Victoria Falls Christie described with such delight in *The Man in the Brown Suit*. Moreover, there was room enough for—

She looked up in surprise. Then pleasure.

Oh yes, indeed, there was room enough.

AGATHA CHRISTIE
TITLE CLUE

Miss Lemon makes a mistake!
Hercule Poirot does a double take.

13

nnie snapped off the dryer and gave a final swipe to her still damp hair. "So Emma's not going to be any help at all." She checked her reflection in the wall mirror. As always, she was surprised at how little outward appearances can reveal. She looked cool and summery in her lemon crew neck sweater and red-and-blue patched Madras shorts. Perhaps the only hint of recent passion was the softness in her eyes.

Max, cool, crisp, and, as always, Joe Hardy handsome in white shorts and a navy crew neck, rustled his sheaf of papers, some of them newly water-spotted, and said, "Emma must know that the trouble between Calloway and Bledsoe isn't common knowledge. I didn't pick up anything about it. We can check with Laurel, see what she's found out about Fleur in her calls."

Annie checked the water she'd put on to boil. "How's everything going at the office?"

"At last count, Lady Gwendolyn's dart score was eighteen thousand and climbing."

"Isn't she doing any work?" Annie dropped a quart-size bag into the pitcher.

Max leaned against the counter and watched as Annie poured the hot water over the tea bag. "Periodically, she drops her directives on our desks, enough interviewing ideas to keep us busy well into the twenty-first century. I can see why she has seventy-five books to her credit." He rubbed his ear. "Do you think it's getting a cauliflower look?"

Annie inspected it, almost added a kiss, decided Max might be too easily distracted from serious pursuits, and murmured, "Looks healthy." She found sliced limes and fresh mint in the refrigerator. Someone at the Palmetto House was definitely into sensory delights.

She put their huge glasses of iced tea on the table beside the wicker sofa, plopped down, and patted the cushion beside her.

Max settled down comfortably, perhaps only a little too close, and handed her the sheaf of papers.

Just to keep things on a businesslike plane, she pushed his thigh away from hers. Sipping her tea, she began to read.

NEIL CAMERON BLEDSOE. *Born January 11, 1948, in Chicago, Illinois. Mother, Juliette Hailey, 34; father, Cameron Bledsoe, 39. Mother a blues singer. Never made it beyond the Midwest nightclub circuit. Father a trombonist in a band. Neil's early childhood spent in series of hotels. Band leader's wife, Gloria Franz, remembers him as "a skinny little kid with huge hungry eyes. Never smiled. Juliette was always on his back. Hangovers. Lousy way to wake up. Made her mean. Then when Cameron ran off with a waitress in Cincinnati, she took it out on Neil." Bledsoe was made a ward of the children's court in Chicago when it was learned (a teacher complained) that a boyfriend of Juliette's burned him with cigarettes. The court papers read: Child repeatedly subjected to abuse for refusal to cry when punished.*

"Oh, God," Annie murmured.

Max slipped his arm around her shoulders.

She looked up at him with haunted eyes. "No wonder," she said simply. "Oh, Max, how can people be so dreadful?"

"Violence always has a long history," he said soberly.

Annie laid the sheaf down. "I thought if we found out enough about him, we might find a way to reach him. But he's been angry for a long, long time." A twisted, scarred man. Was that why he was so intent on destroying the reverence so many millions feel for Christie? Or was it simply a matter of money? . . . *a lot of money . . .*

The living and the dead. What mattered? Who mattered?

Neil Bledsoe, alive with all the possibilities and glories that life could offer.

Agatha Christie, dead and gone, but living still in the minds and hearts of her readers.

Annie picked up the sheets and determinedly began to read:

On an east coast tour, Juliette left Neil with her brother, Frederick, and his wife, Kathryn. Juliette never came back for her son. Frederick Honeycutt was a small-town lawyer in Connecticut, earnest, serious, successful. Kathryn was his secretary. They were prosperous, decent, respectable, and totally unable to deal with the teenaged Neil, who alternated between outbursts of high energy and episodes of malevolence. Neil was a bright, quick student, but teachers and classmates alike feared his vicious sarcasm and outbursts of fierce hostility. He sought out challenge and seemed impervious to fear. On a dare, he once drove his motorcycle to 110 miles an hour. A scar on his left forearm was the result of a knife fight in college, reputedly over a gambling debt. Attended Berkeley on a scholarship at the height of the sixties. Degree in journalism. Counterculture reporter for various tabloids in the early seventies. As the greening of America turned brown, he moved into publishing. Made a fortune in the late seventies with a magazine aimed at mercenaries, Have Gun, Will Travel. *A friend from Berkeley days, Wallace Mercer, said, "I swear I don't get Neil. So there aren't any hippies anymore. But he was damn near a Weatherman in the sixties. So how could he peddle guns to right-wing killers? I asked him and he laughed and said you might as well be dead as cling to dead ideas. He said everything's corrupt, both the Left and the Right, and at least the Right can pay for what it wants." Gambling got him in trouble again, in the early eighties. He bet a quarter million on the black at Vegas and it came up red. Had to sell* Have Gun, Will Travel *in 1981 to pay it off. Had no choice, pay up or die. Word on the street had it that he was in deep again, had a deadline to meet.*

Annie reached over, edged the pen out of Max's pocket, and circled *deadline.*

But it seemed so futile. She almost put the papers down. What was the point in knowing more about Bledsoe? No appeal to his better nature or to his commitment as a critic to truth in publishing would have any effect. Not with this man.

But the sheets held the same riveting fascination as a James Ellroy novel. How dark could a life be?

She found her place:

Bledsoe has made the circuit in publishing since his sale of Have Gun, Will Travel, *working briefly as an agent with Masters and Wright* [Margo Wright? Annie would check], *as an editor with Hillman House, as a bookseller with the now defunct Ex Libris in New York, and, presently, as editor and publisher of* Mean Streets, *a journal devoted to the mystery.*

Annie's hackles rose at that. As if there were only one kind of mystery. Realism? Private detectives as knights errant, tilting courageously against an evil and corrupt society? Ah, the male fantasy novel, full of swashbuckling blood and guts with liberal splashes of female bashing and bedding. (Translate *barefoot and pregnant* to *backhanded and screwed.*)

"Max, can you believe this!" and she pointed at the offending line. "About as close to real life as a Rambo movie. Do you want reality?" she demanded.

Max nodded obediently. He'd heard this diatribe before.

"Read Christie! There's reality. Her characters are people everyone knows. Respectable people driven by lust and hatred and greed and dishonesty. That's reality." The fire in her eye was replaced abruptly by amusement. "I love it, the way some hard-boiled writers swagger around, as if *they* were the only true mystery writers. But ask any bookseller. Who sells? What sells? Christie sells. One *billion* books. They won't sell a billion Hammett books in a thousand years!"

Her good humor restored, she resumed her reading:

Bledsoe married twice. First wife, Susan Figaro (m. 1973), divorced him 1975. No children. She is a flight attendant for Buena Vista Airlines and presently lives in Miami and flies the South American route. On layover now in Caracas. Hotel room didn't answer. Married his second wife, Pamela Gerrard Davis, 1982. A divorcee with an eighteen-year-old son, Derek.

"Derek Davis," she said aloud. "Max, that has to be the publicist with Hillman House. My God, Bledsoe's his stepfather!"

"Former stepfather," Max clarified.

Derek Davis, young and eager—until he saw Bledsoe. Davis had done nothing to help when Bledsoe careened down the hotel stairs in the throes of a panic attack.

Annie read on:

Pamela Bledsoe died of a fall in 1985. Reportedly lost her balance and fell down a flight of stone stairs on the patio of their home in Stamford, Connecticut. She had been drinking heavily. The postmortem revealed a blood alcohol level of .12. As Pamela Gerrard, she had enjoyed a successful career as a women's novelist with several novels (notably Farewell, My Love, Forever) *reaching the* New York Times *hardcover fiction bestseller list and selling in excess of 400,000 copies.*

"I remember her," Annie said abruptly. "I saw her on *Good Morning America* once. She had such a *cheerful* face."

The memory sharpened in her mind. But the face that came clearly was Derek's, roundish, snub-nosed, wide-spaced hazel eyes, a sprinkling of freckles. He was, as sons so often are, the image of his mother.

"A fatal fall," Annie said thoughtfully.

On the surface the all-English dinner was a rousing success. Everyone was having a wonderful time, that was clear from the rapid chatter and bursts of laughter. The hotel had come through magnificently. Beneath the chandeliers, china and crystal glittered on shiny damask tablecloths. The food was perfect, succulent, and authentic: oyster soup, roast beef of Old England, Yorkshire pudding, roast potatoes, curried chicken with rice, syllabub or tea, and, of course, a hearty serving at meal's end of clotted cream and fresh strawberries or sherry trifle. Lady Gwendolyn enjoyed it so much, in fact, that spatters of the golden cream adorned the front of her pink-flowered lavender dress.

But, as she scraped the last microdot of cream from her dish, the old author swept the table with a troubled glance. "The brew is bubbling."

Annie stiffened. Max frowned. Laurel bent forward in rapt attention, but Henny only half hid a yawn behind her napkin.

Lady Gwendolyn absently swiped her spoon again in her empty bowl.

Laurel murmured, "Banting, you know. I'd be so happy to give you mine. It's quite untouched," and she offered her dessert.

The old lady happily plunged her spoon into the full bowl. "I do abhor waste." Not quite indistinctly, despite the deployment of her spoon heaped with golden cream, Lady Gwendolyn continued thoughtfully, "I took the opportunity prior to the opening session to visit with those who have been linked to Bledsoe." She smiled almost shyly. "One of the fruits of longevity—often unappreciated both by its possessor and recipients of the resulting pearls of wisdom—is the ability to judge character."

Annie wanted very much to derail these observations. Talking about Bledsoe and his adversaries detracted from the glow of this marvelous dinner, but she knew that Lady Gwendolyn meant well.

Annie's face must have revealed more than she realized.

Lady Gwendolyn chided her gently. "Remember Arthur Bantry, Annie. It helped him not at all to refuse to see what was happening around him." Those bright, questing blue eyes swept the dining room. "Much is happening around us—all the result of the intermixture of characters assembled here." The old author's tone was somber. "Bledsoe, of course, is the focal point."

With an effort of will, Annie managed a strained smile.

Lady Gwendolyn absently smoothed her upswept hair. "Oh, Bledsoe's obviously posturing, but I sense a purpose, a plan. At this point, I've been unable to determine his true objective. Whatever it is, I fear he will achieve it at all costs." She said it coolly, without great dramatic flair, but Annie's skin prickled. It was as ominous as a muffled roll of drums. "And the rest of them, bound to him by ties we cannot see. Fleur Calloway—such a charming woman, but she's shackled by misery. I see it in her eyes. She needs to break free of the past, live again. Emma Clyde—oh, she's immensely clever and she knows it. A bad enemy. Derek Davis—life is hard on the young. His emotions are raw. He's living on the edge. Natalie Marlow—gauche." Lady Gwendolyn reinserted a bronze bobby pin in her braids. "She doesn't know how to be a woman, but she wants to be, a very dangerous combination. Natalie's ripe for the picking. Margo Wright's a cool customer. She doesn't miss much. Nathan Hillman—assuredly a very civilized man, but his feelings run deep. Victoria Shaw—her dead husband is more real to her than the people here. Resentment can fester, twist even a gentle nature."

"Brilliant," Laurel breathed admiringly.

Henny rolled her eyes.

Max cupped his chin in his hand. "So you think there's going to be trouble, Lady Gwendolyn?"

"Yes."

Annie winced. The old lady didn't have to sound so damned positive—and so convincing. As a matter of fact, tonight's bash was about as far from trouble as possible, and Annie was beginning to hope that perhaps the quick and thorough police response—thanks to Chief Saulter—to the incident at Death on Demand had made the perpetrator realize the seriousness of breaking the law and that nothing further would occur to mar the conference. Besides, Annie, perhaps a little superstitiously, didn't want to court trouble by thinking about it.

She popped to her feet. "Got to check on the band."

As she passed through the dining room, she knew her guests were having fun:

"Obviously Marple is the superior detective. Poirot just postures."

"I beg your pardon. Think of his brilliance in solving *Sad Cypress*."

"I'd love to see a revival of *Spider's Web*. She wrote the play especially for Margaret Lockwood, and when it was produced it ran simultaneously in London with *The Mousetrap* and *Witness for the Prosecution*. How many playwrights can equal that?"

"Sometimes a woman's hunger for children can be destructive— think of Rachel Argyle in *Ordeal by Innocence*."

"By far the most unforgettable figure of evil in all of Christie's work is Mrs. Boynton in *Appointment with Death*."

"It would be too dangerous—think of the libel problems—to pattern a character today after someone as openly as Christie patterned Louise Leidner in *Murder in Mesopotamia* after Katharine Woolley."

"*Endless Night* is a psychological *tour de force*."

The band leader assured Annie that the musicians were prepared; there would be plenty of Cole Porter and George Gershwin. (Whenever she heard Porter's "I Get a Kick Out of You," she thought of the marvelous 1982 film version of *Evil Under the Sun*. She'd have to check the schedule at the movie room. Maybe she could take time to drop in and watch at least a little of it.)

As she turned away, Chief Saulter came up, and he wasn't wearing a happy face.

"What's wrong, Frank?"

"Nothing the end of your conference won't solve." At her startled look, he shrugged. "Sorry, Annie. I know how much all of this means to you, but I got some bad news."

She suppressed a groan.

"There wasn't any gun on the bottom of the harbor." He tugged on his black bow tie as if the unaccustomed evening dress choked him.

"Billy may have missed it," Annie suggested.

"Maybe." The police chief surveyed the festive dining room. "Dammit, I've got a bad feeling. I've been looking these people over today"— Annie didn't have to ask for names—"and I smell trouble."

First, Lady Gwendolyn. Now, Frank.

"Oh, Frank, everything's going great."

And it was, she insisted to herself as she started back to the table.

The man at the center of this spider's web seemed, to all intents and purposes, at peace with the world, his buccaneer's face genial as he talked with Natalie. Although seated at a large round table, they sat with their heads close together, ignoring the other guests. Bledsoe spoke only to Natalie, his deep voice subdued. One hand rested on her arm. Annie glimpsed the young author's face and almost flinched at its eagerness and vulnerability.

Annie had read Marlow's debut novel. A young wife and mother, isolated in a country home, hears a voice warning her not to open the cellar door. It is a voice she knows, that of an elderly woman who had once owned the house—and been murdered in it. The murderer was never found. The young mother does open the cellar door—Annie tried to will away her memory of Marlow's brutal, unforgettable, macabre prose. She piled horror upon horror upon horror. Even Ruth Rendell might blanch when reading this.

As she watched, Marlow's fingers reached up, tentatively, slowly, to touch Bledsoe's face. His hand caught hers; his lips touched her palm.

Annie turned away. No business of hers, but that young woman needed a refresher course on Jerks, How to Spot Them. And perhaps a seminar on Appropriate Behavior at a Banquet.

Nathan Hillman wasn't engaged with the bonhomie at his table. The seat next to his was empty. Every so often, he looked tensely toward the doors.

Margo Wright, her face gentle and kind, sat beside Victoria Shaw. The author's widow was animated, her usually faded cheeks touched with spots of color. Every so often Margo nodded in agreement. Occasionally, unobtrusively, she glanced toward Bledsoe and Marlow.

Emma Clyde's voice always carried. "Fleur, don't do this to yourself. Let's go for a drive."

Fleur Calloway should have been spectacularly lovely, her slim body sheathed in a beautifully cut white satin gown, but her face was as empty as a windswept moor, the muscles slack, her eyes somber.

Suddenly, Nathan Hillman shoved back his chair and hurried past Annie.

Turning, she saw him grab Derek Davis's arm.

Derek wavered unsteadily on his feet. "Let go," he muttered. "Let go."

Annie and Frank reached the two men at the same time.

"Problem here?" Frank asked quietly.

Hillman tried to put a good face on it, though he didn't loosen his tight grip on Derek's arm. "It's all right. Derek's had a bit too much to drink. I'll take care of it."

But Derek was too drunk or too upset to care that he was struggling with his boss.

"Let go of me, Nathan. Lemme go. Maybe you don't give a damn, but I do. He's a shit. I tell you he's a shit." His voice became shrill. "He killed my—"

Hillman clapped his hand roughly over Derek's mouth. "Derek, listen to me. Wait a minute, listen. I'll go over there. I'll ask Natalie to come join us. But promise me you'll wait here and keep quiet." The stocky editor's face was shiny with sweat, and he looked imploringly at Annie and the chief. "Look, Derek," Hillman said with false joviality. "Here's Mrs. Darling, you know who she is—the organizer of the conference. The bookseller. She's going to sit down here with you. And I'll go ask Natalie."

As Hillman loosened his grasp, Derek wavered unsteadily.

Annie reached out, took his arm, and smiled up into alcohol-dulled eyes. "Tell me about the novels you're promoting right now."

She wasn't even certain he heard her. He pulled free and, unexpectedly, careened into a shambling run, lurching past Hillman and stumbling to a stop beside Bledsoe's table. He reached out a trembling hand. "Natalie." His voice cracked. "Natalie, he'll hurt you. Please, come away with me. He's—oh God, Natalie, he's evil."

The young writer's head jerked up. She stared at Derek in surprise, then an angry red flush suffused her face, vivid in the light from the chandeliers. "Derek, for God's sake, be quiet."

Bledsoe leaned back comfortably in his chair and looked up with an amused smile. "Drunk again, Derek? How sophomoric. But then I suppose you can't get away from your genes, can you?"

Derek made a noise low in his throat and flung himself on Bledsoe, his hands scrabbling for the big man's throat.

Bledsoe grunted. Although Frank and the harried editor both lunged forward, the encounter was over before they could intervene. With apparent ease, Bledsoe chopped upward with his forearms, brutally breaking Derek's grip, then one huge hand grabbed Derek's tuxedo jacket and flung him backward onto the floor.

Bledsoe erupted out of his chair and stood, legs braced, glowering down at Derek. For a moment, Derek lay flat on his back, stunned, then he rolled over and struggled awkwardly, painfully to get to his hands and knees. His face was crimson with fury and frustration.

Bledsoe glanced at Hillman. "Get him out of here, Nathan, before I have to hurt him."

Derek lurched to his feet and once again, mindlessly, flung himself at Bledsoe. Frank and Nathan grabbed him, but Derek continued to struggle, head down, drunken arms flailing helplessly, trying to get to Bledsoe.

As the older men hustled him out of the dining room, Annie walked away. She didn't want to see any more of Bledsoe. She hated his look of smug amusement. It was in such sharp and ugly contrast to Derek's tear-streaked, maddened face.

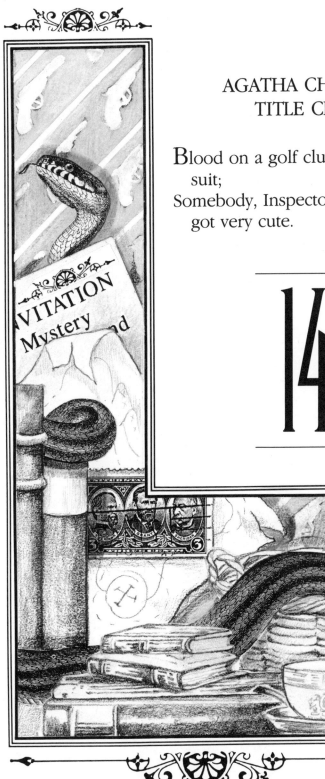

AGATHA CHRISTIE
TITLE CLUE

Blood on a golf club, blood on a
 suit;
Somebody, Inspector Battle thinks,
 got very cute.

14

Annie, Anniieeeee . . ."

Her name, huskily, throatily, penetratingly voiced, buzzed in her ear with the persistence of a mosquito.

Annie said, "Mmmhph," and sleepily pawed to her left. The rumpled sheets were cool to her touch. She reluctantly opened one eye and turned her head. No Max.

"Annie, Anniiieee . . ."

Annie lifted her head and peered through the shadows toward the windows opening onto the balcony.

The call came again. Annie knew who it was, of course. In all the world, there was no other voice quite like Laurel's, a combination of Dietrich sultriness, Bacall sensuality, and wood nymph innocence, a beguiling, enchanting, bewitching triad—but not at sunrise.

The call came again, clearly from outside.

Their room was on the third floor. Sleep fled. Both eyes snapped open. Surely—

Annie rolled out of bed and trotted to the balcony. Peering out, she saw Laurel on the next balcony. Oh, good Lord, she hadn't realized her mother-in-law's room was that close to their own. And they'd left the balcony doors open both nights. . . . Annie's ears flamed.

Laurel, with the eyesight of a marsh hawk, hadn't missed the telltale movement. She waved energetically to summon her daughter-in-law, and the folded sheet of yellow paper fluttered in her hand.

Annie peered out once more, this time surveying the darkened Palmetto Court below and the untenanted nearby balconies, then, with a shrug, padded barefoot in her shorty pajamas to the railing.

Laurel didn't *say* anything, but her brief glance at Annie's pajamas moved the flush from Annie's ears to her cheeks.

Laurel's eyebrows rose just a fraction; she gave an infinitesimal sigh and headshake.

So what was wrong with Bugs Bunny pajamas! Annie liked them. But she knew that once again she'd failed to pass muster. She was quite certain that Laurel, in her many marital outings (five, for heaven's sake), had always worn the daintiest night things imaginable. Actually, the Bugs Bunny p.j.'s were Annie's concession to the married state. Previously, she had preferred a cotton T-shirt and shorts.

Annie opened her mouth, then closed it. She had no intention of discussing her nocturnal fashion choices. Dammit, surely Laurel hadn't rousted Annie from her slumbers merely to glance askance at her choice of lingerie. Not any of her business, anyway. "Yes?" she snapped.

With a sweet smile that exuded patient forgiveness of early morning irritability in less gracious creatures, Laurel announced firmly, "Annie, we *must* confer. I shall fly to your door." Whirling, with the grace and effortless speed of a ballerina, Laurel pirouetted back into her own apartment.

Annie was not slow-witted, but her unexpected awakening, the vision of Laurel, bright and eager in a delicate shell-pink warm-up, and the unaccustomed misery of awaking first (Max *always* got up and put the coffee on and had it ready when she stumbled down the stairs. Really, that instantly available cup of coffee the first thing in the morning was one of the greatest plusses of the married state.) combined to make her less than alert.

So it took a minute or so for her to respond to the steady knock at the suite door.

Laurel sped inside, taking time only to scoop up another sheet of yellow paper from the floor just inside the door. Adding that to the sheet she'd fluttered from her balcony, she stalked to the center of the living room and clapped the squares of paper dramatically to her heart.

"Annie, Agatha is being Griswolded."

Annie stared at Laurel. Her head was beginning to throb. Coffee. God, how she needed a cup of coffee. Of all the mornings for Max to go for an early morning walk. Coffee . . . where was the coffeemaker . . . ?

"Coffee," she moaned, heading blearily for the kitchenette. As Annie yanked open cupboards, Laurel skipped to her side, eyes downcast.

"Truly a dreadful occurrence and a heartrending story. Even now, more than one hundred and fifty years later, it brings tears to my eyes." A tear dutifully rolled down her lovely cheek.

Annie ignored the tear and her mother-in-law and grabbed the canister of French coffee. Brought from home, of course. She ignored the container of Kona. This morning she needed a sharp, heady, dark, *strong* brew.

". . . almost seems beyond belief that there could be such wicked misrepresentation of a poet's life. It is truly a scandal that generations of American schoolchildren should be taught that dear Edgar was a drug addict and a drunk, a wastrel and a degenerate! All because of Rufus Wilmot Griswold. That dreadful man."

Annie lifted the pitcher of fresh orange juice out of the refrigerator. "Juice?"

"Thank you, darling. I'd love some."

Annie filled two glasses, slumped into one of the kitchenette chairs, and downed half a glass at one gulp.

Laurel joined her. She dropped the folded sheets of paper on the table and picked up her juice. She sipped dreamily. "My heartfelt desire is that the world should know the truth about dear Edgar."

"Opium," Annie muttered, "all those horrid visions—"

"My dear, that's *Griswold*."

Annie blinked. "I thought," she said distinctly, "we were talking about Edgar Allan Poe." She almost demanded to know *why* they were talking about Edgar Allan Poe and his opium proclivities at—it took character but she steeled herself and looked at the wall clock. God!—at six-fifteen in the morning.

"My dear, it's just like Bledsoe with Agatha." Laurel hitched her chair closer to Annie's. "You see, when it started out, they were friends—"

"Bledsoe and *Agatha*?" Annie demanded. If the coffee would just perk . . .

"Edgar and Rufus," Laurel explained patiently. "They met in Philadelphia in 1841 when Rufus was twenty-six and Edgar was thirty-two." She clapped her hands together. "Poe at the peak of his genius! Not knowing he had only eight years left to live. Poor dear boy." A lowering of her eyes and an instant of reverential silence. "Anyway, in 1841 Griswold was putting together an anthology. Young Poe gave him several poems and recommended some other poets. Griswold took Poe's poems, but he ignored Poe's suggestions. And he didn't pay Poe a cent for his poems! When the anthology came out, Poe reviewed it—favorably—but he did say that some of the poets included were 'too mediocre to entitle them to particular notice.' Annie, can you believe it? Griswold never forgave Poe for that single line of negative comment!"

Having overheard authors discussing reviewers, Annie could believe it.

"It's such a shame that Griswold could not have patterned himself after our dear Agatha. Although, of course, he couldn't, since he was alive first. But you know what I mean . . ."

Annie had no desire at all to know what her mother-in-law meant.

"When you think of that really intemperate essay by Edmund Wilson—and how many people today recognize *his* name—but dear Dame Agatha never, to my knowledge, made any comment at all about the nasty piece. However, her sterling example came much too late to help Edgar. Although Griswold was so 'literary,' perhaps he wouldn't even have read her. In any event"—Annie's head definitely ached—"worse was to come. In 1843 an unsigned review sharply criticized Griswold's anthology. Griswold was convinced Poe wrote the review, though no one's ever known for certain."

"So Griswold didn't like Poe. So he said so. So what?" Annie asked, but her tone was more amiable because the coffee was ready. She poured each of them a cup and never in her memory had there been a scent to compare with the heady, heavenly aroma of the French roast brew.

"Oh, my dear. It is even worse than our present instance because dear Edgar *trusted* Griswold. Before they became enemies, Poe even asked Griswold to serve as his literary executor, and Griswold accepted." Laurel's spectacularly lovely blue eyes flashed. "Griswold began his character assassination of Poe two days after the poor man died in 1849. He wrote an account of Poe's life and career for the *New York Tribune* that began this way, 'Edgar Allan Poe is dead. He died in Baltimore the day before yesterday. This announcement will startle many, but few will be grieved by it.' " A soulful sigh. "Annie, it was a vicious diatribe against the greatest poet America ever produced. Griswold wrote that Poe 'had no moral susceptibility . . . and little or nothing of the true point of honor.' "

Annie swallowed a wonderful warming jolt of coffee and began to pay attention. It slowly dawned on her that Laurel was drawing a parallel between the past and the present. She looked sharply at her mother-in-law. "Are you saying all this stuff that's hung on Poe all these years—drink, drugs, less than honorable relations with his mother-in-law—that none of it's true?"

"None of it. Oh, it's accurate that the poor boy didn't handle liquor well. He had an extremely low tolerance for it. But according to many of his friends, he rarely drank. And certainly not when he was working. As for the rest, it is a fraud upon his memory."

Laurel's quiet words hung between them.

"He was a dear boy, and he tried so hard," Laurel said softly. "Such a sad life. His mother deserted by his father when Edgar was but a year old. His mother, a wonderful young actress, dying of tuberculosis, when he was not quite three. A wealthy, childless Richmond, Virginia couple, John and Frances Allan, adopted Edgar. Oh, there are so many interesting stories about his youth. He was a handsome, athletic teenager, good at running, swimming, boxing. But he and his foster father were never close. A merchant, John Allan couldn't understand a young man so interested in poetry. But Annie, the way Griswold twisted the facts . . ."

Laurel ticked the charges off on her fingers. "In his biography of Poe, Griswold claimed he had been expelled from the University of Virginia because of drinking. Not true. Griswold said Poe deserted from the army and was expelled from West Point. Not true. He insinuated Poe was an opium addict. Not true. He wrote—and this was utterly without foundation—that Poe 'had criminal relations with his mother-in-law.' No one had ever suggested any such thing, until Griswold said that it was commonly understood and believed.

"Oh, Griswold was a man without character. He destroyed letters of Poe's which would have contradicted his calumnies. He added sentences in letters to put Poe in a bad light." Laurel's eyes widened. "But worst of all, his biography was considered the *authorized* biography of Poe. For many years it was included as a preface in all editions of Poe's work. So when Poe's friends—and he had many—claimed Griswold's attack was untrue, they were ignored. Griswold achieved his revenge. Even today many teachers believe all those dreadful accusations. Oh, Griswold was a scoundrel."

"That's really too bad." Annie commiserated. It was certainly a shame. But it was a long time ago and she suspected Poe would care more that his work was still revered, especially by the European literati, and care less that his personal reputation was stained by Griswold's machinations. Evil, after all, would come as no surprise to Edgar Allan Poe.

"Poe's friends came to his succor too late. But Christie's admirers shall speak now!" Laurel snatched up the folded sheets of paper and thrust one at Annie.

Annie's slowly mounting sense of well-being, a product of the excellent coffee and a conscious decision to go with the flow (i.e., indulge Laurel), evaporated faster than Lady Frankie Derwent driving her large green Bentley down country lanes in *The Boomerang Clue.*

Annie stared at the yellow flyer.

---

behind the
FALSE FACE

DISCOVER THE TRUTH ABOUT

AGATHA CHRISTIE

Subscribe now ($24) to *Mean Streets* and be among the first to read *behind the FALSE FACE* by Neil C. Bledsoe, the dramatic and revealing tell-it-all, no-holds-barred biography of the so-called First Lady of Crime. To be serialized in *Mean Streets,* beginning in the December edition.

Find out Christie's relationship with the well-known novelist Eden Phillpotts. Christie's first love affair. The truth behind her disappearance: who was driving the car, the ultimate plan, how it came undone. How well *did* she know Sir Leonard Woolley before that first trip to the Middle East? The real reason why she used Katharine Woolley as the victim in *Murder in Mesopotamia.* Who really came up with the plot idea behind *The Murder of Roger Ackroyd?*

LOVE · BETRAYAL · FURY · HEARTBREAK ·
SERENDIPITY · A SECOND SPRING

All of this and more in

behind the
FALSE FACE
by Neil C. Bledsoe

Annie was on her feet, brandishing the sheet and heading for the door when it swung in.

Max reached out and caught her. "Annie?" He looked beyond her at Laurel, who was smiling encouragingly at her daughter-in-law.

"So nice to see young people with so much spirit. I, for one, have not lost hope in the younger generation. There is indeed passion in—"

Annie was struggling to get to the door. "I'll false-face him. Wait until I get my hands on him. I'm going to obliterate that man."

Understandably startled, his hands full with an enraged Annie, Max left the hall door open.

"My dears, forgive me for intruding at such an early hour." The light, sweet voice spilled from the doorway. Lady Gwendolyn, in a baggy gray tweed suit and sturdy oxfords, looked like an academic out for an early morning stroll, except that her vivid blue eyes crackled with determination. She flung a crumpled yellow sheet to the floor with finality. "This is absolutely reprehensible. We cannot—we will not—permit such vile muck to be circulated. We must act immediately."

Annie stood beside the pool and seethed.

It wasn't quite ten o'clock on Tuesday morning, and the Palmetto Court resembled the ground floor of the R. H. Haymaker Department Store when silk stockings went on sale in *File for Record* by Phoebe Atwood Taylor writing as Alice Tilton. The only difference was one of tone. Rather than battling, as did the war-deprived women, these were good-natured, orderly line-standers, bathed in the warm September sunlight and fortified by the conference-provided hearty English buffet breakfast of eggs, bacon, kippers, cold grouse, and York ham. Those who had indulged in the English breakfast were relaxed to the point of somnolence. Obviously, many of the morning panels were going to be ignored in favor of Bledsoe's appearance. He was throwing a monkey wrench into the flurry of investigating underway at Confidential Commissions, too. Not even Laurel would agree to forsake the hotel this morning until Bledsoe made his appearance. Lady Gwendolyn understood, and they all agreed that inquiries would resume as soon as possible at Confidential Commissions. Annie pointed out further that she needed everyone's attendance that afternoon at the Agatha Christie Treasure Hunt. Lady Gwendolyn suggested that Annie could handle the hunt alone. "Have you ever," Annie inquired, her tone strained, "participated in a mystery convention contest?" That won over Lady Gwendolyn immediately. "My dear, there was a Mystery Weekend in Wales, and before it ended, there were three kidnappings, one case of amnesia, and two elopements. Such excitement. By all means, we must stand ready to assist you in your hour of travail."

The lines wound through the Palmetto Court to Neil Bledsoe's table. The table was untenanted at the moment, but Annie could see stacks of the yellow flyers, an ample supply of pens, and a pile of subscription blanks.

So now they knew Bledsoe's real reason for attending The Christie Caper. It wasn't to torment his enemies or to sabotage the conference. If such were the by-products of his scheme, no doubt it would be added pleasure. But these weren't his primary interests. As soon as possible, Max would dig deep into Bledsoe's financial situation, but Annie was sure she already knew the truth: Bledsoe was in trouble over a gambling debt or *Mean Streets* was in a hole. Bledsoe desperately needed money—and lots of it—and was willing to stoop to any level to increase the number of subscribers. Everything in magazine publishing hinged on the number of subscribers: advertising rates, ad linage, lender confidence.

If all of these people subscribed . . .

She glared at the people in the lines. Dammit, what kind of loyalty were they showing to Christie? And what could she do about it? And where the hell was Lady Gwendolyn, after all her fine talk about taking action? Not that she'd come up with any concrete plan before they parted. Annie scanned the court again. Not a trace of the English author. Annie didn't doubt the author's determination to foil Bledsoe. But where was she?

Well, somebody had to do something!

Annie marched to the deep end of the pool and climbed swiftly up the ladder to the ten-meter diving platform. She walked out onto the board. Now the lines snaked past the tables and around the shallow end of the pool, almost to the boardwalk.

Annie pulled a crumpled yellow flyer from the pocket of her white cotton slacks. She took a deep breath and shouted:

"DON'T GRISWOLD AGATHA!"

She hadn't known that's how she would begin. The words popped unbidden into her mind. But once started—and startled faces turned up to watch—she sketched it for her audience, just as Laurel had for her. At one point (shaking her fist over the gutter-inspired tactic of inventing slander then attributing it to "common knowledge"), Annie heard a husky "brava" and looked up to see Laurel clapping energetically on her balcony. On the adjoining balcony, Max raised his hands above his head and clasped them in a victory stance. Lady Gwendolyn flashed a brilliant, approving smile.

Laurel and Max and Lady Gwendolyn were not the only balcony observers.

Neil Bledsoe, a cigar poking jauntily from the corner of his mouth, leaned casually against a blue vase, arms folded, and listened intently.

Annie held up the yellow flyer. "This is a scam!" she shouted. "Don't waste your money. I can answer these questions for you.

"What was Christie's relationship with Eden Phillpotts? It was," Annie said clearly, "simply that of a novice who shyly sought advice from the then-famous novelist, who was a neighbor of her family. Upon reading her first novel, *Snow upon the Desert,* Phillpotts took the time to write the eighteen-year-old Agatha a very thoughtful, encouraging letter. In it, he noted that Agatha had 'a gift for dialogue,' and so he was the first critic ever to recognize one of Agatha's greatest talents as a writer. In a second letter, he offered a good deal of insightful technical advice. Finally, Agatha wrote asking him what she should be doing with her life. Phillpotts warned her that 'art is second to life—' "

"All this talk about a writing mentor," Bledsoe boomed.

The faces below swung toward him.

The critic leaned forward, his massive hands on his railing. "Funny question to ask *him,* what should she be doing with her life. We all know," and his deep voice dropped suggestively, "those of us with any sophistication, that old men do enjoy young women. This is a question I pursue in *False Face.* Subscribe now to make sure you can get your December issue and find out the truth."

In a clear, ringing shout of outrage, Lady Gwendolyn announced, "Phillpotts had *gout!*"

The faces below swung toward Lady Gwendolyn.

"That's in the feet," Bledsoe replied pointedly.

A titter ran through the crowd.

Lady Gwendolyn enunciated icily, "Double entendres are the product of a second-class mind incapable of producing substance."

Annie shouted, "Bledsoe's trying to make something out of nothing."

The audience swung about and looked toward the diving board.

Annie rattled the flyer. "All of these questions, hinting that there's more than on the surface. Her first love affair? It certainly wasn't an affair as we use that word today. Agatha's first serious suitor was Bolton Fletcher, a colonel in the Seventeenth Lancers, fifteen years older than she. He deluged her with love letters, chocolates, flowers, books, and other gifts. He proposed the third time he came to call at Ashfield, but, fortunately, Agatha's mother felt this was too much too soon, and proposed a six-month ban on visits or letters. At the end of the six months, the colonel sent a telegram asking if Agatha would marry him. She declined."

Bledsoe pushed away from the balcony railing and stood to his full height and clapped enthusiastically.

Before Annie could erupt, he trumpeted, "By God, this is a good forum. But there's a better forum—*Mean Streets*. Here's what I propose, Lady Gwendolyn, Mrs. Darling." He half-bowed toward each. "My chapters in one issue, your responses in the next. I will provide readers with psychological insights into the life of this peculiarly educated, abnormally reclusive woman, and you can respond with the materials so conveniently approved by Christie's family."

Bledsoe looked down at the upturned faces and gestured toward the table with the flyers. "There's the place to sign up. Be a part of the great debate on Christie. I'll be right down, and I won't leave until every person in the hotel's had a chance to subscribe."

Annie, goaded past endurance, yelled at his back as he ducked into his suite. "Wait a minute. I won't do it. This is criminal. I won't be a party to—"

Too late she realized she was moving forward. She wavered, her arms pumping wildly, trying to regain her balance, then toppled to her right. As she plummeted down, she glimpsed Lady Gwendolyn, eyeing her with distress, but her pink lips twitched with amusement. It was almost a relief to smack into the water.

"So I blew it." Annie savagely raked the brush through her hair, then threw the brush down on the balcony table.

"It's not a total disaster, Annie," Henny soothed.

Annie sneezed. "Lady Gwendolyn obviously thinks I'm a complete incompetent."

Room service, dispatched at Lady Gwendolyn's behest, had arrived with tea cosseted in a cosy and a note suggesting Annie take a spot of rest. After all, hypothermia could be so dangerous.

"Annie, that was a thoughtful note!" Laurel exclaimed. "I know she would have dropped by to check on you, but I'm sure she's busy planning some way to thwart Bledsoe."

Laurel's confidence in Lady Gwendolyn—and obvious dismissal of efforts by Annie—rankled. Though Annie certainly had too much pride to reveal her hurt.

Henny, however, was definitely not on her ladyship's bandwagon. "Annie's made progress, Laurel. After all, at least we'll have some rebuttal against his slanders."

Nothing Henny could have said would have made her feel worse. It would only add an aura of acceptability to Bledsoe's calumnies if Annie or anyone else took them seriously enough to answer.

Annie clapped a hand to her head. "Henny, no! Don't you see what that will do? People will take it as a legitimate debate. They'll think the questions he's raising have merit. It will be just like Griswold slimily saying an unpardonable offense was common knowledge!"

"Oh." Henny had come directly to the hotel from a board meeting at the hospital. She looked superb in a green linen blazer, daffodil yellow blouse, and beige skirt. She fingered the heavy twisted-rope gold chain at her throat. "I see. But, Annie," she asked reasonably, "isn't it better to take an opportunity to refute slander? If it's ignored, some people will assume it's right merely because it's printed."

Annie, freshly dressed in a blue-on-white cotton sweater and a short polka-dot navy skirt, dropped into the wicker chair opposite Henny's and glared morosely down into the Palmetto Court. "Look at him. Swollen with ill-gotten success, like a nasty bloodsucking leech."

Laurel glanced down into the court, but she didn't look worried at all. No doubt confident that her ladyship would soon settle the matter.

Indeed, Bledsoe did look larger than life, his ruddy face flushed with excitement, his huge hands dwarfing the subscription slips as he counted them. It was almost noon and the last persons in line had reached his table, made out their checks, and received receipts. He made yet another stack in front of him and spoke to Natalie Marlow. The young author smiled.

Annie did not consider herself a critical person. She couldn't help thinking, however, that Natalie Marlow looked about as attractive as an inmate at Tehachapi. Her bilious-green khaki shorts flapped just above bony knees, and a pink tank top emphasized her equally bony shoulders. A sex symbol for a grasshopper, maybe.

Yet Bledsoe was focusing his not inconsiderable sex appeal on her as if she were the kind of voluptuous blonde so beloved of pulp-fiction writers. No white suit for Bledsoe today, but still all white. His polo shirt and polished cotton shorts set off his impressive physique.

He leaned forward, stared into Natalie's eyes, and spoke.

The writer's angular face glowed with happiness, she nodded several times, pushed back her chair and hurried off into the hotel.

Bledsoe bent back to his counting.

Annie didn't want to know how many subscriptions he'd sold. *Beaucoup*, obviously. Did each stack hold a hundred? Dammit, it wasn't accomplishing anything to sit here and watch the sorry bastard in his triumph. Besides, it was almost time to meet Max at the registration table and get the Christie Treasure Hunt under way.

Suddenly, Henny drew her breath in sharply. "Oh my God!" she cried.

Laurel gasped and pointed toward the roof.

Annie looked up and watched in frozen horror.

A blue vase along the roof wall teetered for a long, heart-stopping instant, and then it began to fall, slowly, almost lazily.

Directly below, Neil Bledsoe was just pushing back his chair.

A woman screamed.

AGATHA CHRISTIE
TITLE CLUE

Dolly Bantry's worried sick;
She recruits Miss Marple quick.

15

he huge vase, a blur of sapphire and red, exploded on impact. Bledsoe's table crumpled beneath the crushing weight. Fragments of pottery and clumps of dirt and geraniums rose in a shower of debris.

"Oh my God," Henny said again, but this time in awe, not horror.

"Why, look at him climb!" Laurel exclaimed.

Alerted by the scream of a waitress, Bledsoe had looked up just in time to fling himself backward to safety, and now, his face blood-red with anger and exertion, he was swarming up the carved pillars that supported the balconies, from the ground floor to the roof. He made that climb look easy, his huge hands seeking fingerholds among the protruding curls and knobs of the hyacinth-decorated pillars, his sneaker-clad feet finding one perilous foothold after another.

The man, Annie realized, was one hell of an athlete. Bledsoe reached the roof edge and flung himself over it. He was so big that even in a menacing crouch, he was still clearly visible from below. His head swung back and forth as he searched the roof. Finally, his chest heaving from exertion, he slowly stood erect. With an angry headshake, he turned and glared down at the Palmetto Court and his mesmerized audience.

Thwarted fury roughened his deep voice. "Somebody call the god-dam cops—and don't touch a goddam thing down there."

Yellow crime scene tape fluttered both on the roof and around the impact area in the Palmetto Court. A hastily drawn sign on cardboard directed guests seeking service to the picnic area adjacent to the board-walk where the hotel was providing a buffet luncheon free of charge.

As Annie skirted the cardboard sign, she was glad to see that Frank Saulter had his back to her. She didn't have time to talk to Frank right now. He had plenty of witnesses, of course. She wasn't necessary to this particular investigation, but she didn't kid herself. Frank would want to talk to her. But later was better. The Agatha Christie Treasure Hunt was scheduled to begin in fifteen minutes. She'd seen no reason to cancel. After all, the crashing vase had caused some damage, but no one was hurt. Annie took a tighter grip on the cardboard box with the Clue Sheets and the Title Slips as she hurried into the lobby. She'd taken no chances with these, leaving them in the storeroom of Death on Demand until now. (Agatha had frostily ignored her visit. Fairweather friends deserved no better. Besides, Agatha wasn't fond of Max's secretary, Barb, who was provisioning the water and food bowls this week. Barb, Agatha was prone to growl, talked too much and had the effrontery to pick up cats without permission.) Annie had known better than to leave the Clue Sheets and Title Slips at the conference registration desk at the hotel. She was experienced at mystery events, and, much as she hated to ad-mit it, some people would do anything to win, including attempting to rip off the clues in advance. It had come as no surprise to hear from Ingrid that the boxes behind the registration desk had been moved about, obviously as the result of a midnight search. But she wasn't born yesterday.

"Mrs. Darling!" The manager bounded across the lobby to block her way. Thirty-fivish and already balding, Ed Merritt looked as aggrieved at the misfortune striking his hotel as Jenny Cain's father when any kind of crass reality intruded into his carefully manicured, socially vetted world. Merritt's voice cracked with outrage. "This willful destruction of property must cease. Immediately."

As if, Annie thought furiously, any of this were *her* fault. She glared at Merritt. "Vandalism is not included in the program."

The pudgy manager glared back. "I've already had three checkouts this morning. We'll probably get sued by some nut who claims the vases were improperly secured and the crash has caused him to develop a phobia about sitting beneath balconies. Listen, that vase *couldn't* have fallen by itself. But the police won't even let me out on the roof to look at it."

Annie tried tact. "Don't worry. Nobody thinks it was an accident.

Everyone can relax. That vase was aimed at Neil Bledsoe, no one else. So—"

Merritt blanched. "Oh, Jesus, attempted murder?" he wailed.

It occurred to Annie, belatedly, that her efforts at reassurance had backfired.

"What's going on here?" the manager demanded frantically. "Is this some kind of crazy Christie *cult*? Is there a real murder planned? My God, lady, you can't really *kill* people!"

"Not to worry," she snapped. "The police will handle everything. Now, I've got to take the Clue Sheets to the registration table."

As his eyes bulged, she added, over her shoulder, "Clues to the treasure hunt. Not murder."

She had expected the treasure hunt to be popular. She had not expected the lobby and the hallway to the registration area to be swamped with contestants. Not all of whom were remembering their manners.

A tall, virago-faced redhead almost dislocated Annie's shoulder with her determined grip. "Rank unfairness, that's what this is!" She gestured venomously at the mob.

"Huh?" Annie tried to squirm free.

"The people at the front of the line have an incredible advantage," the woman hissed.

"If life were fair," Annie rejoined, lurching away, "no mysteries would ever have been written."

Two plump matrons executed as neat a sequestering as Annie'd ever seen outside the pages of a Mafia book, one fore and one aft.

"Such a lovely conference, Mrs. Darling." Peppermint breath and a mammoth bosom overwhelmed Annie. "I know you will agree that working together is surely the American way."

"Goldie and I always work together," Aft confided chummily over Annie's shoulder. Whatever charm that entailed was canceled by unrelenting pressure on Annie's back.

"The more the merrier," Annie replied heartily. "After all, Agatha's father was an American." That puzzled them enough that she managed a sideways lunge and broke free.

She was almost to the table and she'd spotted Max, head high, searching for her, when a natty old boy in knickers reached out, grabbed her hand, and shook it. "Tremendous excitement generated. Deservedly, of course. But, one can't help but be concerned. Disputations will undoubtedly arise. Who are the marshals?"

This was a new one. She took in his neatly trimmed Vandyke, horn-rimmed glasses, and terrifyingly intelligent eyes. An academic, of course. "The members of the Broward's Rock Agatha Christie Centennial Society," she replied smoothly, inventing it on the spot. She pointed at Henny, who was also battling her way through the crowd. "There's the president, the lady in the green linen blazer. Direct any questions to her."

The natty old fellow nodded happily. "Sound organizational structure, that's obvious."

When Annie reached Max, she looked at him anxiously.

He gave a reassuring nod, and she sighed with relief. That meant Max had mounted the posters, each containing hints to a particular Christie title. Each poster served as a Hunt Station and was manned by a volunteer from Henny's book club.

There were twenty-five posters scattered at various points on the ground floor of the hotel.

So that was done. All that remained now was for Max to deliver to each station the Title Slips for that book (actually, twenty-four books and one short story; that was to keep everybody loose) and for Annie to release the Clue Sheets. But, first, it was time to explain the rules. She looked at the surging, intense crowd and realized that she and the box she clutched to her bosom were the cynosure of all eyes. She smiled brightly at Max and handed the box to him, announcing loudly, "The programs for the banquet Saturday night."

Although Max was never one to worry, he glanced up at the clock above Meeting Room A. The treasure hunt would begin in ten minutes. "But I thought—"

Without moving her upper body and with her bright smile still in place, Annie kicked him fiercely in the left shin. Before she turned to face the restless crowd, she spoke without moving her lips. "Floor. Hand me Clue Sheets. Deliver Title Slips." It sounded like a cross between a Hungarian with lockjaw and a teenager just home from the orthodontist. She accompanied the request with a brief downward nod, then whirled to face the restless treasure hunters.

"Ladies and gentlemen! Ladies and gentlemen, your attention please!" From the corner of her eye, she saw Max drop into a crouch.

AGATHA CHRISTIE
TREASURE HUNT POSTERS

POSTER 1

A cupboard in the corner of a cottage dining rom. It contains sports equipment and relics of the sporting life: two pairs of skis, ten or twelve hippopotamus tusks, fishing tackle, a stuffed elephant's foot, golf clubs, a tennis racket, and a tiger skin.

POSTER 2

The small, mustachioed man on the hotel terrace holds a woman's fawn felt hat in his hands, showing it to his companion. A look of impatience underlies one of concern on the little man's face. One finger is stuck through a small hole in the hat's brim.

POSTER 3

Scissors. Cut-out letters. A young woman standing at an upper window watching, watching. A wasp's nest and a jar of cyanide.

POSTER 4

The old butler peers nearsightedly through the windows at the drive. A looking glass. Wax flowers on a malachite table.

POSTER 5

The smoldering remains of an air crash. Luggage in a hotel lobby. A much battered tennis racket.

POSTER 6

In the candlelight, the body clothed in a black cloak and a black mask looks absurdly melodramatic, but the young man is very dead.

POSTER 7

The black-haired young woman with eager green eyes stares at a ship model behind the plate-glass window of the steamship company. In her hand, she holds a roll of unexposed film.

POSTER 8

A bucket filled with water and bobbing apples.

POSTER 9

An elderly gentleman stands in the hotel lobby, staring in dismay at the Out-of-Order sign on the lift.

POSTER 10

Her elfin face twisted with jealous rage, the angry young woman yanks a pistol from her lap and shoots the athletic, blond man.

POSTER 11

Light from the fireplace flickers on the faces of the bridge players, intent upon their game, and on the Mephistophelian countenance of the man watching from his chair next to the fire.

POSTER 12

Clutching an oilskin packet, the young woman hurries toward the lifeboats as the *Lusitania* begins to sink.

POSTER 13

The hotel counter is not quite seedy, but certainly not posh. On a notice board, envelopes are pinned for hotel guests. One envelope is addressed to Miss Carnaby.

POSTER 14

The scene aboard the airliner is quite peaceful. Two passengers appear to sleep: a heavy-set middle-aged woman and a small man wrapped heavily in mufflers.

POSTER 15

The beautiful young woman has an air of quiet dignity and great despair as she stands before the judge.

POSTER 16

Uncertain of the proper demeanor when faced with tragedy, the fresh-faced young man in golf clothes kneels on the cliffside path beside the dying man.

POSTER 17

The old woman is definitely the center of the family group in the hotel lounge. The young people seem indistinct and bloodless in comparison to her monumental bulk and grotesque ugliness.

POSTER 18

The clear-eyed old lady sips a cup of tea and studies the occupants of the old-fashioned, luxurious hotel lounge. Muffins and seed cakes are on the plate before her.

POSTER 19

The elderly man in the white duck suit and panama hat reclines comfortably on the deck chair, watching the sunbathers with interest.

POSTER 20

The young woman's body, dressed in a cheap white satin evening dress, looks completely out of place on the old bearskin hearth rug.

POSTER 21

The melange of objects seems to have no rhyme or reason: a cut-up rucksack, several electric light bulbs, a pair of flannel trousers, one woman's evening shoe, a diamond ring, a bottle of green ink . . .

POSTER 22

The murder scene looks just like a stage setting: the lovely swimming pool, the dark blue water, and the blood from the dying man.

POSTER 23

A speeding car. An old woman staring up at it in horror. A cat with a bandaged ear.

POSTER 24

The old man next to the thornbush looks as though he'd seen a ghost as he stuffs a photograph back in his wallet.

POSTER 25

The dark, pretty girl hurries up the steep path on the limestone cliffs to a rock chamber near the tomb.

With the registration table as his cover, he put the box safely on the floor, opened it, and placed in Annie's left hand, which was also screened by the table, the Clue Sheets.

Annie smiled heartily at the treasure hunters. "Welcome to one of our conference highlights, the Agatha Christie Treasure Hunt. We do have a few rules—"

"Mrs. Darling, pardon me for interrupting. I would appreciate an opportunity to speak with the members of your conference for a few minutes." The knees of Frank Saulter's khaki trousers were smeared with dirt. Despite the air-conditioning which kept the hotel temperature in the low seventies, sweat trickled down his leathery cheeks, and the armpits of his khaki shirt were circled. He gave her a brisk nod and turned to face the crowd.

"I'm Frank Saulter, chief of police for Broward's Rock. I would like to have a few minutes of your time."

Several hundred eyes settled on him.

Max began to edge toward the nearest exit. Annie carefully gave no indication she'd noticed. But she needn't have worried. The advent of a genuine police officer held her conference-goers in thrall.

"Police officers sometimes find it helpful to take the public into their confidence. This," Saulter said grimly, "is one of those times. I need the assistance of every person here to prevent a murder."

Gasps. Rustles. A questioning murmur. Some cynical smiles.

Saulter saw those. "No, this isn't part of Mrs. Darling's entertainment for you. I only wish it were." He paused until it was absolutely quiet. Annie was impressed. This wasn't an easy crowd to quell. "Twice," the chief emphasized, "since this conference opened, murder has been attempted." Quickly, he sketched the shooting at Death on Demand on Saturday night. "Today someone pushed a four-foot vase from the roof above the Palmetto Court. The vase narrowly missed hitting Mr. Neil Bledsoe, who is also attending this conference. Now," Saulter planted his hands on the table, leaned forward, and intently eyed his listeners, "anyone who has at any time ever had personal or professional dealings with Mr. Bledsoe is requested to come to the Card Room, which is directly off the main lobby near the coffee shop. Furthermore, if any one of you has any information about the shooting or the vase incident, please come to the Card Room."

A babble of voices broke out.

Saulter overrode them. "Should it become apparent that anyone here knows Mr. Bledsoe and does *not* come to the Card Room, I will consider that a very serious lack of cooperation with law enforcement authorities and will issue a warrant for that person's arrest on suspicion of murder. Furthermore, I want to make it clear that Mr. Bledsoe is cooperating wholeheartedly with the authorities and has checked the registration list for this conference and indicated the names familiar to him in any way."

So the vase got macho man's attention. It was about time Bledsoe cooperated. And this call for anyone knowing Bledsoe to come forward was a brilliant stroke on the chief's part. Annie hoped Saulter soon discovered the culprit. The person who pushed that vase could not have known with absolute certainty that an innocent victim wouldn't walk into its path.

"Finally," Saulter exhorted, "I want to enlist all of you—and you people can think or you wouldn't read mysteries—I want to enlist all of you as unofficial safety officers. Keep your eyes open. If you see anything odd, suspicious, or unusual, report it to me. Especially keep your eyes open when Mr. Bledsoe is present." He gave a short, sharp nod. "Thank you very much."

He faced Annie, and he was still looking stern and official. "All right, Annie, get this thing started. I'll talk to you later."

"Inspector." Despite the outburst of excited chatter at Saulter's conclusion, Lady Gwendolyn's musical voice was clearly heard. "A curious parallel exists here. I believe it is important to consider the effects of Christie's *modus operandi*—"

Saulter, normally the most courteous of listeners, broke in impatiently. "Lady Gwendolyn, it would be a privilege to discuss Mrs. Christie with you at any other time. Right now I'm involved in an investigation." He managed a tight smile and swung on his heel.

Lady Gwendolyn's plump cheeks puffed and her vivid blue eyes blazed. If she had been a cat, she would have hissed. As it was, she turned toward Annie, her pleasant face uncommonly determined.

Annie held up a hand placatingly. "Just a minute, Lady Gwendolyn. I'd better start the hunt before this crowd explodes.

"Ladies and gentlemen!" Annie shouted. When relative silence reigned, Annie said smoothly, "The organizers of this conference regret very much the unpleasant episodes which have occurred, but we feel confident that Chief Saulter and Broward's Rock can count on all of you to do your duty. Now, for you Christie fans, here are the ground rules for the treasure hunt. I know everyone will observe these rules cheerfully. Some of you have already spotted Hunt Stations. I know you will understand"—a toothy smile which was about as sincere as Lord Caterham's geniality when dealing with George Lomax in *The Secret of Chimneys*—"why our dedicated volunteers are forbidden to exchange even a single word with treasure hunters." Annie leaned forward. "Not. One. Single. Word. O—kay?" Another toothy smile to soften the imperative voice. "Furthermore, anyone attempting to deface, remove, or relocate a poster will automatically be disqualified. As will anyone attempting under any pretext to abscond with the Title Slips." A brisk nod to emphasize the seriousness of these regulations. "Now, here's how the treasure hunt works. The objective is to match up the clues and the posters. Each of you will receive a Clue Sheet." She brandished the bright pink sheets. "There are twenty-five clues. Scattered about on the lower level of the hotel are twenty-five posters. Each is manned by a volunteer. You must find the poster which matches the clue. Upon whispering the correct title to the hunt station attendant, you will receive a slip bearing the name of that Christie title. The first person—or persons, teams are fine—to return to the registration desk with all twenty-five Christie title slips will receive a five-pound box of Godiva chocolates."

Appreciative *ah*'s came from the preponderantly female audience. Some facts of gender are beyond dispute. A passion for chocolate and hormone levels correlate uncannily.

Annie reached beneath the table and brought up the gold-foil-wrapped box of chocolates. "Are there any questions?" she called out over cries of delight.

There were, of course, and some would have taxed the ingenuity of Jacques Futrelle's brainy Professor Van Dusen. Annie avoided complications by stubbornly reiterating the ground rules and refusing to entertain even the slightest modification of the program. She knew only too well what could happen if she did.

"Now that the procedure is clearly understood, I'm going to pass out the Clue Sheets. Good luck and Godspeed."

Annie really was rather proud of the Clue Sheets.

The treasure seekers split faster than John J. Malone could order cold beer for breakfast in *The Lucky Stiff*. One moment Annie was the focus of attention; the next she and Ingrid were alone in a suddenly frowsy hallway, littered with discarded Styrofoam cups, occasional cigarette stubs (this was South Carolina, and, honey, no-smoking bans are a communist plot), and candy wrappers (if God didn't want women to eat chocolate, She'd never have arranged for Columbus to get that loan).

Ingrid grinned. "I'm glad I'm not a hunt attendant. Do you want to bet on some creative ploys to get at the Title Slips?"

"That's one tough group—a couple of junior high school teachers, an IRS agent, a priest, a probation officer, a computer security expert. They've heard it all, Ingrid. They won't be conned." Annie spoke with a good deal more assurance than she felt. She'd tried to warn the hunt attendants—be suspicious of telegrams demanding immediate attendance at a loved one's bedside, don't let anyone get close enough to grab the Title Slips, ignore sirens, dismiss as absurd any rumor that a man-eating anaconda has escaped from a circus train. Her brow crinkled.

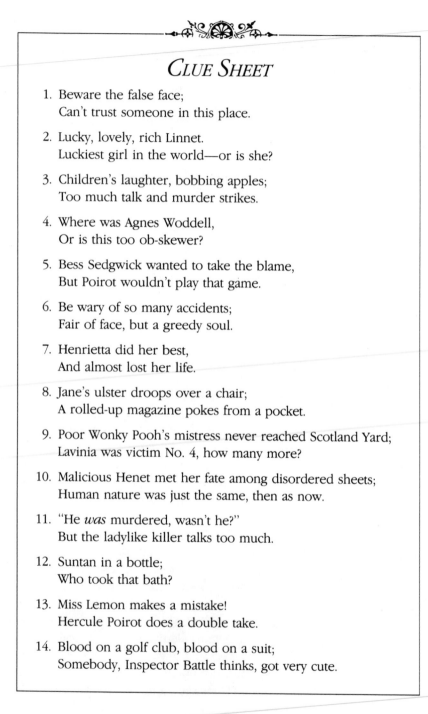

Clue Sheet

1. Beware the false face;
   Can't trust someone in this place.

2. Lucky, lovely, rich Linnet.
   Luckiest girl in the world—or is she?

3. Children's laughter, bobbing apples;
   Too much talk and murder strikes.

4. Where was Agnes Woddell,
   Or is this too ob-skewer?

5. Bess Sedgwick wanted to take the blame,
   But Poirot wouldn't play that game.

6. Be wary of so many accidents;
   Fair of face, but a greedy soul.

7. Henrietta did her best,
   And almost lost her life.

8. Jane's ulster droops over a chair;
   A rolled-up magazine pokes from a pocket.

9. Poor Wonky Pooh's mistress never reached Scotland Yard;
   Lavinia was victim No. 4, how many more?

10. Malicious Henet met her fate among disordered sheets;
    Human nature was just the same, then as now.

11. "He *was* murdered, wasn't he?"
    But the ladylike killer talks too much.

12. Suntan in a bottle;
    Who took that bath?

13. Miss Lemon makes a mistake!
    Hercule Poirot does a double take.

14. Blood on a golf club, blood on a suit;
    Somebody, Inspector Battle thinks, got very cute.

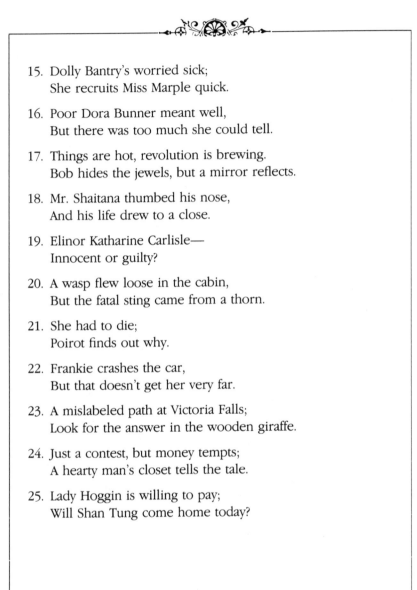

15. Dolly Bantry's worried sick;
    She recruits Miss Marple quick.

16. Poor Dora Bunner meant well,
    But there was too much she could tell.

17. Things are hot, revolution is brewing.
    Bob hides the jewels, but a mirror reflects.

18. Mr. Shaitana thumbed his nose,
    And his life drew to a close.

19. Elinor Katharine Carlisle—
    Innocent or guilty?

20. A wasp flew loose in the cabin,
    But the fatal sting came from a thorn.

21. She had to die;
    Poirot finds out why.

22. Frankie crashes the car,
    But that doesn't get her very far.

23. A mislabeled path at Victoria Falls;
    Look for the answer in the wooden giraffe.

24. Just a contest, but money tempts;
    A hearty man's closet tells the tale.

25. Lady Hoggin is willing to pay;
    Will Shan Tung come home today?

Had she remembered to warn against fainting fits and simulated heart attacks?

"Maybe," Ingrid said doubtfully. "I'd say it's about as likely as either of the Kellermans writing a jolly mystery. Anyway, it's nice to have some breathing space."

"Yes, indeed." Startled, they turned and saw Lady Gwendolyn, almost obscured behind a palm. She stepped forward. "Certainly, you must agree that I *attempted* to merge the investigative efforts. I was, as you can attest, rebuffed. But never, never, never defeated. After all, we can do much on our own, can't we, my dears?"

Annie lurked behind a huge potted palm, observing the rather glum group gathered outside the door to the Card Room. One of them wanted to be a murderer. That was apparent now. The shots at Death on Demand might have been intended to frighten; the vase crashing into the Palmetto Court was clearly intended to kill. Annie had crisp instructions from Lady Gwendolyn: Observe, report.

Nathan Hillman sat stolidly in a red wing chair, ostensibly immersed in a *Fortune* magazine. She could just glimpse his wiry hair and part of his horn-rims. She would have been more impressed if the magazine hadn't been upside down.

Derek Davis, in contrast, was in constant motion, striding up and down. The young publicist's freckled face was puffy. Too much alcohol, too little sleep? What had happened to him last night after his abortive attack on Bledsoe? And wouldn't that be grist for Saulter's mill.

Fleur Calloway, as always, was a book publicist's dream, her finely modeled face hauntingly lovely, her flowing, emerald shirtdress a perfect foil for her tawny hair. She rested casually against the cane chairback, her hands loose in her lap. Her head was slightly bent, her gaze focused on her hands. She looked up briefly when Derek Davis bumped a coffee table. Her eyes were deep and melancholy pools of pain.

Emma Clyde glowered. She had the air of an irate and dangerous Chow looking for trouble. She stood beside Fleur's chair, as if daring anyone to approach. Annie didn't envy Saulter his session with Emma.

Margo Wright sat beside a red-and-gold chinese dragon, and Annie found them both a study in inscrutability. The agent's face was dead white, her brows dark slashes, her mouth a carmine line. An unreadable face. She could as easily have been composing a sonnet, planning an ax murder, or contemplating her karma. So the change was striking when her lips suddenly curved in a smile, her dark eyes softened, and her large hand gestured invitingly. "Victoria, come sit with me," and Margo patted the love seat beside her.

Victoria Shaw took the proffered seat as though it were refuge. She looked especially small and wrenlike next to the imposing agent. And frightened. Her breath came in quick, uneven gasps. "Margo, will I have to tell the police about . . . about Bryan?"

The agent's look was a mixture of pity and sorrow. And something darker, an underlying edge of cold, hard rage. Before she could answer, the door to the Card Room opened.

Every face turned.

Neil Bledsoe filled the doorway. Just behind him, one hand clutching his arm, stood the awkward young author.

As always, Annie felt the inescapable magnetism of the man. And fought it.

Bledsoe's dark eyes surveyed those who had responded to Saulter's call.

"Which one of you fuckers did it?" His tone was insinuatingly conversational. "Was it you, Nathan? You're too soft and gutless to face me. Maybe it's you."

The editor lowered the magazine, closed it, carefully placed it on the side table. "Having fun, Neil?" he asked quietly.

But Bledsoe's gaze was fastened on Fleur Calloway. Her hands came together in a tight, painful grip, but not a muscle moved in her face.

"Not you, Fleur," Bledsoe drawled. "Ice water in your veins."

She looked at him, through him. Once again, he didn't exist.

For just an instant, his fury showed, his dark eyes molten, his scarred face a deeper, redder hue.

Emma Clyde stepped in front of Fleur. "Get the hell out of the way, Neil. We didn't come here to see you." She bent to look past him. "Chief, Chief! You've got some slime obstructing the passageway."

Saulter came along then and broke it up, motioning for Bledsoe to move on, standing aside for Fleur and Emma to enter.

Bledsoe stared at the closing door.

Natalie Marlow tugged at his arm. "Come on, Neil, let's go get a drink."

Annie marveled, not for the first time, at how startling the contrast can sometimes be between an author's persona and an author's work.

Natalie Marlow's book quivered with sensitivity; the writing was somber yet as graceful and fluid and unforgettable as an Edith Piaf melody. Marlow herself had all the charm of a water beetle.

"Neil!" Kathryn Honeycutt rushed up to the critic. The more often Annie saw Bledsoe's aunt, the less she resembled Jane Marple. Oh, the height and the dowdy clothes and the fluffy white hair were there, but she had neither the dignity nor the air of insightfulness so characteristic of the indomitable Miss Marple.

Bledsoe looked down impatiently.

Kathryn's voice was pettish. "Neil, this charade has gone far enough. We must go home."

For just an instant, Bledsoe stood immobile, his dark brows lifted in surprise.

But only for an instant.

"No. Never. I've never run in my life, Kathryn. I won't run now."

Natalie's eyes glowed with admiration. "Oh, God, Neil. You make other men look like shadows."

"Neil—" Kathryn's voice was a despairing cry. "Please, you must listen to me, you must do as I say." Her mouth trembled. "I *know* something dreadful's going to happen. I feel it. It's surrounding me. Evil, Neil. I swear before God, something dreadful will happen if we stay."

Annie felt a ripple of foreboding, as distinct as a clap of thunder, as hard to define as a scarcely glimpsed figure in the fog.

"I won't run. Never."

Kathryn Honeycutt pressed her hands to her face, then turned and stumbled away.

Bledsoe scowled, lifted a hand as if to call her back, then angrily shook his head. "Come on, Natalie. Let's go get a drink. And have some fun. This is a vacation, isn't it? We're all having fun, aren't we?"

AGATHA CHRISTIE
TITLE CLUE

Poor Dora Bunner meant well,
But there was too much she could
tell.

16

Annie hesitated to leave her post behind the palm. After all, Lady Gwendolyn's charge had been explicit: Observe, report. But Annie had a distinct feeling she'd better check on the treasure hunters, especially when she heard shouts and cries of "Not fair! Not fair!" emanating from the main lobby.

Skidding to a stop beside Hunt Station 6, she found a bookseller from Boston with her back to the wall. The bookseller, when accused of attempting to deface the poster, was unrepentant. "Surely when the safety of conference attendees hangs in the balance, no one can complain if a poster received some damage when I attempted to squash that hideous centipede on it!"

That no one else had seen the centipede ("Horrible, actually. Orange feelers and a citron body!"), the bookseller attributed to poor eyesight and a widespread conspiracy to drive her out of the hunt.

Unmoved by her pleas, Annie disqualified her on the spot.

Lady Gwendolyn nodded in satisfaction at the scene of organized activity underway at Confidential Commissions.

Laurel's husky voice oozed charm. "Mr. Ranklin—oh, may I call you Grant?—yes, Grant, I am a free-lance feature writer, specializing in the mystery field. I understand you are a longtime acquaintance of Neil Bledsoe?"

At the next telephone, Max wrote rapidly on his legal pad. "Then who do you think might know the whole truth? One of the editors at Pomeroy Press?"

Lady Gwendolyn was pleased to see Henny deep in conversation, too. Henny was the least tractable of her researchers, quite miffed at leaving the hotel before the treasure hunt ended. Of course, when Lady Gwendolyn pointed out that Henny, as a conference organizer, couldn't be *approved* as part of the competition . . . But now Henny was well into the spirit of inquiry. For an instant, Lady Gwendolyn was a bit puzzled. Surely that wasn't a Brit accent Henny was affecting. . . .

The treasure hunters ran the gamut. Many gamuts. From the reasonable to the absurd, the jolly to the morose, the intelligent to the obtuse, the perceptive to the paranoid.

At Station 4 Annie was forced to disqualify the Matheson sisters (sixty-five-year-old twins with matching Sherlock capes are no damn joke) when they tried a variation on the shell game in an effort to obtain the Title Slips.

There was a mass disqualification at Station 9. It was hard to believe a group of librarians from Baltimore would connive in such a base fashion (informing the hunt attendant that a Department of Energy inspector had declared this portion of the hotel a contaminated area and immediate evacuation was underway).

As for the melee at Station 18, the less said the better.

But finally, shortly after five o'clock, a triumphant claimant emerged, one Millicent Arrowby Truelove.

As the crowd—and the narrowed eyes, jutting jaws, and dark frowns reminded Annie anew that Americans are not the best of losers—gathered at the registration table, word having spread with the rapidity of Mike Hammer surveying a buxom blonde that an announcement was imminent, Annie studied the name carefully.

Truelove.

Oh, sure, she almost said.

Truelove was the name of the child's cart in *Postern of Fate,* the last novel Christie wrote, and was from the author's memories of playthings at Ashfield, her beloved childhood home.

"Millicent Arrowby . . ." Annie hesitated, looking at the incipient winner, whose fulsome smile rivaled a horse's death grimace. "Truelove?"

Willowy Ms. Truelove simpered.

Annie had never actually seen anyone simper. But no other word could better describe Truelove's modestly downcast eyes, inordinately self-satisfied smirk, humbly tilted head, and arms and hands intertwined like ivy run amok. The entire effect was enhanced by her period clothing, a full-skirted brown poplin dress with a lace-edged bodice and an enormous mauve hat with one portion of the brim pinned to the crown.

"I understand, Ms. Truelove, that you are the very first person to turn in a complete set of Title Slips to the desk."

Truelove writhed demurely.

Annie wondered if it was too late to lace the candy with paprika. But it wasn't necessary that she *like* the winner. Clearing her throat, Annie read the Title Slips with the correct posters and clues in order.

"*Murder at Hazelmoor,* Poster 1, Clue 24.

"*Peril at End House,* Poster 2, Clue 6.

"*The Moving Finger,* Poster 3, Clue 4.

"*Funerals Are Fatal,* Poster 4, Clue 11.

"*Cat Among the Pigeons,* Poster 5, Clue 17.

"*A Murder Is Announced,* Poster 6, Clue 16.

"*The Man in the Brown Suit,* Poster 7, Clue 23.

"*Hallowe'en Party,* Poster 8, Clue 3.

"*Towards Zero,* Poster 9, Clue 14.

"*Death on the Nile,* Poster 10, Clue 2.

"*Cards on the Table,* Poster 11, Clue 18.

"*The Secret Adversary,* Poster 12, Clue 8.

"*The Nemean Lion,* Poster 13, Clue 25.

"*Death in the Air,* Poster 14, Clue 20.

"*Sad Cypress,* Poster 15, Clue 19.

"*The Boomerang Clue,* Poster 16, Clue 22.

"*Appointment with Death,* Poster 17, Clue 21.

"*At Bertram's Hotel,* Poster 18, Clue 5.

"*Evil Under the Sun,* Poster 19, Clue 12.

"*The Body in the Library,* Poster 20, Clue 15.

"*Hickory Dickory Death,* Poster 21, Clue 13.

"*Murder After Hours,* Poster 22, Clue 7.

"*Easy To Kill,* Poster 23, Clue 9.

"*A Caribbean Mystery,* Poster 24, Clue 1.
"*Death Comes as the End,* Poster 25, Clue 10."

Annie reached out to shake hands. "Congratulations, Ms. Truelove."
Truelove untwined sufficiently to lay limp fingers delicately on Annie's palm.

Her smile a trifle strained, Annie picked up the box of chocolates. All hell broke loose.

"Disqualification! Disqualification!" The virago-faced redhead screeched like the Simplon–Orient Express rounding a Turkish mountainside. "*Book* titles. *Book* titles!"

Truelove shed her amiability faster than Miss Marple knitted in *The Tuesday Club Murders.* Snatching the box of candy from Annie, she clutched it to her bosom and snarled a vulgarity at the redhead. Not a term in common use by ladies in period costumes.

It was at that point that a bellhop edged near with a message for Annie. Grabbing it, she stuffed it in her pocket and turned back to the fracas, which had escalated into body contact that would have shamed a hockey goalie.

When Annie, with Ingrid's help, separated the two women, the box of candy was split open, the redhead was nursing a black eye, and Truelove's display of gutter language surprised even Ingrid, who read the hardest of boiled (Valin, Izzi, Ellroy, Thompson).

The redhead wasn't a quitter. "You said book titles. I distinctly heard you say book titles. 'The Nemean Lion' is *not* a book title. *I* turned in the book title, *The Labours of Hercules.*"

"Title, smitle," Truelove snapped. "The clue and poster represent the story 'The Nemean Lion.' I figured it out first. I turned it in first. The candy is *mine.*"

"The *book* title is *The Labours of Hercules,*" the redhead replied stubbornly.

The cry was taken up, people separating into for and against, pro Truelove or pro Redhead. Shouts reverberated as opinions clashed.

"A pottery store," Annie muttered. "Why don't I run a pottery store?"
The redhead lunged again for the candy.
"Mine!" squealed Truelove.
"Mine!" proclaimed the usurper.
Or perhaps a shoe store, Annie pondered.

The claimant lowered her head and butted Truelove in the chest. Truelove screeched, "Murder! Help!"

"Point of order," Annie bellowed.

The two women turned to look at her.

That had been so successful, Annie wished she knew more parliamentary terms, but her repertoire was exhausted.

Her forefinger extended, Annie stalked to the redhead. "No one," she intoned, "who commits forgery can be eligible to win."

"Forgery? I? Forgery? Are you blackening my good name?"

Annie almost told her, à la Miss Marple, that she was a dead ringer for the biggest cheat in Annie's high school, Cinda Mae Coldspot, but bypassed that pleasure for the blowaway.

"You turned in a slip with the title *The Labours of Hercules*?"

"I certainly did and . . ." The redhead realized her peril, and changed course. "You can't ignore the fact that you said book titles, and 'The Nemean Lion' isn't—"

Annie faced the crowd. "Forgery in the first degree. There is not, never has been, and never shall be an official Christie Treasure Hunt Title Slip by that name. The *official* slip, available only at Hunt Station Number Thirteen, reads 'The Nemean Lion.'" Whirling around, Annie yanked up Truelove's arm and waggled it in the air. "The winner, the champion, the world-class treasure hunter, Miss Millicent Arrowby Truelove." A pause. There were, of course, some catcalls and an ominous rumble of dissent. "Tea and crumpets," she yelled, on a desperate impulse, "in the lobby. Courtesy of Death on Demand."

A battle station call on Alistair MacLean's *H.M.S. Ulysses* couldn't have cleared the decks any faster. Once again, Annie and Ingrid held dominion over a deserted land.

Avoiding Ingrid's pitying gaze, Annie busily righted a chair that had been knocked over in the excitement, then began scooping up the Clue Sheets littering the floor. Finally, she couldn't stand it any longer. "Okay, so it will take a month's gross to pay for what that ravening herd is going to consume. What the hell else could I have done?"

Annie ordered a chocolate soda by the swimming pool and dropped wearily into a deck chair. What a day, from Bledsoe's triumphant subscription sale to the treasure hunt. Ever afterward in her mind, the afternoon would be remembered simply and eloquently as the Hunt.

The lengths to which people would go to win! As for Bledsoe, what was she going to do? It was unthinkable that he should succeed in his plan to fabricate ugliness about Christie. But what in the world was she going to do about it?

As she sipped the luscious concoction, a tiny wriggle of energy returned. She sat up straighter and felt a sharp edge of paper in her skirt pocket.

It was the message the bellboy had handed her before the treasure hunt erupted. The signature was indecipherable, looking somewhat like a beetle wearing a crown, but scanning the spidery, ornate handwriting, much like that of Emily Arundell in *Poirot Loses a Client,* Annie had no doubt as to the author of the missive.

The message was quite direct: REPORT TO YOUR SUITE UPON RECEIPT.

If Annie hadn't been so weakened by the treasure hunt fray, she might have ignored it. But she needed help. Maybe Lady Gwendolyn would have some ideas on how to combat Bledsoe. Though it did seem to Annie, as she punched the elevator button, that perhaps Lady Gwendolyn had presumed a bit on Anglo-American relations in setting up shop in her and Max's suite.

"There you are!" Lady Gwendolyn announced cheerfully. "We can't start without *you,* my dear."

Annie's resentment fled in the face of such good humor and obvious good intentions (not to mention such consummate tact).

Max popped up, smiling.

Dear heart, Annie thought fondly.

Laurel waved an abstracted hello, then bent again to the notebook in her lap.

Henny merely flicked her a grumpy look.

Lady Gwendolyn nodded encouragingly toward the couch. Annie sprawled on it gratefully. Her head was pounding. She was too tired to perk up even when Max joined her.

Lady Gwendolyn rustled her sheaf of papers. "I won't call our meeting to order until everyone has gathered. But this is a good opportunity to organize our thoughts. Annie, if you will, dear, please recap the Wednesday schedule."

Although Annie'd never had any trouble keeping up with Pam North in her thought processes, Lady Gwendolyn sometimes stumped her.

"Wednesday schedule?" She tried not to sound plaintive. "Whose schedule? What schedule?"

"Tomorrow's conference schedule." Lady Gwendolyn's sapphire ring flashed as she poured steaming tea that looked gunmetal gray as it curled out of the spout.

That Annie knew. "There are six panels on Wednesday and a Christie film festival. *The Passing of Mr. Quinn*—1928, *Alibi* and *Black Coffee*—both 1931, *Lord Edgware Dies*—1934, and *Love from a Stranger*—1937."

"Nineteen thirty-seven." Lady Gwendolyn's eyes softened. "Ah yes, that was a very good year. I played at Wimbledon and met quite a handsome chap. Nigel—" A tiny sigh. Then, briskly, "The schedule sounds smashing. Moreover, it frees you for deployment."

Annie stiffened as much as her tired spine would permit. There was something in the sound of "deployment" that she did not like.

A sharp knock rattled the door.

Lady Gwendolyn nodded at Max.

Max opened the door (generous of her to permit Max that privilege) and Frank Saulter looked in.

"Inspector!" the high, clear voice proclaimed.

"Chief," he replied wearily.

The brilliant blue stone flashed through the air as Lady Gwendolyn waved dismissively. "Inspector . . . chief—a rose by any name. You are, indubitably, in charge. I prefer to be open and aboveboard with those in authority. I wish to stress that we in no way intend to obstruct, hinder, or interfere with the due processes of the law. Indeed, our aim is to support, reinforce, and supplement your efforts. But it is always important to coordinate." An *encouraging* smile. "We have much to discuss."

Saulter glanced briefly at Annie, and she could read his thought. He was damn tired, it'd been a long day, and was this woman one of those nutty authors?

The canny writer's quick blue eyes didn't miss a trick. She chuckled. "I quite understand your hesitation, Chief. You are by no means interested in the cogitations of barmy old ladies. Nor am I. I promise no nonsense. And, as we join forces, perhaps you might join us for a spot of supper? Steak and kidney pie." Her pudgy hand gestured toward the buffet.

Annie's mouth began to water. She was starving!

Lady Gwendolyn observed happily, "It does look appetizing, doesn't it? Though I must confess room service was initially recalcitrant. It was necessary to have a bit of a chat with the chap in charge. But we're all mates now."

Was it the old author's self-possession that attracted Saulter? Or the enticing scent of dinner?

As they settled around the table (Lady Gwendolyn at the head), Saulter even accepted a glass of burgundy with his dinner. Thanks to Lady Gwendolyn's artful questions, he sketched the results of the day's investigations.

Laurel stopped eating and listed the chief's information:

1. There were no clear fingerprints on the remnants of the vase. Smudge marks indicated gloves.
2. No one was seen on the roof just before the vase came down.
3. A new crowbar was found on the roof. There were no fingerprints on it. It had obviously been rubbed clean.
4. The presence of the crowbar indicated that the attack had been planned in advance. The vase which had nearly crushed Bledsoe had been secured by four iron clamps. It had been prised up with the bar.
5. Four stairways gave access to the roof. All were unlocked.

Henny sighed. "The culprit had a ridiculously easy time of it."

Annie looked to see if there were any more of the meat dish. It was all gone. Pigs. Disconsolately, she took another serving of boiled potatoes. Unsalted? Maybe room service was having a subtle revenge.

Perhaps a little irritable at not receiving what she saw as her fair share of the steak and kidney pie, Annie mumbled through an interminable mouthful of bland potatoes, "Don't see how anybody could count on hitting Bledsoe with that vase. Maybe it had nothing to do with him."

"No, no, no." Henny came to life. She jumped up, riffled through her purse, pulled out a drawing, and put it on the table between them.

One crimson nail tapped the spot where the vase had stood, then traced the arc down to the table where Bledsoe sat. "I've been up there. Great view. But it's the ground layout that makes it absolutely certain Bledsoe was the intended victim. Number one—The culprit waited until Bledsoe was alone at the table. Number two—There is a fountain directly

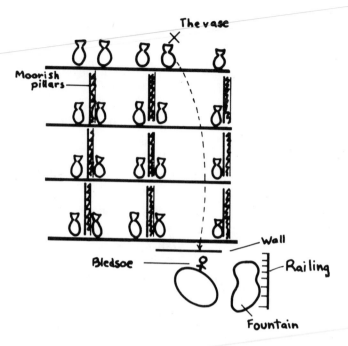

beside the table where Bledsoe was sitting. Number three—Directly-behind the table is the wall that separates the ground floor rooms from the terrace area. In other words, no one could have approached the table without the person on the roof seeing them. Number four—The surrounding tables were empty. Number five—" Henny paused and tried not to look overly smug. She didn't succeed. "I did a little detective work. There's no doubt that particular table was targeted. Someone made a practice run in the middle of last night."

Max put his fork down and stared at her. "Shoved a vase off the roof? Why didn't we hear it?"

Annie heard Laurel murmur, "Night brings with it so many distractions."

"Not a vase," Henny admitted. "A ten-pound sack of sugar. I talked to the cleaning crew." Another shuffle through her papers. "Tommy Loomis found sugar 'to hell and gone' all over the terrace this morning. Of course, he thought it was some kind of prank. He said, 'Listen, you work in a hotel for a while, *nothin'll* surprise you.' So somebody made damn sure of the trajectory a falling object would take. There's no doubt about it, Bledsoe's the intended victim."

Lady Gwendolyn, to Annie's surprise, said nothing. The author's eyes were fixed on the mural on the wall.

Saulter reached out for the diagram and studied it.

"Not an innocent bystander." Laurel admired the high gloss of her pink nails.

"Obviously not," Max agreed. "But it makes our investigation simpler. If Bledsoe's the victim, the possible perpetrators are on a short list. A very short list." He picked up the top sheet and flourished it.

A roll of thunder added dramatic emphasis.

Lady Gwendolyn looked toward the balcony in some surprise. "It was quite clear today."

"Clouds often roll in after dark. Should have a pleasant rain pretty soon." Max glanced quickly at Annie. She had no trouble reading his thought. If there was anything Max enjoyed as much as an afternoon amatory frolic, it was a rainy night frolic. She gave him a tiny wink.

Lady Gwendolyn pushed back her chair. "Believe I'd better trot to my room. I left the balcony doors open."

Henny assured her it wasn't necessary, explaining briskly, "Offshore breeze at night. Balconies face the ocean. The rain won't blow in."

Lady Gwendolyn nodded absently. "Good-oh. It's always best to consult the natives. Now, young Max, let's take a look at your list."

Derek Davis

Nathan Hillman

Victoria Shaw

Margo Wright

Emma Clyde

Annie scanned the list before handing it to Lady Gwendolyn.

"Why not Fleur Calloway?" Annie asked.

Several voices spoke at once, but Saulter's predominated. "Seems obvious the gunplay at your bookstore and the roof incident are connected. A little hard to believe in two separate attackers, and Ms. Calloway was definitely inside Death on Demand when the gunfire broke out."

Lady Gwendolyn studied the list, then looked at Saulter. "I presume you've interviewed all the suspects?" Her tone indicated her confidence this was a totally unnecessary question since Chief Saulter obviously was a first-class police official.

Saulter favored her with a weary but pleased smile.

No flies on Lady G. when it came to dealing with men.

Saulter put down his fork, casting a regretful glance at the empty steak-and-kidney pie dish, and heaved a sigh. "Sure. I'll tell you, those people have got zippers for lips. You'd think they'd taken a crash course in how to talk to the cops and say as little as possible. For Christ's sake, I've never had an investigation where I've got as little out of a bunch of suspects. Just name, rank, social security number. Oh, sure, they admit *knowing* Bledsoe. But nobody will give an inch that they had it in for him. Damn mystery people, they know all the tricks. Good guy/bad guy didn't work with them. Pretending I knew all about their last run-in with Bledsoe, that didn't work. I'm up a creek without an oar."

Lady Gwendolyn put down her wine goblet with a decisive click. "I have in mind a possible solution."

Everyone looked at her.

"First we must accept the obvious: we face a multi-faceted problem."

Annie marveled at the force of personality unleashed upon them. Such a dumpy, soft, gentle-looking elderly lady, but there was no mistaking the authority, the eagerness, and the competence with which she faced problems.

"Mr. Bledsoe has survived two murder attempts. We must forestall a third." Her tone was resolute.

Even Henny was willing to take her lead here. "Lady Gwendolyn's absolutely right. It's just like Poirot in *The ABC Murders*. Why, look at it! The attempts on Bledsoe's life—in effect, they are like the warning letters. If we go at it right, we will be able to *prevent* a murder."

Lady Gwendolyn reached over, gave Henny an approving pat on her hand. "That's the right spirit." She looked confidently at the chief. "We have begun our investigations. We are using the facilities at Confidential Commissions to amass information about the individuals attending this conference who are linked to Bledsoe. However," a meaningful pause, "our task has been both simplified and further complicated by Bledsoe's attack on Christie."

Annie leaned forward eagerly. *Now* they were getting somewhere.

"First, we must refute this scurrilous calumny. Annie can contribute here." Those lively eyes, shining with intelligence, focused on Annie. "It is quite reasonable that Annie appear exercised over Bledsoe's scurrilous attack. Right?"

Annie nodded eagerly.

"That gives her a reasonable basis upon which to approach the suspects. When she does so, however, she will accomplish a dual purpose: she can vet them as possible murderers and, at the same time, gain derogatory information about Bledsoe. The man obviously is a cur. If he attempts to publish scandalous lies about Christie, we can immediately respond with material that discredits him."

"That's brilliant," Laurel enthused.

"Might work," Henny admitted grudgingly.

"Excellent idea." Max nodded. "When we add the results of Annie's interviews to our investigations, we'll probably know at once who's trying to bump off Bledsoe."

Lady Gwendolyn lifted a plump hand. "However, it is clear to me that a grim sequence of events may be underway."

Something in her tone froze each in his place.

"I'm terribly surprised that this possibility has not yet occurred to others. As I attempted to communicate this morning to Chief Saulter, there is a disquieting parallel between the toppled vase in the Palmetto Court and the boulder crashing down at Abu Simbel in *Death on the Nile*."

"Oh, my God," Henny said softly.

In an almost breathless silence, Lady Gwendolyn's soft voice continued stalwartly, "Oh, yes. You see, the attack on Bledsoe came *after* the flyer was distributed. It could well mean that a deranged Christie devotee was taking matters into his or her own hands. We must not leap to conclusions. The gunfire and the vase may not have been the work of the same individual. There is much going on, possibly including much of which we have little knowledge. We must remember Miss Marple's maxim: *Nothing is ever quite what seems to be on the surface*."

• • •

Clouds scudded across the face of the moon. Their footsteps echoed from the wooden dock. To the south, lightning flickered, illuminating a clot of rain clouds dark against the night sky. Thunder rumbled.

"Rain pretty soon," Max observed.

Annie spared a brief thanksgiving the rain had waited until Tuesday night and hadn't ruined the marvelous fête on Sunday, but she wasn't worried about the weather.

She was worried about Lady Gwendolyn's shocking pronouncement.

"Max, you don't really think we could have a furious Christie fan trying to kill Bledsoe, do you?" She tried not to wail.

Although Max never looked for trouble, he didn't flinch from reality.

"It could be, sweetie. But, look at it this way. Isn't it a lot more likely, given the circumstances, that anyone with a rational reason to kill Bledsoe might have the wit to mask a murder behind a facade of madness?"

"Just like *The ABC Murders*. So it still makes sense for me to try and talk to everyone here who knows Bledsoe."

"Sure. Tomorrow." Max slipped his arm around her shoulders as they reached the end of the pier.

Annie relaxed against him.

Suddenly, warm lips touched her cheek. "But for now ... it's getting ready to rain. Let's go in." The urgency in his voice had nothing to do with inclement weather.

Annie was eager, too, as Max unlocked their door. He took her hand, pulled her toward the bedroom, then Annie saw the blinking red message light on the phone.

She stopped, glanced at the light, and almost ignored it.

But she was co-chairman of the conference. It could be important.

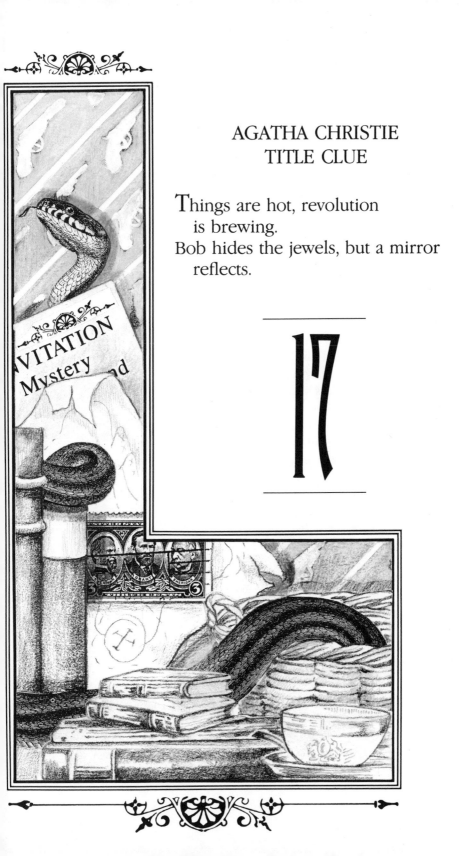

AGATHA CHRISTIE
TITLE CLUE

Things are hot, revolution
  is brewing.
Bob hides the jewels, but a mirror
  reflects.

17

nnie waited impatiently for the elevator, her thoughts churning. Probably this visit would come to nothing. There were always a few nuts—harmless but weird—at any mystery conference. Though that name—James Bentley, James Bentley—seemed familiar. But she'd better check it out.

The elevator doors slowly parted.

Annie rushed in, punched the Close Door button, and the second floor button.

The information from the hotel message center was precise, if not especially revealing: *Message received: 10:49 p.m. To Annie Laurance Darling from James Bentley. I have some information of great interest to the sponsors of The Christie Caper. Please come to room 239 as soon as possible. Desire confidentiality.*

Max had pointed out reasonably that Mr. Bentley could easily contact Annie in the daytime, that it was almost half past eleven, and why not let it go until morning?

Annie understood quite well that none of the above had anything whatsoever to do with Max's desire to ignore Bentley until morning.

She'd grinned. "Love, it won't take long. And that's the price of serving as co-sponsor, on call, day or night. I'll hurry." Max was ready to come along, but she shook her head. What Bentley might divulge to one person, he might be unwilling to tell two. Confidentiality.

The elevator doors opened in their stately fashion, and Annie dashed into the hall—and almost barreled into Lady Gwendolyn.

To say she was surprised put it mildly.

Lady Gwendolyn's suite, the grandest in the hotel, was down the hall from that of Annie and Max on the third floor. Moreover, after the end of their investigative session just before eleven, Lady Gwendolyn departed with Laurel to go down to the bar for a nightcap.

Annie was not only surprised, but suddenly she was tensely aware, just like Bridget Conway in *Easy To Kill,* that something was dreadfully, dangerously wrong.

It was clear from the old author's alert, wary stance—and from the unopened umbrella that she gripped midway down the staff, the knobby walnut handle poised to serve as a weapon. She studied Annie intently for an instant, then returned to a careful perusal of the wall. "Help me look for the blood."

The request, made quietly in Lady Gwendolyn's light, civilized voice, chilled Annie.

Blood—

Then she saw it on the wall—a reddish smear level with her waist. If you hunted, the blood was readily visible, but a casual passerby would never notice the darkish stain against the rattan-colored paint.

"What can it mean?" Annie asked, her voice thin.

"Trouble," came the crisp answer. "I'm afraid we may discover foul play. I've followed the markings from my suite." Gripping her umbrella firmly, Lady Gwendolyn moved on down the hall.

Annie followed.

Given the nature of their preoccupation, it was disconcerting and made their search all the more surrealistic when a couple came out of room 221, laughing and talking, and passed by with a cheerful "Good evening." Annie croaked, "Evening."

The smears appeared every few feet. The farther they went down the hall, the larger and wetter the splotches.

Lady Gwendolyn stopped to study each one, her face expressionless. "When I came upstairs from the bar, I found the door to my suite open— and I smelled blood. It's such an identifiable odor."

Annie suppressed a shudder.

"It was obvious, of course, that something bad was afoot. I pushed open the door and switched on the light." The bright blue eyes paused on another smear, then moved ahead. "I found my cape—I do enjoy capes, they are so comfortable for travel—crumpled just inside the door—and massively stained. I found my response interesting, psychologically. Outrage, followed by fear. It's quite a comeuppance, you know, to realize you are the target of malevolence. That, of course, at the very least. Malevolence and, no doubt, the unmistakable intention to embroil me in a sticky wicket. After all, how could I hope to explain the presence of blood on my cape? But the situation, surely a bizarre one, dictated I should quickly report to your authorities. I stepped back into the hall, intending to go downstairs and alert the desk, when I saw more smears. I began following them. So here I am."

Her light, clear voice betrayed no fear. In fact, Annie was sure she detected a vibrant note of exhilaration.

"And you, dear?" Was there just a hint of reservation in her query? But surely that was understandable.

"I got a message asking me to come to room two thirty-nine. From James Bentley. He said he had important information for the sponsors of The Christie Caper."

"Hmm. So that's where we're going." Lady Gwendolyn picked up speed, brandishing her umbrella.

Annie took a deep breath, then gripped a plump arm. "Lady Gwendolyn, maybe we'd better go down to the desk and get help."

"In due time, my dear. I never ignore a challenge. Someone wants to involve me in this malfeasance. You and I are much too late to help the victim—if there is a victim. And, at this point, I don't expect peril for us. Had there been danger, it would have awaited me in my suite. So, let's play out the hand." She sniffed. "Someone has cleverly intended me to be the scapegoat in this devious plan . . . well, we'll see about that. I may be old, but I am not—as you Yanks say—a patsy."

The door to room 239 was ajar.

Lady Gwendolyn poked the tip of the umbrella against the panel. Slowly, the door swung in.

"Oh, my God." Annie heard her own voice, high and strange.

The old author merely stood there, those brilliant blue eyes absorbing the hideous scene.

A young man's body lay facedown on the pale carpet. A wide scarlet wound curved round the back of his head.

The murder weapon was propped against his hip.

An unusual weapon, shaped like an adz. Although blood clotted along its sharp cutting edge, crimson and blue ornamental stones could be glimpsed in the handle. Made of brass, it was topped by a cocky ornamental brass bird.

"How curious," Lady Gwendolyn observed thoughtfully. "I've never seen a sugar cutter before—but I recognized it instantly."

Annie stared at the bloody weapon. Sugar cutter. Sugar cutter!

Frank Saulter loped up the hallway. The chief stopped at the open door, looked past Annie and Lady Gwendolyn. For an instant, the usual policeman's mask of imperturbability slipped. Astonishment made his face look young and vulnerable, then, once again, the mask returned and he was impassive.

"Have you touched anything?" he asked crisply.

"No, of course not." Annie had hurried downstairs to the desk to make the call, and then quickly returned, to find Lady Gwendolyn still in the doorway. But she couldn't help noticing that her famed companion made no response.

A cluster of curious onlookers was gathering in the hallway. Annie saw a bellhop exit from the elevator, take in the scene, and step quickly back into the elevator. She started to say something, but Saulter interrupted.

"All right. If you'll both return to your rooms—"

Briskly, Lady Gwendolyn succinctly outlined the condition of her room.

Saulter tensed. "You say there's blood on a cape. Your cape?"

Annie intervened. "Now, Frank, it's obvious that—"

"Nothing's obvious, Annie. All right then." He looked grimly at Annie. "If you and Lady Gwendolyn will go to your suite and wait there..." It was nicely phrased. But it was a command.

To say that there was instant antipathy would be to understate.

It was, as Max said later, a glorious effusion of hostile vibrations unequaled since critics attacked *The Murder of Roger Ackroyd* as basically unfair to readers.

Perhaps it was because Lady Gwendolyn eyed Circuit Solicitor Brice Willard Posey upon their introduction with all the enthusiasm of Hercule Poirot confronting a cold draft.

The famous author glanced inquiringly at Annie. "I say, I understood Inspector Saulter to be the man in charge. He's a sensible chap."

That tears it, Annie thought.

And it did.

Posey drew himself up to his full six feet four inches, which was an effort because he was barrel-chested, and glared down at the diminutive writer.

As always, Posey was immaculately dressed, a navy blue suit (taut against his girth) and blue shirt (best for television) and smelled strongly of cinnamon aftershave. "I, madam, am a circuit solicitor for the great state of South Carolina, and I am taking charge of this homicide investigation." His watery blue eyes bulged as he smugly surveyed the room.

It must have been extremely disappointing to his massive ego when he realized his audience consisted merely of Lady Gwendolyn, Annie, and Max, none of whom responded with the anticipated respect.

Posey's glance grew chilly. He flipped open the little notebook in his hand. His mellifluous voice became considerably less mellifluous. "You, madam, are Mrs. Gwendolyn Tompkins of Maidstone, Kent, England?"

"Lady Tompkins," she corrected icily.

"*Mrs.* Tompkins," Posey rejoined stubbornly.

The battle was joined at that instant.

"Can you explain La—*Mrs.* Tompkins, how a garment belonging to you became stained with what is apparently the blood of a murdered man?"

If a plump, Kewpie-doll face could look mulish, hers did. "No." She did not amplify.

There was a tense pause. Annie glanced at Max. But he was watching Posey.

Lady Gwendolyn tilted her head (always a danger with coronet braids) and looked up inquiringly. "Can you?"

Posey gave her an incredulous, indignant glance and took a deep breath. Only Saulter's arrival prevented an explosion. As it was, Posey's face was dangerously red when he swung around in answer to Saulter's call.

"Okay, Brice. Body's gone. Homicide team's still working. The hotel wants to know if they can clean up when we get finished."

"Oh, my dear chap, I must advise against it," Lady Gwendolyn interjected serenely. "And I would like to study the scene as soon as possible. Your chaps may have overlooked some telling detail."

"We may have overlooked—" Posey snorted. "Madam, the day I let unauthorized nonprofessionals into a crime scene is—"

"—the day you might learn something useful, *Mister* Posey. By the by, what is the victim's real name?"

If Lady Gwendolyn wanted a stunned silence, she got it. Unconcernedly, she restored two bronze hairpins to her braids.

"It's not Bentley?" Max asked, puzzled.

Annie clapped her hands to her head. Sugar cutter. James Bentley! Oh, heavens!

Saulter tensed. He looked like a G-man who's just been told Baby Face Floyd is holed up inside a barricaded warehouse.

But it was the sudden transformation of Posey that appalled Annie. The bright red flush faded. His porcine lips parted in a cunning smile. "How very interesting, Mrs. Tompkins, that you know this young man was registered under an assumed name. Surely you want to share with officers of the law the background to your acquaintance with this unfortunate young man."

A sniff of disgust. The coronet braid quivered and slid a bit as she flipped her aristocratic head in irritation. "I say, don't you see the parallel? It's quite blatant. One of Christie's best books: *Mrs. McGinty's Dead.* James Bentley lodged with Mrs. McGinty. He was convicted of bashing her head in with a sugar cutter."

"Jesus!" Posey exclaimed.

"Of course, our crime differs markedly since in this case it is the man known as Bentley who was slain with the sugar cutter. However, it should be obvious that a parallel was intended. Now"—Lady Gwendolyn gestured vigorously with her umbrella (it was perhaps unfortunate that Posey flinched)—"it's interesting here to speculate." A broad sweep of the umbrella punctuated each query.

"Is there an unhinged Christie addict on the premises?

"Was the young man murdered *because* he assumed the name of a Christie character?

"Is the assumed name irrelevant?

"What information did this young chap intend to proffer to Annie?"

And it all came together for Annie. "Bentley!" she exclaimed. "That's the name of the guy who ran up Saturday night and said he saw the gunman in the bushes near the site of the old playhouse!"

Saulter grabbed his notebook from his back pocket and riffled through the pages until he found the one he sought. "I'll be damned. He sure as hell is. *Was.*"

"Now that adds yet another fascinating element," Lady Gwendolyn mused, ignoring Posey. "It puts a new light on tonight's message for Annie. That's the place to start. What did our young victim *see* Saturday night?"

Posey teetered forward, brows drawn in a heavy frown. "Oh no, madam. The place to begin is—with *you!*" And he thrust a beefy forefinger at the fragile old lady.

Wednesday, September 12.

During her months of planning, Annie had envisioned Wednesday, the midpoint of the conference, as a rather low-key day, with plenty of panels available, but with the focus on hard-to-find films of the Christie novels. Her thought had been that some conference-goers might elect to sightsee on that day, perhaps driving to Beaufort or Charleston. It would be a shame to travel all the way to the Low Country and see nothing of two of its loveliest and oldest cities.

It had never occurred to Annie in her wildest flights of fancy that she would, in addition to her conference duties, spend the day on a four-star mission, seeking clues to a totally unexpected murder, continuing her investigation into the mysterious attacks against Bledsoe, vainly attempting to satisfy authorities that Lady Gwendolyn—despite the bloody cape—hadn't swatted a conference attendee with a sugar hammer, and gathering information, hopefully derogatory, to be used in blocking publication of a scurrilous biography of the Queen of Crime.

Wasn't it, in a way, truly a Christie twist that she should be charged with pursuing such complicated and contradictory goals?

Lady Gwendolyn reassured Annie over a hearty English breakfast.

"The more complicated it gets, my dear, the more intriguing it is. However, I fear we have a problem. That fat fool"—this turned out to be her invariable description of Posey—"is concentrating on me, so he will make no progress. But we'll solve it. It's simply a matter of putting our minds to it."

Annie wished she shared the spunky author's confidence. Actually—and Annie was only able to toy with her soufflé au kipper, though it was delicious—every time she remembered the scarlet of that wound and the viscous pool flaring round that blood-drenched head, she felt sick and sorrowful. "James Bentley" had been young and alive. Some human hand had brought that bronze implement crashing down. Why?

"Chin up, my dear," Lady Gwendolyn enjoined, her tone firm but her eyes kind. "We shall prevail." She even managed a chuckle. "It would certainly set the crime writers at home on their ears if I ended up in an American hoosegow. However, I don't intend to afford them such grand entertainment. Surely we can outwit that fat fool."

Murder! A murder in the hotel!

The news spread faster than the rumors about poor Colonel Bantry in *The Body in the Library*.

Annie could feel the covert glances, instantly averted when she looked up to meet them. She could hear the excited buzz of conversations that ceased when she came near.

So the murder was having an effect. But the reactions were exactly what might be expected from people present at the outskirts of tragedy.

A very normal response.

That was the most unnerving facet of the day, its very ordinariness. On the surface, everything and everyone was so ordinary. Several hundred very ordinary people.

Was one of them incensed enough by the attack on Christie to commit murder?

Perhaps that dark-haired woman sitting in a deck chair by the shallow end of the pool. Wasn't that a true crime book in her hands?

Or the academic with the Vandyke beard—hadn't he looked a little strange, walking with his head down and muttering rapidly to himself?

Or the redhead from the treasure hunt. Was the venomous glance directed at Annie a result of yesterday's fray? Or much more serious?

And, once the initial buzz of excitement waned, the continuing everyday sounds of the convention emphasized the stark contrast between the placid course of the conference and the dark bloodiness of murder:

"C'mon, let's hurry. I don't want to miss *Black Coffee*. You've got to see the guy who plays Poirot!"

"Can you believe she was seventy-five when she wrote *Third Girl*, and she was really into the hippie scene!"

"*A Murder Is Announced* absolutely has a fabulous beginning! What a terrific premise."

"You know . . . I've always wondered if she had a fixation on time . . . think of all those alarm clocks in *The Seven Dials Mystery* and the five clocks, all set to a different time, in the opening chapter of *The Clocks.*"

"*Crooked House* will give you cold chills!"

Everywhere Annie went, or so it seemed, she caught a glimpse of Lady Gwendolyn—surveying the breakfast crowd, loping through the lobby, poking a head into the panels, peering over the edge of the reopened roof—and always and ever those brilliant blue eyes seemed to be searching, searching.

Annie looked in on the morning's first panel, Christie and Hammett, Who Wrote about the "Real" World? and Henny pounced on her.

Out in the hall, Henny shot a wary glance in both directions, then hissed, "They've identified the victim!" Henny was vivid in a bright yellow cotton dress. Her dark eyes glowed with excitement. "John Border Stone from New Jersey."

"Who was he?" Annie asked quickly. "A writer? A fan?"

"Don't know. Max said he'd add him to his list to investigate. Anyway, thought you should know. I'll get back to you," and Henny sped off down the corridor. Inspector Slack never moved faster in *The Murder at the Vicarage.*

Annie grinned, but her smile quickly slipped away. Henny meant well, but her fascination with crime suddenly seemed callous. Annie remembered only too clearly that brutal wound which had ended John Border Stone's young life. Each time the image returned, another horrid detail burned in her mind—the class ring on a pudgy, lifeless finger. Annie shook her head and scolded herself. Good detectives kept their emotions in check; they distanced themselves from the horrors they confronted. Witness Bill Knox's Glasgow Detective Chief Inspector Colin Thane and his partner Inspector Phil Moss, and Laurie Mantell's New Zealanders, Detective Sergeant Steven Arrow and Inspector Jonas Peacock. That's why Henny was scouring the surroundings for clues.

Annie walked slowly toward the main lobby.

The unexpected corpse.

If Bledsoe had been found, battered to death. . . . But it wasn't Bledsoe. However, the murder must be linked, somehow, someway, to the attacks on Bledsoe; Annie felt confident of it. All the violence had been directed at the critic. John Border Stone had glimpsed the gunman on Saturday night. He'd been unable to give a clear description.

Had he truly been unable?

Or had he seen only too clearly—and, for reasons of his own, kept quiet? Until someone permanently quieted him.

That made all kinds of dreadful sense.

And validated Annie's quest.

Annie checked the autograph room. Yes, Emma Clyde was there, as scheduled. A long double line of fans inched forward to have their books signed. So, while the big cat was engaged—

Annie searched every likely spot in the hotel. She was ready to give up, when she decided to check the beach. She spotted her quarry at the end of the pier.

Annie walked forward swiftly on the wooden planking.

Perhaps it was the hurried cadence of her shoes that made Fleur Calloway jerk around to watch her approach. Perhaps it was that and nothing more which gave an anxious cast to that lovely face. Yet, even half frowning, the delicate tracery of lines on Fleur's face echoed laughter and sunshine and warmth. She sat on the weathered wooden bench at the end of the pier, shading her eyes from the morning sun.

"Good morning, Mrs. Calloway."

"Please, call me Fleur." A moment's hesitation, then, the author said, her voice troubled, "I understand a young man was killed last night."

"Yes."

"Do the police have any idea what happened?" Was Fleur's question just natural curiosity, or was there an undertone of fear?

"I don't know much about it. He was attending the conference. Someone killed him with a sugar cutter."

"A sugar cutter? How odd. I haven't seen one of those in years." The author smiled wryly. "Yes, Annie, I do know what one is. I grew up in Louisiana."

Annie wished she had the nonchalant demeanor so natural to private eyes. Surely Spenser would have revealed nothing at this disclosure. Obviously, her expression—shock? uneasiness? surprise?—had been too easily read.

"Fleur, I know there has been some unpleasantness between you and Neil Bledsoe."

The wry smile dissolved. Fleur Calloway suddenly looked pinched and old.

"I'm asking because I hope to get a full picture of the man and use it to combat his plan to smear Christie. I hope you'll agree to help me. I know you don't want to see her reputation destroyed. If you could just tell me what happened between you and Neil—"

Fleur pressed a hand against her lips. She wasn't looking at Annie; her eyes were focused on the shore.

Annie felt like a paparazza. And hated it. "I'm sorry. I hate prying." She did. She hated it like fury. "Obviously, this isn't pleasant—" She broke off. Not pleasant! The pain in Fleur's eyes was so deep, the anguish so apparent.

Shock widened Fleur's eyes.

Annie followed her gaze.

Natalie Marlow and Neil Bledsoe, hand in hand, strolled barefoot in the shallows. Her face alive with happiness, the author gazed up adoringly at her companion. She was almost pretty, despite her stringy hair and pale face.

Annie wished she had an afternoon, a beauty shop, a dress store, and Natalie by the scruff of the neck. The author could be attractive. She had a strong, intelligent face, a determined chin. Why did she go around looking like Megan Hunter in *The Moving Finger*? Could it be that Natalie, too, lacked confidence, felt so unloved, so unworthy that she hid her femininity in artful self-defense? Annie didn't quite think in terms of "Oh, pshaw!" But her immediate response was, "The author of *Down These Steps*? No way."

Nevertheless, the writer who had brilliantly plumbed the depths of tortured love and hate in her first novel was clearly besotted with a man almost any woman, from six to sixty, would spot as bad news, despite his undeniable sexual magnetism.

"That's the way Jaime looked at him." Fleur's voice was oddly flat and thin, unlike her usual rich contralto.

Bledsoe pulled Natalie into his arms, her face against his chest, her body tight to his.

He lifted his head and stared out at the end of the pier where they sat. For a long, long moment, across the shimmering water, the critic's eyes taunted Fleur. A triumphant smile curved his lips, then he loosened his embrace, tucked his hand beneath Natalie's chin and lifted her face to kiss it, a long, lingering, passionate kiss.

"Oh, Jesus God." The blood drained from Fleur's face.

Annie reached out in alarm to touch her arm.

Ignoring Annie, Fleur stumbled to her feet and turned away from the shore. She reached out to hold onto the wooden railing of the pier. Her body trembled and her face was ashen.

"Fleur! Mrs. Calloway, . . . are you ill? Please, let me help."

"Have they gone?" It was a tortured cry.

Annie glanced back toward the beach. "Yes. Yes, they've gone." She stared at Fleur. Incredible as it seemed, this beautiful and accomplished woman was physically stricken by the sight of Bledsoe loving another woman. Had Fleur Calloway once loved Bledsoe? Annie stumbled into speech. "I'm sorry."

Fleur looked at her strangely.

"I didn't know—I had no idea you'd ever cared about him."

"Cared about him?" The author's face crumpled. Tears began to spill down her cheeks. "Oh, God, if only I had. If only I had." Her face sharpened, hardened. "I won't see it happen again. I can't bear to see it happen again."

Max once again was king of his domain. Not that Lady Gwendolyn wasn't heartily welcome at Confidential Commissions, but he was just as happy she'd stayed at the hotel today. He studied the number his secretary had found at the telephone company office in Beaufort, the telephone number of Bruno Calavecchia, next-door neighbor to Mrs. Grace Wilton Stone in Brooklyn, New York.

It was ugly indeed, just as Emma had warned.

Fleur told Annie haltingly. Some of it she didn't say, but Annie, looking at faded snapshots, understood.

"This is Jaime in Laguna. She was fifteen."

A vacation shot, obviously. Fleur appeared little different from today, slim and lovely in tennis whites. The girl standing beside her would never, no matter how she might diet or exercise or try, have her mother's grace and beauty. Jaime was big: bulky shoulders, a solid girth, thick almost shapeless legs. She wasn't ugly. In fact, her broad, open face had a wholesome prettiness and radiated good humor. Neither was she overweight, but she had the body build of a fullback, and she was very tall for a woman, a good head taller than her mother. The way Jaime stood revealed so much, head tucked to lessen her height, shoulders slumped to minimize their breadth.

"I wanted her to be proud." Anguished eyes looked out over the water. "But ours isn't a society that values strength in women. The first day at school, she came home crying. They'd made fun of her, called her the Elephant Girl."

It worsened as time passed and Jaime grew, always grew. She was not only big, she was clumsy, not good at sports.

"Her father and I were divorced." The tone was cool, but her eyes were not. "He'd been good at sports. That's all he ever cared about. Remembering how wonderful he'd been. He had no interest in Jaime. Just a girl. Just a big, awkward girl."

Fleur's fingers pulled at the neck of her sweater, as if it choked her. "But Jaime was a wonderful musician. I was so proud of her. I thought perhaps music could make the difference in her life."

A pianist. Some thought a pianist with a brilliant future.

"She was so happy at the piano."

But not away from it. And always and ever, the comparisons by the thoughtless, apparent even when unspoken, to her lithe and lovely mother.

"It ate away her confidence." Tears filled emerald-green eyes. "I kept telling Jaime that when she was all grown, that she would be lovely in her own way. That she should walk tall and be proud. And she should have been proud because she was a glorious, wonderful, grand person," her mother said fiercely. "She could always see the funny side to everything—except her size."

The author lifted a hand, wiped away tears, and shook her head. "We had so much fun together. And that last trip, I talked her into it. She had intended to go to summer school, but I persuaded her to come with me. I thought it would be a glorious experience, a three-week mystery tour of England. I was invited to be the celebrity author." Her cheekbones sharpened, her lips thinned. "A tour planned and directed by Neil." Her voice was steely. "I didn't know anything about him. But he was the same then as now. He despises the kind of books I—" a pause "—I used to write. Thinks they're stupid and feminine and silly. Not serious. Not real. But he still went after me to be the traveling author because I was a better draw than a hard-boiled author." Her mouth twisted. "I didn't know that when I accepted, of course. But it didn't take long for me to figure out what an unattractive man he was."

It started out as only an annoyance, one that she had perhaps often faced, unwanted, persistent attention from a man. "Oh, I could see his appeal. But I wasn't interested. I'd been married once to such a man. Once was enough."

Neil Bledsoe wasn't accustomed to rejection.

Wouldn't accept it.

Didn't accept it.

"I tried to handle it lightly, but, finally, I had enough. I told him he was about as appealing as one of those stupid and childish private-detective heroes. That no woman in her right mind would have anything to do with him."

There were two weeks of the tour left.

"So he left me alone. I felt so relieved. I concentrated on the seminars, on the fans. Behind my back, he was focusing all his attention on Jaime. By the time I knew what was going on, it was too late. Jaime was crazy about him. He was the first man who'd ever noticed her, except as an object of ridicule. And here was a man, not a boy, telling her she was desirable . . . and making love to her."

Annie looked away. She couldn't bear to see Fleur's face.

"So . . ."

A long and dreadful pause.

"I tried to tell her." The tears fell unchecked now. "My baby. I tried to tell her. She was so angry, so hurt, she thought I was jealous. That's what he told her."

This was a girl with no experience, caught up in the first passionate relationship in a male-starved life.

"She flew home with him. Nineteen years old. I never saw her again . . . alive."

"Harvey, I certainly appreciate your taking time to talk to me. But we don't want to focus on anything in Nathan Hillman's life that would cause him pain. That's why I want to check with someone who has known him well and for a long time. You know how these charity dos are, well-intentioned but sometimes not well thought out." Henny sounded like a lifelong member of the Junior League. "Once I was involved in a *This Is Your Life* program and no one had told the producer that the woman being honored had lost a baby in 1978 and he went on and on about what a wonderful year 1978 had been for her and, of course, she completely broke down. It was a fiasco. So, in strict confidence, if you could alert me to any danger areas in Hillman's life—"

•   •   •

"He was such a gentle man. And always ready to help out a friend. Give you the shirt off his back." Victoria Shaw's neighbor was excited to be talking to a real live New York reporter (aka Max Darling to his intimates). "Seemed happy all the time. Until those publishers stopped buying his books. That's when he stopped smiling. One day Bryan was fine, the next he looked like death. And old. Overnight, almost." The voice dipped confidentially. "It was cancer. Came on him about six months after his last book didn't sell." Her voice had dropped so low that Max could scarcely hear her. "When people get real upset, sometimes that's when they get cancer. And they say whether you ever get well depends a lot on how hard you fight."

At least a half-dozen florists' bouquets were scattered around Fleur Calloway's suite. Annie admired the lovely flowers as she waited beside the door. Obviously, Fleur was an author still beloved of her fans even though she had no new books to offer. Annie had time to study the bouquets in detail, time enough to observe every nuance of this suite's mural, a languid lagoon scene: the dark snout of an alligator barely discernible in the murky water, a white ibis with bright red bill and legs, a beautifully plumed Louisiana heron—the bird Audubon called the Lady of the Waters—a diamond-back terrapin, and a sleek brown river otter. Time enough to wonder whether the author had changed her mind. Annie would understand. The offer had surprised her. Annie was reaching for the doorknob when Fleur came out of the bedroom, a faded, tattered cloth book in one hand, a framed portrait in the other. She held out the picture. Annie took it and looked into a smiling face. Such a young, unlined, yet-to-be-marked-by-time face, wide-set cheerful brown eyes, rosy cheeks, thick chestnut hair. Dead-and-gone Jaime Calloway smiled out of the frame. "It was made the week before we left for England." Fleur's voice was brittle.

Annie knew she wrestled with long-unanswered, long-unanswerable laments, the if-onlys that always bedevil survivors. If only Fleur had turned down the trip . . . If only she had responded to Neil, absorbed his desire . . . If only she had been able to find Jaime in time . . .

"She looks very nice," Annie said lamely as she returned the picture.

But what could she say that would be better? Nothing that she offered could ease a mother's grief.

Fleur wasn't listening. The author smoothed the worn cover of the book. "I've never shared this with anyone. But I will now." She handed it to Annie, then turned away, but not before Annie saw her eyes, eyes burning with unquenched, unquenchable hatred. Her head was bent, her back rigid, her words oddly muffled. "When you finish with it, you may leave it at the desk for me."

Annie blinked back tears as she turned to go.

Just a tiny discrepancy. Derek Davis began college in 1982, received his bachelor's degree in 1987. It wasn't too unusual for students to take five years to complete an undergraduate course. Perhaps a change in majors. Perhaps a five-year program. Max checked his fact sheet. An English major. So, not a five-year program. It was a tiny blip in what looked to be an altogether unremarkable, to this point, chronology. Max marked down a question. From tiny blips, enormously interesting personal facts could emerge.

Laurel was firm. "Of course, I understand your reticence, Miss Edwards. But certain accusations were made about Ms. Wright's conduct as an agent, and it would be a shame if she missed receiving the Outstanding Agent Award of the Year on the basis of incorrect information. . . ."

Annie felt like the smile on her face was pasted there as she darted from one panel to another, making sure the panelists gathered and got underway. She moved with a brisk efficiency Anna Ashwood Collins's Abby Doyle might admire. The sooner she finished, the sooner she could get back to her search for the truth about Neil Bledsoe and her sub rosa search for a murderer.

When the last panels of the morning were successfully underway—The Orient Express and Other Journeys with Agatha; Society Laid Bare by Christie, from the 1920s to the 1960s; Dorothy L. Sayers and Lord Peter—she would feel free to steal away and read the last entries in Jaime's diary.

·　　·　　·

"Doctors Berry, Aarons, and Wallis."

Max was brisk. "Federal Aqua Shield Health and Independent Physicians' Reporting Service here. Agent Terence Hopgood from Washington, D.C." It would certainly make his life more difficult if those number-calling machines came into wide circulation. As of now, he could assert that his call was originating anywhere from Bangor, Maine, to Canberra, Australia.

"Yes, Mr. Hopgood?"

"Let me see here. Ah yes. I see from our records that Bryan Shaw was a patient of Dr. Wallis's. We're checking on the length of some of these hospital stays. A question of whether they were in excess of Medicare guidelines." Max picked up his coffee cup, realized it was empty, and poked his secretary's buzzer.

"Please hold for just a moment, Mr. Hopgood. I'll connect you with our hospital administrator, Mrs. Beverly."

With the wind fresh on her face, Annie walked until the hotel was long out of sight. She settled on a huge log, driftwood from far away, and pulled Jaime's diary from her purse.

The late morning sun bathed her in warmth but couldn't dispel the cold horror evoked by the brief entries:

SEPTEMBER 19—*If I weren't so stupid, Neil wouldn't hurt me. I know I'm not good enough for him. I'm so big . . .*

SEPTEMBER 24—*I tried to call Mother, but he found me at the phone. I hurt all over. I want to talk to Mother.*

OCTOBER 3—*I can't go to the doctor. He'll want to know how I got these bruises. I think my wrist is broken.*

OCTOBER 9—*Oh, God, I must be pregnant. I must be.*

OCTOBER 10—*He laughed when I asked if he would marry me.*

OCTOBER 17—*The moonlight is shining on the water. It doesn't look so far down. I wonder what it will feel like when I jump? They say water is like concrete when it is so far away. Then it will all be over.*

That was the last entry. There was an envelope tucked in the back of the diary. The direction on it was written in an almost indecipherable scrawl: *Please give this to my mother.*

Annie smoothed the crumpled envelope. She didn't open it.

She couldn't.

Dear God, if ever there was motive for murder . . .

AGATHA CHRISTIE
TITLE CLUE

Mr. Shaitana thumbed his nose,
And his life drew to a close.

18

nnie, maybe you shouldn't try to talk to those people." Henny's expressive face was worried. "I'll do it."

Annie was startled. "Why ever not?"

Henny looked around, but they stood in a deserted area between Meeting Rooms A and B. Behind the closed doors came the hum of low conversation punctuated by occasional bursts of laughter. The eleven o'clock panels were still in session.

The greatest mystery reader on the island avoided her eyes. "The conference. You've got so much to see to. Don't worry. I'll talk to—"

"Henny."

Her favorite customer reluctantly met her inquiring gaze. "It's not safe. Listen," she pulled Annie behind a pillar and said grimly, "you run a wonderful bookstore. You are intelligent, organized, determined—and just about as subtle as Brother Verber in *Malice in Maggody*."

Annie's eyebrows rose.

"Don't take it personally," Henny said quickly. "I wasn't worried when you agreed to talk to the suspects, to see if you could pick up on unsavory aspects of Bledsoe's past. But that was before the murder. We were just talking a broken window and a smashed vase. This murder changes everything. Nobody with any brains is going to believe that you're *really* trying to save Christie's reputation. They're going to think—especially the murderer—that you're investigating, not just trying to derail Bledsoe's attack on Agatha. And you may blunder along—"

"Blunder?" Annie interjected icily.

"—and scare the murderer and—"

"Henny, slow down. All I'm doing is talking to people—in broad daylight, in safe places. What worries me more is our own wonderful Circuit Solicitor Brice Willard Posey, God's gift to the bar of South Carolina. Did you know he—"

"I know, I know. As if that little old lady could possibly bash anyone's head in. Although it amazes me someone hasn't bashed *her* sometime in the last seventy years!" Henny tossed her head defiantly.

"Why, Henny!" Annie admonished.

The bookstore's best customer did look embarrassed, her cheeks reddening. "Well, I swear, Annie, she just thinks she knows everything!"

Annie thought of Agatha, her gorgeous bookstore feline, and Agatha's fury and heartbreak when a new kitten, Dorothy L., temporarily invaded Death on Demand. Oh, dear. Henny was jealous of Lady Gwendolyn's pre-eminence as a mystery authority.

"But Posey's having second thoughts, painful as that is for him," Henny said dryly. "I mean, he *really* doesn't like Lady Gwendolyn, but he can't ignore Stone's tennis shoes."

Annie stared at her blankly.

The murdered man's tennis shoes?

Annie's obvious lack of comprehension vaulted Henny back into a good humor.

"A competent investigator always has contacts within the police infrastructure," she said complacently.

"C'mon, Henny," Annie said briefly. "Give."

Henny's voice dropped conspiratorially, though, of course, every syllable was perfectly enunciated. "In his room was a pair of tennis shoes, and the bottoms of those tennis shoes have bits of gravel and tar from the roof of the Palmetto House." Henny's dark eyes glittered with intelligence. She savored the moment of revelation. "What does that tell us?"

Annie did not go to the head of the class.

Henny was as confident as Lord Peter Wimsey building a case. "The vase that missed Bledsoe—just barely missed him—was pushed from the roof parapet. What are the odds, Annie, that Stone was on the roof at the wrong time for the person who knocked that vase down? And what are the odds Stone tried a spot of blackmail?"

It was a familiar story to any mystery reader. The murder necessitated by an injudicious use of too much knowledge. *A Caribbean Mystery* popped immediately into Annie's mind. What would the person who shoved the vase do if Stone threatened to go to the police? *"I saw you . . ."*

When threatened, a killer reacted swiftly, with deadly finality.

Annie saw her own unease mirrored in Henny's eyes.

Henny said slowly, with no histrionics, "Annie, I've got a feeling something bad's going to happen." She glared defiantly at Annie. Henny was a pragmatist, not given to indulging in feelings.

And neither was Annie. But darned if she didn't have a tiny prickle down her spine. However, she had no intention of admitting it. After all, she wasn't a beleaguered Caroline Llewellyn heroine. Of course, that accomplished author's protagonists would always be well advised to think twice before plunging into peril.

The prospect of lurking danger seemed absurd in the hotel's elegantly appointed dining room. The curtains were dramatically draped from shiny gilt poles, replicas of those from the Greek Revival period. The deeply beveled mauve gray walls afforded a wonderful setting for the salmon pink hangings.

The dining room was a fit setting, too, for Margo Wright's dramatic beauty. Beneath the glitter of the crystal chandelier, her smooth black hair had the sheen of a midnight sea and her pale face the richness of creamy porcelain.

Annie chattered, and realized she was chattering, about some recent mysteries she'd enjoyed (*Adjusted to Death* by Jaqueline Girdner, *The Chartreuse Clue* by William Love, and *Good Night, Mr. Holmes* by Carole Nelson Douglas) and knew she must come to the point. Their lunch had been excellent, Dover sole, potatoes with truffles and goose liver, and, for dessert, a delectable gooseberry fool, with whipped cream so rich it glistened. As they drank coffee and talked desultorily, Annie still couldn't decide how to begin.

Margo added sugar to her coffee. "It's always interesting to know which books the booksellers are enjoying."

"If only we had time to read more," Annie said, echoing the plaint of all bookstore owners.

The agent stirred her coffee, took a sip, then eyed Annie keenly. "I've enjoyed our lunch, Mrs. Darling. Now, what can I do for you?" Her tone was amused.

So much for subtlety. But, if Margo Wright wanted up-front, up-front she would get. "I intend to do everything I can to prevent Neil Bledsoe from publishing that scurrilous biography of Agatha Christie."

Margo's flamingo bright lips curved into a curious half-smile. "I doubt very much, Mrs. Darling, that Agatha Christie needs any assistance from you."

The waiter refilled their coffee cups.

Margo Wright lifted hers in a mock salute. "Good hunting."

"Hunting?" Annie repeated.

"For the murderer. That's your real objective, isn't it?" She sipped at her coffee but her eyes never left Annie's face.

One up to Henny.

Annie picked her words carefully. "Actually, I'm not hunting for that person. If I discover his—or her—identity, I'll tell the police. I'm interested solely in Neil Bledsoe. Look," she desperately hoped she didn't sound like a snake oil salesman, "I want to know all the dirt about Neil Bledsoe so I can discredit him. Maybe Christie doesn't need any help, but I can't stand by and see her slandered without trying to stop it. Besides, Bledsoe's a louse, and it's time somebody thwarted him."

"I would like that." For the first time, passion resonated in Margo's deep voice. "I would like that very much." Carmine-tipped fingers drummed on the table. "A louse? Oh, yes, my dear, Neil is certainly a louse. But he's managed, one way or another, to become a very powerful force in the mystery field. Longevity, maybe. He knocked from house to house in the early seventies, editing pulp novels. If you can call that editing. Then he came out with that slimy mercenary rag." Her eyes narrowed. "I always wondered where he got the money to start it. Magazines don't come cheap, you know. Not even ten years ago. Anyway, he started it and hit it big. Lots of weirdos out there in the hinterland get their jollies reading about plastic explosives, survival tactics, and how to blow up a train. The next thing I knew, he was out on the street. Maybe he just fronted for somebody all that time. Anyway, he was back to working for a living, like the rest of us."

"And he got a job at the agency where you worked," Annie encouraged.

"How did you know that?" Margo inquired quietly.

Annie widened her eyes ingenuously. "Somebody in the bar."

"Talking about me?" Her voice was even quieter.

"No. About Neil."

"Who was it?"

Since the chatty creature didn't exist, it wasn't difficult for Annie to profess ignorance. A shrug. "No one I know. I just overheard—"

"Eavesdropping?" The skeptical eyes bored into Annie's.

"I'm trying to find out everything I can about Neil Bledsoe." Annie's tone was crisp.

A long, thoughtful pause, then a tiny nod. "I went to work for Bob Masters as a receptionist right out of school. I read manuscripts at night, for a reader's fee. Bob thought I had promise. I worked my heart out. Four years later, he made me a full partner. That was in 1978." The rapid monotone came to a full halt.

"Yes?" Annie encouraged.

"The most exciting days of my life. Beginnings are always wonderful." A tiny smile touched her face, just for an instant, then her somber look returned. "I was too young to know that every beginning leads to an end. But for a while, it was glorious. I discovered Pamela Gerrard. Pamela . . ." Margo fingered the spoon beside her coffee cup. "In 1981, Bob hired Neil. I was against it from the first, but Bob thought he would be a draw for hard-boiled writers." She absently stirred her coffee. "I suppose Neil knew I didn't want him hired. Then I overheard him on the phone, making a date with a young writer who'd sent in her manuscript to see if we'd take her on. Bob was out of town. I really unloaded on Neil." A mirthless laugh. "I thought I'd taken care of it. Funny thing is, it never occurred to me to run to Bob. About a month later, I came to work and there was a note from Bob on my desk. I was fired. For unprofessional activities. Bob left town the same day. He refused to accept calls from me. I cleared out my desk, but I kept writing and calling. Finally, I got it out of a secretary there. About a half-dozen unsolicited manuscripts had arrived. Each author received a letter, signed with my name, asking for a fifty-dollar reading fee. Some agencies do require reading fees, but not the best ones. Certainly not Bob's. And the letter asked that the checks be made out to me. One of the authors called up to complain and got Bob. So he fired me."

"Bledsoe sent out the letters in your name? How could that work? If the authors sent checks, wouldn't they have come to you?"

"I tracked down the receptionist. She said Neil told her to intercept letters from certain people, that I had asked him to take care of those inquiries. It never occurred to her to question it, and by the time I wised up enough to hunt for some answers, he'd already gotten her sacked." A bright flush suffused the agent's cheeks. "He forged my name, cashed the checks. I got through to Bob finally. He didn't believe me." The hurt was naked in her voice, all these years later. "Bob said nobody would go to that kind of effort just to cause someone else trouble. Bob was killed in a car wreck six months later. He died thinking the young girl he'd treated like a daughter had cheated him and made his agency look cheap." She cleared her throat. "So, yes, I know what a bastard Neil is." She looked at Annie levelly. "Neil will lie, cheat, steal, connive, whatever it takes, to help himself."

Annie was quite willing to believe all evil of Neil Bledsoe. "But at least you got away from him when you left the agency."

"Did I? Can anyone ever be free of someone like Neil, as long as he's alive to ruin lives?" Her eyes glittered. "I suppose I've just made myself suspect number one." She looked, just for an instant, quite capable of murder, her face hard, her hands clenched.

Annie thought of the tattered brown diary and briefly shook her head.

The agent relaxed slightly. "But God knows I'm not the only one here who loathes Neil. Poor Victoria Shaw and Nathan Hillman and Derek Davis."

Annie waited.

The words seemed dredged from deep inside Margo. "Neil might as well have picked up a gun and shot Bryan Shaw and Pamela Gerrard."

"Why?"

"Sometimes," Margo said, almost dreamily, "I think Neil takes a sheer, perverse delight in evil, that it attracts him the way a woman does, that there's the same element of lust and exploitation. He despises goodness; he sees it as weak, effeminate. There could be no worse judgment in his mind." Margo lifted her coffee cup, then put it down without taking a sip. "Bryan Shaw was my best client. Almost the only client I had when I started out on my own. I had never expected to be on my own. I'd made no provision for it. When Bob kicked me out, I was so stunned, I didn't even try to take any of my authors with me. Bryan called, wanted to know what happened. I told him. Sometimes, in the middle of the night, I think about Bryan and wonder if he would still be alive and published if he hadn't come with me. You see, Neil left the agency for Hillman House. He replaced Bryan's editor just as I turned in Bryan's latest book. Oh, God, why did Neil do it?"

"Turn down Shaw's last manuscript?"

Margo lifted her cup, drank the cold coffee. "Turning it down wasn't the problem. If he'd just turned it down, I could have sold it somewhere else. No, it's worse than that. I sent it around. Word gets out quickly when a name author is available. This is a small community, you know. We know each other. People talk. And I had no reason to be secretive about where I'd sent Bryan's book. Actually, I talked it up, wanted everyone to know a superb talent was available. So Neil listened, then he had lunch with those editors, and in the course of gossip let it be known, oh so confidentially, that Bryan's sales were down. Way down. That pre-orders for his last book had been embarrassing. So, nobody wanted Bryan. There's nothing worse than the author who leaves a big house, and the word gets out his sales have taken a nosedive. By the time I found out what was going on, it was too late. Bryan was dead." She leaned back in her chair, her face somber.

"And Pamela Gerrard?"

Margo's eyes darkened. "Pamela was ripe for the plucking. Just divorced. You know what happens when women divorce. They lose twenty-five pounds. Their makeup is perfect. And they are as brittle as those gorgeous, dying leaves in the fall. Showy and colorful and break-able. She'd just made the bestseller list for the first time. But all that does is terrify an author. Most of them, at least. This was just before Bob kicked me out. Pamela was in town and I was going to take her to lunch. Neil dropped by my office and somehow without my knowing quite how it happened, he came to lunch with us. It was like leading a lamb to slaughter. He came on to Pam like nothing I've ever seen. I might as well have been invisible. Neil is," she said reluctantly, "a sexy bastard."

Annie made no effort to deny it. Bad and mean and dangerous, but sensually, lustfully, magnificently male.

"They flew to Reno three weeks later and got married. Poor Pam. So beautiful, so gifted. So foolish."

Money was often difficult to trace. But this particular documentation had all the earmarks of fakery. Max finally wormed behind the facade of Allied Everest Company in Dallas, Texas, which had paid Neil Bledsoe more than a half million dollars for "consulting" in 1974. Obviously, this sum was the source for Bledsoe's investment in *Have Gun, Will Travel.* Interestingly enough, the short-lived company had no books that could be traced. Checks with other businesses at that address uncovered no memory that Allied Everest had ever rented there. Max traced ownership of the building to a world famous tough-guy writer whose suicide had shocked the publishing world in 1975.

A tête-à-tête with Lady Gwendolyn reminded Annie of the thrill of riding a roller coaster, the sudden, heart-stopping plunge, the racketing climb to another peak, and the wind-whistling descent. It engendered enormous excitement, although intellectual rather than physical.

"Brava," the old author said, as Annie finished her recounting of her interviews. "Quick, now. Who's most likely?"

"Margo Wright." Annie was surprised at her own answer. In answer to the unspoken question, she added, "Margo holds a grudge. And somehow"—Annie hated saying it—"I can see her tipping that vase, pushing down on the crow bar, and feeling it move . . . and enjoying it!"

"Very interesting." Lady Gwendolyn snagged a spidery handful of Spanish moss, dangling from a live oak, as they walked deeper into the wildlife preserve. On the dike to their left, a wide smudge marked an alligator crossing. A cotton rat darted beneath a clump of saw palmetto. "I've been thinking about our suspects today, and I certainly understand the basis for your conclusion." She reached out, gripped Annie's arm, and pointed toward the half-submerged log in the plant-choked pond.

A pine cone crackled beneath Annie's foot, but she, too, glimpsed the fat, muddy brown cottonmouth just before it slithered into the green-scummed water.

As the ripples faded away, Lady Gwendolyn continued, her voice faintly regretful, "But I'm sorry to say I can't help thinking Fleur Calloway is the likeliest."

Annie hated to hear that, hated it because she liked Fleur Calloway very much and hated it because she had a deep respect for this old lady.

Eyes that had seen much of life and found it both glorious and dreadful focused briskly on Annie. "But the picture is still murky. And I keep having a sense that someone is playing with us . . . and that worries me most of all."

Victoria Shaw followed Annie to one of the poolside tables. Annie chose one with an umbrella to escape the late-afternoon heat. The author's widow was aglow with happiness. As they settled in the shade, she twittered, "Mrs. Darling, I can't ever thank you enough for writing and inviting me personally." She leaned forward to confide, "I almost didn't come, you know." She paused and the happiness fled her faded blue eyes. "But you wouldn't know about—about Bryan's illness."

Annie steeled herself. "Oh, Mrs. Shaw, so many readers miss him and his books." This, at least, was true. But her next words were a ploy, no more, no less. "One fan insists there was a title scheduled for publication before he died that didn't come out." She shook her head ruefully. "Fans are so stubborn. I imagine that it was a work in progress. Certainly if such a book existed, the publishers would have brought it out."

"*The Clue at Hacienda Dolores.*" Victoria fumbled at her straw purse, lifting out a leather cigarette case. She opened it, then hesitated. "Do you mind?"

Annie did, but she was willing to inflict only so much misery. She smiled and murmured, "Certainly not." But she was a little surprised. Although many women of this age group smoked, it seemed out of character for Victoria Shaw.

The older woman, her hands trembling a little, lit the cigarette, blew away a plume of smoke, then said apologetically, "I quit for so many years. Bryan and I both. But since he's gone, it doesn't really matter."

There was no intent in her words to shock or affront. It was merely a statement of fact, and it caught at Annie's heart.

It didn't really matter.

Two halves that make a whole.

Annie understood that. For a terrible instant, she imagined herself without Max. Nothing, then, would make much difference, would it?

It was a moment she would never forget.

Independence, the watchword for today's women. Independence, admired and honored, encouraged and approved.

Could anyone truly love and remain independent?

No.

As for going on alone with any joy at all, that would take grit beyond measure.

"I've thought about having it privately published," Victoria said quietly. "But Bryan wouldn't have liked that. He was a professional."

Privately published. That was the last resort of writers with unsalable manuscripts. Bryan Shaw would have been humiliated.

"You mean the book was complete and his publisher didn't publish it?" Annie simulated shock. She did it without pleasure. Sometimes Lawrence Sanders's Captain Edward X. Delaney didn't like his role, either.

Victoria's thin face turned old as Annie watched, lines of misery etched at her eyes and her lips, the light in her eyes quenched. She drew deeply on the cigarette, suppressed a cough. "It was the last book in a three-book contract. Bryan's editor left for another house. They hired a new editor. Bryan sent his book to Margo to submit. It was the ninth in his Father Corrigan series, and he was pleased with it. But a little worried. You know how authors are."

Annie recalled Emma's words: *It all has to do with vulnerability.*

Victoria didn't wait for an answer. "Authors are so unsure of themselves. They can write a wonderful book and look at you with terror in their eyes. You see, in their hearts they're always afraid this book won't be good, this book isn't right. . . . And yet, they know how well they can write. Sometimes," her eyes glowed again, "Bryan would come out of his study and he'd give me a sheet and ask me to read it and say, 'Oh, God, Torie, it's the best I've ever done. Torie, it's wonderful!' Then he'd look at me with that fear in his eyes."

She dropped the cigarette to the flagstones, used the tip of her shoe to grind it out. "He sent in his last manuscript. To Neil Bledsoe." She slumped in her chair, old, defeated. "Neil Bledsoe killed my husband."

Victoria said it quietly enough, but the hatred was there in a voice tight with anger. "Neil wrote Bryan a dreadful letter. He made fun of his book. You can make fun of anything, you know, if you want to. He made fun of it. But more than that, he berated Bryan, said the book was stupid, tedious, childish, poorly written." Anger burned in her eyes. And murder in her heart?

Hands shaking, she lit another cigarette. "Neil rejected the manuscript. I told Bryan it didn't matter, he could find another house. His agent"—a flicker of energy—"you've met Margo? She was Bryan's agent. She was furious, said it was absurd, that they'd simply take the book somewhere else."

The cigarette smoke dissipated in the bright summer air. "That was in the seventies. A bad time for mysteries. No one else bought it. Bryan got cancer." She looked at Annie steadily. "He died within six months. Because he didn't want to live any longer. You see, he was too proud to keep on writing if no one wanted his books . . . and he couldn't live without writing."

Annie's stride checked, but her eyes didn't deceive. Laurel was entering the hotel beauty salon, certainly no surprise. Annie had once accompanied Laurel on a shopping trip through the cosmetic section of Lord and Taylor's in New York. She was glad, for Max's sake, that his mother was independently wealthy, both from her own family and five lucrative marriages. Not, of course, that Laurel would be so crass as to consider wealth a prerequisite for marriage. But she had told Annie once, "My dear, love and marriage are so much more successful when everyone is *comfortably* situated. Impecunious young men can be very charming, delightful companions on a rainy fall afternoon, but not suitable for a long-term commitment. Poverty is so *tiring*. And only for the young, one always hopes." Annie had wondered to herself how any commitment from Laurel could be considered long-term, but had been wise enough not to comment aloud. So, it came as no surprise to see Laurel wafting into the expensive salon. It startled Annie considerably that she was accompanied by Natalie Marlow, who looked exceedingly scruffy in contrast to Laurel's as ever elegant appearance. Annie couldn't resist sidling closer. Laurel's husky contralto was unmistakable: "... such a pleasure to spend time with such extraordinarily talented people. I do so admire your great gifts."

Annie poked her head inside just long enough to see Laurel grip Natalie's elbow firmly and sweep her into a carrel.

Annie paused irresolutely. It was none of her business. But what had possessed Laurel to try and improve Natalie's looks? Annie, too, felt that the right styling and makeup could transform a very ugly duckling. But to what avail? To make her even more attractive to Neil Bledsoe? Annie shook her head in dismay and backed out of the salon. The author wasn't her problem.

Max skimmed the entry in *Twentieth-Century Crime and Mystery Writers:*

SPENCE, BURKE EDWARD. America. Born in Richmond, Virginia, 9 March 1943. Graduate William and Mary. Served in the United States Army during Vietnam War. Honorable discharge, second lieutenant. Advertising copywriter, New York, 1967–70. Novelist, 1970 on. Died December 4, 1975. In the span of five years became the most successful hard-boiled novelist in the United States.

Max's eyes dropped to the short list of books, a total of six. All published by Pomeroy Park Press. Max buzzed for his secretary. When Barb came on the intercom, he said briskly, "Barb, drop over to the bookstore. I need a list of senior editors at Pomeroy Park Press. Check *Literary Market Place.*"

Annie waited outside Conference Room B as the panel entitled Mysteries in the '90s—Bigger, Better, or a Bust concluded to a burst of applause. Her practiced eye checked the crowd. Not too many here, mostly booksellers and unpublished authors. She noted the empty chair on the podium and checked her program. Hmm. Derek Davis had been a no-show, but the other two panelists were there, Nathan Hillman and Jane Casey, an editor at Millington Books. She waited until the last straggling questioners drifted out and approached Hillman.

"Mr. Hillman, may I speak to you privately for a moment?"

The chunky editor eyed her unenthusiastically. "About . . . ?"

Annie gambled. Would bitterness win out over caution? "About Pamela Gerrard . . . and the ugly way Neil Bledsoe treated her."

"Why?" Distaste flickered on his face.

"I'm going to publish the truth about Bledsoe. I'm going to tell the world what kind of man he is."

They were alone in the conference room now. The last stragglers had wandered off, to the bar, to other panels, to the beach. They had the room to themselves.

Hillman shrugged. "What good will it do? It won't bring Pam back."

Annie waited.

The editor turned away from Annie and began to pace, head down. "Pam. Oh, Christ, Pam. Maybe if I tell you, tell somebody, maybe it won't hurt so goddammed much. You're supposed to break open pockets of infection, let all the nasty, foul-smelling pus seep out, but I've never talked to anybody about it. Not even Derek. Especially not Derek. He was at school. He didn't see the way his mother began to break apart. It was like watching silver tarnish. Everything bright and shiny and beautiful and then one day the darkness starts to spot and grow and pretty soon all the shine is gone." Hillman slumped into a chair on the last row, fumbled in his pocket, and pulled out a pipe. But he simply held it in his hand and stared down at the gleaming bowl. "I suppose if I were a 'real' man," his voice put corrosive brackets about it, "the kind Bledsoe talks about, I would have driven out there and grabbed Pam and thrown her in the car, taken her the hell out of there, gotten her away from Bledsoe before it was too late."

Annie looked away from the soul-deep agony in his eyes.

"But I didn't realize how bad it was. Then, too, I thought that, hell, she'd made the choice, picked him, not me. You see," his voice dropped almost to a whisper, and Annie knew it was because he couldn't trust it not to break, "we were just getting to the point where we both knew that maybe we were going to have something together, something special—then she met Neil." The hand holding the pipe tightened until the knuckles whitened. "I'm a pretty ineffectual bastard, in comparison. Pam and I went to the opera together. We took walks in Central Park; we made love once on a beach in Saint Lucia. But I never took her white-water rafting on the Snake River or on a rock climb in the Tetons or elk hunting in Canada."

He turned his face away and Annie scarcely heard him say, "I just loved her very much."

"Bledsoe—" Annie didn't know how to say it, but she had to try, "Bledsoe has a kind of magic, even when you know he's everything you despise."

Hillman looked at Annie with reddened eyes. "Yeah. I give him that. But I should have seen it, understood it for what it was. Almost a sickness. I shouldn't have given up on Pam." He jammed the pipe back into his jacket. "I didn't know what was going on. Not for a long time. I'd turned her over to another editor. Saved myself pain, that's how I looked at it. But Judi saw what was happening. She went up to Stamford, to their place, for a conference about the next book, and when she came back she came in to see me... and said Pam was a mess, fat and no makeup and drunk the whole weekend and Judi sure understood why, the way that jerk rode Pamela, one nasty, vicious jibe after another. I called Pam and she was sober, I swear it. I laid it on the line. I told her I loved her, that she was the loveliest woman in the world, the best writer I'd ever known, that I knew she was sick and I was going to come and get her and bring her home with me." His face broke into angles of sorrow. "Jesus, Little Mr. Do-good, announcing his arrival. Why the shit didn't I just get in the car and go get her? Why did I call?"

Annie watched with dawning horror.

"She was dead when I got there. She fell down the goddammed stairs. Drunk, they said. That's what they said." He buried his face in his hands.

Max held the telephone receiver away from his ear. The voice, deep and angry and violent, spilled into his office. "Aren't you fuckers satisfied? Spence is dead. Isn't that goddam well enough?"

Max interrupted sharply, "I couldn't agree more. But times are different now. Maybe if the truth about Burke Spence came out, what happened and why, maybe it could cause Bledsoe trouble. Have you ever thought about that?"

Annie checked all the late-afternoon panels: Die Laughing—Peters, MacLeod, Hess, and Cannell; The Butler Didn't Do It—Millar, Du Maurier, Hintze, and Muller; and Those Brits—Moyes, Cody, Porter, and Caudwell. She looked in the bar. She walked a half mile in either direction on the beach. She inquired at the car and bicycle rental offices. Finally, the obvious occurred. Derek Davis was probably in his room. Dashing down the corridor to the now deserted conference registration table, she checked the master list of attendees and their room assignments, then scooped up the phone.

As the elevator door began to open, Annie saw the housekeeping cart sweep past. She was halfway down the opposite hall before the import of the scene registered. Whirling around, she broke into a run.

The cart was parked outside suite 315.

The door was closed.

Maids—genuine maids—left doors open when cleaning rooms. Didn't they?

Grimly, Annie punched the buzzer.

When the door opened, Annie glowered.

Henny had established a new dress standard for maids with her smartly-fitting gray chambray uniform accented by a dainty white apron.

"Costume from *The Importance of Being Earnest?*" Annie snarled.

Henny's eyes glinted with irritation. "Shh. Come on in," and she yanked Annie over the threshold and closed the door. Annie reached for the knob. "Oh no, I'm not going to be found breaking into—"

"So who broke in? You rang, the maid answered. Cool it, Annie. Listen, I can't find a trace of any information in this suite that pertains to Agatha Christie, except some of those flyers. What do you think of that?"

"I think whatever work Bledsoe's done is at home in his computer terminal." Annie grabbed a bony elbow. "Come on, Henny, let's get out of here."

Henny resisted. Her bright eyes roamed restlessly around the suite.

Annie looked, too. Jean Hager's Chief Mitch Bushyhead could tell a lot from the contents of a room. But this was a hotel room, lovelier than many, but still carrying little impress of its occupants' personalities. The bedroom doors were closed. The foyer was identical to that in Annie and Max's suite. An ornate black iron grillwork separated the entryway from the living area. Vivid pillows emphasized the crisp white of the wicker furniture. A canvas carryall on the coffee table gaped, revealing a jumble of paperbacks. A neat stack of paperbacks sat atop the small breakfast table. Even at the distance of fifteen feet, Annie recognized the top cover, one of the rare Green Door mysteries. As she recalled, most of the Mr. Moto books had appeared in those editions. Kathryn Honeycutt's purchases from the bookroom, no doubt. Too effete a selection for Bledsoe. His taste would run to Jim Thompson and Jonathan Valin. The *New York Times* was tossed carelessly on the floor beside the divan. A damp black-and-orange beach towel hung from the back of a breakfast room chair.

"No papers here at all," Henny muttered, "except for the subscriptions sold for his newsletter. Boy, he really cleaned up. Forty-eight hundred dollars' worth."

Forty-eight hundred dollars earned by promising to trash Christie. Annie jiggled impatiently from one foot to another. Henny was off on the wrong track. Nosing around Bledsoe's suite wouldn't get either of them anywhere in their quest. She yanked open the door. "If you've got any brains," she warned inelegantly, "you'll blow this pool hall right now. See you later."

•   •   •

If Derek Davis's hand hadn't clung to the doorjamb, he would have slid right down to the floor.

Drunk.

Very drunk.

He stared at her with red-rimmed, muzzy eyes and with no flicker of recognition. The publicist's uncombed hair flared in tangled clumps. He hadn't shaved. He was wearing a soiled, wrinkled shirt, trousers that had been slept in. He was barefoot. The sour odor of whiskey clung to him.

"Yeah."

"Derek, I need to talk to you."

Derek blinked, wavered, clung to the door.

"Yeah."

"About Neil Bledsoe and—"

Derek's face twisted. Tears brimmed in his eyes. He turned away, stumbled, careened into a chair, then dropped heavily onto the couch. He hunched awkwardly over the couch arm, his shoulders heaving.

Annie slowly followed. She stood by the couch, looked down, and a rivulet of anger snaked through her mind. How much heartbreak and agony could one man cause?

"Derek!" came a low cry from behind Annie.

She turned.

Fleur Calloway stood in the door that Annie had left ajar. She looked past Annie at Derek's beaten figure. "My daughter," Fleur said brokenly, "Pamela's son, and that young author, Natalie Marlow." Her lovely face hardened. "It must stop." And her face no longer looked lovely. It was as stern and cold and merciless as that of an avenging angel.

AGATHA CHRISTIE
TITLE CLUE

Elinor Katharine Carlisle—
Innocent or guilty?

19

As she and Max slipped out of the hotel surreptitiously, Annie thought fleetingly of Selwyn Jepson's Commodore Rupert Gill and his penchant for "imported" brandy. Yes, the illicit definitely had its charms. Annie knew she should be at the hotel, on call, for any or all emergencies, but she needed a respite. She *had* to be up for the Agatha Christie Trivia Quiz at eight o'clock. God, she said simply, only knew what some people might do.

It should have been a wonderfully relaxing evening. Conference-goers were free to explore the island's restaurants before returning to the hotel for the evening's entertainment, the Trivia Quiz, in the main ballroom.

Truth to tell, Annie was delighted to be away from the hotel and even from her beloved conference for a while, and there wasn't a single conference attendee in evidence at the Island Hills Golf and Country Club. She and Max sat on the terrace, and a gentle breeze swept over them with the heavy scent of honeysuckle as they studied their menus. Among the Wednesday-night specials was beef Wellington, Annie's favorite entree. So pastry and beef were heavy on cholesterol. So who cared? Annie refused to be intimidated by the health police.

But she couldn't leave her worries behind.

She poked at her beef Wellington and even the luscious gravy trickling down the sides of the pastry didn't help.

"Max, what do you think's going on? Did somebody kill John Border

Stone because he was on the roof at the wrong time? But why was he registered as James Bentley? And every time I think how he was killed—with the murder weapon actually used in that novel, though not on Bentley—it gives me cold chills. Did it make somebody mad that he was registered as that particular Christie character? And why in God's name *did* he register as that particular character?"

"Maybe he particularly identified with Bentley," Max suggested. "Liked him and—"

"Honey, even James Bentley didn't like James Bentley." She shook her head impatiently and absently chewed, then said indistinctly, "I keep thinking it will all make sense." She drank a sip of chablis. "A sugar cutter! Max, that's crazy. And Lady Gwendolyn's cape—that's even crazier!"

"Or someone wants us to think the circumstances are crazy." He squeezed more lemon on his red snapper. "After all, mystery nuts aren't really nuts."

Annie didn't comment. The memory of the treasure hunt was too fresh and her forebodings about the trivia quiz too intense.

"The discouraging thing is, I talked to everybody—" she paused. Actually it had hardly been a conversation with Derek Davis. "I saw all of those people today, the ones who have reason to hate Bledsoe, and, Max, they all hate him so much, it is frightening." She put down her fork, pushed away her plate.

That's when the maître d' interrupted. "Mrs. Darling, I have a message for you."

Annie felt a painful constriction in her chest. The last time she received a message. . . . She ripped open the envelope:

"Dear Hearts," she read aloud, *"do enjoy your evening, for I fear we must gird for intense effort. I've scheduled a meeting in your suite Thursday morning. Breakfast is already ordered. Ciao, Lady Gwendolyn."*

Annie looked at her husband in utter astonishment. "How the hell did she find us?"

Nathan Hillman politely stood aside for Fleur Calloway and the bookstore owner from Honolulu, Sherry Wilson, to climb the steps to the platform. Fleur Calloway paused midway up the steps, hesitated for just a moment, then, chin up, walked on.

In the front row, Neil Bledsoe watched Fleur's every move. His aunt, Kathryn Honeycutt, flashed him a sidelong glance, then gave a tiny sigh. She pushed her glasses higher on her nose and moved slightly in her seat, as if disassociating herself from Bledsoe.

Annie started toward him, but Max reached out and stopped her. "He'd love it, Annie."

Max was right. If she tried to evict Bledsoe from the Christie Trivia Quiz, it would only give him another opportunity for public notice.

She realized, too late, that she should have found a replacement for Fleur. Bledsoe had no intention of easing his pressure on her. But Annie had to admire the author's élan as she bent her head to listen attentively to the bookstore owner as if this were the loveliest of evenings and the most perfect of audiences.

Lady Gwendolyn hadn't missed that byplay either. The old author's shrewd eyes studied Bledsoe with undisguised contempt. As she settled into a seat next to Annie in the first row, just a few seats away from Bledsoe, she commented in her aristocratic, carrying voice, "Bad manners spring from a corrupt heart."

Bledsoe continued to spread blight wherever he went. Margo Wright sat at the far end of the ballroom, her attention resolutely focused on the platform. But she knew Bledsoe was there. It was so apparent in the impassivity of her face, the tension in her slim shoulders.

Victoria Shaw was a few rows behind Bledsoe. She glared at the critic angrily. God, she hated that man.

And Nathan Hillman and Fleur Calloway, sitting on the platform, so carefully did not look at the front row.

Annie scanned the audience. She didn't see Derek Davis. One plus for the evening. The publicist couldn't possibly have sobered up yet. Talk about trouble waiting to happen. . . .

Almost all the seats were taken now. Annie glanced back at the platform. Yes, the contestants were there for the amateurs. Oh Lordy, the sixty-five-year-old twins from Minneapolis, Ursula and Selina Matheson! After her earlier encounter with them, Annie now regarded them with a healthy respect. The amateur trio was completed by Ivan Lungard, a librarian from Provo, Utah.

As the auditorium filled, Annie noticed absently that Bledsoe was waving inquirers away from the empty seat next to him. It was almost time to start when a young woman walked slowly up to him. Annie noted the peacock-blue silk noir slacks with a matching jewel-neck blouse, accented by a navy and red scarf over one shoulder and a dramatic silver shell belt.

"Seat taken," Bledsoe grunted.

"Neil." Even her voice was different, lower, a little breathy.

Realization struck Annie and Bledsoe at the same time.

Annie poked Max in the ribs. "Wow, look at Natalie!"

Bledsoe stared up at the transformed author. Her chestnut hair now clung to her head in chic sophistication. Artfully applied makeup emphasized her luminous dark eyes and high cheekbones.

She waited for his response, a shy, eager pride in her eyes.

His face hardened, his lips turned down in a furious scowl. "Who tarted you up? That little prick, Derek?"

Beside him, Kathryn Honeycutt gasped, then pressed a hand against her lips.

Natalie's face flushed, then paled. Her eyes changed as Annie watched, the softness consumed by white-hot anger.

Annie was on her feet. She rushed to Natalie's side. "You look lovely," Annie said furiously. "Absolutely lovely," but the author turned away. Head down, she strode toward the exit, eyes blinded by tears of rage.

Annie had had enough. "You're the most despicable man I've ever met. Murder's much too good for you." She realized that those sitting nearby, which included the redhead Annie had disenfranchised from the treasure hunt, were listening avidly while feigning indifference. She was too mad to care. "I wish one of those serial murderers you're so crazy about would trap you in an attic and chop you into little pieces while recording the screams. Try that on for size, big boy."

She wouldn't have stopped at that. She had a few more choice bits in mind until she realized a discomfiting fact: Bledsoe was enjoying this scene. Getting a hell of a bang out of it, actually. His greedy eyes gleamed with satisfaction; his pouty lips curved in a half smile. Well, damned if she'd give him any more pleasure. Whirling on her heel, she called to Max, "Hold my seat for me!" then dashed up the aisle, moving against those arriving. But once outside the ballroom, she looked in vain for Natalie Marlow.

Promptly at eight o'clock, Henny stepped to the center microphone. "Ladies and gentlemen, welcome to the World's Most Challenging Agatha

Christie Trivia Quiz, the ultimate encounter between amateurs and professionals. Who knows the most about Agatha and her works? Tonight will determine the answer to that question."

She introduced the Professionals (loud clapping) and the Amateurs (vigorous cheers, aided by shrill whistles from the Matheson sisters).

Henny explained the rules: the first contestant to punch his buzzer and provide the right answer would receive twenty-five points and a chance at a bonus question.

Annie tugged at Max's sleeve. "Listen, if the jerk tries anything, we'll give him the bum's rush, right?"

"Right."

Annie tried to relax. She was unwilling to meditate upon a mantra, Laurel's solution to stress. And Max's attempts to soothe were well meant but ineffectual. She was *mad*. And irritated with herself. She should have moved more quickly. Annie wished she'd been able to find Natalie Marlow. But, finally, she felt her face cool, and she was able to watch the proceedings with pleasure.

Ruling with an iron hand when disputes arose, Henny skillfully controlled the pace. Ingrid stood at the back of the stage, posting the scores on a blackboard. It was neck and neck between the Amateurs and the Pros until the amateurs bobbled a query on Ariadne Oliver. The Pros came through: Oliver had only one solo appearance without Poirot and that was in *The Pale Horse*.

Fleur took the bonus question: What was the origin of that title?

"From the sixth chapter, eighth verse of the Revelation of Saint John the Divine: 'And I saw, and behold, a pale horse, and its rider's name was Death, and Hades followed him . . .'" Fleur continued, "*The Pale Horse* was a wonderful book. Christie considered it one of her best." A tiny smile. "Her sixty-seventh book. She put us all to shame, didn't she?"

In the audience, fans applauded.

Bledsoe made a thumbs-down gesture and hissed.

Boos rocked the room.

Henny lifted her voice, ignoring the interruptions. "Who does George Barton consult when he receives two poison pen letters about the death of his wife, Rosemary?"

The Matheson sisters, Ursula and Selina, still in their Sherlock capes, smacked their buzzers at the same time. They spoke in unison, too. "Colonel Race!"

Ingrid marked the scores. It now stood at Amateurs—250, Pros—275.

The sisters answered the bonus question correctly: Parker Pyne was the Detective of the Heart who advertised his aid to the unhappy in the personals column of the *Times*. But the Pros scored on the next question, identifying *Third Girl* as the Christie title which explored the druggy, unkempt culture of the sixties.

The quiz ended on a note of high excitement.

Amateurs—325, Pros—325.

"A toss-up," Henny challenged. "Whoever answers the next question first and correctly will be declared winner and all-around Agatha Christie Trivia Champion!

"For fifty points: What wealthy, crochety old man makes a posthumous—"

The Matheson sisters' buzzers shrilled.

"Jason Rafiel in *Nemesis*!" they chorused.

"Correct." Henny waved three envelopes above her head. "And each of our knowledgeable fan participants will receive a very special gift—a free tour of five Low Country houses which are reputed to be haunted."

"Haunted houses." Bledsoe's sardonic drawl carried over the scrape of chairs and buzz of conversation. "Not so goddammed much fun when you live in one."

That, of course, caught the attention of those nearby. One of the Matheson sisters hurried to the edge of the platform. "Is your house haunted? Tell us about it."

"Sure is. Every Sunday night you can hear the scream. Real eerie."

"Whose scream?" the other twin demanded excitedly.

Annie knew what was going to happen just an instant before he spoke. But it was too late. There was no way to stop Bledsoe.

Kathryn Honeycutt knew, too. She held up both hands, as if to block her nephew's words.

"My second wife, Pamela. Fell down and broke her crown—actually, her neck—about ten o'clock one night. She was expecting company." Bledsoe's eyes flicked over the platform steps where Nathan Hillman stood. "Cops think maybe she was going to meet a lover and hurried too fast down the stone steps. And now, all that's left of Pamela is this spooky scream on Sunday nights. Hell of a deal."

People looked toward him, uncertain whether to commiserate or laugh. A tragic tale, if true. But surely, the tone in his voice—

Kathryn Honeycutt's lips quivered. She didn't look like Miss Marple now. Instead, Annie thought again of poor Dolly Bantry, distraught over the ugly rumors swirling around her dear Arthur, suspected of murdering the blonde in their library. "Neil, Neil—I wouldn't have thought even you could be so heartless. I've just had enough. You've ruined my holiday. I'm going home in the morning." Tears spilled down her pale cheeks. She turned and hurried away.

Bledsoe reached out, as if to stop her, then dropped his hand and shrugged. His dark eyes glittered.

Lady Gwendolyn swept toward him. People parted to make way for the small, plump, determined figure. Her hand swept up, the sapphire flashing on a pudgy finger as she tapped Bledsoe on the chest. The old author's bell-like voice carried throughout the room. "Young man, the mills of the gods grind slow, but they grind exceedingly fine."

"No wonder people are trying to kill that man!" Annie exclaimed. "I may lead the pack before long." She dropped into a wicker chair in their living room and stared without favor at the two blue-backed folders on the coffee table. "Lady Gwendolyn strikes again," Annie muttered. She picked one up. "Honest to God, if it were just Bledsoe, I wouldn't even try to find out who wants to kill him." She opened the folder. A five-by-seven class photo of John Border Stone looked up at her. Annie bit her lip. Stone's plump cheeks spread in a happy smile. But it wasn't just Bledsoe. Not anymore.

"Time to get to work," she said crisply, thumbing through the bio on Bledsoe.

Max nuzzled the back of her neck. "All work and no play make Jack a dull boy."

Annie shook her head. "Max, we need to read these before—"

His hands slipped over her shoulders.

Annie held onto the folder for a moment more. Duty called.

But so did love.

The folder slipped to the floor.

Five A.M. was not an hour Annie enjoyed.

Max kept tugging at the sheet. "Annie, Lady Gwendolyn called. They're all arriving in just half an hour."

"Ughmmph."

"Annie, we didn't read the bios last night."

She was too sleepy to point out the responsibility for that.

Another fifteen minutes, two cups of coffee, a glass of orange juice, a too-brief shower, and she was awake enough to glower at the door as the busboy arrived, a contingent of disgustingly bright-eyed investigators right behind him.

It was a hearty feast spread on the buffet. Annie studied one dish with especial care.

"Kedgeree," Laurel said carelessly.

"What?"

"Kedgeree, of course." Laurel with a Brit accent was nauseating before breakfast. "A mixture of smoked haddock, hard-boiled eggs, and rice. A glorious by-product of our colonial days." Those dark blue eyes widened ingenuously. "From India." She scooped a heaping serving onto her plate. Annie hoped it resulted in deserved indigestion. "And these Singin' Hinnies are especially delicious," Laurel murmured.

Annie had to admit there was plenty for everyone to enjoy. She opted for the grilled tomatoes, French toast served with raspberries and cream, and a sausage turnover, and if anyone thought that a curious assortment, so be it. At five A.M., both body and soul required substantial sustenance.

Lady Gwendolyn beamed at the heaping plates. Her own bore a barely balanced mound of golden brown crumpets, which almost made Annie rethink her choices. But she wasn't tempted in the slightest by the old lady's strong amber-colored breakfast tea.

Annie wondered if Lady Gwendolyn and Laurel considered themselves to be *pukka sahib* representatives at an outpost of the empire (pronounced *em-pah,* of course). Their khaki shirts and slacks would be perfectly appropriate on a safari in Rhodesia (now Zambia and Zimbabwe), but perhaps a bit much for a rather elegant hotel suite, notwithstanding the ceiling fans and shuttered doors.

Clearly, both meant business.

Lady Gwendolyn sat at the head of the table. Laurel slipped into the seat beside her, after placing blue manila folders at each place.

Lady Gwendolyn flipped open the cover of her folder and scanned a page covered with spidery handwriting, while quaffing her tea.

Laurel drew pale blue glasses from her pocket and perched them on her nose. If, Annie thought, it was an attempt to appear businesslike, it failed miserably. Max's mother looked about as businesslike as the elfin Lady Lucy Angkatell surprising her guest Midge Hardcastle before breakfast in *The Hollow.*

Annie dropped into her seat, next to Henny and across from Max. Henny, she was glad to see, was sturdily herself, wearing an elegant pale lemon warm-up and a yellow calico headband.

"Bledsoe," Lady Gwendolyn said pensively, surveying them in turn. "What role does he play in our drama? Villain? Victim? Smoke screen? And, of course, let us not overlook the late John Border Stone, who masqueraded as James Bentley. Why was Stone murdered? Did he see more than he admitted outside the bookstore Saturday night? Was he present on the roof when the vase crashed down? What information had Stone planned to give to Annie? Can we prove a connection between Stone and any of our suspects? Or is Stone's death a separate issue from the melodramatic attacks on Bledsoe?" A plump hand reached up to reinsert a dangling hair pin. The coronet braids still looked quite tidy. But it was, of course, early hours.

Lady Gwendolyn smiled sweetly. "But we must not think we have divined the truth, or that we even have a clear idea of our quest. We must be certain to look beneath the surface. *Something* is in the process of happening; something as yet obscure. So what can we do?"

As far as Annie was concerned, not even a delicious breakfast made up for a variation on Twenty Questions at this ungodly hour of the morning. Her vocal cords weren't even up to a growl, much less insightful suggestions.

But Lady Gwendolyn, with a cherubic nod, was quite happy to provide an answer. "We have one major recourse—we can analyze our suspects. Like hardy trackers across the Serengeti Plain, we can use our skill and knowledge to pick up the spoor of our quarry. And here"— she lifted a blue folder—"is the fruit of our investigations." She nodded at Max. "Our first report, please."

Annie didn't pay too much attention to Max's report. She already knew about Bledsoe's sorry past. As she finished the delectable toast, she struggled for clarity. Okay, it was early Thursday morning—God yes, it was early morning, not even a finger of dawn perceptible—and the vase had come tumbling down Tuesday morning. Tuesday night, she and Lady Gwendolyn discovered the body of John Border Stone, alias James Bentley. Was it important that the vase fell on Tuesday morning and Stone was killed that same evening? Annie made a note on the fresh notepaper that had thoughtfully been tucked into the inner front-cover pocket of the folder.

Max finished reading the bio on Bledsoe. He thumbed through several sheets. "Here's some information that came through late yesterday about Bledsoe's funding for *Have Gun, Will Travel*. I traced it back to a sham company: Allied Everest. The company used the address of a building that belonged to Burke Spence. Spence wrote six books that earned him more than five million dollars. His readership was predominantly male. His series detective, private investigator Mick Bolt, operated out of Port Arthur, Texas. He carried a Colt Special .38, played rugby for fun, and had a woman in every coastal town on the gulf. Every five pages offer a grunt-and-gouge fight or a give-it-to-'em-quick sex scene. Spence, like his protagonist, was a rugged athlete, played tackle on his college football team. However, unlike his detective, Spence's sexual preference was for other brawny males. According to a publishing figure who insisted upon anonymity, Spence was involved with a series of male lovers. He made a mistake—he went after Bledsoe. The informant said he'd bet the farm that Bledsoe came on to Spence. Anyway, Bledsoe hired a private detective, got the facts on Burke's liaisons, and threatened to go public. Spence paid Bledsoe a half million. Once the magazine was underway and successful, Bledsoe published an article about Spence entitled 'Tough-Guy Writer Dishonors Craft.' Spence blew his brains out two days after publication."

"That's dreadful," Annie exclaimed.

"Diabolical," Lady Gwendolyn pronounced.

Henny shrugged. "So what else is new. This guy's lower than a snake."

"Yes," Annie said quietly, "yes, he is," and she told them about Fleur Calloway and her daughter, Jaime.

"God," Henny said. "That explains a lot in her bio." She found the right page, cleared her throat, and read:

"Fleur Romney Calloway was born in 1935 in Bogaloosa, Louisiana, the youngest of five children. Four older brothers. Father owned the local bank, mother a nature artist. Grew up on a plantation, Romney Hall, overlooking a marsh. Expert horsewoman. Excelled at fishing, loved canoeing. Graduate Randolph Macon, master's in English from University of Mississippi. Upon graduation, she married Jack Calloway, former fullback at the university, the assistant football coach. Divorced three years later, shortly after the birth of daughter, Jaime Noel, in 1960. Never remarried. Returned to Louisiana and lived upon another small family plantation, Strawberry Hill. First mystery, *Death, My Sister,* published in 1964, received the Edgar for Best First Mystery. Seven mysteries, all well received (except for reviews by Bledsoe and a few other antiwomen critics), published between 1964 and 1978. None since then. During her productive years, she was active in book circles in her hometown, a fund-raiser for the local library, member of the parents' groups in Jaime's schools."

Henny paused for a sip of—Annie was glad to note—coffee. "Here's what the head librarian said, 'Such a gracious woman, always so kind and friendly to everyone. I tell you it's a shame how hard she's grieved for her girl. Closed her doors and hardly came out again. Most people in this town don't know her anymore, just heard about her, the beautiful, quiet lady who lives at Strawberry Hill. My grandson works summers at the cemetery, says she comes every evening at dusk and puts a fresh rose on her daughter's grave and stays there a long time, then walks home again. I tell you, it's a crying shame how kids don't realize they're loved till it's too late. Nobody can believe Jaime would jump off a bridge—and what was she doin' in New York, anyway? There's stories— but there's always stories.' "

Henny turned the page. "Jaime's best friend remembered, 'We had so much fun growing up at Strawberry Hill. Barefoot all summer. Picnics at the lake. One summer it seemed like all it did was rain and we were in the house a lot and Jaime's mom told us lots of stories 'bout when she was growing up and how she and her brothers played so many jokes. One time she and her brother Alex smuggled a bull frog into Sunday school and it almost caused a riot. We laughed 'til we cried. That was the summer before Jaime died.'

"Her agent, Evan Parker: 'Oh sure, I've tried. But Fleur just says she can't write anymore. I don't know whether it's grief or guilt. I don't know what it is. But I could sell a book by her tomorrow. Hell, today.'

"Fleur's lifelong friend, Consuelo Magrane: 'Fleur—she was always so full of love, but it's almost as if she's been frozen, ever since Jaime died.' "

Henny pushed her wire glasses up on her nose. "There should," she said crisply, "be a special place in hell for Neil Bledsoe."

"Emma Clyde's opinion precisely," Annie interjected.

"Ah, yes, Emma Clyde." Lady Gwendolyn shot a quick glance at Annie. "I found it quite interesting that Emma Clyde has a biographical sheet already extant, from a prior investigation." She found the proper page and began to sketch her fellow writer's career. "Author seventy-six mysteries—"

Annie interrupted to keep the record straight. "Seventy-nine. The eightieth, *Sing a Song of Sorrow,* is due out in October."

"Hmm. Emma has won two Edgars and a Grand Master Award." Lady Gwendolyn nodded. "I enjoyed winning my Edgar. One." Was there a tart ring to her voice? "I haven't been named Grand Master." Her tone indicated it was only a matter of time.

As she continued, Annie nodded. She knew all about the island's celebrity author, creator of Marigold Rembrandt and rich beyond the dreams of most mystery writers. Her seventy-ninth book, *The Grinning Skull,* had been published only six months before. A competent, intense, domineering woman. Army nurse, World War II. Married briefly to a Tennessean she met on a troop ship coming home from North Africa. A second brief marriage not too long ago ended with her husband's death (some believed murder) when he mysteriously fell from the stern of *Marigold's Pleasure* and drowned. Emma hadn't been pleased when she discovered he was cheating on her. A tough lady.

Emma was quite capable of any amount of devious planning, but surely Emma wouldn't commit murder because of a friend's mistreatment? And no author would commit murder over bad reviews.

Would they?

After some of the bitter comments she'd overheard during the conference, Annie wasn't absolutely certain of that conclusion.

"*Such* a wonderful writer." Laurel fingered a khaki button on her shirt. "Contradictions, aren't we all such a mass of contradictions! Surely a disquieting aura of suspicion clings to our dear Emma. And Henny's view of Bledsoe is *so* understandable, but let me tell you of my research." She turned several pages. "Let's begin with Derek.

"Derek Davis was born in 1964, in Springfield, Illinois. Father, Donald Davis, an accountant; mother, Pamela Gerrard Davis, a novelist. Parents divorced in 1981. Pamela met Bledsoe at her agent's office the following year and married him only weeks later." Laurel lifted an angelic head. "Marry in haste; repent at leisure."

"There is surely much truth in old sayings," Lady Gwendolyn agreed.

Annie stifled a catcall. Wasn't it Laurel's third marriage, to that Italian race car driver, Roderigo, that took place two weeks after she met him?

Laurel smiled beatifically and resumed her report. "Second marriage difficult for Derek. Bledsoe treated his stepson with open contempt, claiming that young Derek was girlish with his love of poetry and painting. Derek's high-school grades were spotty. He excelled in English and art, barely passed math and science. He attended a noncompetitive Midwestern college. He was in his last year when his mother died in a fall. Three weeks later, he dropped out of school. Fraternity brother Bill Elliott: 'Derek went bananas when his mom died. He always drank too much, but so do a lot of guys in college. But he stopped going to class, stayed drunk. The dean of men, though, is a good guy. He understood, got Derek out on withdraw/passing for the fall semester. Derek kept saying his stepfather killed his mom. I don't know, maybe so. I went home with Derek a couple of times and that guy was a real asshole. Bullied Derek's mom. She got drunk every night. Maybe she did fall down the steps. Who knows?' "

Annie knew how hard it was to lose a mother. How much worse would it be if you blamed someone else for that death? And perhaps blamed yourself because you weren't there to prevent it.

"Poor Derek," Annie said quietly.

Laurel flashed her a warm and understanding glance, and Annie remembered once again why she loved her mother-in-law, despite her dingbat proclivities.

"Such an unhappy story," Laurel commiserated. "Derek showed up intoxicated at his mother's funeral. He tried to attack Bledsoe. Some of the funeral home employees hustled him outside. After that, the boy dropped out of sight. His mother's editor, Nathan Hillman, found him four months later living on the streets of Chicago. In a holographic will dated a week before her death, Pamela Gerrard Davis left her entire estate to Bledsoe with directions that he provide for Derek. As far as we can determine, Bledsoe never made a penny available to his stepson. Apparently Bledsoe used some of Pamela's money to fund his latest venture, *Mean Streets,* but he lost most of it gambling.

"However," Laurel continued more cheerfully, "Hillman paid Derek's tuition the next fall. Derek graduated in the spring and moved to New York. He attended the New York University Publishing Short Course, then started to work for Hillman House." Laurel looked over her glasses and reminded her listeners. "They had published his mother's books. Derek's done very well, recently receiving a promotion and a raise. The last few months, he's been very attentive to a rising young star at Hillman House, Natalie Marlow." Laurel sighed. "Until this week and his encounters with Bledsoe, Derek had had no further drinking problems."

Laurel took off her glasses, dropped them in an outsize khaki pocket. "Now, to be the devil's advocate. I helped Max tie up some loose ends on his report on Bledsoe. So I tracked down an old friend of Bledsoe's— Taylor Graham."

Annie sat up straight at that name. "Graham's wonderful! The best private eye writer since Chandler. He's done for El Paso what Loren D. Estleman did for Detroit and Les Roberts for Cleveland and Carl Hiaasen for Miami and Sara Paretsky for Chicago and George V. Higgins for Boston. He's just superb." She smiled with remembered pleasure. "And such a sweetheart. He did a signing at Death on Demand, and everyone fell in love with him." Her smile faded. "He's a friend of Bledsoe's?" Disbelief tinged the disappointment in her voice.

Laurel looked ever so slightly reproving. "We must give everyone a fair appraisal. Not even Neil Bledsoe is *all* bad."

"So Hitler loved children and dogs. Aryan children, of course. So what?" Annie muttered.

A swift glance from the vivid blue eyes at the head of the table quelled her. But she was glad to see a brief thumbs-up gesture from Henny.

"Bledsoe was Graham's agent at one point. Graham said, 'Neil's a funny guy. Go to hell and back for a friend. A bad enemy. A guy has to measure up, you know. No leeway. But he's a hell of a lot of fun at poker. Takes you to the cleaners, of course. Goddam brave. Rode some rapids with him once that turn most people white-haired. He just laughed. Always felt sorry for him. First wife screwed around on him. Second wife a lush. He had a German shepherd that was his best buddy. He loved that goddammed dog. Used to see them jogging in Central Park. Neil jogged winter, summer. Never gave in to cold or heat. Always took Willie with him. Anyway, damn hot day. High nineties. High humidity. Willie dropped dead of a heat stroke. Neil picked him up, carried him off. Cried all the way. I never saw him at the park again.' "

"Too bad he couldn't have shared a little of that love with people," Henny observed acidly.

"That provides a fascinating glimpse of the man," Lady Gwendolyn commented placidly. "But, we should all remember, there is a special relationship between a man and his dog. Perhaps that day in the park, Bledsoe grieved for himself, not the dog. Now, it's time for a most essential, determinative inquiry, one which I am very surprised that no one else has, as yet, called for." She looked inquiringly at each in turn, then gave a slight shake of her head (the braids quivered but held). Annie was afraid Lady Gwendolyn was disappointed in her staff. Was she thinking back to the good old days of World War II intelligence when she had better aid than a fey, Johnny-come-lately Christie enthusiast, a rather grumpy mystery expert even though the best customer at Death on Demand, a mystery bookseller, and a very low-key counselor. (Max avoided the use of the term "private eye." South Carolina was very particular in its licensing laws of private investigators.)

Of course, as Lady Gwendolyn well knew, one had to make do with what fell to one's hand.

"The victim," the old author said with a sly smile. "Therein, my dears, is sure to lie a tale."

AGATHA CHRISTIE
TITLE CLUE

A wasp flew loose in the cabin,
But the fatal sting came from
a thorn.

20

must say," Lady Gwendolyn continued serenely, "some extremely interesting information has been turned up by our investigators." She favored each with a warm smile. Laurel looked as though *she'd* been awarded the Croix de Guerre. Max rubbed his ear reflectively. Henny gave an all-in-a-day's-work shrug. "I know, of course, that it isn't unusual for people in the mystery field to be acquainted. It is, after all, a very small world. However, I think it is quite remarkable that the murder victim was personally acquainted with Bledsoe, Wright, Hillman, and Davis. This gives us much food for thought." With scarcely a pause for her listeners to digest this offering, she added dramatically, "Moreover, it behooves us to recall Poirot's dictum, *The seeds of death can be found in the victim's life.*

"John . . . Border . . . Stone." The old author's voice was as chilling as a footfall in a house thought to be empty.

Laurel gazed at Lady Gwendolyn adoringly.

Henny's fox-sharp nose twitched in irritation.

Max listened with rapt attention.

No wonder that Lady Gwendolyn's books sold so well, Annie thought grimly.

"His was a short life. It ended in violence." Lady Gwendolyn spoke quietly, but there was, for an instant, a clear sense of her anger, anger at that kind of death, ever, for the young or the old. "Stone was born twenty-five years ago in Brooklyn, New York. Father, a real estate salesman; mother, a junior high-school English teacher. He was the youngest of four children. His older sister Mimi: 'I *told* Johnnie he should stay away from mystery writers. What a bunch of weirdos—people who write and think about nothing but murder. He went to a banquet once and you know who the speaker was? This ex-medical examiner from L.A. and he showed the most awful slides of the latest serial killings out in California. Slides of the victims! I told Johnnie people who liked to talk when they're eating dinner about semen stains and the way bodies swell in water had to be whacko. He wouldn't listen to me. The last time I talked to him, two weeks ago, he was all excited. He told me about his trip to this meeting and how it was going to make such a big difference in his career. He kept saying that it was going to make it possible for him to sell his book. Oh, yes, he'd written a mystery. He showed me the first chapter once and it was awful, all about this man who gets his foot chopped off when he's a teenager, some kind of silly dare about a train overpass and he didn't run fast enough and so he blamed the other guys with him. There was the girl who was hot for his body, but she can't stand deformity, so the romance is all off. He sets out to get revenge, and he plans how he's going to kill them one by one and chop off a foot each time. I didn't tell Johnnie what I thought, but honestly, the writing was awful.'

"His older brother Bud: 'So I should be surprised, right? Tell you Johnnie was a great guy, something like this should never have happened to him, right? Wrong. Dead wrong. Johnnie had a real talent for palling around with lowlifes. Johnnie would've cheated his own mother at cards. Johnnie was a sneak, mister, a real sneak.'

"I'm sorry to say," Lady Gwendolyn said gently, "that Bud's conclusion comes as no surprise to me. Look at these." Lady Gwendolyn held up two photographs.

Annie's folder contained the pictures, one in cap and gown taken at Stone's college commencement, the second a somewhat out-of-focus snapshot. The formal picture gave little sense of personality, curly brown hair bunched beneath the mortarboard, a pudgy, self-important face striving for dignity. But the snapshot—John Stone was leaning back in a wooden chair, holding a stein of beer, laughing boisterously. He looked cocky, self-absorbed, and a little cruel. It was the irresponsible cruelty of the obtuse.

Lady Gwendolyn tapped that photograph. "When you know how a man laughs, you know how he lives." She glanced back to her papers. "A transcript of Stone's undergraduate work at New York University shows a C minus average. After graduation, Stone attended the NYU Publishing Short Course. Among those on the faculty that summer were Neil Bledsoe, Margo Wright, and Nathan Hillman. Derek Davis was a classmate." She let them think about this information for a moment, then she added, "I must stress that these are not the only people attending this conference who are known to us. Two more editors who are in attendance at this very conference served on the faculty of that same short course. However, neither of these people"—she peered at the paper—"Jean Reinhardt and Terry Abbott, has any apparent connection with Bledsoe, and it remains my conviction that Bledsoe is central to our present investigation. We won't, of course, ignore any possibilities, but we'll discuss those later.

"Stone worked as a messenger at CBS. He seems to have made no special impression on anyone. He was often late to work, and he was finally warned that he would be sacked if the pattern continued. His personnel folder reveals no other problems, no achievements.

"Stone had no special woman friend, and no close friends of either sex. He often dropped into a sports pub near his apartment house. The barman, Pat Russo: 'The guy loved the Knicks.'

"A friend of Stone's mother said: 'Johnnie was a little silly, you know, always thinking this time he'd win the lottery. I mean, not kidding about it.' "

Annie looked again at the graduation picture. Saturday night outside Death on Demand, after the shots were fired, his cheeks were cherry from exertion. He'd reported excitedly about what he'd seen, yet, boiled down, he had told them little of substance: a shadowy figure, a figure so indeterminate it could have been either a man or a woman.

What if Stone clearly saw the marksman?

What, indeed, would he do if he knew who shot at Bledsoe?

Would he lie?

Oh, he might, he might.

People so often lie, for good reasons or bad.

If Stone knew who had shot that .22, might he have kept an eye on that person? If so, it would explain why Stone's tennis shoes bore tar and gravel from the roof. If so, Stone's presence on the roof owed nothing at all to chance. And, if he saw the vase levered loose to tumble down onto Bledsoe and didn't inform the police—Annie sat up very straight—why then, what happened next was obvious indeed. A call to the culprit, a request for money, an agreement to meet Tuesday evening in his room.

"But, my God, that's why it doesn't make any sense at all!" Annie exploded.

Four polite faces awaited further comment.

"The sugar cutter!" she said forcefully. "Look at it—someone *had* to have brought it here specifically because it was the weapon in *Mrs. McGinty's Dead.* Nobody hauls ornamental brass sugar cutters around like loose change. That would mean someone *came* to the conference with murder already in mind. So how could Stone's death be the result of what he saw, either Saturday night or Tuesday morning?"

"Perhaps it isn't such a conundrum." Those brilliant blue eyes turned to Annie. "Yes, the cutter obviously was brought deliberately— but perhaps it was intended for a different victim."

"Oh." Annie was quieted. But not convinced.

"However," Lady Gwendolyn beamed an encouraging smile at Annie, "your point is well taken, my dear. The possibilities are indeed complex." A pudgy finger tapped the table as she enumerated.

"One—Stone's murder was premeditated and the cutter intended for him. If this proves out then Stone was the killer's objective all along.

"Two—Stone's may have been an ancillary murder. If this is so, I very much fear that the primary murder will yet be attempted. Our present knowledge would suggest that Bledsoe is the primary victim.

"Three—There may be absolutely no connection between the murder of Stone and the attacks on Bledsoe.

"Four—Premise three suggests that a fanatical Christie fan may be responsible for Stone's death and that a personal motive accounts for the attempted murder of Bledsoe."

Those far-seeing blue eyes narrowed. "Or none of the above. In any event, we must plumb the personal relationships of those who are involved—Hillman, Wright, Shaw, Marlow. And of course, Mrs. Honeycutt."

They all looked at the old lady in surprise as she pronounced the final name.

"Mrs. Honeycutt?" Annie said faintly.

Lady Gwendolyn looked especially cherubic as she gently chided them. "As Miss Marple always stressed, never assume that surface appearances are correct. We must by all means include Honeycutt. Now, Henny, what do you have on Hillman?"

Of course, given the opportunity, Henny was incapable of not taking center stage, and her exquisitely modulated voice now milked every nuance from her material. "Nathan Hillman born 1940 in Kenosha, Wisconsin. Father, Elway, a high-school principal; mother, Martha, piano teacher. Only child. Excellent student. Editor high-school newspaper, outstanding student. Majored English at Princeton, B.A. in 1961. One of earliest Peace Corps members, two years Nigeria. M.A. in English, Columbia University, 1966. Joined small publishing firm, Loman Brothers, in 1966. Moved up through editorial ranks, executive editor 1978. Firm prospered. Upon death of founder, Joseph Loman, in 1986, employees bought company from heirs, elected Hillman president and CEO. Beneath surface, bitter battle between Hillman and another senior editor, Francis Morissey. Morissey was ousted in bruising stock battle." Henny paused, then said, almost reluctantly, "Hillman is quite likable—but this gives us another view of him. He's ruthless in business. Does that carry over into his personal life? It's something to think about. Now, under Hillman's leadership, the company's percentage share of the market increased three-fold, accomplished primarily by expansion of its paperback arm. Hillman is well liked by most of his employees. Always genial, personable, pleasant. However, he expects total loyalty to the company, long hours, and books that make money. An editor with more than three money-losing books is encouraged to look for another job. Despite heavy managerial responsibilities, Hillman still edits a number of the house's major authors. In personal life, he has had several serious relationships but only one seemed headed for marriage, that with Pamela Gerrard Davis. But Davis, unexpectedly to those at the firm who knew her, instead married critic Neil Bledsoe. Since the abrupt end of that relationship, Hillman has been periodically involved in casual affairs. At work, Hillman is presently especially interested in the career of Natalie Marlow and—in-house—with the progress of Gerrard-Davis's son, Derek."

Lady Gwendolyn's coronet braids held firm as she nodded to herself and made a notation on a pad. "Well done, Henny."

Henny's eyes slitted again, although Lady Gwendolyn's tone wasn't the least bit patronizing.

The old author checked her notes. "Ah yes, Laurel, what do you have on Margo Wright?"

"Such an interesting young woman. Such a *strong* personality." Laurel beamed at her audience. "So marvelous the way women now can participate openly in every arena in the world. Although certainly it is a grave mistake on the part of today's youth to assume women were *subjugated* in the past. Women have always had the faculty of exercising control in their lives but through *subtle, adroit, social* means. And truly," her husky voice took on a confidential tone, "*I* think the millennia of experience gained by women in such skills as negotiation, diplomacy, and—"

"That is certainly an interesting thesis. There is much to it. But for the moment, perhaps we should confine ourselves to our subject." Such was Lady Gwendolyn's charm that the reproof actually sounded like a compliment.

"Of course," Laurel replied happily, not in the least quashed.

Annie wondered how it would be to go through life not only gorgeous, rich, and ebullient, but armored with impenetrable aplomb.

Not, of course, that she had any desire at all to emulate her mother-in-law. The very idea made her dizzy.

"Margo Wright," Laurel continued obediently. "Margo was born in 1956, the oldest of five daughters, to Harold Wright, a shoe salesman. Her mother, Mary Ann, was a homemaker. That word," Laurel pointed at the text with a shiny pink fingernail, "holds a *world* of meaning. It signifies a kind of dependency quite foreign to—"

"Perhaps we might focus on Margo," Lady Gwendolyn remonstrated gently.

"So *interesting* sociologically . . ." With a cheerful smile, Laurel capitulated. "Ah yes. Margo was a serious student, not especially popular with other students, but respected. President of her class all three years in high school. A scholarship to college. Unfortunately, she had to turn it down because of her father's terminal illness and her mother's inability to earn enough money to support the family. Margo started at the Masters Literary Agency as the receptionist, but her quick intelligence soon won Robert Masters's attention, and he gave her the opportunity to read manuscripts. She excelled, not only having a good sense of what makes books work but an excellent instinct for books the market would reward. In 1974, Margo married an advertising executive, Larry Bynum. He was almost twenty years older than she. They had no children and divorced eight years later. At the office, Margo prospered until—"

Bledsoe's attempt to torpedo Margo's career was old news to Annie. Though Laurel had picked up a bit of additional information which was fascinating indeed.

Her face solemn, Laurel confided to the little group in the suite,

"Another agent working there at the time remembers the incident well. She said, 'Margo never forgets an ill turn. I saw her later that year—after she learned it was Bledsoe who had set her up and driven her from her job. Margo told me, "Someday, someway, Neil's going to pay for this. You can count on it." The way she said it—if I were Neil Bledsoe I wouldn't walk down a dark alley if I thought Margo was anywhere around.' One satisfied author describes her as his New York barracuda. 'Margo never forgets a favor, always repays a slight.' She is an accomplished runner, twice finishing the Boston Marathon in less than three hours." Laurel closed the folder.

Max looked at their leader. "I believe I'm next. But, first, could I get everyone some coffee. More tea, Lady Gwendolyn?"

Dear Max. How had he sensed her desperate need for an infusion of caffeine? Annie immediately held up her empty cup. With her fresh cup of coffee and the paling of the sky beyond the balcony, she began to feel much more human.

"Victoria Shaw—" Max paused. "Honestly, I can't believe this woman could ever hurt anyone."

Lady Gwendolyn smiled at Max benignly. "Your gentlemanly response is certainly to your credit."

Max's ears turned pink. Annie loved it.

"However," Lady Gwendolyn continued, "we must remember that a genteel facade can mask murderous passion." How could anyone who looked so much like a Dresden shepherdess speak so easily of passion and evil? But that was the fascination of Miss Marple, wasn't it? A gentle nature so alive to the reality of evil.

Max avoided Annie's glance and concentrated on his report. "Victoria Shaw was born in 1925 in Willow Spring, North Carolina. Her father, Edward Murray, was a Methodist minister. Her mother, Louise Winton, died when Victoria was four. Victoria was a sweet, good-natured child. She attended the University of North Carolina at Chapel Hill. She met a young teaching assistant, Bryan Shaw, and they married upon her graduation. Bryan pursued an academic career, teaching English, emphasis upon nineteenth-century novelists. He taught at the University of the South, Southern Methodist University, and the University of Georgia. Upon his success as a mystery writer, he retired from teaching in 1974 and they settled in Willow Spring. They had three daughters, all of whom are now grown. Victoria always encouraged her husband in his writing, and she edited and typed his manuscripts. Bryan Shaw died of cancer in 1983. Since his death, she has dropped out of most of her activities. A neighbor: 'Poor Victoria. She used to be so bubbly, so energetic. Before Bryan died. She's almost a shell of the woman she once was. And she's sick so often. Pneumonia twice last year. She only goes to the doctor if her oldest girl badgers her. I was so happy to see her go to this mystery convention. Why, it's the first time she's seemed almost like her old self.' "

"And when Victoria got here, who did she see?" Annie said angrily. "The world's first-class bastard, Neil Bledsoe."

The old author pursed her lips. "Indeed. But, after all, my dear, Bledsoe's name *was* listed in the material sent to all conference attendees. It's difficult to believe Victoria didn't notice it. Don't you think?"

Henny scowled. "But couldn't that be said of all of them? Why, then, did Fleur Calloway come to the conference, if she hated him so much?"

A damn good question.

Laurel's reverence wasn't restricted solely to Lady Gwendolyn. "Oh, I can see how Fleur might have missed it. Why, she's so famous, I doubt if she even bothered to read the list of those coming. *She* isn't a fan."

Maybe. Maybe. Maybe.

But every person coming to The Christie Caper had plenty of opportunity to see Neil Bledsoe's name . . . and make any preparations they wished.

Including the purchase of a .22 pistol and an ornamental bronze sugar cutter.

And God only knew what else.

Annie shivered and quickly drank more coffee. It didn't help this kind of chill.

"We must be certain to balance," Lady Gwendolyn urged, "the information in the reports against events at the conference, including our own observations and conclusions. Character, after all, is the key." A rustle of her papers. "Now, Natalie Marlow."

Annie wanted to protest. Surely Natalie was the least of their suspects! After all, Natalie—until last night—had been so obviously infatuated with Bledsoe. And the first attack on the critic came last Saturday night. But Annie said nothing. Lady Gwendolyn would only point out that appearances can be deceiving. Annie settled back to listen.

"Natalie was born twenty-four years ago in Richmond, Virginia. She was an abandoned infant, found in a church foyer." Lady Gwendolyn's precise voice didn't reflect the tragedy in that last sentence, but the words struck Annie with almost physical force. Oh, Lord. Oh, dear Lord. "She lived in the state orphanage until she was fourteen, then she ran away. She worked a series of low-paying jobs. She never finished high school, but became an omnivorous reader. When she wandered from town to town, she spent every free minute in the library. Befriended by a small-town librarian who gave her a place to live in return for light housekeeping. Started writing *Down These Steps* when she was seventeen. The librarian sent a copy to an editor with whom she was acquainted. And the rest is publishing history. *Down These Steps* was the first book accepted over the transom by Hillman House in the past fifteen years. It became a major best-seller. And the whole movie industry is buzzing over the upcoming release of a major feature film of the book. Young Natalie is going to be a very rich young girl indeed."

When she had read Natalie's novel, Annie wondered how anyone could pack that much misery into three hundred pages. Now she knew. Knowing made her that much angrier at Bledsoe.

She thumped her fist on the table. "Bledsoe's despicable."

"You know," Henny cupped her chin in one hand, "I don't think I'd worry too much about Natalie. You saw her reaction last night?"

Annie had indeed. When Bledsoe insulted her, Natalie's eyes had glowed with the wild look of an enraged animal. Unreasoning, unthinking, pulsing with hatred. That was bad. Worse was Annie's memory of Moira, the protagonist in *Down These Steps*. Goaded into a frenzy, Moira snatched up a paring knife and stabbed a rapist repeatedly. It was an unforgettable reading experience. Natalie's searing prose made the ragged edge of every wound a pucker of pain, the spurting of fictional blood a red glory, the stench of death unmistakable.

"Certainly she is a young woman to reckon with," Lady Gwendolyn concluded, nodding. "Now," and the high, clear voice took on an instructional tone, "I must point out that the prognosis of the situation is unclear. All may well be as it appears: Bledsoe is on bad terms with the individuals we've just discussed and on fairly good terms with his aunt. But, it may be that his and Honeycutt's relationship is different indeed. What if *Honeycutt* came to this conference planning to kill her nephew? We cannot rule out that possibility." A sharp nod to Henny. "Your report."

It was hard for Henny, but she grudgingly admitted, "There are a couple of curious points that have arisen, although certainly there is no overt evidence even *hinting* at any kind of vendetta against Bledsoe by Kathryn Honeycutt."

Annie exchanged glances with Max. Something unexplained in a life that seemed so normal?

Henny did love the limelight. She spoke with a storyteller's verve. "Kathryn was born in 1924 in Van Nuys, California. She met Sergeant Frederick Honeycutt at a USO dance in Hollywood when she was nineteen. They married four months later in September 1943, just before his unit shipped out to the Pacific." In two simple sentences, Henny splendidly evoked the romance and excitement and fear of a young couple in love in wartime. "After Frederick's discharge from the marines in 1945, she went with him to his hometown, worked as a secretary while he went to college on the GI Bill, continued working while he was in law school. Worked as his secretary when Honeycutt opened his own firm. Widowed in 1985. Active in the Christian Science Church. No children. A member of two local book clubs, the garden club, the Business and Professional Women's Organization, the legal secretaries club, the bar auxiliary, a hospital volunteer. Past ten years served as treasurer for local philatelic club. Collects stamps, especially early American, and mysteries. Has first editions of all Patricia Wentworth mysteries—"

Annie was impressed. Wentworth wrote sixty-five mysteries, starting with *The Astonishing Adventure of Jane Smith* (1923) and ending with *The Girl in the Cellar* (1961). Her last book was published the year she died.

"—also all of the Agatha Christies, though not first editions. Especially enjoys the Marple books as Kathryn bears a remarkable resemblance to Christie's maiden lady detective, tall, with fluffy white hair, and blue eyes.

"In recent years, Kathryn has worked one day a week at a food canteen for the homeless. Her health is fairly good, but she is losing her eyesight. Refuses to undergo cataract surgery. Despite her years of activity in her community, she is considered fairly retiring in the sense that she rarely discusses personal matters with acquaintances, or even with friends of long standing."

Henny paused until every eye was on her. "Through artful interrogation of a bank manager's rather indiscreet wife"—the aforementioned artful inquisitor darted a glance at Lady Gwendolyn, who gave Henny a warmly admiring look, and even Henny looked pleased—"I have learned that Kathryn inherited a substantial estate upon her husband's death. Something in the neighborhood of seven hundred thousand dollars. However—" another pause for dramatic emphasis, "that estate has dwindled drastically, with the withdrawal of substantial sums at erratic intervals. The bank manager's wife sniffed, 'My George tried to talk to Kathryn about it—he was afraid some fast-talking, unethical investment counselor might be taking advantage of her, and, of course, George is quite capable of advising the bank's clients on good investments. But Kathryn got downright snippy, said what she did with her money was her business and no one else's, so of course George didn't say another word. But he told me it looks real funny, she goes along for months and has just her usual expenditures, then she'll draw out a cashier's check made to bearer for as much as sixty or seventy thousand dollars.' "

"That's quite interesting." Lady Gwendolyn's eyes glowed. "It could be blackmail. It could be the purchase of anything from diamonds to drugs."

"Drugs," Max repeated. "Kathryn Honeycutt?"

Lady Gwendolyn chuckled. "You'd be surprised what old ladies can do, young man."

This time, Max's ears turned crimson.

"Why, it's so simple," Laurel suggested.

Everyone looked at her. Laurel so often struck the truth in an oblique fashion that it never paid to dismiss her ideas.

Laurel smoothed back a wisp of golden hair. "Neil Bledsoe's certainly been accused of far worse. Perhaps he talks Kathryn out of the money, perhaps he demands it!"

Oddly, it was Annie who had to defend Bledsoe here. "No. I'll admit that sounds likely, but Kathryn told me she always turns him down when he asks for money and he usually *does* need money. As for this conference, she thought perhaps that's why he invited her, so she asked him. In fact, she offered him money. Bledsoe seemed very surprised by the offer. He even admitted to her that he was in a hole financially, but he told her he had a plan to get it; he didn't need any from her." Annie frowned. "And it turns out he really does have a plan—that nasty biography about Christie!"

Lady Gwendolyn tapped the table thoughtfully.

"People do reveal themselves in conversation. That's quite an important fact you gleaned, Annie." She gave each of them an approving nod. "I wish to compliment all of you upon your excellent efforts. We've certainly made good progress."

Her pink lips curved in an enigmatic smile. "Now, I do have a final note which isn't included in our papers. Local authorities have set in motion an intensive investigation of myself. I spoke to an old friend at Scotland Yard prior to our meeting this morning." Her blue eyes twinkled. "He had a bit of fun at my expense. He told your inquisitive circuit solicitor all about my recent book in which the victim, a young man, is bludgeoned by an old lady." Almost as an aside, she added, "I don't like age discrimination. Passion, sex, and vigorous activity should not be barred to the elderly." A pause. "And I learned that Posey inquired most insistently about my health and was told that I continue to ride to the hounds."

"You still jump?" Laurel asked, her eyes wide.

"Certainly. I haven't lost my seat. The point, however, is that the American authorities are seriously considering me for the role of chief suspect. The blood on my cape, which should be obvious to a child, is that of Stone. There would be no point to it otherwise. It is apparent to me that someone entered my suite prior to Stone's murder for the express purpose of obtaining apparel suitable for marking with incriminating bloodstains. That definitely reveals the Stone murder was premeditated. That fat fool seems to believe I sallied forth in my cloak and rather messily dispatched that poor young man."

Their immediate and indignant outburst included even Henny.

Lady Gwendolyn held up her hand. "Thank you. Thank you. A show of support is always appreciated. However, our current investigation is *not* an effort to clear me. Our sole purpose is to prevent another murder." She leaned forward and looked soberly at each in turn. "Here is my plan."

AGATHA CHRISTIE
TITLE CLUE

She had to die;
Poirot finds out why.

21

rasher of bacon, a Belgian waffle with whipped cream, applesauce, and a big glass of orange juice," Annie said pugnaciously.

If Max had reservations, he kept them to himself. Picking up the telephone, he punched the button for room service and cheerfully repeated her order.

When he hung up, Annie snapped, "Why didn't you get something for yourself?"

"Annie, we've already had breakfast. But I'll make some fresh coffee."

As if a few more cups of coffee would be enough to restore the energy leached by several hours of consultation with Lady Gwendolyn, Laurel, and Henny. Of course, she and Max were lucky the trio had departed, each with a specific objective. But, first things first. "Max, that was *hours* ago. *Nothing* eaten before seven in the morning counts." She glanced at the clock. Almost ten. And she had *so* much to do. Lady Gwendolyn seemed to have forgotten that Annie was still running a conference. It was Thursday, and this morning was devoted to current, well-known mystery writers, especially Elizabeth Peters/Barbara Michaels and Charlotte MacLeod/Alisa Craig. Even thinking of them put Annie in a better humor. And this afternoon would focus on Tony Hillerman and Aaron Elkins, two of the most likable best-selling authors she'd ever encountered. Oh, her wonderful conference. She felt a pang of guilt. A young man's murder needed to be solved, and, perhaps, another murder

prevented—but it *was* a wonderful conference. And tomorrow night—
Friday night—was the *pièce de résistance,* the wonderful, glorious Agatha
Christie Come-as-You-Wish-You-Were Ball. It wasn't wrong to look forward eagerly to that grand moment. And it gave her even more impetus
to try and solve the crime as quickly as possible.

So, somehow, between sessions, Annie must discharge the task Lady
Gwendolyn had assigned. Although it was flattering to be chosen, she
still wondered at the reason why. Lady Gwendolyn's brisk comment—
"Annie, my dear, you won't be misled by nuances"—mystified her.

What nuances?

Jean Reinhardt's tight blond curls quivered as she shook her head.
"No, I don't think I know . . ." She turned the graduation photo of Stone
to better catch the light in the foyer outside Meeting Room B. "Wait a
minute. Yes, yes, yes . . . at the publishing course. Oh, Jesus. The guy
with the manuscript with all the missing feet." Her nose wrinkled. "Honest to God, you wouldn't believe some of the manuscripts we get. No
expletives deleted, and the way some writers confuse reality with de-
scriptions of body functions . . ." A sigh.

"Have you seen this morning's paper?" Annie asked.

The editor nodded. "Sure."

"You missed his picture?" Annie asked, surprised.

The editor was surprised in turn. She looked at Stone's photo again.
"In the *Times*?"

"Oh, no, the local paper. The *Island Gazette.*" Annie whipped a
copy from under her arm. Stone's murder, of course, had run in the
Wednesday paper, but it was still the top story in today's.

Reinhardt took the paper. "Well, I'll be damned. So this is the guy
who was killed. Small world."

"What did you think about him?" Annie asked.

A shrug. "Not much. Harder to shake than plaster of Paris. Seemed
to think taking the course gave him every right to try and waylay you
after work to talk about his book again."

"Did you know he was here at this conference?" Annie asked.

"Lord, no." She scanned the story at an editor's whip-flash reading
rate. "Funny. I would have classed him as an obtuse jerk. Who would
ever have thought he would end up murdered?"

· · ·

In the dealers' room, Annie stopped at the Death on Demand booth which Ingrid's good friend, Duane Webb, was minding. Annie hoped that Duane, a former newspaperman, an ex-drunk, and not a sufferer of fools, was also minding his tongue.

"How's it going?" She straightened the front row of second-hand paperbacks, all in good condition and priced at three dollars each, noting a few titles: *Dead Letter* by Douglas Clark, *Too Hot for Hawaii* by Thomas B. Dewey, *Bitter Finish* by Linda Barnes, and *Somewhere in the House* by Elizabeth Daly.

"Gangbusters." There was a note of bravado in Duane's gravelly voice. "Except . . . uh . . ." He smoothed his balding head sheepishly. "Could've sold all the Shaw books." He pointed at the top row of the case to his left. Annie had displayed separately books by conference attendees or those being especially honored. "Told the guy to fuck off."

Annie waited. She couldn't read Duane's eyes behind the thick lens of his glasses.

"The jerk that's causing all the trouble, threatening to slander Christie," Duane explained.

"Oh, Duane." She leaned forward and kissed his cheek. "You wonderful S.O.B."

She was still grinning when Henny pounced on her as she came out the door.

Grabbing Annie's arm, Henny tugged her behind a pillar. "Annie, you're not going to believe this!" Outrage warred with amusement in her tone.

Such words could only herald information about a particular circuit solicitor. "Let me guess. Posey's arrested Fleur Calloway!" Among those known to dislike Bledsoe, Fleur alone had to be considered free of suspicion. She and Annie were standing at the coffee bar in Death on Demand when the shots rang out Saturday night.

"It's not that bad. But it's the damndest thing. For starters, Posey's just back from a law enforcement conference that stressed multiple lines of inquiry in a homicide investigation." Henny looked bemused. "His new favorite expression is, 'In the alternative . . .' "

"You mean he hasn't glommed onto one theory to the exclusion of all others?" Annie asked. Actually, such open-mindedness would be a marked improvement for her least favorite circuit solicitor.

"By no means. Okay. Theory Number One: Lady Gwendolyn, a known Christie partisan, is so immersed in Christie lore that she has crossed over the edge of sanity and is committing murder using methods in Christie novels."

"Lugging an ornamental bronze sugar cutter all the way from England, of course," Annie said sarcastically. But, if that was Theory One, surely Posey was much closer to reality with Theory Two. "I suppose he's checking out everybody to see if someone's trying to hide behind the crazed-Christie image to get at Bledsoe?"

"No such luck. No such sanity. No such sensible alternative inquiry," Henny sputtered in disgust. "No, Posey's Theory Number Two: Stone was the victim of a drug war!"

"A drug war?"

"Yes. And guess who's in on it?"

Annie scarcely knew where to start. With Posey, anything was possible. Laurel. The president of the local PTA. The diocesan bishop.

"Bledsoe!" Henny whooped. "Oh, God, is he pissed! Posey's been grilling Bledsoe all morning. Posey's alternative theory is that the attempts on Bledsoe's life and the murder of Stone are the action of a drug ring trying to discipline its members."

Annie had the same sense of unreality she sometimes experienced in second-rate hard-boiled novels. The words were presented in utter seriousness, and they were absurd. (*The slug caught him just below the shoulder. Threw him back against the wall. He shoved away from the wall, caught the first thug with a karate chop to the neck, kung fu'd the second guy, looked for a way out. In a haze of pain, sweat beading his face, he tumbled through the window onto the fire escape, and started up, two rungs at a time, blood spattering as he went. He ignored the shouts behind him. The second slug creased his leg. On the next floor, a scowl twisting his face, he kicked in the window. Rose was waiting. Almost like she'd known he'd come. She lifted her hand in a silent plea. He gave her a tired grin. 'It's too late, sister,' he said softly. He pulled the .45. He hated to do it. God, she was pretty. But the prettiness was all on the outside. The gun bucked in his hand as he shot. He watched her die. Just like she'd watched Al die.*)

"A drug war," Annie repeated. "What led our stalwart officer of the law to that creative conclusion?"

"The autopsy. Posey got the results this morning," Henny explained. "Stone had traces of cocaine in his blood."

"So?" Illegal, stupid, and dangerous, but not surprising in his age group and certainly not evidence of criminal conspiracy.

Henny grinned cynically. "They had a huge cocaine bust on Hilton Head a year or so ago. I imagine Posey's hungering for the kind of publicity that engendered."

Annie remembered the bust, of course. It was the largest haul ever in South Carolina, one hundred million dollars' worth of pure cocaine. A story with some piquant angles. Such as the lawyers found digging in the backyard of one of the defendants. This unusual display of manual labor by members of the bar encouraged digging by the authorities. The result: buried lawn bags stuffed with cash. *Beaucoup* cash.

"I see," Annie mused. "Are Stone and Bledsoe supposed to be smugglers who've fallen out with the Colombian cartel, or independent jobbers in a turf war?"

"Posey hasn't let anybody in on the fine points of his investigation yet," Henny said sardonically. "Of course, he's hacked that Bledsoe's the only person in the hotel officially alibied for Stone's death. Saulter had Billy Cameron on duty Tuesday night, just down the hall from Bledsoe's suite. Billy saw Bledsoe go in his room, even said good night to him. He didn't come out all night."

"Sounds to me like Posey's busy proving he was born without any little gray cells." But Annie was thinking about Billy Cameron's night duty. "So Saulter has Billy watching Bledsoe." It was odd how relieved she felt. She might despise the man, but she certainly didn't want to see him murdered.

"Yes. Posey approves, of course. He told Bledsoe someone would be watching him from now on—so they can break the drug ring when somebody tries again to kill him."

Annie laughed out loud.

But Henny didn't smile. "The problem is, Annie, Posey's told the chief to concentrate on the hotel and question all the employees about possible smuggling activities."

"That will drive the manager bananas."

Henny brushed that aside. "It also means any investigation of the key suspects has come to a screeching halt."

"So?"

"So that leaves it squarely up to us." Henny gave a Bulldog Drummond salute and swung toward the door.

•   •   •

Annie glimpsed the other investigators—Lady Gwendolyn, Henny, Laurel, and, of course, Max—at odd moments during the day. Each was assigned one or two suspects. Their task was simple: To contact their suspects and confidentially, oh, so very confidentially, but with pointed looks suggesting the information might be very important to the listener, report it had been learned that the police knew the murderer's identity and an arrest was imminent.

As the early morning meeting in their suite had ended, Annie couldn't resist twitting Lady Gwendolyn—after all, this was one of the hoariest ploys in the history of fiction (*Flee, All Is Discovered*). "Do you really think anyone will fall for that?" Lady Gwendolyn had grinned impishly. "The point, my dear, is that the guilty flee even where no man pursueth. Of course, no one will quite believe it, but can anyone quite dare to disbelieve it? I don't expect a sudden, guilt-revealing exodus from the hotel. But I do think it might—just might—discourage the murderer from acting again."

Annie found Terry Abbott, the other editor who had been on the staff when Stone attended the publishing course, coming out of the bar shortly before lunch. He glanced casually at Stone's photographs. "Oh, the guy who got killed." So he, at least, had read the *Gazette*. "I remember him. The kid really hounded us editors. He was sure he was the next Ludlum and he couldn't wait to tell you about it. Only one problem: He had no talent."

Neil Bledsoe lounged at his ease in the Palmetto Court, at a table situated precisely where the vase had landed.

Annie held out the photographs of Stone.

His dark brows drew down in a frown. "Yeah. I know that face."

In a now familiar gesture, Annie handed him that day's *Island Gazette*.

"I'll be damned. So that's the chump who got bumped off. Oh, hell yes, I remember him. What a bore. Pestered me for months about his damn manuscript, thought I could get him an editor."

True to her firm instructions from Lady Gwendolyn, Annie tried to analyze Bledsoe's initial reaction. Irritation at being accosted? Yes. And disinterest. Until the realization that this was the murdered guest.

Margo Wright patted her perspiration-streaked face with the thick terry-cloth towel. The waters in the Jacuzzi swirled and foamed around her slender body. "Sure. I remember that creep. So what? I didn't bash his head in."

No trace of concern on Margo's part. Only a sharp spasm of irritation at being questioned.

Derek Davis opened the door to his room, saw Annie, and slammed it shut. But it was hard for Annie to dismiss the haunted look in his red-rimmed eyes. Just what was Derek trying to forget?

Emma Clyde leaned back in the rattan chair on the terrace. The wind rustled the fronds of the palmetto behind her. She took her time studying the pictures. "Never seen him before in my life." She handed the photos to Annie. "You keep on looking for trouble—someday you're going to find it."

Annie looked into the author's pale blue, cool eyes. "Emma, are you threatening me?"

"No. Just warning you, honey. For old time's sake."

"A student at the short course," Nathan Hillman said immediately. "But I had no more contact with him than with any other student."

The waiter skirted Annie to offer Hillman and Natalie Marlow more coffee.

Annie didn't feel especially welcome. Hillman's pleasant face was set in rigid lines, and the young author was clearly disinterested.

Annie held out the photographs to Natalie.

The writer didn't take them. She shook her head. "The guy who was killed? I didn't know him."

·   ·   ·

Kathryn Honeycutt stopped outside Meeting Room C. She bent her fluffy white head and listened politely.

"Oh, that young man who was killed." She took the pictures, held them close to her eyes, squinted. Then she shook her head dolefully. "I'm so sorry, my dear. I just can't see well enough anymore. But I don't *think* I ever met him."

It was late afternoon when Annie found Fleur Calloway. The writer was coming in the main entrance of the hotel, a sun hat in her hand. Her face was flushed with exertion. She stopped by the bank of telephones and listened patiently to Annie's question, then studied Stone's photographs.

"Oh, yes. Yes, I signed a book for him Tuesday afternoon." She shivered. "It seems cold in here after the heat outside. I took a long walk in the forest preserve." She gave the pictures back to Annie. "It's so dreadful, isn't it? Hatred and anger, twisting the world, destroying lives. Why does it have to be this way?"

Lady Gwendolyn was the primary speaker at that evening's after-dinner session. As the conference-goers wandered in:

"I always loved Poirot's description of Ariadne Oliver, an 'original if untidy mind.'"

"Honestly, this guy poisoned six people with thallium and would have got away with it if a forensic specialist hadn't read *The Pale Horse* and recognized the symptoms!"

"Joan Hickson is simply the best Miss Marple in the world."

"I like the symmetry of it, *The Mysterious Affair at Styles* and *Curtain*."

"She wrote the short story, 'Three Blind Mice,' before she wrote *The Mousetrap*. God, *Mousetrap*'s *still* running in London!"

Annie spotted Victoria Shaw.

The author's widow introduced Annie to several women, "fans of Bryan's." She looked happier than Annie had ever seen her. But when she took the photographs from Annie, her smile fled.

"Oh, that poor young man. I still can't believe something like that happened here, so close to all of us!" Victoria shook her head. "No, I've never seen him . . . so far as I know."

· · ·

Laurel clapped her hands. "I've ordered champagne. Such a *superb* speech, Lady Gwendolyn."

Henny ignored Laurel. She had managed a moderately graceful compliment to Lady Gwendolyn on their way upstairs in the elevator. She took her place at the table. "So far, so good today. I mean, no more bodies. But honestly, I can't say I think we made any progress."

Annie handed Max a couple of bowls of nuts to place on the table in the living room, then hurried to take her place. She wondered if the honeymoon suite had ever before served as consultation headquarters in a murder investigation. Not that the amenities of the suite were being—at appropriate times—completely ignored.

Lady Gwendolyn plumped into her chair. She didn't respond directly to Henny's challenge. "Today our ostensible mission was to remind suspects that the investigation is continuing, to imply that an arrest is imminent, and to explore the links between Stone and those attending this conference."

The champagne arrived and Max presented a foaming glass to each.

Lady Gwendolyn lifted her glass. "I commend each and every one of you. Our duties were discharged with élan." She tipped her glass and all followed suit.

Annie sputtered. Champagne always made her nose tickle.

Undeterred by the bubbles, the famed author drained her glass. "You will note that I referred to our 'ostensible' mission. Henny was quick to question the effectiveness. Now, the question arises, what is our *real* mission?" Those bright blue eyes moved from face to face. "We must fight with the weapons at hand from a perilously ill-equipped arsenal. Since the fat fool has focused on me and on a spurious cocaine ring, I am certain our murderer is positively elated. So, we have attempted subtle intimidation and harassment. Were we successful?" The coronet braids wobbled as she shrugged and held her glass out to Max for a refill. "Actually, that success or failure is irrelevant. Our real mission today was to prevent another murder. In that, we have succeeded gloriously. We engaged the attention of all the suspects throughout the day. Tonight we may rest easy. Bledsoe will be under the direct scrutiny and, therefore, the protection of the constabulary. Tomorrow is the last full day of conference. Once again we must serve as guardian angels—and this will be the critical period. If we fail, someone will unquestionably die."

Annie shuddered at the grimness of her tone.

AGATHA CHRISTIE
TITLE CLUE

Frankie crashes the car,
But that doesn't get her very far.

22

She was a hapless egg in a blender, being whipped around and around. She burrowed deeper into the pillow, but the shaking continued. She had been enjoying a lovely dream, a stroll through a Godiva factory. The smell of chocolate permeated the air, thicker than attar of roses. She wanted to go back to that wonderful aroma. She didn't *like* being an egg. Who could possibly like being an egg? Beaten. Discriminated against. Certainly not treasured for scent. The dream segued into a Fourth of July sequence, exploding fireworks and the acrid smell of smoke—

"Annie, Annie, wake up!" She was being pulled roughly out of bed. The *pop-pop-pop!* of fireworks continued.

As Max swept her off her feet and into his arms, she came thrashing to wakefulness. Her nose wrinkled at the sulfurous odor.

"Fire," he said grimly. As he spoke, another flurry of pops sounded, then were overborne by the piercing shrill of a fire alarm. Max kept a tight grip on her elbow and hustled her toward the bathroom. Inside, he yanked down towels with one hand, held to her with the other.

Annie wriggled free. "I'm awake." She pushed the light switch. No light.

"Great," she muttered. A sopping towel was thrust into her arms.

"Hold on to my shorts," Max ordered. "Stay down. We'll try the door."

It was blindman's bluff with a vengeance and darker than the shades of hell (one of Annie's favorite mental images—she could just see gray forms writhing in a stygian dark). Max swore when he bumped into the wrought-iron railing that separated the foyer from the living area.

"The door isn't hot," he announced. "That's a good sign."

But when he edged it open, a stinging cloud of smoke wafted in. He slammed the door shut.

"We'd better try the balcony."

By the time they reached the balcony, the scent of smoke seemed lighter. Cries for help echoed in the night. "Stay right here." Max shouted to be heard over the cacophony of sounds, sirens, cries, calls for help, and the continuing sputter of firecrackers. "I want to see if Laurel's okay," and he turned right.

She still clung to his shorts. "I'll come, too," she yelled.

"Annie, Max, my dears—" The voice sounded almost beside them, husky, disembodied. A beam of light from a small flash shone from the adjoining balcony. It settled briefly on Annie, who was wearing a very see-through shorty nightgown, leapt discreetly to Max. "Such excitement. Why, it reminds me of the fireworks at Cannes. I met such a darling young man there—Georges—the fireworks blazing in the night sky in accompaniment to—" a pause—"oh, look, here are the lights."

They came on in abundance.

Annie had a confused picture of the scene.

In the courtyard below, hotel guests stopped in midflight to look up fearfully.

Guests in assorted kinds of sleepwear, clutching wet towels, crowded to the edge of their balconies on the upper floors.

The night manager, the only person fully dressed, dashed into the courtyard, shouting, "False alarm! False alarm! No fire! Remain in your rooms!"

"There's smoke in the hall!" screeched a woman from a balcony near theirs.

The manager, panting, yelled, "Vandals. Vandals. Smoke bombs. No danger. Stay in your rooms!"

Another siren pierced the air.

The manager lifted his hands. "The police are coming."

"A doctor! Help! A doctor," a deep voice called out raggedly.

Annie turned and reached out to clutch Max's arm.

Three balconies away, Neil Bledsoe wavered unsteadily, visible in the wash of lights from the courtyard. Blood streaked the thick mat of black hair on his heaving chest and the limp form he cradled in his arms.

Annie paced angrily up and down the living room. "Who do they think they are"—her hand waved toward the hall door—"the cops in *Fletch?*"

"Now, Annie." Max yawned. "Crime scene," he observed wearily, stretching his long legs out before him. "How can they investigate if frantic hotel guests are swarming around like lemmings?" He patted the couch beside him. "Come on, honey. Relax. Saulter'll let us out as soon as they finish. Besides, what do you want out for?" he asked practically. He pointed at the shell clock over the wet bar. "It's only a quarter to four."

She plopped onto the couch and stared morosely at the door. "Oh, Max, it's so dreadful. Poor Kathryn Honeycutt. She was so proud of looking like Miss Marple." Tears stung her eyes. "Oh, God, if only she'd really *been* like Miss Marple, able to see and understand evil around her. And we tried, we all tried, didn't we? But we lost. We should have known it wasn't enough, just to have Billy Cameron guarding Bledsoe's door. And, dammit," the tears streaked her cheeks, "even if someone went after Bledsoe, why did they have to shoot *her?* Oh, Max."

He pulled her close to him, and she buried her head in his shoulder.

Max poured the freshly brewed coffee into a thermos and glanced at the honey-blond head bent over a notebook. Dear Annie. She always tried so hard. And she was determined, somehow, someway, to find Kathryn Honeycutt's killer. He poured out two cups of coffee, set one beside her. Without looking up, she nodded her thanks. Max took his cup and returned to the divan. The coffee gave him energy. He picked up his pen and began to write:

SUSPECTS/TIMETABLE

Persons on the island known to have some connection with Neil Bledsoe:

Kathryn Honeycutt
Fleur Calloway
Emma Clyde
Margo Wright
Nathan Hillman
Derek Davis
Victoria Shaw
Natalie Marlow.

SATURDAY NIGHT: Shots miss Neil Bledsoe outside Death on Demand.

Possible suspects: Emma Clyde
                        Margo Wright
                        Nathan Hillman
                        Derek Davis
                        Victoria Shaw
                        Natalie Marlow.

Alibied: Fleur Calloway
                        Kathryn Honeycutt.

TUESDAY MORNING: Vase topples from hotel roof, narrowly misses Bledsoe.
Possible suspects: Margo Wright, Nathan Hillman, Derek Davis, Emma Clyde, Fleur Calloway, Victoria Shaw, Kathryn Honeycutt.

TUESDAY NIGHT: John Border Stone (registered as James Bentley, character in Christie's *Mrs. McGinty's Dead*) struck down with sugar cutter in his hotel room. Lady Gwendolyn's cape found in her room with blood on it. Tests show it is Stone's blood. Blood smears on hotel walls between Lady Gwendolyn's room and Stone's. (Traces of roof tar found on tennis shoes in his room.)
Possible suspects: All of the above.

EARLY FRIDAY MORNING: Attack on Bledsoe; Honeycutt killed.
Possible suspects: All of the above, except for Honeycutt.

Max chewed thoughtfully on his pen. First, cross out the impossibles. Quickly, he marked through Kathryn Honeycutt and Fleur Calloway. That left Emma Clyde, Margo Wright, Nathan Hillman, Derek Davis, Victoria Shaw, and Natalie Marlow.

Okay, here were the suspects. Now to rank them in order of probability—

The phone rang.

Annie reached for it and glanced at the clock. It was shortly after four A.M.

"Outmaneuvered. Outflanked. Outfoxed," Henny announced. "But not outdone."

"Are you out of your room?" Annie demanded, ready to demand her rights.

"Everyone's been sequestered," Henny retorted.

At Max's inquiring look, Annie put her hand over the receiver and mouthed, "Henny. Intrepid sleuth. Tuppence, I think."

"It always helps to know people," Henny continued rapidly. "Good thing I'm on the town council and also chairman of the hospital board."

"Oh. Who did you wake up?" Annie was well acquainted with Henny's methods.

"Vince Ellis. According to him, Bledsoe's already been treated and released. He refused hospitalization and is back at the hotel, talking to Posey and Saulter. Bledsoe's threatening revenge for his aunt's murder."

That was good thinking on Henny's part. The editor and publisher of the *Island Gazette* would be grateful for the news tip and honor-bound to share his gleanings.

"Then I talked to the head night nurse. Bledsoe's injury is painful and he's lost a good deal of blood, but it isn't serious unless infection sets in. He was shot once in the shoulder, but the shot missed the bone. Kathryn Honeycutt was shot three times." Henny paused and added gruffly, "Once in the face, twice in the chest. She was dead on arrival.

"According to the head nurse, Bledsoe gave this account: He was awakened by the fire alarm. He smelled smoke and heard pops, which he recognized as firecrackers. That puzzled him, but he felt the alarm must be responded to. He wet some towels and awakened his aunt. She had a traveler's flashlight. He was opening the door to check the hall when the door was shoved hard against him. Caught by surprise, he stumbled backwards. A flashlight turned on him from the doorway and then a gun fired. He was hit in the shoulder. He dived instinctively for cover. Honeycutt apparently aimed her flash at the doorway, screamed, 'Oh, you—,' there was a flurry of shots and Honeycutt fell. Bledsoe staggered to his feet, dizzy and weak from blood loss, found Honeycutt—her flash was lying by her, still on—picked her up, stumbled out to the balcony and yelled for help."

"Did Bledsoe get a look at their attacker?"

"No. Apparently he dived behind the couch, and the rest of it just took seconds, then he was concentrating on Honeycutt."

"Did anybody see someone running?"

A pause. Henny said kindly, "Dozens, my dear. You've forgotten the fire alarm and the smoke bombs and the firecrackers and the tripped breakers."

"Smoke bombs and firecrackers and an electrical blackout—you know, we need to think about this, really think about it." Annie shoved a hand through her unruly hair. "What kind of person would go to such elaborate—"

Henny interrupted impatiently. "Billy Cameron, of course."

For an instant, Annie thought her best customer had taken leave of her senses. Billy Cameron, Chief Saulter's assistant, was about as imaginative as a Doctor Watson, though incredibly athletic and—"Oh, God, Billy was watching Bledsoe's suite. Wasn't he?"

"You got it. He was pretty relaxed. I mean, nobody'd been out in the hall for a couple of hours. Billy was reading the latest George V. Higgins. Quiet as a graveyard. Then some firecrackers—Billy thought some pretty big ones—went off about a quarter to three. Sounded like it was out near the pool. The lights went out. Billy decided he'd better check it out. He started down the stairs and somebody cracked him over the head. He recovered consciousness at the hospital. Doesn't remember a thing after he started down the stairs."

"Billy's going to be all right?" Annie asked anxiously.

"Fine. Nurse said he'd have a lousy headache for a couple of days, but otherwise he's okay." A pause, and, for a moment, Henny dropped her investigator's persona. "Poor Billy. He figures it's his fault Bledsoe got wounded and Mrs. Honeycutt killed. Billy said he should have realized he was being decoyed, but his first instinct, at the possibility of fire, was to check, to see if he needed to raise an alarm. The chief told him he'd done his best and he was right to think of all the hotel guests and their safety. But Billy's lower than a hound dog's belly."

"Oh, Henny, please tell Billy we're all proud of him. We know he did his best. And listen, he'd better be glad he went downstairs to see if he was needed. If he hadn't, what're the odds he would be dead now, too? This killer doesn't care who gets hurt."

But Annie knew just how Billy felt. To think you might have made a difference was painful, no matter how good your intentions.

Annie's fingers drummed impatiently on the tabletop. "Dammit, Henny, we need to get out of our rooms and find out how the killer did it. Where the fireworks—"

"Nero Wolfe never left the brownstone. At least, hardly ever. And I haven't left this room, but I'm making progress. You can expect a complete report on the deployment of the fireworks within the hour." The line went dead.

Annie stared curiously at the phone, then hung it up. "Henny says she'll call back within the hour and tell us how the killer engineered the firecrackers and smoke bombs—all without setting foot outside her room."

Max chuckled. "If she manages that, we'll have to admit she's the best detective of all."

Annie didn't bother to answer. Certainly, *she* knew who was the best detective—and it was neither Henny nor Laurel nor Emma Clyde nor Lady Gwendolyn, however much each might aspire to that role. Who but Annie was on such intimate footing with the greatest detective of all time? Now, if she were Hercule Poirot, what would she do?

Employ the little gray cells, of course.

But she was already doing that.

Poirot, Poirot—he always enjoined Hastings to study the personality of the victims. Because in their lives were the seeds of their deaths.

But not, she thought dispiritedly, this time.

She picked up the blue-backed folder with the bios. No, it wouldn't help to reread them. Still, she opened it up, flipped through the pages, glancing at the names. Behind some familiar face, hidden behind everyday expressions of anger or concern or despair, was a ravening hunger for revenge. Someone whose name was in this folder was determined to see Neil Bledsoe pay for the evil he had wrought. Who was the wolf among the sheep or, as Christie put it so well, the cat among the pigeons?

AGATHA CHRISTIE
TITLE CLUE

A mislabeled path at Victoria Falls;
Look for the answer in the wooden
giraffe.

23

heriff's deputies were everywhere. Hotel guests were permitted to leave their rooms only after the police completed a room-by-room survey, setting up interviews at ten-minute intervals in Meeting Room A, beginning at nine A.M.

The atmosphere in the Palmetto Court that morning was subdued. Low-voiced conversations, furtive glances, and somber faces created a funereal atmosphere. Every eye watched as Saulter and Posey strode through the court shortly before nine. Saulter's khaki uniform looked crumpled and creased; his lean face sagged with fatigue. Posey lacked his usual sartorial splendor, his tie loose at his opened collar, his un-shaven cheeks covered with stubble.

Lady Gwendolyn's plump, pink face creased in an unaccustomed frown. "I was so confident. And yet our efforts failed. With the tragic addition of an innocent victim. What did I overlook?" She propped her chin in a pudgy hand and sank into a reverie.

Annie started to speak, but Laurel quickly held a finger to her lips. "Thinking," she whispered huskily.

Henny looked up irritably from her sketch pad, sniffed sardonically, then returned to her work. When Annie'd inquired earlier, Henny had briefly replied, "Fireworks placement."

Max gave his mother a quick smile.

Annie finished a last sip of coffee, but she didn't feel her customary morning zing. She sighed heavily. She had come to a decision, and a painful one it was.

"I've made up my mind. The conference is over. Ended. No more." She tried hard to keep the tremor out of her voice.

"Annie, why? Tomorrow's the last day anyway," Max pointed out.

Lady Gwendolyn, deep in thought, ignored them.

Laurel's blue eyes darkened in distress. "Shh, my dears. We must give Lady Gwendolyn every opportunity to exercise her brilliance."

Annie wasn't deflected. She pushed away the plate with its untouched waffle. "I'm not going to be responsible for anyone else being hurt—or killed. If I had cancelled the conference when somebody tried to shoot Bledsoe at Death on Demand or after the vase almost hit him, Kathryn Honeycutt would be alive. Maybe Stone, too."

"Look, Annie," Max said reasonably, "you're not a psychic. Anyone who found those incidents upsetting—including Kathryn—could have left the island. These murders didn't happen *because* of The Christie Caper, and it's unfair to blame yourself."

"Maybe. But I've made up my mind." She avoided Max's glance. He was on her side, and she loved him for it, but she felt responsible for those who had journeyed to Broward's Rock for The Christie Caper. She could no longer ignore danger to them, and it was only too clear after two murders and a wounding that a deadly predator was among them.

Even though it broke her heart to close down her wonderful conference.

Annie posted the last sign on the doors of Meeting Room D:

NOTICE
EMERGENCY MEETING
ALL REGISTRANTS
THE CHRISTIE CAPER
1 P.M. FRIDAY, SEPTEMBER 14
MAIN BALLROOM

She reached out and touched the date. Tomorrow would be the one hundredth anniversary of the birth of Agatha Mary Clarissa Miller Christie Mallowan. Fleur Calloway was scheduled to speak at the closing luncheon of The Christie Caper in honor of the greatest mystery writer of all time. Wouldn't Christie be astounded to know that a meeting to honor her had been cancelled because of murder?

No.

Annie felt certain that Dame Agatha wouldn't be at all surprised. Miss Marple's quiet observation in "The Bloodstained Pavement" rang in her head: "I hope you dear young people will never realize how very wicked the world is."

Annie glanced at her watch. Thirty minutes and The Christie Caper would be history.

A collective sigh from her listeners rivaled the poignant cry of a Carolina dove. Annie steeled her heart. She avoided looking at the front row where Max sat. She might weep. As she scanned the audience, she couldn't help noting particular faces:

Nathan Hillman no longer appeared genial. Tight lines bracketed the editor's mouth, and his eyes were wary.

Derek Davis had shaved spottily and nicked an ugly gash in his chin. Dark glasses hid his eyes.

Natalie Marlow's new hairdo framed a hollow-eyed face. Her mouth was a thin, straight, tight line.

Margo Wright gazed at Annie with utterly unreadable eyes.

Victoria Shaw sat with folded hands, eyes downcast.

Emma Clyde's spiky hair glinted emerald in the light from the chandeliers. It did nothing to add charm to her square, blunt features.

Fleur Calloway stared toward the door, one hand at her throat.

Neil Bledsoe stood there, one heavily wrapped arm in a sling, his white suit jacket loose on his shoulders. The ashy grayness of his face emphasized the rage glittering in his penetrating eyes.

Oh, yes, time and time enough to end this. "I want to thank all of you for being such grand participants," Annie said, "and I regret more than I can say the necessity for ending the conference at this time, but I'm sure—"

"Just one moment, please, dear Annie."

The sweet, light yet authoritative voice would have caught the attention of a court full of justices, a forum filled with Roman senators, a gaggle of five-year-olds at a birthday party.

Annie's immediate, "Now, Lady Gwendolyn..." was swiftly overborne as the elderly author bounded vigorously up the platform steps, moving so quickly her coronet braids seemed to dance atop her head.

Near the open doorway, Posey grabbed Saulter's arm and pointed toward the stage.

Lady Gwendolyn faced the audience with a kindly smile. Her reddish hair emphasized the pink-and-cream of her complexion. Her gray silk dress shimmered like London fog in November. "I feel that we face a simple question here. What is our duty, yours and mine: to stay? or to go?" In her swift and vivid fashion, Lady Gwendolyn captured the hearts of her listeners. Gently shushing Annie's attempts to interrupt, the silver-tongued author built her case, quoting from mystery greats of past and present. By the time she finished, she had the conference-goers on their feet.

Even Henny cheered. "Good show! Bully! Get the blighter!"

Annie made frantic motions at Max, but he lifted his hands to indicate helplessness—and tried not to grin.

"Are we crime experts?" Lady Gwendolyn demanded.

"Yeeees!"

"Shall we show the white flag?"

"Noooooooo!" Some in the back rows climbed on their chairs the better to see.

Annie thought miserably about broken bones and liability insurance.

"Shall we—in the name of all that our dear Dame Agatha treasured—remain at our posts, no matter what the cost?"

A roar of commitment.

"Let us go forth in pairs." Lady Gwendolyn spread her chubby hands wide. "Let us seek answers. Scour the vicinity, leaving not a stone unturned. Bring your reports and clues to Meeting Room D—and tonight! Tonight revel with your fellow investigators at the Agatha Christie Masquerade Ball here in the ballroom, and tomorrow—September fifteenth, the centenary of Agatha's birth—gather for the closing luncheon address by our wonderful guest author, Fleur Calloway." The cheers began. Lady Gwendolyn held up her hands to gain a lessening of the roar. She lifted her voice and announced, "And the luncheon will be followed—" a dramatic pause "—by the grand finale to The Christie Caper, the announcement by myself and my co-hostess, Annie Laurance Darling, of the identity of the murderer who has now struck twice in our midst!"

The huge room resounded with shouts and clapping. Max was clapping too until Annie eyed him sternly.

Lady Gwendolyn clapped happily in time with the cheers. Ardent admirers surrounded the platform. She reached down, shaking hands, smiling nonstop.

Annie glimpsed Saulter and Posey turning away from the doorway, leaving with the crowd. Saulter followed, shaking his head in vigorous disagreement.

At last the big room emptied. Max came up to the platform and looked uneasily from Annie to Lady Gwendolyn.

Annie stood stiff and straight, hands jammed into the pockets of her coral cotton skirt. "Lady Gwendolyn—" It came out a croak.

"I believe in luck, Annie. It's our turn, I feel it in my bones. We shall prevail." Lady Gwendolyn's primrose blue eyes blazed with conviction. She lifted her chin and turned to go.

"Lady Gwendolyn!"

She airily waved a plump hand, the sapphire flashing. "Be of good cheer, my dear. The faint of heart conquer not." A swirl of gray silk, and she was gone.

An almost suppressed chuckle.

Annie whirled and glared at Henny.

Unabashed, the island's mystery expert grinned. "Have to hand it to her, grandstander that she is. Don't sulk, Annie, she's saved your conference." Henny was imposing this morning—no doubt she had a board meeting to squeeze in at some point during the day—in a black silk noil dress accented by a pearl choker and a twisted cerise-and-cream silk belt.

Annie exploded. "Saved my conference . . . Henny, what if someone else is murdered?"

"Annie, my sweet, do stop trying to assume responsibility for the world. Unless you intend to shoot someone between now and noon tomorrow, your conscience should be clear." Henny glanced at her watch. "Come on, let's go to the terrace. I need a cup of coffee."

"Coffee?" Annie's voice cracked. "Is that all you're thinking about, coffee? What about the rest of the conference? Or is that just for me to worry about? And what about noon tomorrow, when we're supposed to magically come up with the name of the murderer? How could Lady Gwendolyn do this to *me*?"

Henny slipped an arm through Annie's. "Pairs, my dear, if they stay in pairs they'll be all right. After all, these are the savviest mystery readers in the world. They know the drill—no midnight forays in a tulle nightgown, no responding to a crumpled note suggesting an assignation in the back of the cemetery, no eating of chocolate creams delivered to the room by a secret admirer."

"Dammit—"

Henny lifted her voice and continued serenely, "As for the un-masking of the murderer, Lady Gwendolyn has you figured out—my dear, you *always* work better under pressure of a deadline. Doesn't she, Max?"

It didn't improve Annie's humor as they walked briskly toward the main lobby and the steps to the terrace café that the world seemed suddenly to have been Arked. Or Noahed. Or whatever one should call a populace abruptly divided into couples. Two by two. She didn't know whether to laugh at the obedient response of the conference-goers to Lady Gwendolyn's commands or to howl.

Howl.

"Henny, Max, my God, what's that noise?"

"Bloodhounds," Henny responded quickly.

Of course. No other dog in the world made quite that distinctive sound.

Her eyes alight, her fox-sharp nose quivering with excitement, Henny bolted ahead. "Come on, you two. Let's see what's happening."

Which was easier said than done.

The terrace was jammed with people. Everyone seemed to be looking toward one of the walls that provided a barrier of privacy for ground-floor rooms in the wings. At the far end of the wall, Laurel sat cross-legged, quite fetching in lime-green linen slacks and a raspberry blouse. Only on Laurel would the combination have been so attractive. She looked like a summer confection, good enough to eat. She saw them and gestured energetically for them to join her.

Annie reluctantly followed Henny and Max—dammit, why did everyone always respond to Laurel as if she were a queen—while searching for the dogs. The triumphant baying apparently was coming from about the center of the wall.

It took all of Max's tact and Henny's determination to edge their way past the thickest clumps of watchers to the end of the wall.

Laurel cooed, "My dears, *so* interesting. To and fro, to and fro. And with such *élan*."

Henny stood on the toes of her sleek black patent-leather pumps. "I can't see a thing," she groused.

Max grinned, scooped Henny up in his arms, and placed her on the wall, next to Laurel. They were a perfect foil for each other, Annie thought grumpily, elegance in sports attire and elegance in dress attire. Max turned to give Annie a hand. She ignored him, scrambling up by herself. He grinned and pulled himself up to join her. Even from this vantage point, there wasn't much to see. Three droopy-eared, slick-coated, abysmally homely hounds continued to bay, but the object of their attention was an apparently unremarkable spot of ground at the center of the wall upon which the quartet of observers sat.

"Exactly," Henny observed.

Annie looked at her expectantly.

Henny merely nodded importantly.

Laurel clapped her hands. "So perceptive of you, dear. Just like Miss Marple when bird-watching in St. Mary Mead."

Annie gritted her teeth. Someday Laurel was going to go too far, and that day might be imminent. As for Henny, this was maddening. Obviously, to discover what Henny meant, Annie was going to have to ask outright, thereby revealing that she hadn't the faintest idea what was interesting or why.

Annie's eyes slitted.

It could be a bluff.

If Annie asked and Henny had truly deduced something from the hounds' puzzling behavior, Annie lost face. (Shades of dear old Charlie Chan, a face-saver in the grand tradition.)

On the other hand, if Annie asked and Henny's Holmes-like behavior was shown to be a sham, Henny lost face in a big way.

"Exactly what?" Annie inquired in a dulcet tone.

"The hounds have traced the killer's route to that spot," Henny announced confidently.

Laurel beamed her approval. "Oh, my dears, such excitement." She turned to Annie. "I did hate to miss the meeting, but I felt sure Lady Gwendolyn would prevail."

Annie fought off an attack of apoplexy. So Lady Gwendolyn's appearance on the platform was not fortuitous. Somehow that made it worse. What gall. What arrogance. What infuriating chutzpah. And Laurel had connived in the treasonous plot!

Oblivious to Annie's mounting displeasure, Laurel chattered on. Even more displeasing, Henny and Max hung on her every word.

"... overheard Mr. Posey ordering the dogs. I awaited their arrival and followed their progress. Circumspectly, of course."

Oh, certainly, Annie thought. Nothing could possibly be more circumspect than an elegant blonde in a raspberry-lime combo atop a wall.

Suddenly authoritative, Laurel reported crisply, "During the early morning search by investigators, while we were restricted to our rooms, two items of especial interest were found, a pair of soft brown cotton men's gardening gloves, which unfortunately will not yield fingerprints, and—" here she paused for effect "—a twenty-two pistol."

"Where?" Annie demanded. So much for her resolution not to feed Laurel's pampered ego.

Laurel pointed over the heads of the crowd toward the center of the café area. "They found the gloves and gun there. They took the dogs up to the third floor to the Bledsoe suite and let them smell the gloves. Such sweeties," Laurel cooed, "especially the one with the mottled splotch over one eye that makes him look quite quizzical." Her glance swept over Annie. "Rather like Annie when she's puzzled. Dear fellows, all three."

"The hounds smelled the gloves," Max prompted gently.

"Oh, yes, of course." Laurel resumed her crisp tone. "The dogs went down the hall to the stairs, down the stairs, stopped and set up a lovely howl outside the closet with the breaker switches, then trotted outside to the terrace and went there and there and there"—Laurel waved gracefully, raspberry nails glistening in the sunlight, at various points around the perimeter of the terrace—"where the firecrackers and smoke bombs went off, then stopped at the center of the wall. And that's where they've stayed."

Annie and Max stared at the blank, unrevealing wall.

Henny snapped open her gleaming black patent-leather purse, pulled out a scratch pad, and began to draw. "Let's see, they started here..." A dark head and a blond head bent in consultation.

"I'd say the dear fellows could use some more scouting lessons," Annie said dryly. "I mean, why stop at the wall? That's a dead end." She leaned forward, and Max reached out to keep her from falling. "Oh, hey, why don't they take the dogs and go around to the other side? Maybe the murderer went over the wall there."

As if on cue, the handler motioned for the people pressing close to step back. The dogs broke into a trot. As they passed, it seemed to Annie they were tugging their handler along. They were close enough to see their reddish brown eyes, shiny black noses, and low-hanging ears. The dogs reached the end of the wall, turned, sniffed down the inside of the wall—and did not stop at the spot opposite their initial stand.

But Annie wasn't following their progress now. "Uh-oh," she warned, poking Henny with her elbow.

"I see him," Henny replied.

Brice Willard Posey, the circuit solicitor from the mainland, hustled importantly after the handler and his dogs. When the dogs passed the area opposite their sighting, Posey pompously exploded, "Those damn dogs have smelled too much dope. They didn't even hesitate where he must have jumped down."

The dogs had reached the other end of the wall now and were returning. They didn't stop at any point on the inside of the wall. Reaching the first end, their handler swept them around it and once again, yelping in delight, the hounds trotted straight for their original, unremarkable, unrevealing position and bayed energetically.

Hurrying in their wake, Posey's always red face turned yet a brighter hue. He stopped and glared at the yelping dogs. Hands on bulbous hips, watery blue eyes bulging dangerously, he berated the dogs' keeper. "Useless. Worse than useless. They're supposed to be able to smell something the killer's worn and track him. Right?" The circuit solicitor poked a stubby forefinger into the chest of the handler.

An arc of brown spit from the wad of smokeless tobacco in the dog owner's cheek curved dangerously close to Posey's dark blue suit. The wad shifted. "Did," came the laconic answer. The handler, whose mustache drooped in a manner of which Hercule Poirot would have stringently disapproved, pointed toward the middle of the café. "Gun. Gloves." Then he half turned, pointed across the terrace, close to the table where Bledsoe had been sitting when the vase fell. "Smoke bomb. Firecrackers." Turning, he pointed toward the end of the hotel wing behind the interested quartet. They craned to see better. "Breaker panels." The finger moved again, jabbing at the wing. "Interior stairs. More smoke bombs, firecrackers. Third floor, ditto. That's the route." He bent and stroked his dogs. "Good going, boys." Rising, he turned and began to stride toward the parking lot, the dogs trotting obediently beside him, with the look of choirboys who'd sung like angels.

Posey bellowed. "Wait a minute! What the hell did the guy do when he got to the wall? Sprout wings? Listen, this is a gyp. Where did he go from here?"

The handler didn't even break stride as he flipped one at Posey.

On the wall, the four tried to smother whoops of laughter.

They didn't quite manage.

Ponderously, Posey swung toward them. He glared for a long moment, then lumbered over to them.

Annie resisted the impulse to wish him a good day.

"Mrs. Darling." To say his tone held little warmth was to put it very nicely indeed. Since Annie was atop the wall, looking down, Posey had lost his usual psychological advantage of height. "I understand you had an altercation with Neil Bledsoe over the book he's going to write about Agatha Christie."

Annie's jaw jutted out. "You bet I did."

"Are you interrogating my wife, Posey?" Max dropped lightly down to the ground. His tone was pleasant.

Posey was taking a deep breath, preparatory, Annie felt sure, to a grand pronouncement of the duties and obligations of the circuit solicitor for this particular circuit in the sovereign State of South Carolina, when Frank Saulter, his crumpled uniform in sharp contrast to Posey's still crisp blue suit, hurried up. "Brice, a guest on the second floor thinks she saw the murderer last night, says he went past her balcony—"

"Did she say what size wings he had?" Posey's thick lips split in a derisive smile. Looking up, he gestured toward the hotel facade.

Annie looked up, too.

Lady Gwendolyn stood, hands apart on her balcony railing, surveying the scene below.

Trust the canny old author to find a superior vantage point.

"Lady Gwendolyn." Posey almost sounded like he was purring.

Startled, Annie glanced at the circuit solicitor and was immediately unnerved by his expression, a combination of satisfaction, stubbornness, and perverse anticipation.

"Enough nonsense. *I* can't be fooled." Posey turned, still with that air of immense self-satisfaction. "A concerted effort has been made by some to encourage authorities to concentrate their attention upon individuals *presumed* to have reason to kill Bledsoe."

"Oh, the drug runners?" Annie asked innocently.

Posey gave her the kind of look Fletch reserved for cats and ex-wives. "In a multipronged investigation, it is quite obvious that various theories will be considered and discarded before the ultimate focus is made." In other words, the circuit solicitor's hopes of aping the success of the Hilton Head police by uncovering a huge cocaine operation had been dashed by a murder committed with a .22 pistol and the aid of fireworks and smoke bombs. It was embarrassingly obvious, even to Posey, that Kathryn Honeycutt's murder, whatever its origins, certainly didn't involve ordinary, run-of-the-mill street criminals. Annie could imagine the incredulous response of a drug runner handed a .22 and a handful of firecrackers. Anyone who regularly read about the exploits of hoods such as Banana Bob and Ferocious Frankie knew the artillery was heavier and the action—grunt, slash, slam, and boom—straightforward.

However, since the suggestion of drug-related violence had been headlined in the *Island Gazette* after Stone's body was found, Posey couldn't disavow his initial statement.

Henny, who often displayed the compassionate instincts of a shark, now positioned herself for the kill. "Autopsies are such an aid to investigators, aren't they? Cocaine in Stone's bloodstream, Valium in Honeycutt's. Do you think a gang that handles both street and prescription drugs is involved?" Her smile rivaled that of a sand tiger shark when sighting its next meal.

Annie turned toward Henny in surprise. "The autopsy's already been done on Kathryn?"

"Underway." Henny tried not to sound overly pleased with herself. "The blood tests have been completed. Other work's continuing."

Annie had to hand it to Henny. Talk about contacts. Probably the tip had come from Vince Ellis at the *Gazette*, and Vince must have a real pipeline into the medical examiner's office.

Saulter tried to deflect an outburst from Posey. "If you've heard some of the autopsy results, Mrs. Brawley, you'll know Mrs. Honeycutt had ingested approximately five milligrams of Valium, which is well within the ordinary dosage prescribed by physicians. And as you may recall, Mrs. Honeycutt was considerably upset at the close of the Christie Trivia Quiz last night. She may reasonably have taken the Valium for a better night's sleep."

The pleasure in baiting Posey abruptly fled. Annie all too clearly remembered Kathryn's distress the previous night and the woman's announcement that she would leave the island this morning. Had she packed her bags, readied herself for bed, and taken the tranquilizer to ease into sleep, thinking tomorrow would be better, that tomorrow she would be rid of Neil Bledsoe and the island?

Posey ignored Saulter's efforts at peacemaking. He paced right up to the wall next to Henny. "Already know some stuff out of the autopsy, huh? Think you're pretty smart. Well, we'll see just how smart all of you people are." Posey's face rivaled a stormy sunset, interesting splotches of red vying with purple. Imperiously, he snapped at the unhappy Saulter, "Round them all up. Meeting Room C."

Annie couldn't help it. Like almost everyone in the meeting room—except Lady Gwendolyn, who sat perched on a front row chair, apparently in a state of suspended animation. "Thinking," Laurel explained admiringly—Annie kept glancing covertly at Neil Bledsoe.

Bledsoe was well aware of the glances. His angry eyes challenged his foes. The critic's usually ruddy complexion was ashen; he looked fatigued and crumpled. Unshaven, his jowls were almost obscured by bristles. The white suit jacket around his shoulders bunched over the bulky bandage beneath a polo shirt; his once crisp white trousers bore dark splotches and smears. His blood? Kathryn's blood? Annie looked away, looked back. Whatever he had suffered, Bledsoe had lost none of his combativeness. As each person entered, he raked them with a harsh, questioning gaze, as if demanding, Are you the one? Did you try to murder me? Did you kill Kathryn?

Annie leaned over to Max. "Posey shouldn't do this, he shouldn't put all of them in one room together."

"It's deliberate," Max said quietly. "Deliberate—and vicious."

Startled, Annie looked toward the front of the room.

Posey waited behind the lectern, watching avidly as each of the suspects entered, his watery blue eyes darting from each face to Bledsoe and back again. Occasionally, he reached out, made a notation upon the legal pad on the lectern. Frank Saulter stood on the platform, too, but, hands clasped behind his back, the police chief stared down at the floor, repugnance evident in every rigid line of his body.

In they came, one by one.

Nathan Hillman's squarish face bore no traces of geniality. The editor met Bledsoe's gaze with a somber look of distaste.

Her scarlet caftan almost matching the high color in her cheeks,

Emma Clyde stumped in, ignored Bledsoe, and marched directly to the front of the room. "Posey, I don't like a deputy sheriff arriving at my house and ordering me to accompany him. I want you to know that under no circumstances would I be here unless served with a warrant except for Fleur Calloway. I intend to make very certain that you treat Mrs. Calloway with respect. Do I make myself clear?"

Emma was one of the island's many millionaires. She was also a rabid Democrat with a multitude of personal contacts in the legislature.

Posey forced a conciliatory smile. "Mrs. Clyde, please, do take a comfortable seat. Certainly there is a misunderstanding. You are under no compulsion to be here. I merely thought you would want to be present in the interests of your friend, Mrs. Calloway."

Emma wasn't charmed. "Mrs. Calloway will answer no questions without the presence of an attorney." Turning, she stalked back to the last row and plopped down. Her green spiked hair quivered.

Victoria Shaw edged open the door, saw the others assembled, and scuttled inside. The widow sank timidly into another back seat. But the faded eyes that fastened on Bledsoe were stern with hatred.

Natalie Marlow stopped in the doorway. The young writer was once again dressed in faded dungarees and a mended khaki man's shirt, but Annie was pleased to see that her hair was smoothly brushed and her new makeup in place. She gave Bledsoe one scathing glance, then moved—and Annie almost smiled—with her shoulders up and her head high to sit next to Hillman, who reached over to squeeze her hand.

Both the editor and Emma Clyde stood when Fleur Calloway entered. Fleur was so remarkably lovely that even in these unpleasant circumstances there was, just for an instant, a sense of lightness and peace. The author's finely modeled face was grave, her lovely eyes weary and touched with sadness. She smiled at Nathan but slipped quietly up the last row to join Emma.

Not once did Fleur give any indication that she was aware of Bledsoe's presence.

Not by a turn of her head.

Not by a flicker of an eyelash.

Bledsoe's face turned an ugly muddy color. The anger in his eyes was frightening.

Posey marked vigorously on the legal pad.

Margo Wright stood in the doorway. The agent was a regal figure, her midnight black hair smooth, her handsome face impassive, her bright red, full lips firmly set. She shot an openly contemptuous glance at Bledsoe.

"Don't have too much fun, Neil." There was no mistaking the taunting edge in her voice. "It might come back to haunt you."

Posey pounced as she took a seat on the row in front of Annie. "Are you *threatening* Mr. Bledsoe, Ms. Wright?"

She regarded the circuit solicitor steadily. "Am I? Oh, certainly not," she replied sardonically. "I always have Neil's best interests at heart. Just as he does for all of us."

Posey placed his hands on the sides of the lectern and leaned forward. "It has appeared that someone, Ms. Wright, most certainly does not have Mr. Bledsoe's best interests at heart."

The agent ignored him. Opening her purse, she pulled out a compact and began to freshen her vivid makeup.

Posey flushed. He glanced at his legal pad, tapped his pen against a list. "Frank, I want everyone here. Where's Davis?"

The chief conferred briefly with a deputy at the door, then rejoined Posey on the platform.

The circuit solicitor surveyed his hostile audience with satisfaction. "I've called all of you here—"

"Rather unorthodox, isn't it, Mr. Posey?" Henny's player's voice carried beautifully. "Aren't you afraid that counsel ultimately may claim that you've prejudiced the defendant's case, subjecting him or her to questioning without benefit of either the Miranda warning *or* any opportunity to seek legal representation?"

Annie promptly forgave Henny any and all annoying attributes. "Way to go," she hissed enthusiastically. Carolyn Wheat's rough-and-tumble lawyer Cass Jameson couldn't have said it any better.

Posey's grip tightened on the lectern, but he kept his voice in check. "It may interest you to know, Mrs. Brawley," he said with heavy sarcasm, "that no Miranda warning is required when the investigator questions individuals in an attempt to gain information and not with the objective of filing charges."

Saulter stared at the tips of his boots.

"In fact, we have here an extremely unusual situation." Posey's voice took on the mellifluous, liquid, pompous tone of an orator enamored with the sound of his own voice. "We have an instance where murder is attempted, not once, not twice, but three times, and we *believe* we know the intended victim. Death strikes, yes, indeed, but each time the killer is thwarted, his true quarry escaping. What does this make possible?" His voice boomed with evangelical fervor. His pleasure in his own performance was not diminished in the least by the lack of response from his captive audience. Annie had seen alligators somnolent in the sun that displayed more interest than Posey's listeners. "This makes it possible for an intelligent investigator to learn from the mouth of the victim who wishes him ill—and why."

He had their attention now, all right.

One by one, every face turned toward Bledsoe. Even Fleur's.

Slowly, Bledsoe stood. One hand, white to the knuckles, gripped the back of the chair in front of him.

"Fucking murderer." His voice rasped like metal against stone. "One of you is a fucking murderer—you killed Kathryn." A spasm of pain twisted his truculent face. He stopped, head down for a long moment, then looked up, his eyes again moving accusingly from person to person. "Tried to kill me. When I know who it is—" The threat hung in the air, glinted in his malevolent eyes.

"Mr. Bledsoe," Posey intervened pompously, "the law will see that justice is done."

Bledsoe's spiteful eyes touched briefly on Posey. "When I know—"

Posey's hand swept the room. "Here they are, Mr. Bledsoe, each and every one of our suspects. Who hates you, and why?"

Bledsoe used both hands now to brace himself against the chair in front of him. He was breathing heavily. As his chest rose, his shirt pulled taut against the bulky bandage. Annie marveled at the man's enormous control. Obviously, he should be in the hospital. Obviously, he would never give in to pain. She felt a grudging admiration, even though he was a man who more truly than most was reaping what he had sown.

"Could it be you, Nathan?" Bledsoe jeered. "I don't think so. No guts. You never had any guts. Crazy about Pamela, but too gutless to do anything about it. I can tell you one thing, you didn't miss much. She had about as much spirit as a wet rag. That's what going to bed with her was like—"

"Stop it, goddam you!"

Hillman was on his feet. His face stripped of every defense, pain and anguish and heartbreak plain to see, Hillman turned maddened eyes to Posey. "You've got to stop this. I don't have to listen to—"

"Sit down, Mr. Hillman," Posey ordered, "unless you want to go to jail for obstructing an investigation."

"Go to hell," the editor said shakily. "I'd rather go to jail," and he started up the aisle toward the exit.

The deputy at the door glanced questioningly at Posey, who slowly shook his head.

"Maybe a few guts." There was almost a tone of admiration in Bledsoe's voice. "Maybe we can't scratch Nate boy yet."

"We can scratch this entire unsavory and disgusting episode!" Emma rose swiftly, with surprising agility for a woman of her bulk. "Come on, Fleur. We're leaving."

Fleur stood, too, and the two writers started toward the aisle.

"Now you two just wait—"

Emma swung on him venomously. "Be careful, Posey. Be very, very careful."

As the two women continued up the aisle toward the exit, Bledsoe's goading voice followed implacably. "Emma's got spirit, all right. Emma's a dark horse. Made her mad when I said Marigold Rembrandt was just a tired retread of Miss Marple. As for Fleur, she didn't like it when I screwed her daughter." His hateful voice boomed off the walls. Annie shuddered. Never had she been in a room that contained so much emotion, so much evil. "Her great big horse of a daughter. But Jaime liked the hell out of it."

The door closed on his poisonous insinuations. Emma and Fleur were gone. Bledsoe's mouth thinned, and hard white patches at the corners told of pain. Then, abruptly, the door burst open and a deputy shoved Derek inside. "Found him in the bar, sir. Tried to resist. Arrested him for drunk and disorderly conduct."

Derek swayed unsteadily.

Natalie jumped up. "Derek, are you all right?"

Derek obviously was far from all right. His eyes were glassy, his face was slack.

Bledsoe lifted an arm in mock greeting. "Oh, the screw-up's pride and joy, that wonderful little mama's boy, Pamela's good son, Derek."

Annie struggled to shut out the ugly words. But worse than the words was Bledsoe's vicious pleasure in the pain they inflicted. She

could see it in the tiny satisfied curl of his lips, in the hot glitter of his
eyes. He was having himself a hell of a time.

Natalie reached out for Derek's arm. The young man shrugged her
away, shook loose from the deputy. "I can walk," he said with sodden
dignity. The publicist started down the aisle toward the podium one
lurching footfall after another. His drunken eyes never left Bledsoe's
face. "I swore I would kill you, Neil. I swore it the day Mother died."
His mouth trembled, tears began to spill down his unshaven cheeks.
"You killed her. I know you did. I swore I'd make you pay—and I will."
Derek fumbled inside his coat. He drew out a gun, its shiny blue black
metal glinting in the overhead lights.

Bledsoe's head jerked up, his eyes widened in naked surprise.

The deputy launched himself into a brutal tackle. Derek came crashing down into the aisle, his head striking the seat of a chair. The gun
clattered harmlessly to the floor.

For a moment no one spoke.

Margo Wright was the next to stand as she drawled, "I think I can
bypass this little comedy."

"A comedy," Posey repeated loudly. "That's what all of this has been,
because the murders have nothing to do with Neil Bledsoe."

If Posey's intention was to shock, it was an unqualified success.

Everyone gaped at him in stunned silence. Including Neil Bledsoe.

"When every path leads to the same door, the *intelligent* detective
becomes suspicious." Posey smoothed his thinning blond hair. Was he
imagining the whirr and clatter of news cameras? "But what is the sole
relationship between the two victims?"

The only response was a heavy sigh from Saulter.

Posey smiled avuncularly at the police chief. "I am indebted to my
co-officer of the law for unwittingly having shown me the way."

Saulter stared grimly at the floor.

"John Border Stone and Kathryn Honeycutt"—Posey intoned the
names like a bailiff—"were guilty, in the eyes of the murderer, of a
heinous crime: daring to take on the appurtenances of Agatha Christie
characters! John Border Stone registered at this convention as James
Bentley, the lodger in a book entitled *Mrs. McGinty's Dead*. Kathryn
Honeycutt had the temerity to emulate Christie's most beloved detective,
Jane Marple. A grave mistake on their parts. The result: a sentence of
death."

Max stood, and there was nothing easygoing about him now. "Hold it, Posey. This sounds crazy, and it sounds—"

"Not crazy, Mr. Darling. Arrogant. Supercilious."

Posey jumped down heavily from the platform and strode to the front row. His finger stabbed at Lady Gwendolyn. "Who is the world's foremost authority on Agatha Christie? Who became incensed when Bledsoe threatened to write a nasty biography? Whose cape was stained with the blood of a young man who should have had many years yet to live? Whose latest book, *Death of a Nabob*, includes firecrackers thrown as distraction and a light pistol as the murder weapon?"

Annie glanced frantically at Henny, who reluctantly nodded.

"Who—" Posey paused dramatically, "threatened Mr. Bledsoe last night? Came up to him after the program and all but informed him his days were numbered?"

"No. Never."

Annie had never thought *neow, nevah* could sound so valiant.

The aged author slowly rose. She hardly came to the prosecutor's imposing midriff. "There *is* an interesting parallel between *Death of a Nabob* and this crime." Her tone would have been appropriate at a symposium.

Annie had had enough. "Wait a minute, Posey. This is *crazy*. For starters, Lady Gwendolyn wasn't even on the island Saturday night—"

A mischievous grin lit the pink-and-cream face. "Actually, Annie dear, I did happen to be here. You see, I always avoid cocktail dos. Besides, I was determined to have an absolutely smashing arrival at the fête. In fact, I was in the vicinity of your bookstore during the attack. It quite took me back for a moment to my days in France during the war. However, I must announce that I am the victim of circumstantial evidence. Don't you know, that's such an intriguing situation for a mystery novelist!"

"Lady Gwendolyn Tompkins, you are under arrest. Before we ask you any questions, you must understand . . ."

The Miranda warning. Annie had never expected to hear it like this.

AGATHA CHRISTIE
TITLE CLUE

Just a contest, but money tempts;
A hearty man's closet tells the
tale.

24

arly on in the planning for The Christie Caper, Annie realized that the committee for the Agatha Christie Come-as-You-Wish-You-Were Ball (composed of Henny, Laurel, and Ingrid) was out of her control.

Out of all control.

At that point, besieged for decisions regarding printing, brochures, reservations, meals, cocktail parties, panels, author signings, program copy (why did some authors assume that surely they would be included and damn surly if they weren't if they mailed it in the week before the conference?), treasure hunt clues, and questions for the Agatha Christie Trivia Quiz, Annie had wished the committee Godspeed.

So the transformed ballroom was as impressive and exciting to her as to the conference registrants. The ballroom was divided, by means of decorated screens, into fourths with an unusual difference. The band-stand was in the center of the ballroom, and the screens ran flush to the platform, so that each area was open to the music but self-contained with its decorations. Each square thus formed represented a particular kind of Christie mystery, the Country House, Travel, St. Mary Mead, and Adventure. It was cleverly done, the watercolor murals on the screens given substance by a few appropriate stage pieces: a fireplace complete with hearth rug and a country gentleman's desk; luggage and a Model T Ford, an elegant mockup of a railroad dining-car table with fine china and a damask rose in a silver vase; a mud-spattered bicycle leaning against the painted fence in front of a cottage and tennis rackets propped carelessly against slatted wooden lawn chairs; a sealed oilskin packet and a crate filled with carved wooden animals from Africa.

By the time Annie and Max arrived, the ballroom was jammed, most of the three hundred costumed party-goers opting to display their cleverness in the appropriate arena. Annie and Max were running late because it had taken time to convince Ingrid that she no longer needed to guard all the flotsam turned in to Meeting Room D by the conference clue hunters.

Shouts were required to be heard over the excited din and the tea dance band music (heavy on Cole Porter, which vividly evoked the marvelous 1982 film version of *Evil Under the Sun*).

Annie and Max came as Tommy and Tuppence Beresford, emulating the jaunty versions done so well on television by Francesca Annis and James Warwick. (Though, as all Christie readers know, Tommy is a redhead.) Max's thick blond hair wasn't appropriate either, but Annie was confident that otherwise Max was a quintessential Tommy, brave, stalwart, and forever admiring of Tuppence. As a couple, the Beresfords did not engage in mawkish shows of affection, "Good show, old bean," was high praise. At the beginning of their collaboration in detecting, they'd scrambled for funds, Tuppence a parson's daughter lately of the VAD (Volunteer Aid Detachment) and Tommy a newly discharged war hero without prospects. All they'd had (in common at that moment with Agatha and Archie Christie) was youth and love, but that, Annie thought, was the best the world could offer.

On one point, however, Annie had prevailed with the committee: Name tags identifying the character portrayed were required at the ball. That made encounters a great deal of fun. A bookseller from Denver was a marvelously effective Poirot, complete with black bowler, luxuriant black mustaches, and shiny black patent-leather shoes. A librarian from Downers Grove, Illinois, a feather duster tucked beneath the bow of her apron, was superb as the refreshing and unconventional Lucy Eyelesbarrow, who helps Miss Marple confound a murderer in *What Mrs. McGillicuddy Saw!*. A local bank vice president (whom Annie had always considered a bit of a stuff) revealed an unexpected capacity for playfulness. His name tag read EDWARD ROBINSON. As he tangoed past, his companion adorned with a magnificent (paste, no doubt) diamond necklace, Annie recalled the short story "The Manhood of Edward Robinson" and wondered what that indicated about the banker's psyche.

Max looked at her anxiously. "Having fun?"

"Sure." She tried to sound lighthearted.

"Annie, relax. Everybody else is." But Max's blue eyes were understanding. "You know Lady Gwendolyn would exhort us to keep a stiff upper lip. And there isn't anything else we can do tonight. For her or Derek."

Annie was still bemused at Posey's unexpected (and surely unintentional) emulation of a classic Poirot turn-the-tables confrontation that morning, and its shocking outcome: Derek Davis arrested for assault with a deadly weapon; Lady Gwendolyn under arrest for the murders of John Border Stone and Kathryn Honeycutt.

The rest of the afternoon, Annie'd fumed and paced and railed: How could Posey not see the forest for the trees?

But tonight she wished she had a better capacity for compartmentalizing her emotions, because the Agatha Christie Come-as-You-Wish-You-Were Ball was truly spectacular. The decorations perfectly caught the tone and times of Christie's novels. And she loved the characters-come-to-life, especially, of course, Henny as an untidily coiffured, cardiganed, lisle-hosed, apple-laden Ariadne Oliver; Ingrid as prim, grizzle-haired, angular-bodied, pince-nezed Miss Lemon; and Laurel—[honestly, Annie was willing to indulge fantasies; that was the name of this game, but surely there were limits?]—as the Countess Vera Rossakoff, the only woman Poirot ever loved, the flamboyant jewel thief, the proprietor at one time of a cabaret known as Hell. But damned if Laurel, in a dark wig, a satin gown, and six-inch heels, didn't look the part! Laurel daintily tipped her fan as she danced past.

Max was right. Everyone was having a jolly good time.

For the mood of the conference-goers had lightened considerably when news of the two arrests swept the hotel. As far as most of the Christie fans were concerned, the terrifying specter of murder no longer hung over the hotel, and the dreadful events were considered closed. Though an angry contingent of Lady Gwendolyn's fans was at this moment (Vince Ellis had told Henny who told Annie) marching (in costume) with placards outside the jail, protesting their beloved writer's innocence. Would Lady Gwendolyn be amused or touched?

Everyone at the ball, however, seemed to be in high spirits. Annie sought out those who had been present when Posey arrested Derek Davis and Lady Gwendolyn. Victoria Shaw was a surprise in a sandy wig, a spattering of fake freckles, and a sensible traveling costume. Her name tag read MRS. UPJOHN, ON A BUS IN ANATOLIA. Annie was charmed. What kinship did this reserved and unhappy woman feel with blithe, adventurous, lively Mrs. Upjohn, Julia's mother in *Cat Among the Pigeons*? Emma Clyde, monstrous in a heavily padded dark dress, her hair blackened and drawn back in a tight bun, was an almost too-successful replica of the dictatorial Mrs. Boynton in *Appointment with Death*. Margo Wright as a blonde was a shock, but Margo Wright as Victoria Jones (*They Came to Baghdad*) was fascinating. Victoria Jones, impulsive, a fluent liar, eager for adventure—what a contrast to Margo's unshakable control and reserve. As for Fleur Calloway—certainly she was as elusively lovely as Elinor Carlisle in *Sad Cypress*—but did she feel an affinity for Elinor in the dock or Elinor broken free from a living nightmare?

There was no sign of Natalie Marlow or Nathan Hillman. A fox-trot ended, the crowd shifted, and Annie spotted Frank Saulter, not in his official khakis but in country tweeds. "Frank!" Annie exclaimed. She tugged on Max's hand and plunged into the crowd. They came up behind the police chief.

Annie, as always, didn't weigh her words. "Chief, listen, Lady Gwendolyn didn't do it."

Saulter turned to face them. His tag read MR. SATTERTHWAITE. Annie knew that Frank was just as curious as that longtime associate of Mr. Harley Quin's, but certainly wasn't as fussy and prim.

Frank gave a rueful shrug. "Posey's closed the investigation. Told me to keep my nose out of it." His right eyelid dropped in a careful, conspiratorial wink. "He'd raise hell if he thought I was here to keep an eye on things." The chief surveyed the gaily decorated area. "Heck of a show tonight. Guess you two put this together?"

"Actually, no," Annie admitted. "Laurel and Henny and Ingrid planned the ball. Do you like it?"

Just for an instant, his tired face looked cheerful. "Oh, yeah. Did you see the way the caboose on the Orient Express lights up?"

"No," Max exclaimed, craning his neck to look. Max was a train *nut*. He could recite innumerable facts about the fabled Orient Express, which first left the Gare de Strasbourg in Paris for Constantinople on October 4, 1883, and made its final regularly scheduled run in May 1977.

Annie was determined to forestall that. "Chief, wait a minute. Has Posey had Lady Gwendolyn arraigned for murder?"

Saulter shoved his hands into his trouser pockets. "Yep. Four o'clock this afternoon. Charged with the murders of John Border Stone and Mrs. Honeycutt, attempted murder of Neil Bledsoe." Saulter kept his voice even. "You'll read all about it in the paper in the morning." Annie could imagine the Class A press conference Posey must have held.

Max peered over the heads of the crowd, looking for the caboose. "What about Derek Davis?" she asked.

"Oh, sure. Attempted murder of Bledsoe. They found the pawn-shop in Savannah where Davis bought the gun—"

Max looked back at the chief. "First murderer, second murderer," he murmured skeptically.

"Which gun?" Annie demanded.

"The one he pulled this afternoon in the meeting room. Now, sorry as you may feel for that young man, Annie, I'd like to remind you that he rented a car, drove thirty miles, used a false name, and purchased a gun, a gun that he pulled out of his coat right after threatening to kill his stepfather."

"Former stepfather," Annie clarified.

Max was impatient. "Seems like too many guns in this case. What about the gun that killed Kathryn Honeycutt? Have they linked it to Lady Gwendolyn or to Derek?"

"Nope." It was a wry, dry disclaimer that spoke volumes about Saulter's attitude toward Posey's theories. "A search warrant didn't turn up anything in Lady Gwendolyn's suite. Anyway, nothin' more we can do tonight, so we might as well have some fun." He didn't look like a man embarked on a delightful social evening. His face creased in a frown. "That young woman, the writer, Miss Marlow, if she's not careful Posey's going to throw her in jail. She raised all kinds of hell, swore Derek never did it, that even if he bought a hundred guns, he couldn't have killed anybody, said we were blind fools, that Derek was so drunk he wouldn't have gotten the gun pointed at Bledsoe before Bledsoe would have decked him, told Posey she'd see him in hell before she'd ever let Davis stay in jail, then she stormed out. Made Posey damned mad. If you see her, you might tell her to lay off. No sense her going to jail, too."

"Yeah, we will." Max had restrained himself as long as he could. "Hey, where's the caboose to the Orient Express?"

"This way." Saulter jerked his head.

Doors appropriate to the various murals—a pantry door beneath a staircase in a village house, a stateroom door aboard a ship—opened between the screens so revelers could slip from area to area, perhaps pretending for a moment that they were walking into one of Christie's novels. (Annie was sure she detected Laurel's hand. Another of Laurel's enthusiasms was Andrew Lloyd Webber. "My dear, he is to stagecraft what Von Braun was to rockets!") Annie was smiling as she followed Max and Saulter. She was almost to the door when a hurrying figure brushed roughly past her.

Startled, she looked around.

"Chief!" Ed Merritt, the hotel manager, kept his voice low, but he couldn't control the tremor. "Chief!"

Saulter jerked to face him.

"Chief, oh, Christ, it's awful—on the terrace—that guy, the one all the trouble's about—"

"Bledsoe?" Saulter looked older than time, his yellow, wrinkled skin taut with foreboding.

"Jesus, the way he fell—blood and—"

"Fell? Where'd he fall from?" Saulter snapped. "When?"

"Now. Just now. From the balcony of his room," the hotel manager said. "You didn't hear the scream in here? God, I'll hear that scream the rest of my life."

"A doctor? Have you called a doctor?" Annie demanded urgently.

"Doctor?" Merritt's eyes skimmed over her vacantly. "What for?"

It was hard to remember, looking at Neil Bledsoe's broken body, how much bigger than life he'd seemed.

Annie held tight to Max's hand. After one quick look—and that look remained indelibly in her mind, the blood pooling beneath the crushed head, the unnatural angle of the neck, the splintered bone protruding from his calf—she stared up at the balcony. It was easy to spot the place—a portion of the railing was askew, bulging out from the balcony. Bledsoe must have fallen almost headfirst.

Saulter swore in a tight, hard monotone, then, crisply, he issued orders: "Merritt, get some of your people out here, arrange the tables and chairs as a barricade—oh—ten feet each way. That's first. Second, call the mainland, get word to Circuit Solicitor Posey, tell him we need the homicide crew and at least a half-dozen deputies. Max, with Billy in the hospital, I'm damn short on staff. Will you and Annie serve as deputies, secure Bledsoe's room? Make sure no one enters, nothing touched or changed until I can get people up there. You know the drill."

•   •   •

A white-faced bellboy turned the key in 301. As the lock clicked, Max, using his handkerchief, eased the knob to the left. The door opened an inch, then jolted to a stop.

"I'll be damned," Max murmured. "The chain's on."

It took time. A call to maintenance. The hinges removed, the door propped to one side.

To Annie, the suite smelled of death, though, to her surprise, almost all vestiges of the bloody shooting had already been erased, the carpet shampooed (damp splotches still evident). Of course, once the investigation of a site was complete—photographs made, surfaces dusted for prints, sketches done—there was no need to maintain the appearance of the crime scene. This was, after all, a hotel, and these rooms, after Bledsoe's departure, would be routinely readied for new guests.

Bledsoe's departure.

Via the balcony.

So the murderer had, after all, triumphed.

But, at the least, this should mean Lady Gwendolyn's prompt release and perhaps even Derek Davis's.

The bedroom door to the left of the living area was closed; the door to the bedroom to the right of the main portion of the suite was open. Max poked his head in that bedroom. "Bledsoe's stuff's in here. Let's check out the balcony first."

Annie paused in the entryway, picturing the scene the night Kathryn Honeycutt died and Bledsoe was wounded.

The physical layout of the suite was exactly that of Annie and Max's.

A small square entryway, a closet to the right, the decorative wrought-iron room divider to the left, separating the entryway from the living room.

Straight ahead a short hall. A door to the right opened into a bedroom. Bledsoe's room, Max said.

To the left of the divider was the living room. A closed door in the far wall led to the second bedroom; Kathryn's room.

The suites were arranged with a bedroom to each side of the living room. Balconies opened off of both the living area and the bedrooms.

Late Thursday night. The fire alarm. Smoke. No lights. Bledsoe had opened the door to the hall. A flashlight glared in his eyes. Shots. Hit in the left shoulder, he'd reeled backward, taken refuge behind the couch. Even wounded, Bledsoe could have covered that distance in one stride.

Kathryn must have turned *her* flashlight toward the door at almost the precise moment Bledsoe was shot. Otherwise the attacker could have pursued Bledsoe and pumped more bullets into him.

Instead, Kathryn aimed her flashlight at the attacker, and the gun was turned on her. Bledsoe was saved.

Annie knew where Kathryn had fallen. Just a foot or two past her bedroom door. The shampooed rug told the story.

By then the hotel was in an uproar. The killer fled, running down the stairs. Once on the terrace, mingling with other guests rousted by the alarms, the killer tossed the gun and gloves.

In the suite, Bledsoe staggered to his feet, found Kathryn, and carried her out onto his balcony. Annie could see the damp carpet splotches leading into his room.

As for tonight, there was nothing disarranged in the living room, and the only item not ordinarily in place was the open picnic basket on the coffee table. From here, it appeared—

"Hey, Annie, come on out here."

As she walked through Bledsoe's room, she noted that the mattress on the bed was askew, a chair in front of the desk overturned, one of the French doors to the balcony hung unevenly. On the balcony, a chair and the table were overturned. The railing bowed out sharply.

"A hell of a struggle," Max said. "Who was big enough and strong enough to manhandle Bledsoe over the edge?"

"How did the murderer escape?" Annie looked back toward the living area. "The door to the suite was not only locked, it was chained."

They looked through the suite. Annie had noted the signs of struggle in Bledsoe's room. Otherwise, it was the room of a man who had packed his bags in preparation for checking out the next day, an open suitcase neatly filled, his shaving kit on the dresser, litter discarded in the waste-basket, a *New York Times*, a *Business Week* magazine.

Kathryn's room—the room she had used—was bare and clean, as devoid of personality as all untenanted hotel rooms. There was no evidence anyone had entered it.

The kitchenette, too, was clean. A single glass, ice melting, sat on the counter. Max sniffed. "Scotch."

In the bathroom, used towels hung from the rack. On the lavatory lay a toothbrush, paste, shaving cream, razor, stick deodorant.

Nothing was knocked over in the living room. Annie walked to the coffee table. The picnic basket was nothing out of the ordinary, woven brown wicker, rope handles, a red-and-white checked cloth inside and— she looked more closely. A single yellow rose lay on the somewhat rumpled cloth.

Behind her, Max said, his voice puzzled, "Annie, I don't get it. Where the hell did the murderer go? And how?"

"*Accident!*" Annie erupted.

Posey rocked arrogantly back on his heels in the center of the suite's living room, but his blue eyes bulged dangerously. "Mrs. Darling, I am fully capable of carrying out the duties of circuit solicitor for this county in the great State of South Carolina *without* assistance from either you *or* Mr. Darling, notwithstanding your sudden commission as deputies. In fact, Chief Saulter can now relieve you of this burden since I have arrived on the island with sufficient law enforcement personnel to complete our investigation into this unfortunate accident."

"Accident!" Annie repeated furiously. Max would have to restrain her if she got much angrier. The man was an idiot. "Someone's been trying to murder Bledsoe for almost a week, they finally succeed, and you call it an accident!"

"Mrs. Darling, you have been misled, intentionally misled, as it were, by the crafty and cunning perpetrator of these crimes. Have we a shred of proof that Mr. Bledsoe's demise was ever the murderer's goal?"

"The bookstore—the vase—Bledsoe shot first—"

Posey raised his hand imperiously. "Ah, the vase. A red herring, I believe that's what crime writers call it. And should it surprise us that this particular crime should contain such an element of deception? I believe not. Further, there can be no other reasonable explanation of the unfortunate death of Mr. Bledsoe. The door to the suite was chained on the inside, as you yourself, Mrs. Darling, will have to testify. Moreover, we have an eye witness, a waiter stacking chairs on the terrace, who saw Bledsoe storm out onto the balcony, crash into the railing, and such was the force of that collision, he shot over the railing— 'almost like a dive'— and crashed down to the terrace. Headfirst. And there wasn't another living soul on that balcony."

Annie tried not to wriggle. But she couldn't sleep; absolutely couldn't. She thumped her pillow furiously. That pigheaded, idiotic, infuriating moron Posey! He was so determined not to be proved wrong in his arrest of Lady Gwendolyn that he wouldn't even consider that Bledsoe had been murdered.

For it was murder, she knew it in her bones. Even if no one else *was* on the balcony when Bledsoe dived over it. Not even Posey had tried to suggest suicide. No one would ever believe Neil Bledsoe was a suicide. Annie's thoughts continued to churn. Accident! Somehow that "accident" had been staged. But how? There wasn't, and Annie wasn't even grudging in admitting it, a man or woman in the world from whom Bledsoe would have run in terror—

Annie sat bolt upright.

Max stirred. "Hmmph."

Annie evaded his touch. Talk about waking Max up, that's all it would take. She edged out of bed, dropped to the floor (the height of old-fashioned four-posters always surprised her), and padded softly into the living area, easing the bedroom door shut.

Annie paced.

The chained door.

The picnic basket.

Bledsoe careening over the railing.

Was it possible that the secret to Bledsoe's death might even yet be in that suite?

She frowned at the wall clock. Twenty minutes after two o'clock in the morning. A hell of a time to call someone she didn't know well.

But time might be critical.

She fumbled with the telephone directory, flipping the pages until she found the name she sought. She didn't need to look up the second number; she knew it by heart.

Saulter got there first. A Leica hung from a leather strap around his neck. His eyes were bright and eager. "I think you're onto something. Damn clever." He rubbed the back of his neck. "Posey'd have my ass if he knew I was here." The chief didn't sound overly worried at the prospect. "So, might as well be hanged for a sheep as a lamb." He dug into his khaki pants pocket and pulled out a wrinkled, many-folded sheet of notebook paper and handed it to Annie.

Annie stopped her nervous pacing—what if Rhonda Kinkaid didn't come?—and took the small square of paper. She unfolded it and strained to read the spidery, oft-underlined message:

The solution is clear. Apply logic. What did the murderer ACHIEVE with shots, vase, Stone, Honeycutt?

Achieve was underlined three times.

There was a scrawled postscript:

Bledsoe dead! The mills do grind—

It didn't matter how many times Annie reread the simple missive, she couldn't fathom Lady Gwendolyn's intent, yet she felt certain that she held in her hand the signpost to a murderer. "The solution is clear. . . ."

The elevator door opened. Annie stuffed the note in the pocket of her white pants.

A skinny, high-energy redhead in faded Levis, sneakers, and a ratty old army sweatshirt charged up the hall, her arms full of paraphernalia. She skidded to a stop in front of Annie and Saulter. "You did call me, didn't you? I haven't dreamed this?"

Annie and Saulter watched as Rhonda Kinkaid dismantled the heating-cooling unit in the living room, then put it back together. They followed her into each bedroom. Kinkaid worked swiftly. Annie envied her dexterity. It took less than five minutes to search those units. The kitchenette offered more scope. Beneath the refrigerator. Behind it. Even a quick survey of the cabinets. "Sometimes there are holes you don't notice," Kinkaid explained. It took longer to disassemble and restore the stove.

Saulter had hung close at the beginning, but finally, yawning wearily, he stretched out on the couch in the living room.

Annie glanced at her watch. A quarter to four. Maybe there wasn't anything to find.

Kinkaid started on the living room curtains next, then both bedrooms.

Annie leaned against the doorjamb to Bledsoe's room. Almost every square inch of the suite had been covered.

Kinkaid stood in the middle of the bedroom floor, hands on hips, her eyes flicking about the room. She looked up, and her mouth curved in a grin. Moving with frenetic energy, she dragged a desk chair next to the canopied four-poster. Hopping up, she stood on tiptoe. "Oh yeah," she cried. "God, what a beauty." She glanced down at Annie who'd hurried to the bedside. "Would you get the cage, open it, please."

Kinkaid swung a pronged stick over the top of the canopy and in one swift, competent move transferred the sleek reptile into the opened box and immediately slid shut the top. She grinned with delight. "Sometimes it's neat to be the island's best-known herpetologist. Now, tell me—what the hell is that red rat snake doing here?"

The adrenaline pumped. Annie didn't even consider going back to bed. So she'd guessed right. Murder by snake. Chancy, to be sure, but it had succeeded superbly. But she still didn't know who. Or why Bledsoe hadn't been wary enough to avoid the trap.

The list of suspects was shorter.

Not Derek Davis. He was in the county jail when Bledsoe died.

Who did that leave?

Annie sat down at the desk. She looked at her notebook and Max's, at the stack of biographical sheets, at Bledsoe's crumpled flyer promising the "truth" about Christie, at the copy of the autopsy on Honeycutt (Saulter was treading on dangerous ground to make it available), at the puzzling missive from Lady Gwendolyn, "*What did the murderer achieve*..." Lying atop the bio stack was the key to Meeting Room D where Ingrid had stored all the odd bits and pieces turned in by the conference "detective teams" in their search for clues.

Annie picked up a pen and found a clean sheet. She wrote swiftly:

> Nathan Hillman
> Margo Wright
> Victoria Shaw

A short list. A very short list.

After a moment's hesitation, she added:

> Natalie Marlow

And, in a moment:

> Emma Clyde
> Fleur Calloway

Some problems with the last three. Natalie, so far as anyone knew, was thoroughly caught up in Neil's spell until the evening of the Agatha Christie Trivia Quiz, which was long after the shooting at Death on Demand, the dumping of the vase, and Stone's murder. So, Natalie was very unlikely. Annie thought a moment, scratched through her name.

And, of course, Fleur had been in full view of Annie and Saulter when the shots rang out that night at Death on Demand. Annie's pen hovered over her name. But did anyone on this island have more reason to hate Bledsoe than Fleur? Annie left the name untouched.

Emma Clyde. Emma was tough, smart, and crafty. Her name stayed on the list.

All right, all right. Look at the more likelies.

Margo Wright. One imposing woman. Clever. Strong. But strength had nothing to do with Bledsoe's death. Still, on the night Kathryn was killed and Neil shot, the murderer had to move quickly, decisively. That fitted Margo, certainly. But was the loss of respect and affection from Margo's boss and mentor reason enough to kill? Of course, Bledsoe had compounded her injury by maliciously destroying two of her clients, Bryan Shaw and Pamela Gerrard. Had that moved Margo to murder? Annie added a string of question marks after the agent's name.

Nathan Hillman. He'd loved Pamela. Reason enough for him to hate the man who had driven her to death. Bledsoe said Hillman didn't have enough guts. Had Hillman proved him wrong?

Victoria Shaw. Oh, surely not. Yet Annie remembered the look in her eyes Friday afternoon in the meeting called by Posey. Hatred. Unforgiving, implacable hatred. Bledsoe had taken from her life all the joy, all the meaning. And weren't the somewhat ineffectual attacks almost a parody of murderous intent, the use of a .22 pistol and a vase and fireworks and smoke bombs? Weren't those attacks the kind that a desperately unhappy, sheltered woman might mount?

Annie threw down her pen. Dammit, how was she ever going to figure it all out? The pen clinked against the key atop the stacks of paper— all the information they'd gathered. Annie looked at the stack without enthusiasm. Maybe if she read it all, one more time, maybe she would see something wrong, something odd, something to set her on the trail.

The first pink slivers of dawn streaked the sky as Annie put down the last sheet.

She stared down at her scratch pad on the desk. She'd written one single word: VALIUM.

Because that was wrong, all wrong.

It was in the autopsy report on Kathryn Honeycutt. Not mentioned as important, merely a part of a thorough report. Kathryn Honeycutt had taken a Valium, probably at bedtime, no more than the commonly prescribed five milligrams. No evidence, of course, of drug abuse. Nothing of that sort. Saulter had seen nothing peculiar in it. Kathryn'd had a difficult week, an unpleasant evening. Why not take a tranquilizer at bedtime?

But it was a false note, the one really peculiar fact Annie had found. Kathryn Honeycutt was a Christian Scientist, one so committed to her principles that she was losing her eyesight because of cataracts, yet she would not agree to an operation. Poirot would have sniffed round this fact, just as Annie was.

Would Kathryn Honeycutt take Valium?

No. Annie knew it just as clearly as Miss Marple knew Gladys was innocent in "The Case of the Perfect Maid."

One false note.

If that was false, what else might be false?

Murder by snake. Absurd. Yet, it had succeeded. But—Annie rubbed tired eyes—the person who placed the snake in that hamper had no assurance whatever that it would succeed. A different matter indeed from gunfire and a plummeting vase. And why, dammit, had Bledsoe opened the damn basket? Whatever the man had been, he was not stupid; he was, despite his offensive views, indeed an expert on the mystery. Of all people—

Annie sat very, very still. Another false note. Though it could be argued from Bledsoe's behavior during the week—his attempt to run after the gunman at Death on Demand, his swift scaling up the pillars to the roof after the vase fell—that he was indeed fearless.

But perhaps fearlessness had nothing to do with it. Perhaps the answer was simple, very, very simple and much more illuminating.

But if Annie's surmise were true, it meant that nothing was what it seemed to be.

She picked up Lady Gwendolyn's note:

The solution is clear. Apply logic. What did the murderer achieve with shots, vase, Stone, Honeycutt?

Look at what actually happened, the canny author was saying.

The shots—They were seen as the start of a murderous campaign against Bledsoe.

The vase—Further evidence of deadly intent against the critic.

Stone's death—Stone is silenced. If he knows more than he has admitted about the attempts against Bledsoe, that knowledge is forever lost.

Honeycutt's death—An innocent victim if Bledsoe is the killer's quarry.

Neil Bledsoe wounded—The killer stymied again.

Neil Bledsoe—A man pathologically afraid of snakes. But who could know he would fall to his death to escape one?

Scaled back to the bare bones, what did they have?

John Border Stone dead in his room.

Kathryn Honeycutt murdered.

Neil Bledsoe wounded.

Neil Bledsoe killed in a violent fall from his balcony.

In that order.

Suddenly, Annie understood. Oh, yes, Lady Gwendolyn. Yes, yes, yes. But how had it been managed? Annie closed her eyes for a long moment, picturing again the Bledsoe suite the night Kathryn died and Neil was wounded. For just an instant, she had to admire the guile and care and, yes, courage involved. Not impossible. Difficult, yes. Complicated, yes. Untidy, yes. But life was difficult, complicated, and untidy. Just like rivers running to the sea, human emotion wasn't contained within narrow bounds. It was of these kinds of human emotions, so often doubling and twisting within civilized confines, that Agatha Christie wrote.

Annie knew at least a part of the answer. Now all she had to do was prove it. She got to her feet and restlessly prowled around the living room area, but this time she was looking, studying, imagining. Finally, she stopped to stare at the iron grillwork that separated the foyer from the living room.

And she could almost hear a high, clear voice joyously announcing, "Bully for you, my dear, you've got it."

AGATHA CHRISTIE
TITLE CLUE

Lady Hoggin is willing to pay;
Will Shan Tung come home today?

25

h, Lord." Annie stared in dismay at the tables in Conference Room D. Each table was littered with an assortment of rubbish. Three-by-five cards were taped next to each piece.

Max looked over her shoulder. "Can't say they didn't give it their all."

Chief Saulter sighed heavily. He hadn't been pleased to be recalled to the hotel after only four hours sleep, but that was four hours more than she had enjoyed, Annie had pointed out.

"I thought they kept a clean hotel here," Saulter groused.

The collection of trash demonstrated just how much waste people discarded even in a carefully policed environment. Although perhaps the gatherers of this motley mess had been a trifle overenthusiastic. Indeed, the conference-goers who had participated, two by two, in a search of the hotel, the terrace, and the surrounding terrain yesterday must have left the areas sparkling clean.

Ingrid, of course, had directed the careful deposit of the materials along with the accompanying notes on the tables.

Annie glanced at her watch. It was early, to be sure. Annie had awakened Max with the news of her conclusions, and together they'd planned their approach, then called Saulter. Max insisted upon break-fasting first (he and Inspector Dover scrupulously believed in regular mealtimes), but Annie had scarcely been able to eat. There was so much to do and so little time. The conference ended today with the noon luncheon. Their little comedy must be played out by then. But the evidence came first. That was essential.

It took time, so damn much time. Max started at the back of the room, Saulter in the middle. Annie was still on her first table: cigarette packages and butts, crushed drink cans, wadded tissues, pennies and nickels and dimes, buttons, combs, slips of paper, fishing weights, a subway token, lipstick case, chewed gum, a paperback mystery (Graham Greene's *Stamboul Train*), five assorted bookmarks (where authors gather, bookmarks appear as if by magic), an empty condom package, a man's ornate class ring (Annie must remember to announce its finding at the luncheon), a pair of broken sunglasses, a thimble, a single silver hoop earring (ditto), a pocket-size New Testament, a pair of tweezers—

"By God, here it is. Here it is!" Saulter boomed.

Annie and Max reached him at the same time.

The loose coil of wire was among the more nondescript items on that table. It was a dark gray, perhaps a quarter-inch thick, flexible.

Saulter leaned over to read the notation on the three-by-five card. "Found 9/14/90 atop shrubbery in center of the Palmetto House Hotel terrace. Alleyn J. Forman, 1733 North Eighteenth Street, Little Rock, Arkansas. Annie, damned if I don't think you're right!"

"Don't you want to come?" Max asked in surprise, standing by the chief's car.

Annie yawned and rubbed her eyes. "You and the chief can take care of it. I know what the results are going to be." She glanced at the paper sack on the front seat of the car. In it reposed the treasured wire, on its way to the mainland and tests for nitrate residue. She bent to look in the driver's side. "Chief, you will bring it back for the meeting, won't you?"

"Sure. You rest up while we're gone, Annie. You look mighty peaked. We'll be in Meeting Room A," he glanced at his watch, "no later than ten forty-five. I'll bring Lady Gwendolyn, and I'll have a deputy get in touch with everyone." Saulter's lips twitched. He might have been hiding a smile. "Including Posey, of course."

As the car pulled out of the hotel drive, Annie waved good-bye. She maintained her weary, going-to-take-a-brief-nap demeanor until the car was out of sight. Then she set off at a trot. Tired, sure. A nap. No way. There was much to do before Max and Saulter returned.

As she let herself into the suite, she wondered briefly if they'd not thought beyond the proof they were going to validate. Didn't they see what a Pandora's box it opened?

She saw.

And she wanted to think it through.

The picnic basket. A single yellow rose.

The field was wide open:

Nathan Hillman. He still berated himself for not snatching Pam to safety.

Fleur Calloway. Bledsoe's treatment of Derek and Natalie inflamed a never-healed wound.

Emma Clyde. How deep could a critic's barbs go? A dangerous woman to cross.

Margo Wright. She had good reason to loathe Bledsoe—and a reputation for toughness.

Natalie Marlow. She lacked social graces, but she'd been many dark places.

Victoria Shaw. Even the meek can be pushed only so far.

Once again Annie looked through the bios. Only one really fit. Only one.

Annie buried her face in her hands.

What now?

Derek Davis was shackled to a deputy. The young publicist looked almost frail in the too-big pair of orange jail coveralls. He stared at the room full of people with scared, defiant eyes.

Natalie Marlow jumped to her feet when he entered. "Derek, Derek, it will be all right. It will be."

Davis blinked uncertainly, then, reluctantly, irresistibly, his face softened.

Lady Gwendolyn stepped as elegantly as if she were garbed in mink and not an orange jail shift. She flashed a brilliant smile at Annie and winked one large blue eye. She was not, Annie was glad to see, shackled to a deputy, although she walked behind the deputy and in front of Posey. As they passed, she gave Annie a thumbs-up salute.

The deputy looked at Posey, who was a walking thundercloud,

shoulders tightly hunched, face drawn in a scowl. "Yeah. Anywhere," Posey snapped.

Annie couldn't imagine how the chief had wangled Posey's presence, but he had.

Posey and his entourage had been the last to arrive.

Annie wanted to grab hold of the podium and hang on for dear life. So much depended upon how she marshaled the facts, and how persuasive she was.

Annie cleared her throat. Not for silence. It was very silent in that small meeting room. Nathan Hillman eyed her warily, no trace of the editor's usual charm in his manner. Margo Wright was as impassive as a statue. Victoria Shaw nervously opened and closed the clasp of her purse. Emma Clyde reminded Annie of an alligator at rest, watchful, observant, and very, very dangerous. Fleur Calloway's lovely face was worn and pale. Derek Davis watched Natalie Marlow. Natalie hunched forward, her face intent. Henny's vivid eyes flicked from face to face. Only Laurel and Lady Gwendolyn appeared serene.

She began: "I appreciate everyone coming this morning. I thought all of you would want to know the truth about the deaths of John Border Stone, Kathryn Honeycutt, and Neil Bledsoe." Annie was proud of her even, unemotional tone. "This is a complicated story, one composed of a great deal of hatred and viciousness allied, oddly enough, with discipline and brilliant planning. I'd like to go back a few months, if you will. Neil Bledsoe was in financial trouble. I suspect, when the investigation is done, it will turn out that he was in very serious financial trouble. Bledsoe learned of the conference planned for this fall—our conference—to celebrate the centenary of the birth of the world's greatest writer of detective stories, and Bledsoe conceived an audacious plan to make himself rich. He knew when he signed up for this meeting that it would draw many people who hated him. He knew, in fact, that Fleur Calloway"—the author stared down at her tightly clasped hands—"was to be the featured speaker. He knew that Lady Gwendolyn Tompkins was serving as co-hostess. Lady Gwendolyn is one of today's most famous mystery writers. Bledsoe knew that. He read her latest book, *Death of a Nabob*. He made plans to come to the conference, inviting his aunt by marriage, Kathryn Honeycutt, a true Christie fan, to accompany him. His troubles started soon after his arrival on the island. Emma Clyde came within inches of running him down. Gunfire erupted when he left my bookstore Saturday night. On Sunday, he made an obvious play for a new young writer, Natalie Marlow." Natalie turned brooding eyes toward Annie. "On Monday after Lady Gwendolyn's address, he disrupted the conference by criticizing Christie. On Tuesday, he unveiled his plan to publish a vicious biography of Christie. Later that morning a vase was shoved from the roof. It narrowly missed Bledsoe."

No one could have asked for a more intent audience. They knew the story—but not the end of the story.

"Death struck Tuesday night—but Bledsoe was not its target. Dead, murdered, was a young man attending the conference. He had registered as James Bentley, a name drawn from Christie's *Mrs. McGinty's Dead*. His real name: John Border Stone. Stone desperately wanted to be a mystery writer. Saturday night, he ran up to the bookstore to say he'd seen the gunman. When he was subsequently killed, everyone assumed he'd recognized the person who shot at Bledsoe and that Bledsoe's assailant murdered Stone to prevent disclosure.

"There were many here who could be suspected of wishing Bledsoe dead: Fleur Calloway, whose daughter lost her heart and her life because of Bledsoe." Annie saw Emma reach out to grip Fleur's arm. "Nathan Hillman, who loved the woman Bledsoe married and whom Bledsoe may have pushed to her death. Derek Davis, Pamela Gerrard's son. Derek hated Bledsoe, blamed him for his mother's disintegration into alcoholism and her death. Moreover, Bledsoe had attracted a young woman whom Derek was beginning to care very much about." Natalie Marlow's hands clenched. "Victoria Shaw. Bledsoe took away Shaw's reason for living. And," Annie looked into hostile cornflower blue eyes, "Emma Clyde. A great many people," Annie said deliberately, "think it's quite unwise to anger Emma."

A tiny smile touched the lips of Emma Clyde.

Max shot Emma a wary glance.

"All the suspects. But," Annie's tone sharpened, strengthened, "not quite all. Because everyone here, all of us, from the people I've mentioned to Chief Saulter to Circuit Solicitor Posey, who followed yet another false scent—the murderer as a crazed Christie fan—have had our eyes focused on the wrong elements. Instead, here is what mattered."

Turning, Annie grabbed up chalk and rapidly wrote on the blackboard available for business meetings:

1. The shots at Death on Demand. Bledsoe goes after the assailant.

2. The vase misses Bledsoe; he climbs up the ornate columns of the balconies to the roof.
3. Stone's murder. Killed because he knew too much.
4. Roof tar on John Border Stone's tennis shoes.
5. Kathryn Honeycutt's murder; Bledsoe wounded.
6. The bloodhounds baying at the wall on the terrace.
7. Valium taken by Kathryn Honeycutt.
8. Bledsoe opens a picnic basket left at his door.

"Now when you study this list, you will see that the murderer doesn't accomplish anything—oh, a lot of noise and confusion and semblance of threat—until Stone is murdered. Why was Stone murdered? The police determined that Stone's tennis shoes have roof tar on them. He was the person who claimed to have seen the gunman outside Death on Demand. The assumption was made that Stone got a better look than he admitted, that he watched the gunman and was also present when the vase toppled."

A high, clear voice intervened. "Good show, young miss."

Annie felt a surge of elation—and gratitude. "You tell them, Lady Gwendolyn. You set me on the right track."

The British author bounced to her feet. Every eye turned to her.

"We so often do *not* see the forest for the trees." Lady Gwendolyn turned bright blue eyes toward Posey. "Think of this—who was on the roof when the vase came down? Young Mr. Stone. So who pushed the vase?" Lady Gwendolyn began to nod. "Why, yes, the answer has stared us in the face all this time. John Border Stone pushed that vase."

Posey jumped up, his face reddening. "Wait a minute. This is a whitewash, and it won't work. If Stone was trying to kill Bledsoe—which I don't believe for a minute; *I* know the truth and it's all tied up with this crazy mystery business—well, if Stone was the one trying to kill Bledsoe, he sure couldn't have shot Bledsoe and Honeycutt. Because Stone was already dead by then!" he concluded triumphantly.

But Lady Gwendolyn gave him a cherubic smile. "My dear chap, most certainly that is quite true. You see, Bledsoe murdered Stone."

The circuit solicitor rolled his eyes. "First you got Stone trying to kill Bledsoe, then you got Bledsoe killing Stone. Next thing I know you'll have Bledsoe killing himself!"

Annie said firmly, "No. Bledsoe *wounded* himself. He killed Kathryn Honeycutt."

"Oh, for Christ's sake!" Posey exclaimed.

With Lady Gwendolyn nodding her approval, Annie laid it out: "Bledsoe played a role from the very beginning. There was no reasonable excuse for him to attend this kind of conference so he provided himself with an impeccable purpose—the character assassination of the world's most beloved mystery writer. He knew a great deal about Christie. At some time in the past, he'd run across a sugar cutter like the weapon used in *Mrs. McGinty's Dead*. He probably bought it just for his own amusement, but when this plan came into his mind—"

"This plan, this plan!" Posey expostulated. "You claim a man went through this elaborate ruse—attending the conference, faking attacks on his life—for what? Why? There's no rational reason in the world—"

"Money." There was a world of sadness in Annie's quiet response.

Posey clamped his hands to his hips. "Whose money?"

"His aunt's. Kathryn Honeycutt's."

The circuit solicitor looked like he'd just picked up a hand with thirteen spades. "Would it interest you to know," he inquired sarcastically, "that Mrs. Honeycutt *wasn't* a rich woman? Oh, she had been at one time. But we've talked to her bank, checked out her estate"—condescendingly he looked around the room—"amateur detectives lack the resources to fine-comb a victim's background—"

"Stamps." Annie spoke with finality.

Posey sensed trouble. "Stamps?"

"American mostly. She collected. Bledsoe knew it. I have no doubt that when the contents of her home are evaluated, there will be a fortune in stamps. She once told me, 'It's my money. I can spend it any way I want to.' And a fortune in stamps was even better for Bledsoe's purposes. What are the odds those stamps would have quietly been lifted and no account given of them in the estate proceedings? Oh, there's money there. And Bledsoe very deliberately, very cold-bloodedly went after it. He brought the sugar cutter to the conference, knowing that its use as a weapon to kill Stone would confuse the police and perhaps divert the investigation entirely toward Christie fans. He came to this conference knowing that his criticism of Christie would infuriate everyone here. He knew another natural line of inquiry would be directed at his enemies, and he knew that many of those he'd injured in the past would be at this conference. Good, more motives. He persuaded Stone—and I'm sure it will turn out that he took advantage of Stone's hunger to be published—to fake the 'attacks.'" Annie's face tightened. "I imagine it was easy for Bledsoe to convince Stone that the attacks on him were part of a publicity build-up, certain to enhance interest in Bledsoe's upcoming biography of Christie. Bledsoe must have promised to help Stone meet an editor. So the attacks occurred—and Bledsoe was clearly the object of two murder attempts. All attention was focused on Bledsoe, who was so obviously the killer's target. At that point, Stone's fate became certain. He must not be alive when Honeycutt is murdered and Bledsoe wounded. Because Stone alone knew that the first two attacks were bogus. So Bledsoe arranged to meet Stone in his room Tuesday night. Bledsoe knew his own room was being watched—a protective measure—so he went out via the balcony. He detoured by way of Lady Gwendolyn's room (she'd left her balcony doors open), on an impulse took her cape, then climbed down to the next floor, and hurried to Stone's room. He had the sugar cutter with him. Probably he made some kind of joke about it. He offered Stone cocaine, then struck him down with the cutter, using the cape as protection against bloodstains. He then smudged the bloody cape against the wall in a trail leading back to Lady Gwendolyn's room. He'd unlocked her door earlier—what could be easier than tossing in the bloodied cape? Then he regained his own room via the balcony."

"He was an agile, clever fellow, but altogether a blackguard," Lady Gwendolyn commented. "At that point the stage was set for the main murder—the death of his aunt."

"That was quite a production," Annie said soberly. "Bledsoe was busy as hell the night he killed Kathryn. From the autopsy report, we know that she had spaghetti, a green salad, and ginger ale for dinner. Bledsoe slipped a Valium into her ginger ale. She was a Christian Scientist, had no prescription for Valium, and in fact never took medicines of any kind. But Bledsoe had to be sure she slept deeply that night. It was that single dose of Valium that started me on the right trail. Because it was wrong. And if that was wrong, how wrong were we about everything else? Bledsoe dressed in dark slacks, pullover, sneakers, and the brown cotton gloves that were found on the terrace. Again he left his room by the balcony, without being seen by Billy Cameron, who was on protective watch duty in the hall. That suited Bledsoe fine; Billy would provide him with an unimpeachable alibi. He climbed down the side of the hotel—"

Posey had had enough. "You sure Clark Kent wasn't out there that night?"

Annie ignored him. "We all saw Bledsoe go up the side of the building after the vase was pushed over. Without having seen that, I might never have figured it out. But Bledsoe couldn't resist posturing, demonstrating just how brave he was, and revealing just how athletic he was. That explains the bloodhounds, Posey. Bledsoe came down the side of the hotel, climbing down those ornate pillars (and that's why the lady on the second floor was right; she *did* see the murderer go by), and then he jumped to the top of the wall and dropped onto the terrace. The bloodhounds picked up the murderer's trail—Bledsoe's trail—where he *started*, not where he stopped. He ran fast, throwing firecrackers and smoke bombs, hurrying to the closet where he pulled the breaker switches, then up the stairs—more firecrackers and smoke bombs—and here came Billy. Bledsoe knocked him out and the coast was clear. Running up to the third floor, he opened his door, woke Kathryn. She would have been very muzzy, very sleepy. He got her up and as far as her door, then he sprinted a few feet to the foyer, turned, pinned her in the flashlight and shot her. Then he stripped out of his clothes, dropped them in his room, got a wet towel, returned to the living room—"

"You amateurs." Posey luxuriated in his disgust. "Think you're so smart."

Lady Gwendolyn sniffed. "Annie is absolutely correct on all counts."

Posey directed a supercilious smile at the English author. "Your lack of knowledge about police work is astounding, madam. Any doctor knows the difference between a contact wound and one from a distance of six feet or more. And Bledsoe was shot from a distance of at least six feet."

Lady Gwendolyn threw up her hands. "My dear man, obviously Bledsoe took this into account."

"He didn't forget that." Annie shivered. "He didn't forget anything. He dropped the towel by Kathryn's body in readiness, wired the gun (he still wore gloves, of course) to the iron grillwork, attached a string to the trigger, carefully stepped off the distance, and pulled the trigger."

"Shot himself?" Henny asked. Then, she answered herself. "Of course. So macho and a hell of an alibi."

"It must have hurt like hell." Annie remembered the little boy who'd refused to cry so long ago. "He didn't have to hurry now. He picked up the towel, used it to staunch the blood, undid the string from the trigger and the wire from the gun, went out to the balcony and tossed the gun and wire and gloves into the night. You remember there were no lights in the hotel. People were screaming, running across the terrace. It was absolute chaos. Hurrying back to Kathryn, he picked her up, and stumbled out to the balcony."

"The wire that was found on the terrace," Saulter didn't give further provenance, "tested positive for residue from gunpowder."

"Neil had himself a damn good time, didn't he?" Hillman said bitterly. "Except—what the hell happened to him?"

Annie looked at the editor in surprise. "But that's already been made clear—thanks to our outstanding circuit solicitor." She managed to sound admiring without gagging. "As Mr. Posey insisted—since the door was chained and no one else was visible on the balcony—Bledsoe's death was most certainly accidental."

Max's lake blue eyes narrowed.

Annie faced Posey. "Of course there *was* a reason why Bledsoe ran to his death. However, we may never know quite how or why it happened. My guess is that he found a picnic basket outside his door. He brought it inside and opened it and—"

Chief Saulter reached down behind the podium and picked up a finely meshed wire cage and dropped open the door. "Handsome fellow, isn't he? A red rat snake. We found him curled up, fast asleep on top of the four-poster in Bledsoe's room. Red rat snakes climb real good."

Someone in the audience said, "Jesus, look at that bloody thing!"

Annie wasn't fond of snakes. She didn't look. "Yes, that snake was in the picnic hamper—and Bledsoe was pathologically terrified of snakes. When he opened the basket, the snake must have slithered over the side, and Bledsoe quite simply went into a state of blind panic, reeling away from the equally frightened snake, running, careening from wall to chair, across his bedroom and out the open French window and onto the balcony—to his death."

Laurel gasped dramatically.

She stood up, pressed a hand to her heart.

Annie jolted to a stop. "Laurel, what—"

"Oh my dears, I am stricken." Laurel closed her eyes, then opened them to look piteously about, tears brimming in her huge blue eyes. "To unwittingly cause a fellow creature such horror, such fear—to indirectly be responsible for another's death—I don't know if I can bear it." She pressed a dainty lace handkerchief to her face.

Max jumped to his feet.

"Well, I'll be double damned!" Emma Clyde exclaimed.

Annie darted across the room, pulled her mother-in-law into her embrace. "Dear Laurel..."

Her mother-in-law lifted her chin, stared bravely at the shocked faces turned toward her. "I had no idea that was Bledsoe's room." She pulled away from Annie. "Oh, Henny, why didn't you tell me you'd changed rooms?"

"Oh my God, so that's how it happened!" Annie exclaimed.

"Wait a minute." Posey gaped at them. "You mean she"—and he pointed at Laurel—"put a damn snake in a picnic basket and put it there for this guy to get when he's scared to death of snakes? Wait a minute!"

"How tragic," Henny said somberly. "Laurel, I am so sorry." She turned to Posey. "It's so simple, really. You see, I was originally in the suite taken by Bledsoe and his aunt. They were assigned to 313, which has a mural with an alligator in it, and it threw Bledsoe into a state of panic. That's when I offered to trade suites. I took 313 and gave my suite, 315, to Bledsoe. Unfortunately, poor Laurel didn't know of the room change." Henny reached out to take Laurel's hand. "I'll bet that lovely red rat snake was a present for me, wasn't it?"

"A present?" A stunned Posey peered toward the cage where the red splotched snake coiled, head up.

Laurel dabbed at her moist eyes. "Moles. Red rat snakes are so effective with moles, and poor dear Henny, a new lawn just *filled* with mole tunnels. Those pesky little rascals. I took a little picnic over to the forest preserve Saturday afternoon, just for a few moments by myself with nature and I enjoyed it so much—chicken salad sandwich and kiwi—just a light repast..."

"And you got that *snake*?" Posey eyed her belligerently.

"One must seize opportunity," Laurel replied with great dignity. "Red rat snakes are great climbers, you know, but this one must have been full, for he was curled up right on the first branch. I saw him and I immediately thought, 'Henny!'" Laurel clapped her hands together. "It was but the work of a moment. I just scooped this dear fellow right into my basket and popped shut the lid." She beamed, looking around for approval. Then her lovely face settled into sad and pensive lines. "Such a tragedy that I didn't know Henny's room had been changed."

"So," Annie concluded heartily, "Circuit Solicitor Posey was absolutely right—Bledsoe's death *was* an accident."

Lady Gwendolyn rushed to Annie and gave her a quick hug. Then she turned to the circuit solicitor. "One has to wonder about fate—and the mills of the gods. Don't you think?"

The phone rang.

Annie rose stiffly. Shelving books had to be the hardest work ever devised and she'd been at it for days now, replacing the books they'd offered at the book room during the conference. Sales had been excellent, but there were always plenty that came home.

She reached the phone as it rang again.

"Death on Demand." It felt good once again to be at work in the finest mystery bookstore this side of Atlanta. The Christie conference—aside from the unexpected traumas, and she would be a long time forgetting some of them—had been a fabulous success. But Annie was ready for a little peace and quiet. Perhaps she'd have a chance to read some of the books just in, the latest from Julie Smith, James Yaffe, and Caroline Graham.

"I just keep having the most *marvelous* ideas for a new book." The line crackled.

"Lady Gwendolyn, where are you?" No answer would have surprised Annie—in a commune, atop a fire lookout tower, nursing a gin gimlet at Raffles in Singapore.

"In flight. They have an air phone. I just couldn't resist."

Annie had last seen her visitor at the Savannah airport en route for New York.

"Are you going home?" With most people, it was a natural assumption.

"No."

It was a beautifully modulated *Neow*.

"I decided to visit your West Coast. I understand there are many writers there. I will be attending a retreat." A burble of laughter. "I've already come up with the title for my next book—*The Christie Caper*. Do you think it has a certain ring?"

Static exploded on the line. Annie held the receiver away from her ear and faintly heard, "After that, *Death of a Fat Fool*. So I'm thinking of coming back by your island on the way home. A spot of research."

It was not the most direct route to England. But Annie was thrilled. "As soon as you can," she urged.

Annie was smiling when she returned to her task. Lady Gwendo-lyn—brilliant, jolly, intrepid—a co-conspirator to be prized.

The front doorbell rang.

Still on her knees, Annie twisted around, then scrambled to her feet. "Mrs. Calloway, how nice of you to come by."

Fleur Calloway, slim and lovely in a lemon blazer, a cream blouse, and daffodil skirt, hesitated in the doorway. The late afternoon sunlight turned her gloriously red hair to flame. She said, abruptly, "I wanted to see you before I left the island."

"Let's have coffee," Annie urged, and she led the way to the back of the store and the coffee bar.

As Annie poured almond mocha into their mugs, she said warmly, "Your speech at the luncheon was just wonderful. It was a perfect ending to the conference."

"Lady Gwendolyn's closing remarks," Fleur said quietly, "were well received."

Annie had been delighted to give the speaker's role to Lady Gwen-dolyn so that she might make good on her promise to announce the name of the murderer at the luncheon's end. The doughty author held her listeners spellbound with her account. Neil Bledsoe, murderer. And so the story ended, a murderer who escaped men's justice in an odd twist of fate. "But," Lady Gwendolyn had concluded, "can we doubt that the mills of the gods grind exceedingly fine?"

Annie looked directly into Calloway's luminous, questioning eyes. "I'm very glad it's over." She knew that Fleur Calloway understood that she was not talking about the conference.

Fleur Calloway, who had loved her daughter so much and every day placed a single yellow rose on her grave.

Fleur Calloway, who grew up in the bayous of Louisiana with four rambunctious brothers.

A snake and a single yellow rose.

The author's lips trembled. "How? How did you and Lady Gwen-dolyn and—is it your mother-in-law and—"

"It wasn't difficult. Once I knew what must have happened—"

Fleur pressed a hand against suddenly trembling lips—"I talked to Laurel and Henny." Annie paused. "Laurel has three daughters. She loves them very much. And Henny was adamant that the truth would do no one any good. They agreed at once to my plan."

Fleur stared at her with luminous eyes. "I still don't see why you would take such a risk . . . for a stranger."

"Because we felt it was right," Annie said simply. She put down her mug. "Just a moment." Hurrying up the aisle, she scanned her almost reshelved Christie section and found the title she sought. Returning, she placed it on the coffee bar. "I'd like for you to have this. It's a story of people working together to see justice done. This is a first edition. To remember . . . Death on Demand."

The author looked down at the cover, at the copy of Christie's famed *Murder on the Orient Express*, the indescribably brilliant and touching novel in which Christie made it very clear that law and justice are not always synonymous.

Calloway's eyes had the bright shine of tears when she looked up. "I see—and the three of you conspired—"

"Four," Annie interrupted. It would never do to leave out Lady Gwendolyn. Then, briskly, she asked, "Are you on your way home?" To say too much would be a serious mistake.

"Yes." The author took a deep breath, looked away, her gaze sweeping the back of the bookstore. "Oh, your watercolors. They are so well done. Who won the contest?"

"Do you know, we forgot to ask people to turn in their lists!"

Fleur Calloway pointed in order. "*The Mysterious Affair at Styles, The Murder of Roger Ackroyd, And Then There Were None, Mrs. McGinty's Dead,* and *What Mrs. McGillicuddy Saw!* Among Christie's finest."

Annie clapped her hands. "Now you've won. You get free coffee and a book."

Calloway slowly picked up *Murder on the Orient Express.* "I *will* take this one." She held it tight to her body. "I can never thank you enough," she said softly, her voice breaking. She gave Annie a swift hug, then turned and walked away.

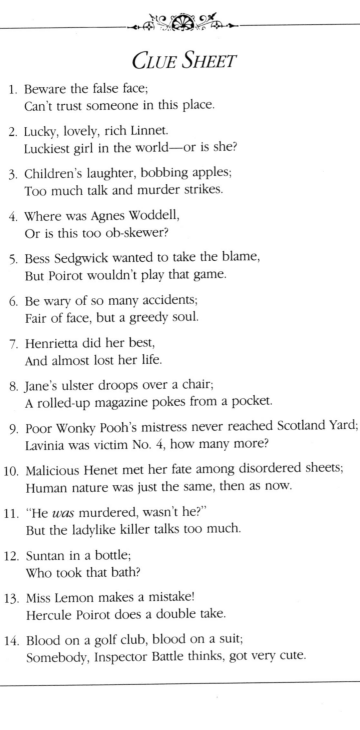

CLUE SHEET

1. Beware the false face;
   Can't trust someone in this place.

2. Lucky, lovely, rich Linnet.
   Luckiest girl in the world—or is she?

3. Children's laughter, bobbing apples;
   Too much talk and murder strikes.

4. Where was Agnes Woddell,
   Or is this too ob-skewer?

5. Bess Sedgwick wanted to take the blame,
   But Poirot wouldn't play that game.

6. Be wary of so many accidents;
   Fair of face, but a greedy soul.

7. Henrietta did her best,
   And almost lost her life.

8. Jane's ulster droops over a chair;
   A rolled-up magazine pokes from a pocket.

9. Poor Wonky Pooh's mistress never reached Scotland Yard;
   Lavinia was victim No. 4, how many more?

10. Malicious Henet met her fate among disordered sheets;
    Human nature was just the same, then as now.

11. "He *was* murdered, wasn't he?"
    But the ladylike killer talks too much.

12. Suntan in a bottle;
    Who took that bath?

13. Miss Lemon makes a mistake!
    Hercule Poirot does a double take.

14. Blood on a golf club, blood on a suit;
    Somebody, Inspector Battle thinks, got very cute.

15. Dolly Bantry's worried sick;
    She recruits Miss Marple quick.

16. Poor Dora Bunner meant well,
    But there was too much she could tell.

17. Things are hot, revolution is brewing.
    Bob hides the jewels, but a mirror reflects.

18. Mr. Shaitana thumbed his nose,
    And his life drew to a close.

19. Elinor Katharine Carlisle—
    Innocent or guilty?

20. A wasp flew loose in the cabin,
    But the fatal sting came from a thorn.

21. She had to die;
    Poirot finds out why.

22. Frankie crashes the car,
    But that doesn't get her very far.

23. A mislabeled path at Victoria Falls;
    Look for the answer in the wooden giraffe.

24. Just a contest, but money tempts;
    A hearty man's closet tells the tale.

25. Lady Hoggin is willing to pay;
    Will Shan Tung come home today?

AGATHA CHRISTIE
TREASURE HUNT POSTERS

POSTER 1

A cupboard in the corner of a cottage dining rom. It contains sports equipment and relics of the sporting life: two pairs of skis, ten or twelve hippopotamus tusks, fishing tackle, a stuffed elephant's foot, golf clubs, a tennis racket, and a tiger skin.

POSTER 2

The small, mustachioed man on the hotel terrace holds a woman's fawn felt hat in his hands, showing it to his companion. A look of impatience underlies one of concern on the little man's face. One finger is stuck through a small hole in the hat's brim.

POSTER 3

Scissors. Cut-out letters. A young woman standing at an upper window watching, watching. A wasp's nest and a jar of cyanide.

POSTER 4

The old butler peers nearsightedly through the windows at the drive. A looking glass. Wax flowers on a malachite table.

POSTER 5

The smoldering remains of an air crash. Luggage in a hotel lobby. A much battered tennis racket.

POSTER 6

In the candlelight, the body clothed in a black cloak and a black mask looks absurdly melodramatic, but the young man is very dead.

POSTER 7

The black-haired young woman with eager green eyes stares at a ship model behind the plate-glass window of the steamship company. In her hand, she holds a roll of unexposed film.

POSTER 8

A bucket filled with water and bobbing apples.

POSTER 9

An elderly gentleman stands in the hotel lobby, staring in dismay at the Out-of-Order sign on the lift.

POSTER 10

Her elfin face twisted with jealous rage, the angry young woman yanks a pistol from her lap and shoots the athletic, blond man.

POSTER 11

Light from the fireplace flickers on the faces of the bridge players, intent upon their game, and on the Mephistophelian countenance of the man watching from his chair next to the fire.

POSTER 12

Clutching an oilskin packet, the young woman hurries toward the lifeboats as the *Lusitania* begins to sink.

POSTER 13

The hotel counter is not quite seedy, but certainly not posh. On a notice board, envelopes are pinned for hotel guests. One envelope is addressed to Miss Carnaby.

POSTER 14

The scene aboard the airliner is quite peaceful. Two passengers appear to sleep: a heavy-set middle-aged woman and a small man wrapped heavily in mufflers.

POSTER 15

The beautiful young woman has an air of quiet dignity and great despair as she stands before the judge.

POSTER 16

Uncertain of the proper demeanor when faced with tragedy, the fresh-faced young man in golf clothes kneels on the cliffside path beside the dying man.

POSTER 17

The old woman is definitely the center of the family group in the hotel lounge. The young people seem indistinct and bloodless in comparison to her monumental bulk and grotesque ugliness.

POSTER 18

The clear-eyed old lady sips a cup of tea and studies the occupants of the old-fashioned, luxurious hotel lounge. Muffins and seed cakes are on the plate before her.

POSTER 19
The elderly man in the white duck suit and panama hat reclines comfortably on the deck chair, watching the sunbathers with interest.

POSTER 20
The young woman's body, dressed in a cheap white satin evening dress, looks completely out of place on the old bearskin hearth rug.

POSTER 21
The melange of objects seems to have no rhyme or reason: a cut-up rucksack, several electric light bulbs, a pair of flannel trousers, one woman's evening shoe, a diamond ring, a bottle of green ink . . .

POSTER 22
The murder scene looks just like a stage setting: the lovely swimming pool, the dark blue water, and the blood from the dying man.

POSTER 23
A speeding car. An old woman staring up at it in horror. A cat with a bandaged ear.

POSTER 24
The old man next to the thornbush looks as though he'd seen a ghost as he stuffs a photograph back in his wallet.

POSTER 25
The dark, pretty girl hurries up the steep path on the limestone cliffs to a rock chamber near the tomb.

TREASURE HUNT TITLES

Murder at Hazelmoor, Poster 1, Clue 24.

Peril at End House, Poster 2, Clue 6.

The Moving Finger, Poster 3, Clue 4.

Funerals Are Fatal, Poster 4, Clue 11.

Cat Among the Pigeons, Poster 5, Clue 17.

A Murder Is Announced, Poster 6, Clue 16.

The Man in the Brown Suit, Poster 7, Clue 23.

Hallowe'en Party, Poster 8, Clue 3.

Towards Zero, Poster 9, Clue 14.

Death on the Nile, Poster 10, Clue 2.

Cards on the Table, Poster 11, Clue 18.

The Secret Adversary, Poster 12, Clue 8.

"The Nemean Lion," Poster 13, Clue 25.

Death in the Air, Poster 14, Clue 20.

Sad Cypress, Poster 15, Clue 19.

The Boomerang Clue, Poster 16, Clue 22.

Appointment with Death, Poster 17, Clue 21.

At Bertram's Hotel, Poster 18, Clue 5.

Evil Under the Sun, Poster 19, Clue 12.

The Body in the Library, Poster 20, Clue 15.

Hickory Dickory Death, Poster 21, Clue 13.

Murder After Hours, Poster 22, Clue 7.

Easy To Kill, Poster 23, Clue 9.

A Caribbean Mystery, Poster 24, Clue 1.

Death Comes as the End, Poster 25, Clue 10.

AUTHOR'S POSTSCRIPT

If *The Christie Caper* conveys to the readers even a particle of Agatha Christie's brillance as a writer and charm as a person, I will have succeeded in my effort. I hope it will also excite readers' interests in learning more about Christie. I would highly recommend the following titles:

Agatha Christie, An Autobiography, Dodd, Mead, 1977.

Agatha Christie, A Biography, by Janet Morgan, Knopf, 1985.

A Talent to Deceive, An Appreciation of Agatha Christie, by Robert Barnard, revised and updated, The Mysterious Press, 1987.

Come, Tell Me How You Live, by Agatha Christie, Dodd, Mead, 1946.

Mallowan's Memoirs, by Max Mallowan, Dodd, Mead, 1977.

The Agatha Christie Companion, The Complete Guide to Agatha Christie's Life and Work, by Dennis Sanders and Len Lovallo, Berkley revised trade paperback edition, 1989.

The New Bedside, Bathtub & Armchair Companion to Agatha Christie, second edition, edited by Dick Riley and Pam McAllister, Ungar, 1986.

Agatha Christie, First Lady of Crime, edited by H.R.F. Keating, Weidenfield and Nicolson, 1977.

Murder She Wrote, A Study of Agatha Christie's Detective Fiction, by Patricia D. Maida and Nicholas B. Spornick, Bowling Green State University Popular Press, 1982.

The Agatha Christie Companion, by Russell H. Fitzgibbon, Bowling Green State University Popular Press, 1980.

Agatha Christie, The Woman and Her Mysteries, by Gillian Gill, The Free Press, 1990.